perchance to dream

Cover designed by Najla Qamber Designs.
(najlaqamberdesigns.com)
Photo by Wm Russell Photography. Model: Courtney Boyett.

Published by Snowy Wings Publishing.
www.snowywingspublishing.com

ISBN: 978-1-946202-52-9

perchance to dream

*Classic Tales from the Bard's World
in New Skins*

edited by LYSSA CHIAVARI

Snowy Wings
PUBLISHING

Contents

"In black ink my love may still shine bright."
- WILLIAM SHAKESPEARE

Introduction

T he blame for this story collection can be placed squarely at the feet of the late Mary Stewart. Sort of.

It was the summer of 2014, and I had just finished rereading her novel *This Rough Magic* for what must have been the third or fourth time. Though Stewart's suspense novels tend to have contemporary bases (and, arguably, a very young adult flair to them), most of them also have threads of classic literature woven through them. *This Rough Magic* is thematically based on Shakespeare's *The Tempest*: not only are lines from the play excerpted at the beginning of each chapter, but the characters reference the play, and events from the story find themselves being worked into the overall mystery of the novel.

I remember being struck by how one work could have influenced another and led to a brand new story that was vastly different, but just as enjoyable as the original. Stewart's books are by no means unique. Different interpretations and retellings of Shakespeare are all around us, from the 1950s musical *Kiss Me, Kate* to modern webseries adaptations like *Nothing Much to Do*. People who grew up in the nineties (and who are geeky like me) may even have noticed the confluence of multiple Shakespearean storylines in the Disney cartoon *Gargoyles*.

William Shakespeare is arguably the most influential English writer of all time, and much of this is due to the universality of the themes of these stories. Though the stories were written over four hundred years ago—and many of them are inspired by events that took place centuries before that—so much of society is still the same. The issues of prejudice and discrimination tackled in *Othello*, the themes of grief and revenge found in *Hamlet*, among others... these are all still extremely relevant in the modern world. Because of this, Shakespeare's plays often feel oddly timely.

As I worked on other projects of my own, I kept thinking, in the back of my mind, how much fun it would be to reinterpret Shakespeare in the same way. The idea kept coming back to me over a span of several months, unrelenting, until I finally gave in and emailed a few other authors, asking them if they would be interested in participating in an anthology based on Shakespeare's plays and sonnets.

The response was overwhelming.

The stories presented here are amazingly unique. From sci-fi to contemporary to historical fantasy, and featuring characters from all walks of life, I was astounded by the variety of story ideas that everyone was able to dream up with no other prompt than "based on Shakespeare." The authors collected in this volume come from vastly different backgrounds, perspectives and worldviews, as you can see just from reading their stories; but a love of the Bard's classic tales managed to inspire each, leading to eleven beautiful and richly varied tales. I hope you will enjoy reading them as much as we enjoyed writing them.

Rosemary for Remembrance

JESS R. SUTTON

"'Tis not alone my inky cloak . . .
Together with all forms, moods, shapes of grief,
That can denote me truly: these indeed seem,
For they are actions that a man might play:
But I have that within which passeth show;
These but the trappings and the suits of woe."
- HAMLET, *THE TRAGEDY OF HAMLET*

There was no right weather for a funeral, Mel thought as she stood outside the church. Sun was no good, of course, and rain always felt like God was trying too hard. She was grateful that it wasn't snowing, at least; her mother hated the snow. A thunderstorm might have felt right, but there was no storm. Gray clouds hung heavy in the sky, threatening rain that wouldn't fall, like an absolution never granted.

She adjusted her pouf slightly, grateful in some corner of her mind that she'd left her hair natural this morning. Then again, it wasn't as though she had the presence of mind to even find the flat iron this morning, let alone use it.

"It's time." Aunt Clara squeezed her shoulder and walked through the doorway, into the church. Mel followed, closing the heavy wooden door behind her. Her uncle Joseph was already sitting in the front pew, holding a box of tissues. He passed them over to Mel. She wouldn't need them. She'd cried every tear she had in the last two days. There was nothing left.

Reverend Gorka stood at the pulpit and looked out at the funeral attendees. His eyes were red-rimmed, and Mel remembered that he'd worked with her mother on local charity events.

3

Almost everybody knew Rosemary. Mel's skin seemed to vibrate with the overwhelming numbness of it all. Why would a woman so loved take her own life? *And why would she leave me?* The question hung heavier than the rainclouds.

"Dearly beloved," the reverend began, and Mel discovered that she did, in fact, need the tissues.

The sermon was nice, although she didn't really remember what was said. Aunt Clara gave a short eulogy, led by a story from their childhood. She choked up briefly in the middle but cleared her throat and carried on. Mel had been asked to speak, but she knew she wouldn't be able to.

Afterward, she stood outside again, her aunt and uncle by her side. They shook people's hands and thanked them for coming, and Mel kept wishing she knew a spell to make the clouds break. Anything would be better than this grayness.

"I'm so sorry, Mel," a voice said, and before she could quite process who the speaker was, the handshake had turned into a hug. Before the woman pulled away, Mel recognized her spicy perfume.

"Thanks, Hannah," she said.

Hannah held on for a moment longer, then squeezed Mel's hand. "My ima wants to bring some food over tomorrow. A casserole, maybe some fresh bread, she said. Is that okay?"

"Of course. And could you—" Mel stopped short.

"She's already spelled the potatoes for strength."

"You're the best. Thank her from me, would you?"

"You got it. I'll see you tomorrow in the studio, yeah?"

"Yeah, I'll try." Mel managed a smile as Hannah walked away. She'd only met Hannah's mother a few times, mostly when the arts and magic studio Hannah managed put shows on, but she was somewhat of a local celebrity when it came to her kitchen spells. No magic could make her heart stop breaking, but maybe the casserole would keep her from feeling like she was about to fall over just from standing.

"You're going to the studio tomorrow?" Aunt Clara asked.

"I always work Sundays."

"Are you sure that's a good idea?"

"Why not?" Mel's question fell from her tongue like a knife. If her aunt wouldn't let her go…

"You know why not, Mel." Clara paused, shook another hand, received another hug.

Mel shook her head. "It's not like we have to sit shiva or anything. Just because my best friend is Jewish doesn't mean I am."

Clara turned and looked Mel in the eye. "I don't mean that. I just don't know if you should be going out so soon."

"It's not 'out.' It's to the studio."

"Honey," Joseph interrupted, his hand on Clara's shoulder. "Perhaps you should continue this in the car?"

"Yes, of course."

Mel could tell that her aunt was watching her, but she didn't want to know if it was with frustration or with pity. She wasn't sure which would be worse. Instead of looking to confirm, she shook the last person's hand, thanked Reverend Gorka, and sat in the car until Clara and Joseph joined her to drive home.

The little bell jingled as Mel opened the door to the Glass Shard Studio of Arts and Magic. She breathed in the familiar smells—paint, glue, something resembling burning toast. She kept meaning to figure out what was letting off that particular odor.

"I'll be right with you." Hannah's voice came from the back office, and her body followed quickly after. She looked up. "Oh, hey! I'm glad you came."

"You know me," Mel said with a shrug. "I never miss a shift."

"I appreciate that." Hannah handed over the handful of paintbrushes she'd been carrying. "Would you put those up for me?"

"Got it." Mel walked over to the wall and started sorting the brushes by size. The pottery painting was one of the most popular aspects of the studio, although Mel had never tried it herself. She preferred to keep her mediocre sketches to scraps of paper and the edges of her biology notes until she'd had a little more practice. The back room was the real reason she was here—space to work on her potions without any questions.

The two women worked in silence for a quarter hour. Mel could tell that Hannah was shooting her glances every few moments.

"I'm okay, you know," Mel said aloud.

Hannah blushed. "I'm sorry. Are you sure this isn't something you want to talk about?"

"What is there to say? She's dead. My mother is dead. And no spell or potion is going to bring her back. So that's all there is, isn't it?"

"Just because that's all true doesn't mean it doesn't hurt. You're allowed to grieve."

Mel straightened a stack of colored paper. "So what if I grieve? Still won't change the fact that my mother killed herself. Jumped off that bridge for God knows what reason and left her sixteen-year-old daughter behind. And I'll have to live with that question forever regardless. So what's the point?"

"Mel—" Hannah moved to give her a hug but was shrugged off.

"I'm going to go clean up the potions room. There aren't any clients in there right now, are there?"

Hannah sighed. "No, it's empty. Go ahead." Before she'd even finished, Mel was gone.

The back room was dimly lit, although there were desk lamps at intervals along the tables for individual use. Mel grabbed a rag from a bucket at the front and began to wipe down the tables. Some of them had indelible stains on them, of which Mel was quite sure she'd caused more than one. She was still honing her skills, which sometimes meant that certain potions were more dangerous—or just messier—than she anticipated.

Along the side wall were lockers, most of which were used by regular customers like Mel. She spun her combination and looked at the collection of bottles. Half the bottles were full, with masking-tape labels stuck on haphazardly. While the large majority of her potions were still a little too experimental to use safely, her energy potion had been well-tested. Sure that there was a bottle in there somewhere, she shuffled through the clinking glass until she found it.

She poured a few drops into a drinking glass, added water from the tap, and downed the concoction. Fortunately, it was tasteless, and she soon felt a little bit of warmth in her extremities. That would help get her through the rest of her shift.

The room, which was hardly messy to begin with, was now spotless. Mel returned to the front, where Hannah was helping a young boy choose a plate to paint.

"They're all infused with self-healing spells, so if you chip it or crack it, just put it in a safe place for about twenty-four hours and it'll be good as new," Hannah said to the boy's mother. "If it's completely shattered, though, that's beyond the abilities of the spell."

"I wanna paint the cup for Dad!" the boy said, pointing at a coffee mug.

His mother nodded at Hannah, who pulled down the mug and set the boy up at a table. Mel began refilling the paint jars, as some of the primary colors were nearly empty. It was always the parents, rarely the children, who threw tantrums when colors weren't available. After six months at the studio, dealing with those people was practically second nature, but still something to avoid if possible.

Hannah joined Mel at the counter. "You doing okay?"

"Yeah, I'm okay." She nodded. "Sorry about earlier."

"No need. I understand."

Mel half-smiled her thanks. As she gathered up an armful of paint jars to return to their shelves, Hannah touched her arm.

"Oh, your girlfriend called."

"What? Why'd Lea call here?"

"She knows you don't have your cell on you during work. Anyway, she said she'd be dropping by your house this evening, and to call her if you didn't want her to come."

"Oh." Mel set half the bottles down and wiped her forehead. "Yeah, okay. Thanks. That should be fine."

An hour later, after the boy had painted a nearly-recognizable dinosaur on the mug and left it behind to be baked, Hannah came up to Mel, who was sorting receipts.

"If you don't mind my intruding…" Hannah paused.

"You know you can say anything to me."

"Why wasn't Lea at the funeral?"

Mel shrugged. "She's the lead in *The Taming of the Shrew* and they had a matinee. She's got an understudy, but everyone knows she's the best. I told her to stay. It doesn't really matter. She doesn't like churches anyway."

Hannah pursed her lips. "Okay. I was just curious."

"It honestly doesn't matter. I could barely handle talking to my aunt at the funeral. Lea would have been too much." Mel's throat constricted at the thought.

"Fair enough."

The rest of the afternoon was blissfully busy, with half a

dozen regular customers coming in to use the workshop spaces in the potions room or the airy side room for spell practice. Mel could see Hannah breathing a little more easily after each customer came in; without the regulars, she knew this studio wouldn't survive long. Fall always saw a sharp drop-off in patronage after the busy summer, and it was hard to push through until the holiday season.

When Hannah sounded the chimes to mark five o'clock, the last few customers paid cheerfully and left. The door closed, its tiny bell echoing in the now-empty space, and Hannah slumped into a chair.

"You okay?" Mel asked.

"Yeah, just tired. And worried. It'll be better come November. It always is." She took a breath and pushed herself up. "Let's get this cleaned up and go home."

Clara was sitting at the kitchen table waiting when Mel walked through the door.

"Oh, good, you're home," she said, pushing her chair back. "Come have a seat."

Mel tensed. "Hold on, let me put my stuff up." She dropped her purse on her bed and kicked off her shoes. It still felt strange to have her aunt and uncle in her home for so long. They lived near enough that visits had always been short, a night at most. Then again, having them here now helped to fill the emptiness.

On her way back to the kitchen, Mel stopped before her mom's room. The door was closed—at least her aunt and uncle had taken the guest room instead of this one—but she pushed it open. Of course everything looked the same as it had before her mother died. Glasses on the bedside table, clothes in the hamper. As though she'd be back in a moment. There was a framed picture of her parents on the chest of drawers, from back when

Mel was just an infant. They were both smiling, and her father's glasses were slightly askew. Her mother looked the quintessential Black woman of the '70s, complete with afro and clenched fist on her t-shirt, despite the photo being taken nearly two decades after that style had passed.

Her dad had died just six months after that photo—the last time Clara had come to stay for an extended period. Mel didn't remember, of course, but there were a few photos, the occasional story, just enough to feel like that time had existed.

"Mel?" Clara called out. Mel started and stepped out of the room. Dealing with Mom was going to be a lot harder than when Dad died, she thought. And this time, with sixteen years' worth of memories, there was no hope of forgetting what had happened.

"What's up?" Mel asked as she filled a glass of water and sat down beside Clara. Joseph sat across from them, grading spelling tests.

"Now that the funeral's done…" Clara paused a moment and took a deep breath. "Right. Now that the funeral's over, we need to talk about what's going to happen in the future."

Mel blinked. "Now?"

"Better sooner than later," Clara said. "Now, your mother had a will made up after your dad died."

"Yeah, she told me. Said you never knew when tragedy would strike and you had to be ready."

"She was right. Now—"

"Not really," Mel interrupted.

"Sorry?"

"Well, it's not like she didn't know this would happen, right? She made this choice."

"Mel," Clara began. "You and I both wish this hadn't happened the way it did. But we still have to deal with the consequences. That's what I want to talk to you about."

"Fine." Mel stared at the table. It was still unfathomable that her mother had left her. Mel couldn't count the number of times they had talked about the future, about Mel's college plans or career goals. Why would she leave when she knew exactly what she'd be missing?

"Now, your mother named me and Joseph your guardians in the event of her death, as I imagine you've gathered."

"Yeah, and?"

"Mel," Joseph said warningly, having looked up at the sound of his name. "Your aunt is just trying to help."

She looked down at the floor. "I know. Sorry, Aunt Clara."

Clara continued, "The main issue now has to do with where to live. We can't all fit comfortably in Joseph's and my apartment, and it's not in the zone for your school. And we certainly can't leave you alone here, since you're still a minor. It looks like the only option is for us to move in here with you and sublet the apartment until our lease runs out. How would you feel about that?"

Mel sighed. "Does it matter?" The thought of living in this house without her mother made her chest pull tight. This was the home they'd made together, just the two of them, in the years after her dad died. They'd chosen curtains that three-year-old Mel loved, and the walls were decorated with a collection of art pieces they'd picked up at various fairs throughout the years. She couldn't stay here without her mom, but she couldn't leave either.

"It matters to me." Clara's face was placid as she reached out to touch Mel's hand.

"I mean, it sounds like you've made your decision, haven't you? And you're right, it's the only choice."

"It's your life too, though."

"Only for a couple more years."

Clara put her fist to her forehead. "Yes, that's true, but Mel..."

"Look, do what you want, okay?" Mel stood up. "Lea's coming over in a bit and I have to clean my room."

"We are not finished talking about this!" Clara's voice grew in volume as she pushed back her own chair.

Mel spun around and walked out of the room, fuming. It wasn't even a discussion, so why bother pretending it was? She heard Joseph's low, thundering voice talking Clara down but didn't stop to hear his words.

Once in her room alone, she shut the door and moved to sit on the bed. Before she got there, her knees gave out. She crumpled onto the carpeted floor, drawing her knees to her chest as her lungs heaved. For the first time since she'd heard the news, all the awfulness seemed real. Only a handful of tears fell from her eyes, but she could hardly draw a breath. She curled in tighter, trying to stop the room from spinning.

The door opened and a body sat down beside her.

"Hey, it's me," Lea said.

Mel turned, her body still a tense ball, and leaned against her girlfriend. She felt arms wrap around her shoulders and rock her gently until the tightness in her chest subsided.

She sat up, coughing a little. "Hey there."

"I'm so sorry, Mel." Lea kissed her forehead. "How are you feeling?"

Mel laughed shakily. "Well, I was doing okay until about five minutes before you came in."

Now finally able to breathe steadily, she stood and held a hand out to Lea. Lea was white, a full five inches taller than Mel, and much more muscular. Mel liked that they looked like opposites in the mirror. "Opposites attract, right?" she'd said to Lea on their first date.

"I mean, I don't know how I'm feeling," she continued. "The only reason I got through today at work was because of the energy potion. Otherwise I don't think I could have kept from falling down."

"Are you sure that's wise?" Lea pursed her lips.

"What are you, my mother?" The words fell from Mel's mouth without passing through her brain, and she froze. "Right. Of course not."

"Here, come sit down." They sat beside one another on the bed, fingers intertwined. Lea stroked Mel's hand with her thumb.

"I just don't believe it," Mel burst out.

"What do you mean?"

"How could she have done it? I know my mom. I know her. She wouldn't have killed herself, it just doesn't make sense."

Lea breathed out, heavy and deep. "It seems pretty clear she did, though."

"Does it?" Mel turned toward her, legs crossed. Her eyes were bright, and only partially from the tears she'd cried. "I mean, think about it. It doesn't make any sense for a woman who is happy, well-paid, and involved in her community to do this. For a mother to do this. Right? There's no reason."

"We don't know if she was really happy."

"You think she wasn't?" Mel scoffed. "She spent practically half her time singing, she was so happy. And the bridge…"

"Mel, don't go there."

"No, I'm serious, *think*." She grasped Lea's hand in her own. "You remember that psych class we took last year? When we talked about suicide, one of the things Mr. Williams said was that women don't kill themselves like this. They don't—it isn't messy."

"That's just a trend, it isn't always true."

"But you knew my mom, she was... To jump off a bridge? Onto asphalt?" Mel sat up straight. "There's no way. It must have been foul play, it must have."

Lea's jaw dropped. "That's ridiculous."

"Haven't you been listening?"

"I have, and you're being absurd." She furrowed her brow in concern. "I know this is hard for you, but that doesn't mean you can just go making ridiculous claims."

"It's not ridiculous!" Mel snapped. "Look, you don't have to be involved in this, whatever."

"I'm not going to." Standing, Lea shook her head. "Get some sleep, okay? Maybe things will look clearer in the morning."

"Yeah, maybe," she said, unconvinced. "I'll see you in school tomorrow?"

"I'll see you then." Lea leaned forward and kissed her gently. "Take care of yourself."

"I will."

The following Wednesday in geometry, Mel doodled stars on the edge of her notes. She listened idly to the lecture, aware that she should be paying much closer attention but unable to summon the will. When she walked into class, Mrs. Irwin had had pity in her eyes, and Mel knew she wouldn't be penalized for her inattention. Her stomach felt like it was full of rocks, and soon her eyes unfocused from the little drawings. Up through Sunday, grief had felt like numbness. Now, after the weekend's breakdown, she felt the full weight of everything that had happened. The words she was supposed to say bubbled up from her throat, acidic and foul, whenever people asked how she was doing. The bitterness that coated her skin had rubbed off, and even moving felt raw.

Blissfully, the bell rang. Mel put her nearly-blank notes back into her folder and rose from her desk. From the front, Mrs. Irwin called her name.

"Mel, could I speak to you for a moment?"

Mel's stomach would have dropped had there been anything left to feel.

"Sorry I spaced out in class," she said preemptively. "I didn't..."

"I know." Mrs. Irwin nodded. "I just wanted to let you know that it's fine if you can't get the homework in for the next couple of days. I'm surprised you're even here."

Mel shrugged. "My aunt said it would be best."

"She may be right. Just make sure you're taking down the assignments, and turn them in when you can."

"I will."

"Okay, enjoy your next class."

Mel hoisted her backpack higher as she stepped out the door. In the hallway, Lea stood, waiting.

"Oh, hey. You waiting for me?"

"I figured I'd walk you to Spanish like normal. That okay?"

"Yeah, thanks."

The two girls walked in silence. Some of Mel's hair had come out of her ponytail and dangled in front of her face. She twisted it around her finger, watching it bounce back into its curl when she let go.

"Hey, watch out!" someone shouted.

Mel stumbled and spun around, barely missing a trash can.

"Sorry," Lea said for her, taking Mel's arm and walking her past. "You okay?"

She nodded, still walking. Lea's face creased in concern as they turned the corner, but Mel shrugged it off.

"I'm okay, I promise."

Lea squeezed her hand and nodded at a classroom. "That's

your class."

"Right." They parted ways, Mel still fiddling idly with her hair.

When lunch came around, Mel sat with her usual group, munching quietly on her turkey sandwich at the end of the table. Nobody spoke to her. She couldn't really be bothered to care. It wasn't as though she had anything to say to anybody. Lea didn't join them for lunch most days because of rehearsals or drama club meetings, for which Mel was secretly glad. She knew Lea worried.

As she ate, her conversation with her aunt from the previous night came back. Clara was right about there being no other realistic option, but, God, the idea of somebody other than her mom living in that house with her was unnerving. To call it a stain on her mother's memory seemed melodramatic, and yet the image still wrapped around her heart like a boa constrictor. There was no real comfort in their presence.

It should have felt better to have people who loved her around. That's what everybody said, what the books said. Everybody was wrong. It didn't do any good. Joseph was always wrapped up in his grading and planning, and Clara—whatever she was, she wasn't a mother. They'd chosen not to have kids, and Mel knew the idea of raising her now had to be a bitter pill.

At the bell's ring, she tossed her banana peel in the trash and trudged to her next class, head still foggy with thoughts of her future. The rest of the day passed in the same thickness, for which she was grateful.

After school, Mel dropped by the theatre room and gave Lea a quick hug before leaving for the studio. Once outside, she leaned against the wall and pulled out her cell phone. Maybe Lea thought she was simply consumed by grief, but the conditions of the suicide continued to nag at her. It didn't make sense.

She looked up the local police department's number and dialed, focusing on keeping her breath even.

"Hello, Glenwood Police Department. How may I direct your call?"

"Hi, my name is Melanie Daniels, and I was hoping to talk to the officer who came when my mom, uh—when my mother, Rosemary Daniels, committed suicide."

There was a brief pause. "What date did the suicide occur on?"

"Um, last Wednesday." The sound of long nails clicking on a keyboard came through the phone. Mel tapped her foot on the ground.

"Okay, that'll be Detective Rosen. She's not in today. Would you like to leave a message?"

Mel's heart fell.

"Could you just have her call me back? Any time is fine." She rattled off her cell number. This was not the kind of call she wanted to get through to Clara.

"I'll let her know. You won't get a call before tomorrow, though. Is there anything I can do for you in the meantime?"

"No, thanks, that's all. Goodbye." She sighed as she hung up the phone. The report had already been filed, but maybe she could convince the detective to investigate further. *Like on those crime shows Mom watches*, she thought, then caught herself. *Right. Used to watch.*

When Mel walked into the studio, Hannah was deeply engaged in an insistent conversation with two young girls. They were waving paint-stained hands around and talking animatedly over one another. Hannah shot a worried glance at the nearby ceramics, so Mel rushed over and stood between them and the shelves.

"Girls, come on over here and just wait for everyone else to arrive. Please, just"—Hannah took in a deep breath—"just sit for a few minutes. I promise we'll start soon."

Once she had the girls settled, Hannah came over to where Mel was now wiping down the tables in the middle of the room.

"Thanks for that. I was sure she was going to knock half those mugs down."

"No problem. First timers?"

"Yeah, their mom dropped them off twenty minutes early and bolted." Hannah rolled her eyes. "She's got a lot of chutzpah."

"Delightful. Hopefully the girls are more respectful than their mom."

"It is what it is. Are we good to go?"

Mel glanced at her watch. "We're at T-minus ten minutes," she said. "The tables are almost all cleaned off. Do we need the tarps on the ground today?"

"Yeah, we're painting with the kinetic paints. We're going to do landscapes on paper, since this is the first time any of them have worked with this medium."

"Got it." Mel started spreading plastic sheets around and beneath the tables. Even though the floor was linoleum for this very reason, sometimes it was easier just to use disposable sheets with this many children involved. The after-school program was only once a week, and they had between fifteen and twenty-five local children each session. Hannah had started the program after learning that none of the elementary schools in the area had any arts education.

"It's unfair to them," she'd said to Mel when she first started working there. "Art makes a difference, you know? I can't know that they don't have any way to access this and not care. I have to do this." She'd insisted on making the program free despite the fact that the studio wasn't exactly a financial success. The area was definitely lower-income, and most of the families who sent their kids here couldn't have afforded a traditional art camp, especially not one that lasted all school year.

The door jingled, and Mel snapped out of her reverie to see a pair of twin boys walk in the door.

"Miss Mel! Miss Mel!" they yelled, starting to run over to her but then skidding to a stop at her raised eyebrows.

"We're not supposed to run," one half-whispered to his brother.

"Good memory, Brian," his father said, trailing them a few steps behind.

Mel grinned. "Hi, Brian. Hi, Xander. How are you?"

"We got to make volcanoes in school today!" Xander burst out. "It was so cool!"

"That sounds fantastic. We're painting moving nature scenes today. Maybe you can paint a volcano!"

"Yeah!"

"All right, go sit down. Miss Hannah will help you get settled, okay?"

They scurried off, and their father smiled wearily at Mel. "Thank you both for doing this, as always."

"It's our pleasure."

When three-thirty hit, there were seventeen children scattered around five tables, most chattering loudly. The benefit of having the same kids every week was that by a month or two into the school year, they'd found friends in the group if they didn't already know anyone. Hannah brought out the kinetic paints on a cart, which she placed between the tables.

"Okay, now listen. We talked last week about how we're going to be really careful with our materials, right?" There was a chorus of yeses. "Because today we're going to paint things from nature. You can paint a beach, or a forest, or a lake, or a mountain, or anything like that."

"Can I paint a volcano?" Xander interrupted.

"Yes, you can paint a volcano."

"Can I paint a dinosaur?" another child yelled out.

"Well, we should try not to paint animals. But we've also talked about listening to all the directions before we ask questions, right?"

Another chorus of yeses. Mel smiled, impressed at Hannah's infinite patience.

"What's special today is that we're using something called kinetic paint!" She went on to explain the paint that would move slightly on the page, making the landscapes look a little more real. It was a clever charm that went into that kind of paint. Mel was no good with charms, but Hannah had spent the last month perfecting this one. The paints they were using today were booster paints, purchased pre-charmed from a supplier and amplified by Hannah's spell.

The next hour passed by in a flurry of paint splatters and encouraging words. As their time came to an end, Mel knelt behind the new girls, who had introduced themselves as Thea and Becca.

"How are you two doing?"

"I made a river! Look, the water's moving!" Becca said cheerfully.

"Wow, that's pretty great! You gonna put it on the refrigerator when you get home?"

"Yeah!"

"Mine, too!" Thea said. "It's a forest."

"I love it! You girls did a great job. Go ahead and finish up, and then go wash your hands, okay?" She stood, her knees cracking, and ushered some of the other kids toward the sinks.

Parents began to arrive, gathering up children and gushing over paintings. Xander and Brian waved goodbye, the door closed, and Hannah flopped into a chair.

"I always forget how exhausting that is."

Mel looked around the room. "I'm officially glad we put tarps down."

"Tell me about it. They tracked some of the paint on their shoes, of course, but it could have been so much worse." She took out her scrunchie, then retied her hair, pulling the flyaway locks back into submission. "Let's crank out this cleanup so you can go home."

Mel was back in the studio less than twenty-four hours later, this time for her own project. She pulled a pot from the top shelf and began gathering her materials. She'd found an old book of potions in a bookstore a few weeks previous, most of which she'd never heard of. Some of the names for ingredients were old, and some were rare, but she'd flagged a few that looked doable.

The page she flipped to this time held a recipe for a tonic that was meant to be taken to ease the physical symptoms of emotional pain—upset stomachs, headaches, muscle tension. It was irritatingly fitting, and Mel nearly changed her plans out of spite. But she felt her gut tighten at the mere thought of grief, at the barest whisper of her mother's memory. It couldn't hurt to try.

Since there were a couple other people at the opposite corner of the dark room, Mel didn't turn on the radio like she sometimes did. Instead, she put in her headphones and flipped on her desk lamp. The recipe was water-based, so she filled and turned on the electric kettle on the counter.

There was a peace in chopping and measuring herbs, sprinkling them into the pot of hot water at regular intervals. One of the plants turned the mixture a chilling blood red, and Mel hastily added the saffron. Soon, the mixture was a pleasant sunset orange, and she poured more boiling water in to raise the temperature. The potion was meant to sit for a quarter hour after the final water was added, so Mel covered her pot, set a timer on her phone, and began to clean up her utensils.

In the last few minutes before the timer went off, Mel sat quietly in front of the slowly-cooling pot. A reread of the directions indicated that the potion could be drunk as soon as the quarter hour was up, if so desired. She felt another wave of weariness wash over her, tears coming to her eyes and slipping out without a moment's pause. Some hours everything seemed fine, but sometimes she could barely breathe.

The timer dinged quietly. Mel set to decanting the potion, filling three bottles with just enough left over to take now. She scribbled labels for the full bottles and put them in her locker before dipping a finger in the remaining liquid. A careful taste seemed safe, so she poured the few tablespoons' worth into a glass and downed it. It burned going down, and she wished she'd cut it with water, although the recipe hadn't explicitly allowed it. Perhaps it was best this way.

Her stomach knots began to untie slowly as she made her way out of the back room, backpack slung over one shoulder. It seemed to be working, but there was only one way to be sure.

"You leaving for the day?" Hannah asked as she passed by.

"Yeah, I'm..." She hesitated. "I'm going to visit my mom. Her grave, I mean."

Hannah nodded. "Okay. I hope talking to her is helpful."

"Me, too." Mel walked out the door and took a right. The chill wind pushed at her back, urging her along the sidewalk as she made her way to the cemetery. Hannah wasn't entirely wrong about her going to talk to her mother. But what really drove her was the need to see if the potion could withstand the pain of sitting at the graveside.

The gate to the cemetery swung open easily, and Mel made her way among the gravestones to the plot where her mother had been buried. There was only a temporary placard at the gravesite; the headstone would be put in later. She sat on the grass, knees pulled to her chest.

"I miss you, Mom," she said. The words sounded hollow and insufficient. "Aunt Clara wants to move in and I can't stand it. I can't believe she'd try to just fill your place like that. I don't know why you had to go, but I just… I can't believe you killed yourself. It's so cold here." She grabbed a hoodie out of her backpack and pulled it on. "It's colder in the ground. I'm going to talk to the detective who filed the report on your death. I'm hoping I can convince her to start an equivocal death investigation, like in your crime shows."

The chill no longer seemed to be coming exclusively from the wind. Mel shivered deep in her bones, huddling in on herself. Tears fell from her eyes and slid down her cheeks, leaving frosty trails. "You must have been so cold, lying there on the pavement. I know how much you hated the cold weather. It couldn't have been you."

Mel's teeth began to chatter, and she could hardly speak. She tried to stand, but her head spun wildly. She hadn't had a headache before, but now one set in, throbbing and dizzying. *The potion.* She cursed inwardly, unable to keep her head straight long enough to find her balance.

I only took a little, she thought. If she stayed sitting, hopefully it would pass without further incident. Then somebody sat down beside her with a plop. Mel started slightly, then nearly fell over when she saw the person's face.

"Mom?" She blinked furiously.

"It's me." Her mom smiled gently but didn't reach out.

"What…" There was no way to end her question, but it didn't matter. The chill in her head subsided some, and she was able to stop her teeth chattering long enough to focus on her mother.

"I don't have a lot of time. You've got to listen to me."

"Wait, what do you mean, not a lot of time?"

"I can't stay."

"Are you… a ghost?" The word came out choked.

"Something like that. The specifics don't matter."

"But there's no such thing!"

The woman laughed. "Mel, you make potions. There's an intro to spells class at your high school. What makes you think that there can't be ghosts? Anyway, this has to be quick. I just wanted you to know that you're right."

"I'm… right?"

"I didn't kill myself. I shouldn't be there." She gestured to the grave. "This wasn't me."

"Who did? Were you pushed?"

Her mother's face tightened. "Yes. She pushed me."

"Who pushed you?"

"You know we had always struggled…" The image was beginning to fade.

"Who?"

"Me and Clara, of course." And before Mel could squeak out another word, her mother was gone. The headache returned with a vengeance, and she curled up on the grass. This coldness had to end soon. It had to. It had to.

"Mel? Mel!" A voice rang in her ear, and she started awake. Hannah was kneeling over her. "Mel, are you okay?"

"I'm… What happened?"

"I don't know, you were just… Did you fall asleep?"

"I must have. Why are you here?"

"Your aunt called the studio when you didn't answer her calls and didn't come home. You said you were coming here, so…"

Mel sat up and took careful inventory of her body. She seemed to have passed the worst of it, and the heaviness in her stomach was only a result of what her mother's ghost had said. *Clara.* It almost made sense.

"Thanks for checking on me. I think I'm feeling okay now."

"What happened?"

"I just…" Mel sighed. Someone might as well know. "I saw my mother's ghost."

Hannah's facial expression barely changed. "You did? What did she say?"

"She said I was right. She wasn't… Somebody killed her."

This time, Hannah couldn't keep a poker face. "What?"

"Not 'somebody'. Clara. My aunt."

"Mel, what the hell are you saying?" She reached out and took Mel's hand. "You feel warmer. Let's try to stand up, okay?"

"Okay." Slowly, the pair rose, and Mel took a few shaky steps. "I think I can walk now."

"I came in my car. Come, I'll drive you home."

"Thanks."

Once they were in the car, Hannah turned the heat on. "Now talk to me. Your mother's ghost said that Clara killed her?"

Mel relayed the story in halting sentences, pausing frequently to catch her breath and her thoughts.

"Well, that's quite something," Hannah said. "I hate to ask this, but do you think seeing the ghost was part of the side effects of that potion?"

"No," Mel said emphatically. "I knew her. It felt like her. And she was right—why not? Why can't there be ghosts?"

"I'm just a little concerned."

"It makes sense, though. Mom never would have committed suicide, not ever—and not like that. And she and Clara have always had a tempestuous relationship."

"Is that really reason enough to suspect her?"

Mel shrugged. "I don't know. Maybe."

"Just be careful, okay?" Hannah pulled onto Mel's driveway and shifted the car into park. "I worry about you."

"I know you do."

Mel sat at the dinner table, playing idly with her broccoli. Joseph had been telling a story about his students, but when he finished, the conversation had faltered into silence. It hadn't been hard to lie to them, to say that she'd just lost track of time and her phone had been on silent out of respect in the cemetery. Clara had seemed to understand, although she was clearly frustrated with Mel for not picking up.

"So, how were your classes today?" Joseph asked.

"Okay." Mel shrugged and ate the piece of broccoli she'd been pushing around for the last five minutes. "I mean, it was school."

"Anything interesting happen?"

"Not really."

His attempts at conversation having failed, Joseph turned his own attention to the meatloaf in front of him. The ring of Mel's cell phone cut through the silence. She pulled the phone out. The number on the caller ID was from the police station.

"I'm sorry, I have to take this," she said, pushing her chair back.

"Mel!" Clara scolded. "No phone calls at the dinner table."

"Sorry," she said, then walked out of the room as she

answered the call. "Hello?"

"Is this Melanie Daniels?"

"Yes, this is she."

"This is Detective Rosen from the Glenwood Police Department. I was told you called regarding your mother's suicide." Her words were crisp, but they veiled the same pity that was in everybody's voice these days.

"I did. I called because I have reason to believe that her death was not a suicide, and I'm concerned that it wasn't fully investigated."

"What makes you think that?" Now the pity was tinged with skepticism.

"There's no evidence to indicate that she was suicidal, and her method wasn't typical for a woman."

"Ms. Daniels, I'm sorry for your loss, but the situation was fairly clear-cut. I don't think there's any physical evidence for this death being anything besides a suicide."

Mel's chest constricted, and she fought to keep herself calm. "I understand that it looks that way, but I really don't think that's the case. Isn't there anything you can do?"

The detective sighed. "I can come out on Monday and talk to you, if you'd like. But I can't guarantee anything."

"Can't you"—she paused, searching her memory for the words—"do an equivocal death investigation?"

"We'll see on Monday. I'll come to your home around four. Will that do?"

"Yes, that's great, thank you!" Mel breathed a little easier as she hung up the phone. This would finally get things in motion.

When she returned to the dinner table, though, the lightness of her heart vanished. Clara's face was stony.

"You know it's not acceptable to take phone calls at the dinner table," she said. "Who was it?"

"Oh, nobody." Mel knew even as she spoke the words that it wouldn't work.

"Clearly it was somebody important, or else you wouldn't have left the table. Who was it?"

"Um, the police department."

Clara closed her eyes and passed her hand over her face in a gesture of frustration. "The police department?"

"Yes." Mel met her aunt's gaze defensively. If she wouldn't let Detective Rosen come investigate, that would be proof that her mother's ghost had been right. "The detective who handled Mom's case is coming on Monday to begin an equivocal death investigation." Perhaps it was a white lie, but it seemed necessary.

"A what?"

"To see if she really committed suicide, or if she was murdered."

"Murdered!" Clara laughed, sharp and humorless. "Mel, what on earth are you talking about?"

"Mom wasn't suicidal. She didn't do this voluntarily. I think somebody pushed her." She took a few bites of her meatloaf calmly, eyes on her aunt's face.

"There's no reason to think that. Honey, I'm sorry, I really am. What happened to your mom… You're not the only one who's hurting. But you can't make assumptions like that."

All pretense of finishing dinner was now abandoned.

"It's not just an assumption. There are things that don't add up."

"Don't be ridiculous. Call the police department back and tell them you've made a mistake."

"I won't." Mel folded her arms. A part of her was aware that she looked like a typical petulant teenager, but her fury ran over her reason. "Mom was murdered. I know it. And I'm going to prove it."

"Lord, help me," Clara said. "I know you're grieving, but, Mel—"

"I'm going to prove it, no matter what you want." Mel stood and carried her plate to the kitchen. She scraped the remains of her dinner into the trash and put the plate in the dishwasher, then walked back to the dining room. "You can't stop me."

"Melanie Daniels!" But it was to no avail. Mel stomped back to her bedroom, ignoring Clara's calls and locking her door firmly behind her.

The next evening, after a long day at school, Mel waited by the drama classroom for Lea to exit. She came out, spotted Mel, and walked over with a smile.

"Hey, how's it going?" she asked.

"It's okay. How are you?"

"Busy." Lea laughed. "It seems like there's never any break. Even though we just wrapped *Taming of the Shrew*, it's already time to start making decisions about the next play."

Mel listened to Lea chatter about her conversation with the drama teacher as they made their way out of the school and toward a nearby coffee shop.

"In any case," Lea said, "are you… doing okay?"

It was clear that her real question was, "Have you accepted that your mom committed suicide yet?" But Mel had had enough of being disbelieved.

"Better now. I talked to the detective who handled my mom's case, and she's going to come over on Monday and maybe start an equivocal death investigation."

"Oh, Mel." She sighed. "This isn't healthy, you know."

"I really believe this, okay? I…" Mel took a breath. "I saw her ghost."

Lea stopped walking. "Are you serious?"

"Yes, I'm serious. Come on, I'll talk to you about it inside."

When they entered the coffee shop, Lea went off to find a table while Mel ordered a latte and a black coffee. She carried the drinks over to where Lea was sitting, eyebrows skeptical.

"So tell me what happened."

Mel relayed a shortened version of the cemetery story. "It was really her, Lea. I've never been so sure of anything."

"Are you sure it wasn't"—Lea gestured, searching for words—"I don't know, something medical? It sounds like a hallucination."

"I'm certain." Mel sipped her latte. "It was my mom. I know my mom. And she said Clara pushed her."

"This is ridiculous."

"Is it? They've never had the best relationship."

"Neither have my brother and I, but that doesn't mean I'm suddenly going to push Adam off a bridge!"

"I know, but this is different. Anyway, Detective Rosen will come on Monday and…"

"And what?" Lea interrupted. "And you'll tell her that you suspect your aunt of murder because you saw your mother's ghost? How exactly is that going to go?"

"I'm not going to tell her that. I'm just going to tell her I don't think it was suicide. She can figure out who it was for herself—or at least I can start looking for clearer signs."

Lea shook her head. "I can't believe you don't hear how this sounds."

"I know it's a little unexpected, but sometimes I just *know* things, okay?" Mel's voice came out higher-pitched than she wanted, as though she was begging Lea to understand. She didn't want to beg.

"You've said that before, and you're not always right."

"Trust me on this one, okay?"

"I can't." Lea downed the last of her coffee. "I'm sorry. I don't know what to tell you, Mel, but this is so beyond reasonable. And I hope the detective tells you that on Monday."

"How incredibly kind of you," Mel snarled. "I so appreciate your confidence in me."

Lea stood. "I have to get home," she said shortly.

"Fine. Me, too."

"Fine."

Mel sat at the table for a minute after Lea had left the shop, just to ensure they wouldn't run into each other, then started down the sidewalk toward home, fuming all the way. At least Hannah believed her. And come Monday, so would the police.

The school day felt like an eternity on Monday. Mel couldn't manage to focus on any of her classes despite repeated attempts of her teachers to engage her in class discussions. Even Mrs. Irwin got frustrated when she called on Mel for an answer and received a vacant stare and an "I don't know." It didn't matter. She'd get her grades back up in a few weeks. For now, she could think of nothing but the detective's impending visit.

Mel nearly sprinted home after school, arriving a full half-hour before Detective Rosen was supposed to come. Neither Clara nor Joseph was home from work yet, and so she sat at the kitchen table and tried to work on her geometry homework. At a quarter to four, the sound of a car on the street outside made her leap out of her seat. A look out the front window showed that it was only a neighbor pulling into their driveway, and she sat back down.

At four on the dot, the doorbell rang. Mel took a deep breath, noted her thudding heart, and went to the door. Two people stood there, badges out, one of whom was presumably Detective

Rosen.

"Hi, I'm Mel," she said, holding out her hand to shake.

The woman stepped forward and took it. "Detective Rosen. We spoke on the phone. This is my partner, Officer Stern." Mel shook his hand as well and invited them in.

"Please, sit down." They all found seats at the kitchen table. "Thank you for coming," Mel said.

"Of course. Now, you said that you suspect foul play in your mother's death?"

"Yes. I know it seemed like a suicide, but it seems to me that if anybody knew she was suicidal, it would have been me, right? I was her only child, and we've always been really close. She'd never been happier than she was recently. She'd gotten a promotion at work, and we were doing better financially than we ever have."

Officer Stern shook his head. "That's not reason to assume she wasn't suicidal. She was found on a Wednesday morning, right?"

"Yes, sir. Early. Around six, I think." Mel folded her hands in front of her.

"And is your relationship with her the only reason you assume she didn't commit suicide?"

Mel sighed. "Women almost never commit messy suicides like that. Women drown themselves and take pills. This doesn't make sense."

Detective Rosen smiled gently. "Are you a fan of crime shows?"

"Sort of. But it's not just that. I learned about it in my psychology class, too."

"While it's true that women overwhelmingly do not jump off of bridges onto asphalt bike paths, there is literally no evidence to support any other theory."

Tears welled briefly in Mel's eyes. "That's why you have to investigate! There won't be any evidence if you don't look for it."

"Ms. Daniels, I know you're grieving. But please take a moment to think about this."

"I have! I have thought about it, and—" Mel broke off. They waited patiently while she caught her breath. "And I know this isn't just me wishing. She's my mom, all right? And I know her. Knew her."

The officers exchanged a look. "I'm sorry," Detective Rosen said, closing the file she'd had in front of her. "There's nothing we can do. If you find any actual evidence, please do call the station."

She pulled a business card from her wallet and handed it to Mel.

"If you need anything," she added, "please don't hesitate to call me. I know some wonderful grief counselors that I can recommend to you."

"Thank you," Mel said. She ran her fingers through her hair. "I appreciate you coming. I'll let you know when I have more evidence."

Detective Rosen looked at her with sympathy. "Okay. I'll be here."

Mel showed the officers out. Just as they closed their car doors, Clara pulled into the driveway. She walked up to the front door, where Mel was still standing, watching the police car drive away.

"So the police came already," she said.

"Yes."

"And? What did they say?"

"They're not going to help."

Clara's face relaxed visibly. "Good."

"What? Why is that good? Don't you want to know what

happened to your sister?"

"I know what happened. She jumped off a bridge and ended her own life," she said. "I have no doubts."

"Well, I do." Mel spun around and stalked back into the house.

"Mel, come back here right now."

She stopped at the bottom of the stairs. "What?"

"I understand you're in pain, but there is a point at which your behavior becomes unacceptable. You are fast reaching that point. Take some time to think about your actions."

"Fine." Mel turned the corner around the staircase and shut herself in her room. Once alone, she pulled out her cell phone and typed in Hannah's number. The phone rang once, twice. Mel lay down on her bed, head sinking into the fluffy pillows.

"Hello?"

"Hannah, it's me, Mel."

"Hey, Mel. How's it going?"

"I've got even more reason to believe it was… her." Best not be overheard.

"Oh? What happened?"

"The police came by, and they're not going to reopen the investigation." Mel's stomach curdled. *How dare they?*

"I'm sorry. I know that's not what you wanted."

"But when she found out, she seemed too happy that it wasn't going to happen."

"Are you sure she wasn't just hoping you'd move past this?"

Mel tensed. "Are you hoping that?"

"I just want the truth for you. Whatever that means," Hannah said soothingly. "You know that."

"I know. Sorry. But I do think she was too relieved. Like she was hiding something."

"Well, what are you going to do next?"

"I don't know. I'm not giving up, though."

As soon as the bell rang for lunch the next day, Mel ran to Lea's locker. She might only have a few minutes to catch her before she went to the drama classroom.

"Hey, you." Lea walked up and kissed Mel, their fight in the coffee shop forgotten. "I wasn't expecting you here. What's up?"

"Do you have a drama club meeting today?"

"Not officially, but I was going to drop by and talk to Mr. Bell about something. It can wait, though. You seem flushed. You okay?"

"Yeah, I just—can we sit down?"

"Of course." Lea furrowed her brow in concern as they sat on the floor in front of their lockers, several feet away from the nearest group of students. "Now talk to me."

"So Detective Rosen came by last night."

"Oh, God."

Mel could see Lea trying to refrain from rolling her eyes. "Don't do that. Just listen to me."

"I'm sorry," she said. "Go ahead."

"They're not going to do an equivocal death investigation. They're not going to do anything."

"Oh, that's good."

"What?" The word came out like a yelp. "That isn't a good thing!"

"I mean, it kind of is, Mel." Lea smiled. "Maybe now that they've told you it wasn't foul play, you'll believe it."

"But when Clara came home as they left, she asked me about it. And I told her the same thing I told you, and she looked relieved! Like she'd been afraid they would figure out what she'd done!"

"You are making no sense, you know that, right?" Lea shook

her head. "Your aunt did not kill her sister. That's the most ridiculous thing I've ever heard."

"You just don't know them as well as I do."

"And you? You love your aunt, you always have. Wasn't going over to visit her and Joseph your favorite thing to do in the summer when you were a kid?"

"So maybe I was wrong." Mel shrugged. "But this time…"

"No, this time, you're wrong. But, hey, if you don't believe your aunt, or your uncle, or the police—why should you listen to me?" Lea stood up. "I'm going to go talk to Mr. Bell. I've got to run home after school, too. Adam's got soccer practice so I have to let the dog out. I'll see you tomorrow." She left before Mel could utter another word.

Mel looked after her in shock. Nobody was listening to her! It wasn't fair. If nobody would listen, if she couldn't find evidence, if she couldn't find some way to render justice—would she have to live with her mother's murderer for the next two years?

Her head swam with terrifying images: Clara standing behind her mother on the bridge. Clara looking over the dead body. Clara in her house, in her mother's bed, perhaps planning Mel's own death to look like a grief-stricken suicide. It wouldn't be a stretch. Everybody thought she'd lost her mind, especially Lea. Detective Rosen and her partner would be able to testify to her overwhelming grief. The thought was chilling.

When she got home that afternoon, Joseph was just pulling into the driveway. He joined her in the kitchen a few minutes later.

"Would you like some tea?" he asked.

"Sure, that'd be great." Mel pulled out her Spanish textbook and flipped to the vocabulary she was supposed to be studying.

"How was school today?"

"It was okay. I had a fight with Lea," she ventured.

"Oh? Why's that?" Joseph flipped on the electric kettle and took a seat beside her.

"Oh, I don't know. It's just been hard recently." No matter how understanding he was, she couldn't tell him she suspected his wife of murder.

He nodded knowingly. "Relationships are hard enough without grief poking its nasty head in and making a mess."

"You seem to do okay."

"Well, your aunt and I have been together for many years, and we have a lot more experience behind us. That makes a big difference. But even we struggled when your father died." The kettle clicked off, and Joseph stood to finish the tea.

"Really?"

"Oh, yes." He poured the now-boiling water into two mugs and brought them over to the table, his large, dark hands dwarfing the handles. "Your aunt and I had only been dating for a few months, you know. We didn't know each other well enough for me to be able to help her through the mourning process."

"I didn't know that."

"Now, we made it through okay. But it was rough for a while. She loved your father very much, you know."

Mel frowned. "She wasn't…"

Joseph laughed. "Oh, not like that. No, she and your mother had very different taste in partners, which was probably good for their relationship. But the two of them had been getting closer, finally, after the struggle in college, and his death was a huge strain. Your mother had a very hard time, and I think Clara wanted her to move on faster than she was ready."

"Why's that?"

"Your aunt is not the type to wallow. She processes her emotions more quickly than others—sometimes so fast it looks like she hasn't felt anything at all. Don't think she isn't grieving now, though."

Mel took tiny sips of her tea, trying to avoid being burned. The insulation-charmed ceramic mugs were nice when she forgot her tea for forty minutes, but less so when she wanted to drink it immediately. "But what happened in college?" Maybe the issue had come back, and that's what had caused her aunt to… The words were still hard, but she forced herself to think them. *To kill Mom.*

"You know, I never really knew the details. Neither of them ever wanted to talk about it. But something drove them apart for several years."

"Mom never said anything."

"She wanted you to have a good relationship with your aunt." Joseph put his hand on Mel's. "And she still would, despite all of this."

"Yeah, I know." Guilt washed over Mel. She definitely couldn't tell him now.

"She put us in her will as your legal guardians for a reason."

"I figured it was just the only choice."

"No, we had a long talk about it after Clara and I got married. Your mom said she trusted us to be able to raise you if necessary."

Mel's heart sank further. "But you never wanted children."

Joseph shook his head. "That doesn't mean we wouldn't take care of you. That never meant we didn't love you. And," he chuckled, "it's not as though you need a lot of raising now. The diaper-changing, time-out days are long over."

A laugh escaped Mel's throat. "True."

"It is okay with you that we move in here, isn't it?"

She shrugged. "I really don't have a choice."

"I know. But I'd like the situation to have your blessing, even though it doesn't need your permission."

Mel stayed silent.

"Well," Joseph said, standing. "Think about it. I have some papers to grade, and I believe you have homework to do. Let me know if you need a hand." He walked out of the kitchen, leaving Mel with a heavy conscience and a still-scalding mug of tea.

"Why won't you listen to me?" Mel's voice broke as her volume climbed.

"Would you keep your voice down?" Lea hissed, grabbing her arm and dragging her toward the door. "Come on!"

Mel followed, glaring at her girlfriend. Fortunately, the bell had rung fifteen minutes ago and most students were already on their way home.

"There," Lea said once they were in the parking lot. "God, you were practically screaming. Everybody was listening."

"So what?"

"So I don't want to fight in front of them!"

"Fine. But you're still not listening to me."

"Because you have lost your mind. I have no idea how to make it clearer to you. Your aunt did not kill your mother." Lea shook her head. "She did not."

"Why are you so reluctant to believe this?"

"Reluctant?" Lea laughed. "I'm not reluctant. I'm telling you that this is not true. I don't know why you want so badly for this to be true, but it's not."

"You didn't see her!"

"I don't have to."

"She told me..." Mel put her balled fists to her forehead. "My mother told me she was murdered. Told me it was Clara. Clara was way too relieved when the police didn't investigate further. She and my mom had some mysterious fight in college that they never fully got over. How is this not adding up to you?"

"Because you don't even know what this fight was about, and you also don't know that they never got over it."

"My uncle said—"

"Your uncle is a secondhand source of information, and even he never said they weren't over it. Just said they'd had a hard time of it. Well, guess what? That happens a lot. My dad and his sister fought over a boy they both had a crush on in college, and they hardly spoke for a year. One of my friends in seventh grade barely knew his great-aunt because she'd made some snide comment to his grandmother before he was even born, and they didn't invite each other to family events anymore."

"Your point?" Mel snapped.

"People don't kill each other for that!"

"Some do."

"Yes, but you can't just assume…"

"How many times have I told you my reasoning?"

Lea threw up her hands. "That's it. I can't do this. You won't listen."

"What do you mean?" Mel asked, suddenly quiet.

"I'm sorry, Mel. But this is way too much for me. I care about you and I want you to do well. And I had every intention of standing by you through this." Lea sighed. "But I can't do this if you won't listen to reason, if you won't stop blaming your aunt for something it's clear she didn't do. Clear to me, at least," she added.

"Are you breaking up with me?"

"Yes. I am."

The wind whistled through the trees and blew Lea's hair around her face. She brushed it back impatiently and looked at Mel.

"Well, then." Mel nodded. "If you won't support me in this, I suppose that's for the best."

"I would support you. If you were being rational. Which you aren't."

"Thanks for those kind final words," Mel snapped. She walked away, leaving Lea standing there and shaking her head. She knew Lea would have to go back inside at some point, since she'd left a drama club meeting to have this conversation. Normally Mel didn't interrupt her in meetings, but she hadn't been able to find time to talk to her all day. Perhaps this was why.

As she made her way down the sidewalk away from the school, she kicked at the fallen red leaves. So that was it. Lea had bowed out. That was fine.

"I don't need her," she said aloud. There was still Hannah, or so she hoped. Maybe not. Maybe everybody was going to abandon her in this pursuit. It didn't matter. She'd figure it out, no matter what it took, no matter who didn't support her.

Hannah. It's Wednesday. She pulled out her cell phone to check the time. Three-thirty already. She bit her tongue to keep from cursing as she broke into a run, turning the corner so sharply she almost fell over.

She slid in through the door of the studio at three forty-two, apologizing profusely to Hannah before she'd even crossed the threshold.

Hannah looked slightly frazzled, standing over the tables of small children, but smiled at Mel anyway.

"I'm sorry, I'm sorry." Mel quickly washed her hands and jogged over to the tables. "What are we working on today?"

"I figured we'd do kinetic paint again, but this time we're painting animals. Well, mostly." Hannah laughed. "Some of us are committed to landscapes." She gestured to Xander, who was painting a range of volcanoes, all with lava spilling out their tops.

"Got it." Mel slid into camp-counselor mode, shoving all of her anger at Lea to the back of her mind. As she told jokes and cleaned up paint spills, she felt it boiling but shrugged it off. There was nothing she could do.

"I'm sorry I was late," she said to Hannah as they gathered up the finished paintings and hung them to dry in the last few minutes before the parents arrived. "Lea broke up with me and I kinda lost track of time."

Hannah clipped up the painting she was holding, then hugged Mel gently. "I'm sorry. What happened?"

"She thinks I'm being unreasonable about Clara. She said she can't handle it. It's fine. I can be mature about it."

Hannah snorted. "Sorry," she said. "I mean, I do believe you. But I also believe that nobody ever really knows how to be completely mature about a breakup. And I'm sorry that you've lost so much in such a short time."

"Yeah. Me, too."

The sun shone brightly through the window onto Mel's desk, and she leaned forward to feel the warmth.

"Mel? Do you have an answer?" Mrs. Irwin asked.

"Oh, uh." She looked down at her paper. "Two pi?"

"Correct." The teacher cast a worried glance at Mel but continued the lesson without saying anything about it. When class was over, however, she called Mel to the front for the second time in as many weeks.

"Is there a problem, ma'am?" Mel asked as she stood in front of Mrs. Irwin.

"That's what I wanted to ask you. I know you got the answer when I called on you—and before you ask, yes, I *was* testing because I thought you weren't paying attention—but I'm worried about your class participation."

Mel shrugged. "I'm sorry. I've not really been feeling up to it."

"I understand that, but as the semester goes on, it becomes more of a concern. If you don't understand what we're doing now, it'll be a lot harder to catch up later." She handed Mel a stapled packet. "I've got some extra materials I'd like you to look at. Please try to get your late homework in as soon as possible. By Monday, preferably."

Mel blinked in surprise. "Monday?"

"You'll have the weekend, and if you have any questions, you can bring them to me Monday before school. But I need you on track."

"Um, I'll do my best." She put the packet in her backpack. "Thank you."

As she walked through the hallways, she kept half an eye out for Lea. She didn't want to run into her unaware—or, preferably, at all.

Time was running out to do something. The longer she waited, the less likely the police would be to believe her. But the signs had become so painfully clear, even without Lea's support. She felt Clara's guilt every time they shared a meal or passed time in the same room. It weighed on the air and poisoned their conversations. It seemed as though even Joseph was beginning to notice that something was seriously wrong. She wondered if he had any inkling of what Clara had done. What she was capable of.

It was probably easier than she'd imagined. Out for a morning walk, drawn by the promise of intimate conversation and closeness. Just standing there on the bridge, looking at the skinny river below and the wide asphalt bike and walking paths alongside it. Her mother leaning over, pointing at somebody. Laughing. Just a little push. Maybe she hardly realized what she'd done.

And the image of her mother, lying on the ground like the broken swan of so many old poems. Did she know she had been pushed? Did she think it was an accident? Were her final thoughts of fear? Anger? Betrayal? *Did she think of me? Did she have time?*

Mel was called to talk to two more teachers and the guidance counselor before the end of the day, each expressing concern for how she'd fallen behind. She bit her tongue, apologized, promised she'd do better. But they didn't know. She couldn't tell them, not until she had more evidence. If Lea didn't believe her, why would they? They'd tell her to go to the police, and she'd have to admit that she already had. And then what? What could they do? So she kept silent, but visions of justice flooded her mind like ghosts in a graveyard.

Dinner that night was another near-silent affair. Mel poked at her meal, her stomach roiling at the thought of even the blandest food. She saw Clara and Joseph shooting glances at each other and wondered when one of them would say something. It didn't take long.

"Mel, we need to talk." Clara put her fork down with a clink. "We've started advertising our apartment to find a sublessee. There are still six months left in our lease, but we need to be here with you. So as soon as we find one, we'll be moving our things in here."

Mel glared at the plate in front of her.

"Are you listening?"

"Yeah."

"That means we're going to need to rearrange some things in this house. I'm sorry if this hurts you, but sometimes you have to grieve while you get through the rest of life. We can't just set everything aside."

"Honey, you know your mom wanted us to be your guardians," Joseph broke in.

"How do you know what she wanted?" Mel spat. "Neither of you know anything!"

"She was my sister," Clara said calmly.

"She was my mother! And I have just as much right to her as you do!"

"I know you do. Why wouldn't you?" Her aunt's eyes narrowed in confusion.

"More, really." Mel felt her heart racing. "After all, I'm the only one being honest about what happened to her. And she deserved honesty."

"Mel, we've been over this. Your mother committed suicide, and—"

"She did not!" Mel roared. "You know she didn't! You pushed her!"

Silence fell.

"Excuse me?"

"You pushed her." Hands trembling in anger, Mel shoved away her plate. "You pushed her off that bridge. I know you did. Nobody else will believe me, but I know what happened. You were always jealous of her, Mom told me. She said when you were little, you always used to try to take her stuff and the people she loved. And something happened in college—I don't know what, but you never got over it, did you?"

"Melanie!" Joseph rumbled, but Mel barreled on.

"Maybe it was still pure jealousy. Maybe she held some secret over you from college. A crime, or some illegal magic. And you pushed her off that bridge so it would look like she killed herself, but I know my mom! And I know she wouldn't do that. You killed her. Even if nobody else believes me, I know."

Clara stood up, her face hard. "Melanie Daniels, listen to me. You are hurting. You are grieving. And I have given you a great deal of leeway because I know that grief is hard. But this has gone too far. You stand there and accuse me of murdering my own sister? How could you possibly believe that? This is unacceptable behavior. And you need to pull yourself together."

She stared straight at Mel. Neither one broke the eye contact until the clinking of plates made them both glance at Joseph. He was stacking up the dishes and gathering the napkins. He looked at Mel and shook his head, disappointment radiating across his face.

"I can't stay here." Mel ran to her room and threw her wallet and phone in her purse. When she came back out to the hallway, Clara was standing there, daggers in her eyes.

"You are going to stay here and we are going to talk about this."

"I am not." Mel slung her purse over her shoulder. "I'm spending the night at Hannah's."

"Do not walk out that door, young lady."

But Mel walked out anyway.

On the walk to Hannah's townhouse, she toyed with her phone, not sure if she should call first or if that wouldn't do any good. Her feet struck the pavement sharply, her flip flops smacking back against her heels in rhythm. They were the first shoes she'd seen, although now she was mildly regretting not at least putting on tennis shoes. The chill autumn wind whisked around her feet and calves, drawing out the goosebumps.

Arriving at Hannah's without having decided on the phone call was a decision after all, she supposed. She knocked on the door, and Hannah opened up moments later.

"Mel? What are you doing here?"

"I'm sorry," Mel said, shivering slightly. "Can I stay here tonight?"

"Yeah, of course. Come in." She ushered Mel through the door and closed it behind her. "What happened?"

"Well." A shaky laugh caught in her throat. "I, ah, accused my aunt of murder at the dinner table." The phrasing sounded particularly funny, and the amusement mixed with the anger in her chest.

"Oh." Hannah nodded. "Well, yes, I can imagine I know why you're here then. What did she say?"

"Of course she said she hadn't done it. She didn't want me to leave, but I couldn't stay there."

"I understand. Please, have a seat at the table. I'll make us some tea."

Mel nodded and sat, her face in her hands. She watched as Hannah bustled around the kitchen, gathering kettle and mugs and teabags.

"Is Earl Grey okay? I've just got that and green tea."

"That's completely fine. Thanks, you're sweet."

"It's no problem. Now, tell me the story."

Mel took a deep breath and recounted the conversation as close to verbatim as she could manage. "And that was it," she finished. "I just walked out."

Mugs in hand, Hannah joined her at the table. "Hon, I have a question for you."

"What?" Mel asked, dreading what was to come.

"Are you sure your mother wasn't depressed?"

"I've told you already, I'm sure."

"It just seems to me, on reflection, that she had been struggling for a few years now. I know you said her job was hard on her, and I wonder if she was less involved in church committees than she had been before?"

Mel blinked. "I mean, yeah, she didn't spend as much time organizing functions as she used to."

"Did she sleep well?" Hannah asked.

"What? Um, I don't think so. She was always up pretty late. Later than me most nights."

"Those are symptoms of depression. And I bet if you think back, you can find some others. I know how badly you want this not to be true. I know how much it hurts. But I think, just maybe, that you didn't know how much your mom was struggling because she wanted to protect you."

"Oh, God." Mel sank forward and put her face in her hands. "I didn't…"

"You didn't want to believe it." Hannah put her hand on Mel's arm. "I know. But remember, you're not the only person hurting. Your aunt lost a sister. No matter their struggles, your mother was dear to her."

"Oh, God," Mel repeated. The enormity of the accusation she'd made struck her all at once. She couldn't draw breath, the wind knocked out of her like when she used to fall down the stairs as a kid. Hannah rubbed her back gently, and they both waited for her lungs to function again.

"You okay?"

"Not really."

"You don't have to be. But you do have to go back home at some point."

"I can't go back there. How can I face her?"

"You have to." Hannah nudged the mug of tea in front of Mel. "Drink. The warmth will help."

Mel took a few large sips. The heat was comforting, but her stomach still twisted with guilt. She shook her head slightly.

"I was so sure. And the ghost…"

"You said you'd made a new potion that day, right?"

Mel's face burned. "Yes."

"Is there any chance…" Hannah trailed off, letting Mel figure the rest out.

"I feel so ridiculous. I got the recipe from an old book, too. Just something I found at the used bookstore. I didn't think."

"No, clearly you didn't." She laughed a little. "I'm glad you are now, though."

Mel wrapped her hands around the mug to absorb the warmth. "You knew, didn't you?"

"What do you mean?"

"You knew it wasn't her. You knew my mom was depressed a long time before I did."

"I had my suspicions." Hannah closed her eyes and took a long breath. "But that wasn't what you needed to hear."

Mel snorted. "I wouldn't have listened anyway."

"I know." The wind howled outside. Hannah stood and looked out the kitchen window at the swirling gray clouds. "Some things take time. I'm glad you got here when you did."

"Can I still stay here tonight?" Mel asked.

"Of course. Clara knows where you are, right?"

"Yeah. Yeah, I said I was coming here."

"Okay. Let's make up a bed so you can get some sleep. But you have to go back in the morning. Deal?"

"Deal."

The house she grew up in was imposing in the early morning light. She reached out and turned the doorknob. The door swung open, the hinges squeaking almost imperceptibly. Mel took a deep breath and stepped over the threshold.

Clara was waiting in the kitchen, eyes red. She looked up at Mel and shook her head.

"I'm sorry," Mel said. "I…" She held out her arms to her

aunt, who rose shakily and then stepped into the embrace. They stood there for a moment, hugging tightly, before Mel stepped back and wiped away her own tears.

"Mel," Clara began.

"No, hold on. I'm sorry. I don't know what I was thinking. I just… I couldn't believe she'd leave me."

"I couldn't either," Clara said. They sat down again. "Couldn't believe she left you, couldn't believe she left me. Things were finally good with us. We were finally friends. And you—my darling girl, how could she leave you?"

There was no answer.

"I need to know, though. Why did you think it was me?" Clara asked.

Mel buried her face in her hands. "I saw Mom."

"What?"

"I saw her ghost. When I was in the cemetery. I had taken a new potion I made—I guess I messed it up because it made me all cold, and then I saw Mom. And she told me she'd been murdered. By you. After that I guess I was just looking for clues."

"Clues?"

"Yeah, like how relieved you were when the police officers decided against starting an equivocal death investigation. Or the story Uncle Joseph told me about you and Mom having some fight in college."

"Oh, oh." Clara shook her head. "I wondered why you knew about that. I didn't think your mom would have told you."

"What was it about?"

"I got involved in some stuff I shouldn't have. Questionable magic, questionable people. That sort of thing. Probably danger-ous and definitely illegal. Rosemary tried to get me out of it but I wouldn't listen to her. Textbook younger child, I guess. Headstrong and rebellious. But when I finally pulled myself together, we were fine, she and I."

"Oh. I thought you'd fought over… I don't know, Dad or something."

Clara laughed. "No, as much as I loved your father, he was not my type."

"That's what Uncle Joseph said."

And Clara laughed harder. "He did, did he?"

Mel nodded. "I'm sorry, you know. I really am."

"I know you're hurting, Mel," Clara said, "but you can't push me out like this."

"I know."

"No, listen. This is going to be a struggle for both of us. I have to learn how to be a parent without stepping on your mother's toes. But you've got to listen to me. If you don't agree with me, talk to me, but you can't go walking out on me like that."

"I won't." Her face burned with shame.

"Your mother was hurting, too. I don't know what her struggles were, but I know she wanted to protect you."

"Don't do that to me, okay?" Mel said.

"Do what?"

"Don't try to protect me. Not if it means hiding from me."

"I won't. I promise."

They sat together as the sky grew bright and the world awoke. Mel opened the curtains and raised the windowpane. The autumn breeze blew into the kitchen, and Mel breathed it in. Her heart thudded with a dull ache that would never vanish completely, but in this house, in her home, perhaps on the winter wind, she would someday find peace.

Shoulders of Giants

JON GARETT & RICHARD WALSH

"Tut, I have done a thousand dreadful things
As willingly as one would kill a fly;
And nothing grieves me heartily indeed
But that I cannot do ten thousand more."
- AARON, *TITUS ANDRONICUS*

The Last War

Basland was a small, seafaring nation that for generations girded itself against its larger neighbor, East Albion, with superior technology. Its knights carried stronger swords, its caravels fired more powerful cannon, and its jets blasted hotter afterburners.

Basland's first modern military lab was a bunker built beneath a government ministry on the edge of Highdam, Basland's capital city. Then scientists, and the military budgeters supporting them, gained prestige in the national government. The second facility was a gleaming skyscraper in the heart of the city. When the latest—and the last—war with East Albion began, bombing left the capital a ruin.

The third lab was rebuilt in a bunker beneath a government ministry on the edge of Highdam.

Expert panels were convened, and it was agreed: the youth of Basland would be its salvation. New, young scientists would be enlisted in the lab in Highdam, and with them new, fresh ideas to win the war.

East Albion, their foe across the sea, was a culture founded on heroism and the warrior spirit. For generations Albionian boys were raised to revere military service as the most honorable path in life. No greater honor could be earned than giving one's life for the Homeland.

But when Basland bombed their capital city, Newmarket, the nation of East Albion recoiled. For decades their military had paraded about, medals glistening and trumpets trumpeting, while the fighters themselves had become soft and easily cowed.

A great national campaign was mounted to renew the Albionian Spirit, and the military's Top Brass set its sights on the next generation to save East Albion in the nation's ultimate battle with Basland.

Two young adults were called by their countries to fight their war.

Called to Serve

Bridget Bellweather found herself in the lab-bunker in Highdam the week after her sixteenth birthday. Her lab coat was a bit too big, and she kept forgetting on which side of the belt she'd clipped her bio-encrypted entry pass.

She was the Lab Assistant Intern to the Chief Research Liaison. Her boss, the Chief Research Liaison, was Captain Anton Snipes. He was a wiry man with short hair and a straight back. His rank was not just an honorific— he really *was* a captain in the Baslandic Air Corps. He had enlisted fourteen years prior, between wars with East Albion, and had become a bomber pilot before manned bombers became obsolete. He had flown some of the first sorties over the military-industrial Centennial district in East Albion.

Bridget, for her part, had caught the attention of officials just three years earlier when she received a passing score in the national mathematics tests for the third year running. This was considered extraordinary, since fewer than two percent of Baslandic students knew any math. The odds of a student passing three years running were… well, Bridget couldn't perform the calculation off the top of her head, but she presumed the odds were low.

Standing before Captain Snipes, all medals and starch and shoe polish, Bridget had the unmistakable sense that she was about to turn the page to a new chapter in her life: leaving behind the confines of school and entering the world of applied research.

And not just applied research to any old subject, like zoology or pharma or asteroid mining, but applied to *the military*. The schools in her home neighborhood were crumbling, and the monorail running in Highdam was in terrible repair, but the military's lab appeared to be receiving full funding. The test tubes gleamed, and banks of top-of-the-line computers chirped happily as they processed data. She was relieved that she'd been rescued from her mediocre school to help in the war against East Albion. But she worried, momentarily, about her classmates. Where would they end up after graduating?

"Your first project," said Captain Snipes, indicating a pile of gleaming lab implements, "will be Lab Equipment Maintenance Detail." Bridget bristled, despite her moment of gratitude. All the study, the passing math scores, and her talents were to be wasted on cleaning beakers?

"At eighteen-hundred hours," he continued, "we will have a debrief session on *Project Exodus*. Any questions?"

It was more of a statement than a question, so Bridget shook her head and Captain Snipes turned on his heel.

Project Exodus, she thought to herself as she scrubbed a barely-used digital scale. "Exodus" meant a mass departure. Who was leaving? And where to?

Hank Hazlet had not always lived in Newmarket. He had been raised in a village in the highlands of East Albion, but his family had been driven from their lands by a terrible drought. Townsfolk muttered that the catastrophe had been the work of Basland. The highlands were the only stretch of land in East Albion that bordered Basland, and shepherds had reported that a terrific blast had come from the direction of Highdam, the Baslandic capital. Why they'd targeted shepherds, no one knew.

Mere days after the blast the grasses began to wilt, the mud turned to stone, and the Hazlets were driven from their hut in the Highlands to a crowded tenement in Newmarket. Here the effects of the war with Basland were immediately apparent: cathedrals bombed, schools leveled, whole neighborhoods burned to the ground. A shopping mall in the Centennial district had been left in ruins when a Baslandic pilot had mistaken it for a military-industrial complex.

School was not an option for a poor highland refugee, so Hank found work as an errand boy at the Albionian army encampment adjoining the slum his family called home. He cleaned tents and laundered uniforms, marveling at the heavy stitching of the clothes and the waterproof fabric of the billets.

When he turned sixteen he enlisted, joining a unit made up of similarly situated refugee-slumrats called the Highland Sabers.

Two years passed.

"Hazlet," his commanders would call. "Run."

Hank did not ask why. He asked "where?" or, depending on the circumstances, "how fast?"

"Hazlet," his commanders would say. "Cook."

Hank wasn't a cook, but he didn't say that. He would ask "rare, medium, or well done?" or "how spicy?"

He was an eighteen-year-old lance corporal the month the

Highland Sabers were to be deployed as the front force of *Operation Righteous Spear*, a raid on Basland's eastern shore.

Two nights before the deployment, however, Hank's military-issued InstaCot prematurely triggered "Pack" mode. He was still sleeping at the time, and the twisting motion of the automated packing process dislocated his knee.

He was pulled from the final assault on Basland. Instead of loading up for combat with his friends, Hank stood on crutches in the military terminal to watch the Sabers depart. They boarded their brand new invasion craft, one of East Albion's fleet of never-before-seen tilt-rotor assault-helos. Hank watched in awe as each helo's rotors tilted from "Hover" pitch to "Thrust" pitch, and the squadron departed for Basland.

The Albionian Top Brass confidently predicted that Baslandic resistance would melt before the new technology.

Hank was reassigned to a detachment tasked with guarding East Albion's small military lab. In a nation of warriors and soldiers, scientists were not well regarded, but Hank vowed to carry out his duty faithfully nonetheless.

The Albionians' raid went on without him, and word eventually filtered back that his friends in the Sabers had been annihilated. As they'd prepared to land, the rotors of their assault-helo had overtilted, driving the helos from "Thrust" back to "Hover," as expected. But they continued to tilt, first to the previously unknown pitch "Reverse" and then, finally, to "Crash." The few Sabers who survived the impact were mowed down by the Baslandic defenses.

Thinking of his friends killed on that beach, Hank began to understand why East Albionians hated Baslanders.

The Albionian lab's chief scientist was Doctor Peasebottom, a professorial man who walked with a hunch and a cane. He always greeted Hank kindly, and often would tell Hank of new projects that interested him.

"We've begun work on a new weapon," the old scientist said, indicating with his cane a great blueprint tacked on one wall. *"Titan.* A mechanized warrior suit for our strongest soldiers."

Hank couldn't read a simple sentence, much less make sense of the dizzying pattern of technical drawings.

"What about that one?" Hank pointed to a smaller, simpler schematic on the next panel over.

"Ah. The Lilliputianer. A partial success. It was supposed to shrink Baslandic assets. Make them inoperable."

"That is amazing!"

"Should have been. Unfortunately, it's only worked once so far. And only accomplished shrinking one Baslandic factory by seventeen percent. An inconvenience for them, no doubt, but hardly worth our investment."

Hank frowned. Certainly, East Albion's brightest minds were under great stress to keep up with their enemy.

"Titan," said the scientist, coming back to the new project. "This will allow our brave military to do what they do best: direct force engagement. But with robotic suits!"

Direct force engagement. Frontal assault. Ninety percent attrition. The Top Brass always liked to use complex language when it talked about high casualties.

In any case, neither schematic was anything Hank could understand, but he marveled nonetheless. Surely they could prevail. Doctor Peasebottom assured him of just this fact before departing.

Always Faithful

Bridget Bellweather received promotions each of the three years that followed. She rose from Lab Assistant Intern to Senior Lab Assistant Intern, then to Junior Lab Assistant and finally to

Senior Junior Lab Assistant. This was due partially to her adequate mathematical talent and a knack for bureaucratic infighting; but primarily it was because her superiors were being "promoted" and moved out of the lab.

She was surprised to find that now, having been promoted out of cleaning duty, much of her working day was spent completing paperwork instead. There was a form for everything: procurement forms for data consoles that were used to track finances that were used to buy form intakes that were used to process the procurement of new data consoles.

The web of it was beyond her, so she just dutifully took notes during her meetings with Major Snipes and submitted the required forms. Paperwork made the vein in his forehead pop out even further.

On occasion, a lab project's code name would have a connection to its objective, and she would occupy herself trying to tease out these puzzles. For example, *Project Exodus* had been a weapon to drive East Albionian farmers from their farms by causing a drought. Ultimately, it was supposed to have crippled their food supply and ended the war once and for all.

It had been a partial success: *Exodus* had definitely caused a drought.

Unfortunately, the drought had hit the already-arid East Albionian highlands instead of its fertile coastal farmlands. The result had been a migration of useless shepherds. *Exodus* had crippled the Albionian wool supply, rather than its food supply.

Despite the tedium of the work, and the setbacks of good-projects-gone-bad, the lab also opened Bridget's eyes to the good they were doing. She watched project teams working long hours—sometimes day and night—to design systems, build prototypes, and run test scripts. She saw a pair of researchers crack the Xenon Theorem. She marveled at robots that responded to voice commands and rockets that auto-aimed to a specific target's DNA.

Ultimately all of this was for the greater good of Basland and all civilized countries.

She opened the next file to be completed.

"*Project Babel*," said Major Snipes. "The Sonic Disruption Ray is a phenomenal notion. It will eliminate the Albionian ability for verbal communication, such as it is. It could end this war, once and for all."

Bridget shrugged. *Babel* was a tower-mounted weapon that would devolve East Albion's language into an unintelligible system of grunts and gestures, reducing the speakers to primate-level communication. Though it wasn't her decision, she still felt uncomfortable with the notion of transforming an entire nation into jabbering simians.

On the other side of the western sea, Sergeant Hank Hazlet had yet to return to active combat. He completed a year on the lab security detachment and was then moved to a maintenance team supporting the next generation of assault helos. After a year working in this maintenance unit he was transferred again and became a recruiter specializing in middle schools and sports events.

He passed a year as a recruiter before he finally returned to combat duty. After three years of serving in Newmarket, Hank was transferred to a new infantry brigade. The Prairie Dogs were scheduled for deployment to the Highlands of East Albion.

Before their unit left Newmarket, Hank received a call from his old friend at the lab. Doctor Peasebottom invited him to a special event: East Albion's Top Brass were unveiling two of the military's newest inventions in preparation for *Operation Dynamic Furor*, the next offensive into Basland.

The first invention was the Neutronium Forcefield Helmet: a metal crown worn by soldiers that would cast an energy shield to protect their head and upper body from bullets and shrapnel.

The other was the Tactical Psion Antenna, a neurotransmitter that allowed soldiers to telepathically communicate with their officers. Scientists had nicknamed them Thinking Caps. Surely, the military reasoned, Albionian fighters who could read each others' minds would act as a single organism, a unified fighting force against the tyranny of Basland.

The Top Brass presented both inventions to great fanfare. East Albionian innovation, they said, was pushing the limits of science in their nation's righteous fight against the Baslandic lunatics. And *Operation Dynamic Furor* would drive the Baslanders to the edge of surrender.

The Prairie Dogs departed for the Highlands the very next day. They were a band of fearsome Albionian warriors—half of them under twenty years old, most of them from the lowest classes of society, and all of them brave in the face of nearly certain death. They were underfed, undertrained, and—thanks to the chronic wool shortage—underclothed.

But their trip ran late. The northbound train carrying the Prairie Dogs was held up by a scheduling mistake in Southport and then a personnel problem in Portsmouth. At one point, one of the men reported that they appeared to actually be heading the wrong direction down the tracks.

By the time they reached the Highlands, they were a week behind schedule, arriving the day *after* the start of the planned offensive.

The other brigades had been packed up with the Neutronium Forcefield Helmets and shipped to the front in Basland. The Thinking Cap neurotransmitters, which had been on the same train as the Prairie Dogs, were left behind as well.

A week after the offensive began, Top Brass reported in the newsfeeds that the units had faced heavy losses due to "Unforeseen Force Technology Reversals." This, Hank knew, was more complex language, meaning that their own weapons had failed them.

The soldiers in the invasion force had been left defenseless when the Neutronium Force Fields had disintegrated the rifles from the soldiers' hands instead of protecting their heads (and upper bodies) as promised. The Baslanders had mowed them down where they stood.

Honor and Duty

Basland was facing an energy crisis, reported Colonel Snipes, so research resources were being reallocated. *Project Babel* was to be combat tested once as a boost to civic morale and then mothballed so the project team could be broken up and re-assigned.

Bridget Bellweather, now Junior Lab Lead, was moved to *Project Tesla*: the development of Atmospheric Electricity Spools that would satiate Basland's voracious appetite for power.

The official story from government planners was that increased energy usage was being driven primarily by libraries and bookstores in Highdam. They called for the children utilizing the libraries to begin a conservation campaign. This would save electricity until supply could be increased using military technology.

Why the military would be developing a new energy technology to power libraries was a mystery to Bridget.

But the project itself was a remarkable achievement. As Junior Lab Lead, Bridget was assigned a small team of interns and senior interns. They were given research and documentation responsibilities for the Collateral Figmentation Boosters, a critical component of the Electricity Spools' repositioning technology.

Her team worked long hours developing the Boosters, running them through meticulous tests, and filing all of the appropriate development protocols. Each time she had Colonel Snipes sign an approval form she thought she saw one of the crevices next to his eyes deepen. Another project like this one and they'd be able to use his face to test their desert exploration drones!

One evening, as she gathered the day's test results and filed them via the Analysis Phase Technology Development Aggregator, she thought of the quiet, dark evenings in her flat in the city center, where brownouts turned off the lights regularly. She thought of the intermittent monorail service. She thought of the bitter cold winters when heaters didn't work, and the sweltering hot summers when the air conditioners didn't.

The lab was always fully-powered, heated or cooled as needed—how else would they accomplish their mission?—but what if their work could restore full power to *all* of Basland?

That, she decided, was reason enough to finally end this war. Even if *Babel* did reduce East Albion to a nation of grunting primates, at least then *Tesla* could be used to power Basland's trains.

Sergeant Hazlet looked out from his InstaBillet onto the barren hills of the East Albionian Highlands. How strange to have returned here after so many years. He turned to his tent mate, a lance corporal from the slums of Newmarket, to ask about the blinding flash that had just woken them both.

But he found himself unable to utter a word. "Brumph, googa, blump?" was all he could manage.

The lance corporal looked at him quizzically and responded in kind: "Brumph! OOGA. Blomp?"

What had happened?

Hank grabbed his rifle, threw back the flap of the InstaBillet, and emerged into the camp. Other soldiers were milling about, too, their conversations as unproductive as Hank's.

Some of them were pointing to the western horizon, at a place where, apparently, the light had originated. Perhaps some kind of weapon. But no one could speak cogently enough to confirm or to strategize a defense. A Baslandic assault was surely imminent.

Hank racked his brain, searching for a way to communicate with the others. They were nearly all illiterate, so writing wasn't an option.

The Thinking Caps! The military had equipped the expeditionary force in *Operation Dynamic Furor* with the Neutronium Forcefield Helmets, but the neurotransmitters were yet to be generally issued.

Hank grunted and motioned for the lance corporal to follow. They ran full speed into the quartermaster's quonset. He was still asleep, so Hank let himself into the storeroom and rifled through the boxes of gear. There were tents, and a few packs of precious socks, and canteens, and the dehydrated field rations the soldiers ate.

Finally, he found the Thinking Caps. He slapped one on the top of his own head and then one on the lance corporal's.

Can you hear me? he asked telepathically.

Brump? replied the lance corporal.

Hank sighed in disappointment. It had seemed an ingenious plan.

Just kidding, continued the lance corporal. *Yes, I can hear you. Brilliant idea, Sergeant.*

They laughed and together hoisted the box of Thinking Caps up and out of the quonset.

The Few and the Proud

Over the next three years, Bridget Bellweather rose steadily through the dwindling ranks of the lab. General Snipes was under pressure to fill recruiting quotas, so he routinely reassigned lab staff by changing their lab titles to actual military ranks.

Bridget's immediate superior, the lab's Senior Division Supervisor, was made a commander and deployed to St. Rupert's, a village on the Baslandic border with the East Albionian Highlands. So Bridget was promoted from Senior Assistant Division Supervisor. Though still only twenty-four years old, she now had her eyes on a promotion to Senior Division Lead—or even Junior Department Supervisor!

But not all was well. After the failure of their three most prominent projects, the lab's funding had been threatened by some stuffed-shirt politician in the administration bunker on the other side of the capital.

Project Tesla had required more energy to deploy than expected, requiring the government to divert power from an elementary school, a car factory, and a shopping mall. And it had produced less energy than planned, so all three had remained closed thereafter. The good news, Bridget figured, was that the children would be conscripted into the Voluntary Civic Service Corps that much sooner now that their school was closed.

Project Babel had caused a momentary disruption in Albionian communications, as none of the savages were able to speak to one another. But they had unexpectedly already been at work on some sort of telepathy tech. It had not only overcome the Sonic Disruption Ray but had now given the brutish Albionians the advantage of telepathic communication!

And, worst of all, *Project Exodus* had begun to spread. Hitting the Albionian Highlands instead of its farmlands had been just the beginning of their problems. The lab's desertification technology did not understand national origins, or national borders, and the drought had spread across the frontier, back into Basland, and toward their own agricultural belt.

Only the intervention of General Snipes (and the transfer of several fancy computers to important politicians) had saved the lab in the face of so much bad press. Surprisingly, Snipes' wrinkles had smoothed dramatically in the last year. Bridget assumed he was self-administering age-reversing gene therapy.

Now she followed the newsfeeds obsessively, noting how the media reported on their research and the military exploits their research enabled. She ordered her staff to spend time each week writing letters to government media under pseudonyms praising the lab and its efforts. She personally had taken to leaking classified documents to journalists, hoping they would see the inherent value of the various lab projects.

She redoubled her team's efforts. The lab had recently completed *Project Chameleon*, an exciting—and game-changing—technology: the MonoSpectrum Camouflage Suit. This would allow Baslandic soldiers to blend seamlessly with their surrounding terrain. Snipes believed it would be the change that tipped the war in Basland's favor once and for all.

One of her staff approached, dossier in hand for a new project. She flipped it open: *Project Prism*, the Polymorphic Fragmentation Discharge.

It was an audacious program, perhaps the most ambitious they'd ever embarked on.

Lieutenant Hank Hazlet picked through the scrubland of the Baslandic prairie. He was leading a platoon of his thirty fierce Albionian infantrymen nearly a hundred clicks inside the border.

The platoon's mission: find and destroy a supply depot built on the outskirts of St. Rupert's, a village long deserted because of the drought. The depot was guarded by a prominent Baslandic warrior-scientist and a squad of elite troopers.

Hank adjusted his rifle in his hands. It was smaller than he was used to. Seventeen percent smaller, in fact; the result of the Albionians' own Lilliputianer device. The planners in Newmarket had targeted the wrong supply depot at the beginning of the mission, hitting the Albionians' rather than the Baslanders'. Now Hank and his soldiers were issued smaller-than-normal gear.

Sir! A sergeant approached, tugging at the back of his tight pants. He was communicating using the Thinking Cap, since speaking would have resulted in an incomprehensible string of "blergs" and "gloobs". *Recon reports the enemy depot. Two clicks east.*

Move out, replied Hank. He took a sip from his slightly-smaller-than-normal canteen. *And remind the men to use their pinkies to fire their rifles.*

The platoon fanned out across the scrub and approached St. Rupert's. The wind had picked up, throwing up a small dust storm around them.

The supply depot was visible on the edge of the village, and the men began reporting back a strange presence: ghosts.

Most Albionians believed in ghosts, especially citizens who—like Hank—were raised in the country, venerated the old ways, and honored their religion. So these reports were troubling.

Some of the men from the city scoffed. Everyone knew they had scoffed, because they wore neurotransmitters which broadcast their thoughts to all of the other men. The scoff, in fact, was one of the few guttural noises not lost in translation from the Thinking Caps.

A cacophony of psychic chatter filled the airwaves until Hank silenced his men with a stern mental warning. He then motioned to the ghosts on the left of the perimeter.

Do ghosts often carry rifles? he asked.

The men agreed that they did not. Therefore, reasoned one of the older soldiers, the ghosts must actually be Baslanders using some newfangled camouflage technology to lay in ambush.

Hiding was not the way of warriors like the Albionians. They fought with valor and conviction, for theirs was the good fight. The Baslanders, however, lacked honor. They were sneaky and uncourageous.

But their technology had made them overconfident. They were camouflaged yet still plainly visible in the blowing dust of the storm, like a chameleon on a shower tile betrayed by the water running over it. Now even the blindest old crone could have seen them and knocked them down with a well-aimed cudgel. The Baslanders were not simply cowards. They were fools as well.

Cut them down where they stand, ordered Hank.

News of the massacre at St. Rupert's was an embarrassment for the lab. The media, and by extension the lab's political opponents, used the event to call into doubt the relevance of "fancy gadgets" in modern warfare, in particular the MonoSpectrum Camouflage Suit.

Who was to know, Bridget wondered, that camouflage technology could be too effective? That it would be so effective that it would lead users to believe that they were *actually* invisible? She blamed a news reporter who had obtained some of the early leaked development documents and scoffingly referred to the tech as "ghost suits." It seemed a simple enough lesson to add to the tech training, but the fact was that Basland was running out of soldiers to train.

News that the Albionians had been using miniature

weapons—perhaps a cost-saving measure—made the loss doubly embarrassing.

General Snipes arrived at Bridget's office. He had put on weight. No longer wiry, he now carried muscle that puckered the back of this uniform jacket and stretched the collar of his starched shirt. Bridget had the sense that he was training for something. Perhaps a new career as a pit fighter or a Hexagon goalie. However, Bridget wondered if the youthenizing gene therapy had ever been previously tested.

"We need two more volunteers from your team," he said bluntly. "*Prism* has cost us another intern, and the military will not provide any more for the human trials."

Bridget had been ready for this request. In fact, as she'd reviewed the newsfeeds and evaluated her staff on their public relations work, she had begun to see a pattern forming. Several of her interns were not taking their duties seriously. They were not writing to journalists. They weren't telling friends and family about the virtue of the scientists' monumental battle against the enemy. Nor were they informing strangers on the monorail that the lab was developing the tech that would tip the scales for Basland. Instead, the interns were behaving like children. They were messaging one another rather than recruiting younger siblings to join the war effort. They were gossiping in the lab and chattering like squirrels at one another's jokes. They were even going on dates without prior lab approval.

But she knew. She tapped the phone of each new arrival recruited from the high schools. She tracked their activities and kept a log.

And now, when General Snipes needed volunteers for the human trials of *Project Prism*, Bridget Bellweather knew exactly who to commission.

Ultimately, it was good for the lab to weed out the weak and unreliable. And it was good for Basland to advance rationality and science. It was good for the military to move one more step closer to victory over the savages of East Albion.

Lieutenant Hazlet looked over the village of St. Rupert's. With the depot destroyed and its garrison annihilated, Hank felt his lust for vengeance roused rather than sated.

His platoon was on the edge of the prairie. Behind them stretched the vast wasteland of drought, but before them stretched the fertile agricultural heartland of Basland.

He called forward Sergeant Crumb, who generally remained at the back of the unit, for he was carrying East Albion's newest non-combat-tested technology: the Geomorphic Sinkhole Suffoser.

Crumb, thought Hank. *We'll unleash the Devil's Maw here.* The men had taken to calling the device the Devil's Maw, because the sinkhole was not simply a *hole*. It was a living, biological, non-sentient hole. It was a hole that ate men.

Here, sir? replied Sergeant Crumb. His confusion was evident. *I thought we were waiting until the Baslanders sent their reserve soldiers to meet us.*

That's just it, thought Hank. *We'll lure them here.*

How's that, sir?

With the Psych Plants.

Oh. Of course, sir.

Crumb was also carrying an experimental highly-volatile aerosol known as Iterated Psychotropic FloraSpray. All of the control condition results indicated a high level of likelihood that the substance would alter plant-life, causing it to exude a hallucinogenic field. The men called the theoretical results Psych Plants.

If the threat of turning Basland's food supply into a stockpile of hallucinogens didn't lure out the reserve troops, Hank didn't know what would.

A diabolical plan, sir, said Crumb. Of course he'd been able to hear everything Hank had just been thinking.

Thank you, Sergeant. We'll unleash the Psych Plants here, and the Baslanders will have no choice but to deploy their reserves. And then we crush them, and end this war once and for all.

Crumb seemed pleased by the thought.

For King and Country! Hank thought strongly to the rest of his platoon, attempting to ignore the discomfort of his small pants riding up his backside.

For King and Country! agreed the men, knowing full well about his pants.

Project Androidicus was the lab's most secret project. So secret, in fact, that Bridget had never even officially heard of it. She had seen the project's name partially redacted from a PA-989 program funding form, and she'd caught a glimpse of it in the header of a TOP TOP TOP SECRET document on General Snipes' desk once during a review session. But none of that was official.

So it was to her surprise that she was informed that the lab would need to close down *Project Prism* and devote all of its remaining resources to *Androidicus.* After assigning so many volunteers to the human trials for the Polymorphic Fragmentation Ray, these new orders left her sputtering and gibbering in frustration, like the target of a *Babel* blast.

Hadn't *Prism* been the project that would, finally, end the war? They had suffered through the deprivations of the energy shortage, had watched dozens of teenaged intern volunteers march to almost certain death in the testing lab; and for what? For the project to be mothballed like all the others?

She swiveled in her office chair to the nearest terminal and pulled up the testing user interface. The little cursor blinked provocatively. She keyed in a secret override code. The override would only last a minute, but she was familiar enough with the controls for *Prism* that she'd be able to fire off one actual salvo before she was locked out.

She typed quickly in search of a target. "St. Rupert's" appeared. That was the village the Albionians had overrun. The one with the supply depot. The site of the "Ghost Suit Massacre" that had nearly ended all funding for the laboratory.

She scanned the terrain from the geosynced satellite in orbit over the town. Nothing out of the ordinary…

Then she spotted it. A hole. A great, rough, circular crater on the edge of the village. And, in its center, a mouth. A multi-fanged wriggling maw, flexing and pulsing. Until now, she had been certain that she could never be shocked at the depths of savagery that the Albionians would plum for a victory. But in viewing this latest abomination, her stomach turned sour. What had the Albionians created?

She no longer felt the slightest qualm. She centered the Fragmentation Ray on the hole, to destroy the horror, but the host satellite's lateral arrays were not locked. The crosshairs drifted slightly as the satellite orbited. She'd forgotten to fix the array boosters from the test settings, and now it was too late.

She adjusted the crosshairs one more time, attempted to take the drift into account, and pressed the key to fire the weapon.

Then the terminal locked her out.

Lieutenant Hazlet had deployed his troops in a semicircle behind the Devil's Maw awaiting the arrival of the Baslandic troops.

Sergeant! he telepathically called to Crumb, who hurried over. Hurrying over was unnecessary now that they could communicate wordlessly over short distances, but reporting in hadn't completely died out as a tradition. *What's the status of the—*

A beam of multicolored light burst down from directly overhead. Hank was reminded, for a moment, of the religious stories his nana had told him in their village: of angels descending from heaven. Of rainbow bridges and the voice of God.

Then Sergeant Crumb disintegrated into a thousand fragments. Hank winced. Even with all the combat training, he disliked being covered in viscera and carnage. But Sergeant Crumb's fragments were not bloody or gory; instead, he burst into a thousand fragments of *light,* dissipating back toward the heavens whence the ray had come.

The Thinking Caps erupted with activity as all of the witnesses processed their immediate, unconscious reactions to the attack. What a fearsome enemy they faced! Many shrank back in terror.

Hank felt their morale slip away moment-by-moment. He had not led them to glorious victory against Baslandic reserve troops but instead to certain defeat against a faceless rainbow enemy that attacked from the sky! They knew that another attack was imminent, and that it would surely drive them back across the border, to the wastes of East Albion.

Do not fear! Hank cried telepathically. *Our fight continues on. For we have another weapon. One that the Baslanders cannot defeat. The TITAN SUIT!*

He remembered the schematic he had seen so many years before, in that lab in Newmarket. He remembered the power of its mechanized arms and the heavy steel of its thick torso. The bristling radar array and the stout grenade launcher.

The men in his troop were silenced as they watched his mental images. They stood in awe as he imagined himself climbing into the Titan Suit and marching into Highdam. They cheered when he broadcasted a single high-powered neurotransmission back to the command HQ and requested—no, ordered—that the prototype suit be airdropped to their location.

And, to his amazement, HQ agreed. It had been a very, very long time since any field commander had *requested* a prototype from East Albion's military lab.

Bridget rose from her desk, certain that security was en route to arrest her. She decided to meet them halfway. She removed her lab coat and put on her uniform jacket. She holstered her pistol. She hadn't fired it in ten years, but she might as well look the part if she were to be paraded before the cameras.

But, to her surprise, no one arrived.

She let herself out into the hall and looked back and forth. Empty. Now that she thought about it, she remembered the last of the security detail being volunteered to fill in the ranks of the reserve force that was now being deployed to St. Rupert's to face down the Albionian incursion.

Her footsteps echoed on the hallway floor. She made her way to General Snipes' office, but he was gone, too.

The file was still there, though: *Project Androidicus*.

She glanced around, to make sure she was alone, and flipped it open.

Androidicus was a fully integrated combat suit. It stood ten meters tall and was armed with a howitzer, a mortar, and a bazooka. It used the technology from *Exodus* to arm a hyperlethal flamethrower.

It used the technology from *Tesla* to power its sophisticated neuronetwork.

And it used reverse-engineered technology from *Babel* to interface seamlessly with the operator, who was connected into

Androidicus as its brain.

The most amazing innovation, however, was that on its back it carried its own self-contained nuclear fusion unit; a battery containing enough energy to power several small cities—or, if mishandled, destroy them.

She focused on the specs. The development of such a compact nuclear battery would have required absurd amounts of power. It explained the mothballing of *Tesla* and *Prism*, and it was all for this one amazing super-mech. Brownouts and poor monorail service were a small price to pay for such an achievement.

Androidicus, Bridget realized, was going to end the war.

Then she heard a cough. She leapt about a foot in the air, coming to rest where she could now see the other side of the desk. There, on the ground, in his flight suit, was old General Snipes. The suit was a reinforced poly armor, and the general was struggling weakly to right himself, like a long, tanned turtle stuck on its back.

"Help me up," he said, reaching up to her. "I fell."

"What are you doing down there?"

"Trying to get up." He sounded like an old, tired man.

"What are you doing down there in that flight suit?"

"I'm flying it out of here," he said.

"It?"

"The project."

"*Androidicus*?" she said.

He nodded. "It's my destiny," he said. She noticed he was gasping for breath.

She thought of his exercise regimen. The gene therapy. The youthenizing tech. The old man had been trying to get in shape for this moment.

Then she thought of her failed projects. She had been developing technology for him while he built this fancy mech suit for one last glorious mission. All her work for the lab. All her work for Basland!

She deserved to fly *Androidicus*.

"Sorry, sir," she said. "It's my destiny now. Get out of the suit."

He clearly did not understand. "What?" he asked.

"Get. Out." She unholstered her pistol and leveled it at him. "Of. The. Suit."

Now he understood. She helped him unlock and remove the helmet, then the poly armor. She tied up his hands and shoved him into his General-sized closet.

Then she pulled the suit on, yanked the helmet over her head, and followed the coordinates in the folder to the *Androidicus* docking station.

The Baslandic reserve troops arrived in St. Rupert's later that day, just a few hours after Sergeant Crumb's polychromatic demise. They were exhausted from the long march from Highdam.

Hank ordered his men in a wide encircling action and then, having surrounded the Baslanders, pushed them backward into the Devil's Maw. The Albionians' righteous mutant creation ate well that day, devouring scores of Baslanders.

Hank rounded up the rest as prisoners, thinking they could be traded for Albionian hostages. Or perhaps fed to the next Devil's Maw. Hank imagined it planted in the heart of Highdam itself, where they would remember for generations the Albionians as a righteous scourge.

Titan arrived an hour later. The assault-helo that airlifted the huge steel crate did not hover over the drop site for a moment too long. It alighted and buzzed off immediately, as if fleeing the inevitable explosion that would result when the experimental weapon was activated.

But Hank and the Prairie Dogs did not fear *Titan*. They'd seen firsthand the Rainbow Weapon the Baslanders now had at their disposal. They knew *Titan* was their only salvation for vanquishing their enemies.

The men went to work dismantling the heavy shell of the crate. Once they'd opened it, *Titan* stood like a steel gladiator on the cracked dirt of the plain, the harsh sun reflecting off its dull armor. The light contrasted with the craters of hexgun roto-turrets and dilithium rocket cluster apertures that pockmarked its body.

Surely this weapon is unstoppable, Sergeant Bard, who had been field promoted to replace Crumb, thought to the others. *It is our salvation.*

The men cheered their agreement in a long chorus of "blergs" and "moophs". The Baslandic prisoners looked on uncertainly.

I shall operate Titan, Hank announced. None of the men dissented.

They hoisted him up to the command pod. He eased himself into the tight confines, strapped himself in, and took a deep breath. Time to power up the machine. None of the men below had the slightest doubt, and this buoyed him. As Bard had said, surely *Titan* was their salvation. And he, Hank, was their prophet, sent by East Albion to ravage and defile Basland for the sins of the war.

Incoming! one of the men thought loudly, and Hank tried to look up, craning his head beneath his helmet. He could see straight out of the mech's canopy well enough, but he had no visibility above or to either side. He pulled back on one of the levers, hoping to bend the whole robot at the waist. The machine moved, turning to look upward, like an old man with a bad back.

But it wasn't the Rainbow Weapon incoming; it was another

mech, this one long and sleek. Where *Titan* was bulky and solid, with an obvious command pod, this Baslandic design was elegant and human-looking. Its operator was integrated seamlessly.

Hank resolved at that moment to destroy it, to put an end, once and for all, to this war. He would destroy their mech and then march to Highdam and destroy their city as well.

The Ultimate Sacrifice

The battle between *Titan* and *Androidicus* raged for just under fifteen minutes. Bridget landed *Androidicus* safely in front of the Devil's Maw and released a salvo of explosive fire that tore through the Prairie Dogs deployed on the opposite side.

Hank responded by hovering *Titan* across the mouth of the pit and bringing the heavier robot down on top of *Androidicus*. Pinned there, Bridget tried to escape by applying full power to her leg rockets. But the robot wouldn't budge beneath *Titan's* weight, and the blast only served to tear away the edge of the pit.

The two robots began to slide down. Hank attempted to step off of *Androidicus* to the stable ground above, but the servo in *Titan's* left knee blew out under the pressure of the maneuver, uncoiling a long spool of heavy-duty cabling. As he twisted away, panicked by the klaxons now blaring in the cockpit, the cabling wound around *Androidicus*.

Bridget, for her part, tried to eject, hoping to watch from on top of the pit as the two mechs slid to the bottom. The ejection seat functioned as expected, blowing her small pod clear of the robot. But it immediately tangled up in the cabling wound about the mechs. She manually opened the hatch and clamored out.

Hank powered up *Titan's* left arm to push away *Androidicus*, but instead flexed the arm and tightened the cabling further. The escape pod was pulled upward and suspended in the air directly in front of his cockpit. He saw the pilot of *Androidicus* climbing out. He groped about the interior of the cockpit for his own ejection seat. Finding none, he unbuckled himself and pushed open the hatch.

By the time Hank opened *Titan*, Bridget had already leapt from the escape pod to the side of the pit. She looked back and saw the Albionian pilot jump to the other side of the pit and begin scrambling up. She followed suit and started to climb, but the sinkhole was expanding, perhaps trying to accommodate its huge incoming meal.

Hank was exhausted. The sand gave way with every clawing step, and he slid down two meters for every one he ascended. He turned and looked across the Devil's Maw, at the Baslandic pilot on the other side. The pilot had removed the flight suit's helmet, and he saw for the first time that it was a woman his age.

Bridget looked back and saw the Albionian pilot watching her. The climb out of the pit was getting more difficult as the sides grew steeper. She saw that the Albionian mech's left leg, the one that had twisted on top of *Androidicus*, was now dislocated. Its long cabling trailed behind on either side. If the Albionian pilot remotely triggered its booster, it would pull free and provide her—and him—a means of escape from the pit.

She waved to get his attention. "Engage the starboard boot thruster!" she yelled across the chasm between them. "We can pull free with the servo cables!"

She had his attention, but she had no idea whether he'd heard.

"Don't you have a remote ignition device?" she yelled, even louder. "Engage it!"

Hank did not know whether *Titan* had a remote ignition device. Or why it would, since it was intended to be manned by a soldier inside. But he was not an engineer. Perhaps the

Baslandic pilot knew something he did not. Perhaps her plan would work. Perhaps they could escape together.

But they only had a few moments more before both mechs would be pulled into the mouth below. He needed the Baslander's help to figure out an alternative to the remote ignition.

"Blerg?" he yelled back at her. "Moomph ratta moop blamp!"

The hungry beast below them had begun to devour the mechs, rending the metal in its grotesque jaws.

Bridget imagined the pressure exerted by that great mouth and then—too late—remembered the compact fusion reactor on her mech's back. Even if they escaped the pit there would be no escaping the nuclear explosion.

She was aware for a split second of a flash as the fusion unit detonated.

The blast destroyed both mechs along with the two young pilots. It annihilated what remained of the Albionian and Baslandic armies. And it leveled the greater part of the border-lands between the two countries.

It would be another generation before war renewed between the two nations, this time waged with longbows and trebuchets.

Lisbeth

SELENIA PAZ

"What's done cannot be undone."
- LADY MACBETH, *THE TRAGEDY OF MACBETH*

Act I

The tree groaned as it released the last of its leaves to the wind. In the distance the sun was giving in to sleep, the night ready to come alive. The children ran and tossed sweet breads at each other until their mothers slapped their hands, pointing to the graves. Lisbeth kneeled in front of her parents' tombstones, roughly made from stacked concrete blocks and etched clumsily, but luminous with soft flowers and packs of *tamales* tied with ribbons.

She looked around to search for Abuelo's red flannel shirt and Abuela's bright green dress, and, when she was certain they were not near, reached over to touch the tombstones. Closing her eyes, Lisbeth imagined the souls of her parents coming through the concrete, if only for tonight. Her throat tightened and she pulled away.

She felt a hand on her shoulder and looked up. Bianca was wearing her white dress with lace at the bottom. Lisbeth tried not to notice the dirt on Bianca's knees, and rose and brushed off her own. Bianca shivered with excitement.

"So, can you come?" she asked in a whisper.

Lisbeth looked around. She had not asked, but she was sure Abuelo would let her. The tents around the cemetery were almost all up, decorated with bright *papel picado* and glowing lights that were attracting small bugs.

"Come on, I will ask them with you," Bianca said, grabbing Lisbeth's hand and looking around.

Their feet crunched on dirt and pebbles as they walked around the cemetery. Children were already running in and out of tents with candies and drinks, woven cloths and paper flowers. Some sneaked behind trees to eat the candies; others tucked the paper flowers into the crooks of the boughs, only to chase after them when the wind claimed them for itself.

Lisbeth waved as they passed some of the people, trying to smile and nod her greetings while looking for her grandparents. She saw a flash of green and red and pointed. "There!" she said to Bianca, and the pair cut through the trees to catch up.

As they approached, Abuelo turned and raised an eyebrow. Bianca's mouth opened slightly, but she snapped it shut and looked over at Lisbeth, giving her a chance to speak first.

"Can I..." Lisbeth began, but hesitated. She looked over at the tents, and Abuelo smiled a small smile. Abuela nudged him in the ribs and he stuck his hand in his front pocket, fiddling around with papers and tissue and keys and buttons and rocks and who knew what else. He pulled out a few coins and sorted them, handing some to Lisbeth. She looked over them quickly. Ten *pesos*! Almost enough to visit ten tents, if she only went to the cheapest, and enough for more than ten candies in some of the tents.

Bianca pulled her hand and they turned and ran, Abuelo's chuckling laughter following them on the wind. Some people had brought their dogs and cats to visit family, placing them on soft blankets to keep them warm as the night became chillier. Lisbeth rubbed her hands up and down her arms to warm them and hoped it would not rain.

Lisbeth had been to every Día de los Muertos gathering at the cemetery since she could remember, first to remember her dog and the aunt that she never knew, the daughter her grandparents had lost. There was even a small bump in the dirt by a tree where Abuelo had helped Lisbeth bury a baby chick that had died when she was five. Now, she came to see the graves of her mother and father.

Lisbeth looked over at Bianca. Their parents had been riding the same bus to the *consulado* in Juarez when they say it crashed.

Bianca shook Lisbeth out of her reverie. "*Ven!*" she said, her voice breathless. The tents were just outside the crooked metal gate that surrounded the cemetery. She could hear coins clinking and plastic wrappers crumpling. Somewhere, someone dropped a glass bottle and it shattered on the rocks. A boy cried and Lisbeth guessed he had probably tripped and dropped his soda. Her fingers gripped the coins and she looked around, trying to decide which tents to visit.

Bianca pointed to a large white tent with pink paper flowers. *Panaderia Doña Alba,* it read in large pink letters. "Come on!" she said, "I want to buy a *buñuelo* while they're still hot."

The woman behind the counter was wearing a bright yellow dress with black vines decorating the collar. "*Un buñuelo,*" Bianca said to her.

Lisbeth took a step closer, looking at her dress, and the lady smiled. "You can touch the vines, if you like." She bent her neck over the counter. Lisbeth felt the vines, bumpy under her fingers, and she smiled back. She hoped one day she could have something so beautiful.

"*Dos pesos,*" the lady told Bianca, who reached into a small pouch and dropped a coin into the woman's hand.

Reflexively, Lisbeth clutched her hand to her chest and Bianca laughed. "I'll give you some of my *buñuelo* if you want to save your money for the other tents," she said. Lisbeth blushed. Bianca always knew what she was thinking. She took the piece that Bianca offered her and let it sit in her mouth, tasting the warmth and cinnamon and sugar all at once.

Bianca stopped at the next tent and bought a bottle of soda, giving Lisbeth a sip and saving the empty bottle in her pouch to use for *canicas* when she got back home. Lisbeth looked around at the tents selling *tamarindo* and *Duvalín*, sweet *calaveras de azúcar* and porcelain sugar skulls for decoration. Her eyes paused for a moment when she spotted the *mazapan* candies on one of the counters. Two for one *peso*. Lisbeth fiddled with the coins in her hand and looked over at another tent, this one green-and-white striped, with the words *Muñecas del Mundo* on it. She walked toward it, her eyes roaming over all the dolls on the shelves. There were some with pants and shirts and others with bright dresses and others that came with animals: dogs, sheep, and even frogs.

Lisbeth had always wanted a doll. She read the sign on the front of the tent: *diez pesos* each. She looked at the coins in her hand and her heart felt heavy. That was all the money she had.

Bianca came over with two bags full of candies. "Here," she said, handing a bag to Lisbeth. "So you won't miss out on the candies." She looked up at the tent and poked Lisbeth with her elbow. "*Ándale*," she said, pointing to the doll with the dog. "You should get that one!" She pushed Lisbeth forward and the coins jingled in Lisbeth's hand again.

Just then there was a noise to their right. They turned to see a man stumbling out of a large tent with gold *papel picado* all around it. He stood for a moment, looking around, and Bianca pointed. "He bumped into that boy," she whispered. The boy was getting up and the man shook his head and ran off.

Lisbeth moved closer to the tent and saw gold lettering written across the top of the opening: *Las Tres Hermanas*. Lisbeth unconsciously moved forward a few steps, but Bianca pulled her back. The boy who had been knocked over was now going into the tent with a tall woman. Before the flap closed, she looked over at them and winked.

Lisbeth startled, jumping up slightly, and took a few more steps forward. Bianca pulled her back again. "Don't waste your money on that!" she scolded.

"What do you mean?" Lisbeth had heard of the three sisters, but all she knew was that people said they could predict the future. "Maybe they can really see the future," she said quietly.

"Do you think if they could really see the future they would be taking money from little kids like that? Why don't they predict something big and make a lot of money so they don't have to work anymore?" Bianca asked.

"Maybe it doesn't work like that," Lisbeth answered, her eyes brightening.

"Then how?" Bianca asked.

"I don't know. Maybe they can't help themselves like that."

"Well, it looks like they are helping themselves," Bianca said. She sighed. "I think you should get that doll. But if you want to go, get in line already so you can go as soon as that boy leaves, and then we can go see the other tents."

They stood in front of the tent for a few minutes, trying to find a sign that told them the price of a reading.

"Maybe we should leave," Bianca began. "Maybe it's too much."

Lisbeth shook her head. "No, if that boy could go in and pay, I'm sure I have enough."

Bianca said no more, but a small frown formed on her face.

The tall woman opened the tent flap and smiled. "*Lista*?" she asked.

Lisbeth nodded.

Bianca grabbed her arm once more and pulled her back. She

looked around. "But that boy is still in there," she said.

The lady raised one eyebrow.

Bianca looked down. "The boy, the one who went in there before us," she said softly.

"He went another way," the lady answered. "Out the back." Her smile had faded slightly.

She opened the tent flap once more, and Lisbeth followed her inside, Bianca behind her.

"I don't know, Lisbeth. We can still go back, we can…" Her voice trailed off as they stared at the beautiful golden draperies decorating the inside of the tent. There were tables and shelves with trinkets, and a large glass bowl with coins. Two other women sat at a table at the center of the tent. The first woman joined them.

"I am Amana, and these are my sisters, Marzia and Catalina," she said, gesturing first to the red-haired woman and then to the curly-haired woman on the right. A deck of cards sat at the center of the table, and two chairs sat facing the sisters.

"Finally we meet you, Lisbeth and Bianca. We have been waiting a long time," Amana said.

Bianca stepped back, grabbing Lisbeth's wrist. Amana's lips pulled up, and for a moment Bianca thought she heard laughter.

Marzia moved forward in her chair. "We have been waiting a long time to tell your future."

"Your great future," Amana said.

Catalina looked down at the deck of cards on the table. "Sit, please," she said, not looking at them.

Bianca directed her question to her. "But we don't even know how much this fortune will cost, and I used up the last of my money on the candies."

"Oh, it won't cost you any money," Catalina sighed.

"Yes, for you, no charge," Marzia smiled.

"Sit, please," Amana echoed her sister.

Bianca hesitated, but did not want to leave Lisbeth alone in the tent. She looked around, but she couldn't tell if the wrinkles in the cloth walls could be exits or if there really was only one entrance—through the front.

Catalina gathered up the cards and set them aside.

Lisbeth asked, "But how will you tell our fortune without the cards?"

"We have had a message for you girls for a long time now, Lisbeth and Bianca. Now listen carefully, because you will only hear it once tonight," Amana said. She turned to Catalina and nodded.

Catalina unrolled a piece of paper, and the three sisters read:

"You will soar to heights
Only reached by few
You will look forward and not back
A beautiful view
Beloved by the world
You both will be
Embraced by the stars
Embraced by the sea."

Their voices sounded almost like music. Then, just like that, Catalina rolled the paper back up and the sisters rose.

"But wait, there's some more," Lisbeth said, pointing to the paper.

Catalina placed the paper into a metal box behind her.

"We hope you have enjoyed your fortune. We are sure you will do great things," Amana said.

They were being pushed out of the tent.

"But what does that mean?" Lisbeth asked.

"Good night," Amana said, already ushering in another person, the tent flap closing behind her.

Lisbeth and Bianca stood in front of the tent for a few minutes.

"Come on, let's go to the doll tent. You can use your money to buy one of the dolls," Bianca said at last.

"But… but what did that mean?" Lisbeth asked, looking back at the gold tent.

"It doesn't matter. They probably tell everyone the same thing. At least they didn't charge us," Bianca said as she began walking to the doll tent. Bianca pointed to the dolls, but Lisbeth shook her head, still thinking about their fortune.

Act II

Lisbeth woke to the sound of murmurs in the kitchen. She could smell the coffee and the soft tortillas Abuela was making. The crack and sizzle of eggs mixed with the faint coughing of her grandfather. They spoke quietly for a few minutes before Lisbeth heard the scrape of the chair on the floor and, a few moments later, the slight creak of the screen door as Abuelo went outside.

Lisbeth rose and put on her pants and shirt, the front of one of her shoes splitting open as she placed her foot inside. She looked under the bed for the tube of glue and squeezed some on the front of the shoe, holding it closed for a few minutes.

There was a *rap rap rap* on her window, and she knew it was Bianca without looking outside. The front of the shoe seemed stuck together pretty well, so Lisbeth shoved her foot inside and ran to the kitchen. Her grandmother handed her two warm tortillas with soft eggs inside and opened the door, and Lisbeth ran out.

Bianca was waiting near the back fence with a paper bag in her hand. Lisbeth handed her one of the tacos, and they sat on some flat stones to eat them slowly.

"Your grandma makes the best tacos," Bianca said, smiling.

Lisbeth smiled back. She noticed there were small wrinkles under Bianca's eyes.

"Did you sleep okay?" Lisbeth asked her.

Bianca swallowed the last of her taco and breathed in and out slowly, enjoying every last bit of it. Finally she nodded and handed Lisbeth the paper bag. There was a glass soda bottle inside, filled with *canicas*. Two large marbles rolled around in the bag.

"Wow, you filled up the bottle," Lisbeth said. "That was fast!"

"Not really," Bianca replied quietly. "It's been almost a year."

Lisbeth nodded, but said nothing.

"Do you think about them?" Bianca asked. "The three sisters, I mean. Do you think about them?"

Lisbeth grabbed the two large marbles and began to move them around in her palm.

"No," she answered. Then she looked at Bianca. "Do you?"

"I've been thinking about them, yes. I thought maybe you had, too, because of what they said… about our future."

Lisbeth shrugged, the marbles moving slowly around each other in her hand.

"They'll be coming back soon," Bianca said, her eyebrows furrowing.

Lisbeth nodded.

"Less than a month now," Bianca continued.

"Yes, I suppose they will be," Lisbeth said. The Día de los Muertos celebrations were less than a month away. The dry heat of the summer had lifted off the dirt streets in September, and her grandfather didn't come back home so sweaty anymore.

"Maybe we shouldn't go this time," Bianca said softly.

For a few moments, the only sound was the grinding of the two large marbles against each other.

"Why not?" Lisbeth said.

"I don't know. The three sisters, they might be there again. I don't think… I don't think we should see them again," Bianca answered.

"We don't have to go to their tent," Lisbeth said.

Bianca reached over and grabbed Lisbeth's wrist. "But they'll be there," she said in an urgent voice.

"It's okay," Lisbeth said, pulling her wrist away. "It's not a big deal. And besides, maybe you're right, maybe they do tell everyone the same thing. And if they do, then what does it matter? And anyway, they can't make us go in their tent."

"But what if… what if you want to go in to find out what the rest of the prophecy said?" Bianca exhaled.

"What do you mean?" Lisbeth asked. "The three sisters only give a person one prophecy."

"But ours wasn't finished. You saw, there was more," Bianca said.

Lisbeth shook her head and frowned. "No," she said.

Bianca's eyes widened. "Yes, you pointed it out yourself. You even asked them about it."

"No, no, I didn't," Lisbeth said.

"Yes, you did."

Lisbeth rose. "No, I didn't. I think I would remember."

Bianca stared at her for a few moments. Finally, she said, "Come on, let's play," and grabbed a stick, drawing a circle in the dirt. She divided up the marbles, and she and Lisbeth spent one of their last warm afternoons tossing marbles back and forth with their thumbs.

When the sun set, Bianca gathered her marbles in her soda bottle and placed it in her wrinkled paper bag. As she walked home and turned to wave goodbye to Lisbeth, she could not help but notice the lightness of her bag or the heaviness of her heart.

Act III

The night was alive with the smell of damp grass and the embers from fires. The freshly baked bread was still soft to the touch, and the light from the tents shone on the almost-bare branches of the trees, casting long, thin shadows on the ground.

Bianca wore her dark brown dress with the faded yellow flowers and her brown shoes, scratched and scuffed from running all summer. Lisbeth wrapped a knitted gray, black, and white *rebozo* around her pink lace dress to hide the rips and tears. She reached down and tore off a long strip of lace that had been dragging in the dirt and sighed.

They were both almost fourteen now. Four years had passed since their fortunes had been told, and there had been no sign of the three sisters since. Neither had stopped searching, although their reasons for doing so were different.

Bianca could not help but notice that, although time had hardly altered the tall, crooked cemetery, she and Lisbeth had changed far too much to be wearing these dresses. She smiled. "Did your grandma make that dress?" she asked encouragingly, though she already knew the answer. Their grandmothers had made all of their clothes.

"Yes," Lisbeth said. "*Hace mucho, mucho tiempo*," she added with another sigh.

"It's very nice," Bianca said with a small smile. She lifted up her knitted black pouch and shook it. "I've got twenty *pesos* this time," she said.

Lisbeth smiled wide and lifted her white-and-green knitted pouch. "I've got twenty-five."

"Which tent should we visit first?" Bianca asked.

She looked around and pointed to a large red tent where a group of small children were gathered. When they moved, she could see flashes of white feathers and gray and white fur. A man came out of the tent and tossed a handful of grains in the air, and the chickens jumped around and pecked at the ground.

"Let's go over there! We can feed the chickens and pet the goats!" Bianca said, her voice alive. Her eyes shone as she reached over to grab Lisbeth's arm.

"Wait," Lisbeth said. She turned her head, searching each of the tents. Her eyes floated over the sweet breads and candies and sodas, over rag dolls and clay pots and colorful *balero* toys. It was not there.

"Didn't they come every year, before?" Lisbeth asked under her breath.

The light in Bianca's eyes dimmed. "The three sisters?" she asked.

Lisbeth looked down, giving her answer. Her throat felt tight as she pulled the *rebozo* around her. She opened her pouch and pulled out the coins, moving them around in her palm. Then she looked back up at the tents and nodded. "Let's go see the goats," she said, walking forward, her eyes still searching for the beautiful gold tent.

For one *peso* they could get a small portion of hay and feed the goats. Bianca felt a small pang of guilt as she paid for two handfuls of hay, because both of their grandfathers had goats and hay. They saw all of these animals every day. But there was something calming about feeding the goats, and she knelt down and let them take the hay from her hands.

The wind picked up as the night awoke, and soon Bianca was wishing she had brought her own red and orange *rebozo* from home. They walked from tent to tent, Lisbeth's eyes looking but not really seeing, searching for the three sisters and for her future.

When they reached the end of the line of tents, Bianca peeked into her bag. "I only have two *pesos* left," she said, trying to cram her wooden doll and her small package of candies inside. She would save the soft caramels to give to her grandparents.

Lisbeth jiggled her bag. "I have twenty left," she said, smiling.

"Do you want to run through the tents really fast and buy some things?" Bianca asked.

"No, it's okay. I think I should save it," Lisbeth said, placing the long pouch over her neck and tucking it under her *rebozo*.

"Save it? For what?" Bianca asked.

"I don't know," Lisbeth said. "Maybe one day, we'll go north, to the United States, and we can buy some things there. Nice things."

"North?" Bianca asked. Lisbeth nodded. Bianca was about to say that twenty *pesos* was only about two American dollars, but she stopped herself. There was no point. Instead, she smiled at Lisbeth as they began to walk toward their families' graves.

Their grandparents spent most of the night of November First sitting around a small fire and talking softly about their children. They brought beautifully colored flowers—real and paper—to decorate their tombstones. Old black-and-white photographs of small children in chipped oval frames decorated the front of the tombstones. Lisbeth and Bianca knew that when their parents had been teenagers, there had been a few years of dry, harsh weather, when the air was never really clear of the rough dust that floated around, covering crops and asking for water. There were no photographs in those years.

They sat down silently next to their grandparents. Lisbeth's grandfather smiled and winked at them, nodding at Bianca's wooden doll. A good purchase, he thought.

They sat in silence, remembering.

Lisbeth felt the soft wind and recalled the rush of lighting *cuetes* in the new year and to ring in the coming of the *Tres Reyes*. She was so small, and her mother chased her around with a towel, trying to hit her for lighting the firecrackers. "You're going to blow your arm right off, and when you do, I'm not going to feel bad for you!" her mother would scream. Her father would laugh, and together they would run away.

Lisbeth reached into her pouch and pulled out a small brown string attached to a square piece of cloth decorated with the Virgen de San Juan. The string was twisted, and the dark brown color had faded to pink in some areas. She closed her fingers around it as she remembered.

Bianca could see the pictures her mother used to hold up, the bright red book with black-and-white illustrations, a strong and kind *toro* that reminded her of her grandfather's bull. She could smell the paper and feel her heart racing when her mother turned the page. She could remember her father, worried that she was never going to speak, asking her to say anything, anything at all: *perro, gato, mamá, papa.* She remembered the look on their faces when she finally decided to say *toro.*

She reached into her pouch and took out a small brown bear with a red hat. The hat was torn near the spot where it met the bear's ear, and some of the fur had become knotted. The bear had velcro on its back that opened up to reveal a small box with two buttons: one that recorded sound and the other that played it back. Sometimes, late in the night, Bianca pushed the button to hear her mother reading to her. If she listened close enough, she could hear her father talking softly in the background. She held the bear close to her, trying to smell her mother on its fur. Sometimes, she wondered where her parents were now, and what would happen to her when her grandparents died.

As if reading her thoughts, her grandmother tapped her on the shoulder, and she opened her eyes. There were two small envelopes on the ground with their names printed in cursive letters. Lisbeth could tell that her grandmother had written them, because the letters looked as if they were shaking as hard as the hands that had brought them to life.

Lisbeth and Bianca looked at each other. They never gave gifts on this day—only during the Día de Reyes, when they would get a plastic bag with *cacahuates* and other nuts. A thought occurred to Lisbeth and Bianca at the same time: maybe it was from their parents. A letter?

Bianca reached for hers, but Lisbeth hesitated. These weren't from their parents. They couldn't be. How could they have known what would happen? How could they have seen so far into the future to know to write a letter for their daughters, a letter to be given to each when they were no longer around?

Lisbeth reached over and grabbed her envelope. Bianca had waited for her and, in silent agreement, they turned them around and opened them slowly, careful not to tear them.

Lisbeth's eyes widened as they both pulled out a one-way bus ticket to the United States.

Act IV

They were to stay with Lisbeth's aunt Lenna, who was living in the city of Houston in Texas. Lisbeth had only met her once, and she remembered feeling that her aunt was very tired. Lenna had not come back to Mexico very often since she had left, but Lisbeth knew that she sent her grandparents money, and that money was where her Day of the Dead *pesos* came from.

It took Bianca a moment to understand what the ticket meant. It was not a visit. Her grandparents would not be coming with her, and it was likely she would not return for some time.

Bianca had wondered why her grandfather had sold his large bull. She'd thought maybe he was getting too old to take care of so many animals. But a bull could bring in a good amount of money, enough to buy a bus ticket to the United States with a bit extra left in case Bianca needed to buy things for school when they got there. They would have to enroll in high school when they arrived.

Bianca felt a pang of something in her chest—was it longing? Longing for what? Or fear. Fear of leaving her grandparents alone. And guilt. Why should she get to go and not them? But even as her mind asked the question, it also answered it: they would never move away from here. This was their life.

She looked over at Lisbeth and saw a similar mixture of feelings in her eyes as well. Lisbeth's first thought was to decline the tickets, to try to convince her grandparents to get their money back. Not only would they be alone without her, but there was also the fear of living with her aunt, whom she barely knew. Lisbeth was embarrassed. *I would be invading her space*, she thought. *What if she doesn't want us there?*

But there was something else. She was afraid, most of all, of wanting to go. She had wanted to go all of her life. The possibility of having another life—a better life—was too much of a temptation for her to decline. She gripped the ticket even more tightly in her hand, fearful that a gust of wind would come by and take it—and her future—away.

Bianca and Lisbeth could hardly remember the rest of the night. Their grandparents hugged them and told them that when they arrived with Lisbeth's aunt in two weeks, everything would be different. They ate some of the *conchas* Lisbeth's grandmother had made and drank warm coffee. As the night wore on and the wind picked up speed, Lisbeth and Bianca's thoughts intertwined in a mixture of fear and planning.

The next few days were a blur. They filled their small bags with clothes and a pair of shoes. Bianca tried to stuff her plush bear in her bag, but it wouldn't close. She saw Lisbeth put the soft brown necklace over her head and laughed. "You're lucky that's so small, you can carry it anywhere," she said.

"Just leave it," Lisbeth said. "We'll come back, and your grandparents will take care of it."

There was a silence. Would they come back?

Bianca looked into her bag once more, setting her bear aside.

"Okay, ready," she said. Except she wasn't.

As they looked out onto the street where their grandparents were waving goodbye, Bianca cleared her throat to keep from crying. Lisbeth wiped her eyes with her black *rebozo* and exhaled.

The bus rumbled through the bumpy dirt roads, and the concrete buildings turned into shrubs and trees, mountains in the distance. Night fell as they neared the border, bringing with it a cold wind. Lisbeth marveled at the long line of cars ready to enter Mexico, and the long line ahead of them ready to exit.

"Where do you think all these people are going?" she asked Bianca.

Bianca shrugged. She clutched her bear under her *rebozo* and wrapped it more tightly around her. She didn't want to admit it, but she was fearful another passenger would see her with it.

"Maybe visiting family?" she suggested.

Lisbeth nodded. "Sometimes people come to work here, too. From all over the world. But I think mostly it's the other way around."

Bianca nodded. She thought it would be a good time to ask something that had been worrying her the whole time they had been on the bus. "So, what's your aunt like?" She was worried that she might turn out like the women in the fairy tales, the stepmother from *La Cenicienta* and the like.

Lisbeth looked over at her and smiled. She knew, and she

was a little nervous, too. Bianca had never really met Lisbeth's aunt Lenna, and the one time Lisbeth had seen her, she was rushing back and forth, bringing things from her car into the house, hurrying to buy things to take back to Houston. She hadn't stayed long that time, either—less than a week if she remembered correctly.

Lisbeth tried to comfort Bianca with what little she did know about her aunt. "She's a technician or something like that," she said. "At a doctor's clinic, I think." She really didn't know. Sometimes she had caught parts of conversation between her aunt and her grandparents, and she would always hear the word "*clinica*," so she assumed it was a doctor's office.

"She is really nice," she said, trying to convince them both. The truth was, it had been a few years since she had seen her aunt. "I'm sure she's great. But anyway, I'm just worried about whether she'll be able to keep us for a long time. I mean, it must cost money to help us with everything. I have hardly any clothes with me, and what if they are the wrong kinds of clothes? And what about school? Do we have to pay for materials?"

Lisbeth had brought the money she had been saving over the past few years, but in total it amounted to about a hundred and fifty US dollars. She wasn't sure how much that would buy, but hopefully it would be enough so that they wouldn't be too much of a burden on her aunt. She knew Bianca only had about fifty because she had left the rest to her grandparents.

As the sky darkened and the stars came out, the bus creaked on to complete the last leg of their trip. "What are we going to do if my tia Lenna can't keep us too long?" Lisbeth whispered. They had joined their *rebozos* together for warmth, the cool glass of the window beginning to glisten with water drops.

Bianca shrugged. "Come back?" she said. "But thank her, of course. I mean, she got us the tickets and at least a little bit of time."

"But isn't it better to come to school here and stay? To go to a university here?" The wheels in Lisbeth's head were turning. She knew that most of the time, kids left public school and started at a university at about age eighteen. That gave them four years. Four years to save more money, to do well in school, to prepare for their future. Would that be enough time? Could her aunt Lenna support them for that long? And what if they couldn't go to a university?

A slight panicked feeling rose up in Lisbeth's chest. What would happen once they got to her aunt Lenna's home? What would they do? She looked over at Bianca, but Bianca had already drifted off to sleep.

The bus made odd mechanical noises every time it slowed down. As the sun rose, drops of water on the windows streaked down the glass. The passengers all began to stir, and a movie started playing on the television set above the seats. It was about a girl who was in love with a vampire. Bianca watched, thinking about the garlic her grandmother hung over the back door to keep out vampires. She couldn't imagine this boy-vampire the type to hunt them for their blood.

As they grabbed their bags and walked down the metal steps of the bus, Bianca quickened her pace to keep up with Lisbeth. "Wait, Lisbeth," she called. "Wait for me."

Lisbeth had started to jog ahead, scanning the faces for one she recognized, although she couldn't really be sure she *would* recognize her aunt. "I don't see her," she said, and she continued to move forward through the crowd.

Bianca looked around. There was something wrong. The people were gathered in groups and some were moving around to other passengers, talking quickly. She could hear them saying *dinero* and saw them looking through their bags. As she walked forward to catch up with Lisbeth, a woman bumped into her. Her face was wrinkled from the sun. She looked up at Bianca. "My money, all my money, it's gone," she said. "You didn't find any money, did you?"

Bianca shook her head and showed the woman her pouch. "No, I'm sorry. I just have my own money," she said. She moved forward again, but then she turned back to look at the woman who had remained standing there, unmoving.

Lisbeth had moved far away from the crowd into a parking lot until there—there she was, waving. Her aunt Lenna. Almost the perfect image of her mother. Lisbeth's foot moved back and she almost lost her balance. Her heart heavy, she waved as her aunt walked toward her to meet them.

Lenna smiled and embraced Lisbeth. "I am so glad you are here," she said quietly.

It took Lisbeth a moment to speak, but she finally managed to embrace her aunt and nod. "Me, too," she replied.

Her aunt turned and hugged Bianca, who had been hesitating to the side, not wanting to ruin their greeting. "Welcome, Bianca," she said kindly. Bianca smiled shyly. "Do you both have all of your things?" she asked them.

Lisbeth nodded. "Yes. Yes, we do."

Bianca glanced over her shoulder, but said nothing.

"Are you hungry? You must be so tired after being in that bus all those hours," Lenna said.

"Yes, we are," Lisbeth nodded. "Come on, Bianca, let's go," she said, pulling Bianca's arm.

"Well then, let's go get something to eat. Then we can talk about everything we have to do to get you started in the high school near my house. Our house," Lenna added, smiling.

Once they got into the car and began to drive away, Bianca

looked back at the crowd again. As the people moved around and parted, she could still see the old woman standing near the bus, clutching her bag to her chest.

Act V

To say that they enjoyed school would be a great under-statement. Bianca and Lisbeth embraced their new life with vigor, promising each other they would not let their families' money go to waste. The first few years were rocky, but they had soon mastered the English language and were competing with each other for the top spot in their graduating class.

They had made sure to volunteer anywhere they could. Bianca spent many of her weekends at the animal clinic—not doctor's clinic after all—where Lisbeth's aunt Lenna worked, and Lisbeth spent much of hers volunteering at the local science museum, helping groups of small children with activities and giving tours. During the weekday evenings, Lenna dropped them off at the mall, where they both had jobs at clothing stores.

School was out for their final summer as high school students when they heard about the contest the local space center was holding. High school seniors were eligible to apply for one of two spots on the next shuttle mission, where they would spend some of their first year as college students in orbit. The contest would also provide a full scholarship to the student's college of choice, provided the student was accepted to the college.

Lisbeth and Bianca were reading the flyer Lenna had brought home from work. Applications were due at the end of the summer, and applicants would also need to meet certain physical requirements which winners of the contest would work to improve to prepare for conditions in space. Lisbeth looked at herself and then at Bianca.

"What do you think?" asked Lenna.

"That sounds incredible," Bianca said. "But do you think we would get it?"

Lenna smiled. "Why not? You both are at the top of your class, you have a lot of extracurricular activities and you volunteer and work. And you're not in bad shape," she added.

Bianca nodded. Lisbeth remained quiet.

"Imagine what winning this would do," Bianca said. "We could keep working and save more money, for our grandparents," she said.

Lenna smiled. "And for yourselves."

Bianca knew that both of their grandparents were not doing very well, and that although Lenna sent them money, she was not sure it was enough. She had tried giving Lenna money from her own earnings, but she did not make much.

"You should apply. You never know," Lenna said.

Lisbeth looked at her. She knew that Lenna would have loved to apply and had wanted to be an astronaut her whole life. Imagine knowing that your dream was never going to come true. Lisbeth looked away. She couldn't let that happen to her. This was the way. This was the key to a great life, the life she had always wanted. She would apply. And she would win.

As they filled out the forms, Bianca was excited to see how much they had done over the past few years. Their final grade point averages had not been calculated, but Bianca knew that she and Lisbeth scored the same in every class. She tried to ignore the gossip at school, that she and Lisbeth cheated. She knew that Lisbeth's mental ability probably surpassed her own, and that they both stayed up late working on assignments and making sure they were as good as they could be. The circles under their eyes were not from cheating.

As the application deadline loomed, Lisbeth became restless. Applicants would know within a few days whether they were the winners of the contest, because training for the experience would have to begin almost immediately.

Bianca wanted to win more than anything, but she knew that if given the choice, she would give up her spot for Lisbeth. Lisbeth's grandparents were very sick, and although Lenna tried not to show it, Bianca sometimes caught a tight smile or heard a strain in her voice. She thought of her own grandparents, and how she would feel if they were as sick as Lisbeth's. She tried not to show it, but she felt that if her own grandparents were gone, she would surely die. What would be left for her?

She shook her head and tried to think positive. No one was going to die. Lisbeth's grandparents had always been strong. They would get better.

The deadline came and went, and on the afternoon of the seventh day after it had passed, when Bianca had given up on checking the mail, Lisbeth rushed in. In her hand was a large white envelope with a rocket logo on the top left corner.

Lenna stopped scrambling the eggs and Bianca rose, slightly. She grinned. At least one of them had gotten it.

As Lisbeth ripped open the envelope, two booklets and two letters fell out. Bianca reached down and picked them up, seeing her name on one of the letters. The other was addressed to Lisbeth. Before her vision became too blurry, she read the first few words on the letters:

Congratulations on your acceptance to the Hecate mission!

Lisbeth took the sheets from her hands as Bianca sat down. She looked up at Bianca. "We both got in?" she asked.

"No way!" Lenna screamed. She rushed over and looked at the letters, then picked up the booklets, running her fingers over the gold embossed letters: HECATE.

"I can't believe it," Bianca said, her voice barely a whisper.

Lisbeth said nothing.

"We have to celebrate!" Lenna said. She poured the scrambled eggs into her dog's bowl and grabbed her purse. "To the mall!"

Lisbeth and Bianca floated to the car, each lost in her own thoughts.

"I can't believe they picked you both!" Lenna repeated over and over. She looked at them and smiled the biggest smile, the most real smile Bianca had seen in months. *At least for the moment, Lenna can forget about her parents,* Bianca thought.

"Aren't you excited?" Lenna asked Lisbeth, who was staring out the car window.

Lisbeth seemed to wake up. "Yes. Yes, of course!" she answered. But something was wrong. Bianca couldn't put her finger on it, but she felt it.

"Don't tell me you're scared of heights?" Lenna teased.

Lisbeth smiled. "No. I'm not. It's just…"

"A shock," Lenna finished for her. "Well, you're going to need to get used to it. You'll be all over the news pretty soon, for sure! Everyone in the world is going to know who you are."

"Everyone in the world," Lisbeth replied.

There was a large Le Madeleine bakery and café in the mall, along with an assortment of department stores and independent businesses. As they walked through to the bakery, a flutter of movement to the left caught Lisbeth's eye. There was a florist shop at the end of the hallway. She looked up at the sign, decorated with a single golden flower, and stopped. *Three Sisters Flower Shop.*

The glass windows were difficult to see through, there were so many colorful flowers in the way. But the main roses were yellow, and Lisbeth knew they were there, waiting for her.

"Lisbeth, come on!" she heard Lenna say. They had gone on to the end of the main hall and were about to turn right.

"I-I just have to go to the bathroom." She pointed to the left. "I'll meet you there." She turned and walked on, not waiting for a response.

A wind chime jingled as she opened the door and let it close behind her. She looked up. The chime also had a golden flower. She walked through a maze of golden flowers in crystal vases to the counter in the middle. And there they were.

She wanted to ask so many things. Why hadn't they come back to the cemetery all those years? Where were they during that time? Who were they, really?

But most importantly, what was the remainder of the prophecy?

The three sisters looked up. "Lisbeth," they said in unison.

"Where is Bianca?" Amana asked.

"It doesn't matter," Lisbeth said. "You were right. I won. I mean, we won. A contest—to go into space. The whole world will know, they will see us. That's what the prophecy meant, right? You were right."

"We are never wrong," Marzia said, smiling a little.

"So what happens after that?" Lisbeth wanted to ask if she would stay famous, rich even.

"You wouldn't rather know about your grandparents?" Catalina asked solemnly.

"Shush, Catalina. She wants to know the rest of the prophecy. So we will tell her," Amana said as she reached for a scroll on one of the glass shelves.

Lisbeth stood straighter. Amana unrolled the scroll almost completely, and the three sisters read:

"When one takes the place of two
When the sky falls

Amana rolled up the scroll again and held it tightly in her hand.

"No charge," she said, waving Lisbeth away.

"What? What does that mean?" she asked, blinking.

Catalina sighed. "One reading per visit," she said sadly.

"Then I'll pay for another one. How much?" Lisbeth said. "There was more."

"That fortune is not for you," Marzia said. "That is Bianca's ending."

There was a chime and Lisbeth turned. A gray-haired man walked in and picked up a beautiful rose-colored vase filled with red blossoms. When Lisbeth turned back, the sisters were gone, and a tall woman with red hair was walking toward the man.

"Visiting your wife again?" she asked him.

"Every day," he answered.

She jumped a little when she saw Lisbeth. "I'm sorry, Miss. I didn't see you there. Can I help you?"

Lisbeth shook her head. "No, no, thank you," she replied, and hurried out of the flower shop. As she turned the corner and headed toward the bakery, she thought she saw the shadows of three women moving down the hall.

They had gone through the training exercises so many times, Bianca was dreaming about them. They would take off together in one of the first automated shuttles, *Hecate*, and deliver equipment to the International Space Station. They had memorized what would happen in the seconds prior to launch, and knew what to listen for before and after the shuttle lifted off the pad. They would only be in space ten days.

"I can do that," Bianca told herself again and again. There

would be no need for them to learn liftoff and landing controls. The shuttle was also equipped with an emergency escape pod just large enough for two people.

But the pod won't work in space, a small voice in Bianca's head whispered.

Lenna kept reading through the booklet and the brochures. By this time the whole world was waiting for the launch, waiting to see how two teenagers would fare in space, and how the beautiful *Hecate* shuttle would hold up. How many more automated missions could there be after this?

The light of the moon streamed in through the blinds the night before the launch. Bianca thought about saying something to Lisbeth, but what could she say? She was terrified, and the quiver in her voice was sure to give it away. They didn't need to be any more nervous than they already were.

For a brief moment, Bianca wished she was back home with her grandparents. She often thought of going back, but she knew that they were happy to know that she was doing well, that she would have more opportunities in her life than they did. And that her parents had wanted this for her all along. *They'll be watching,* she thought to herself.

She heard a voice, and realized that Lisbeth was muttering in her sleep. *At least one of us is asleep,* Bianca thought.

She reached over to her shelf and grabbed her brown bear, placing him in the bag she would be taking with her. At least the voices of her parents would be with her on this journey.

As the world watched, Bianca and Lisbeth walked toward the shuttle, accompanied by Lenna and several officials from the space program. Bianca could hear one of them, a woman in a green suit, saying, "They're not ready yet. This is a mistake, they are too young. Sally Ride was thirty-two..."

Bianca stopped. "Maybe she's right," she began, but Lisbeth moved past her.

"That was a long time ago. Technology has changed, Bianca. It'll be all right." Bianca thought she saw Lisbeth roll her eyes, eager to keep going. Lenna smiled sympathetically.

As they prepared to separate and leave Lenna at the doors, Bianca and Lisbeth turned. "Good luck! This is going to change everything for you," Lenna said.

Lisbeth smiled. "Yes," she said decisively.

Bianca was not so sure. Her stomach felt like a ball of string, completely knotted up. She wanted to reach out to Lenna, to ask her to drive her to the bus station, back to her grandparents.

And then what? she asked herself.

And then I would be happy, came her reply.

But how could she? With the whole world, maybe even her grandparents, watching, how could she give up an opportunity some people only dreamed about? *But after this, I'll go visit them. I will go see them, spend time there,* Bianca thought to herself. She smiled and returned Lenna's hug, and she and Lisbeth continued on, walking side by side.

Bianca tried to calm herself during launch by telling herself over and over that the computers would do the job. She looked over at the compartment where her bear was stored. It was one of the only things she brought on the shuttle, and as she followed the countdown, it was the one thing that gave her comfort.

Lisbeth's eyes were wide with excitement. She had been more quiet—reserved—since they had won the contest together. There had been times when Bianca thought Lisbeth was angry with her—but they had both won, why would Lisbeth be angry with her? She had begun to spend more and more time alone, and even when Lenna called their grandparents, Lisbeth would only spend a few moments on the phone with them. Bianca was afraid to ask how sick Lisbeth's grandparents were, but she could see the answer in Lenna's face.

"This is going to change my life," Lisbeth said quietly, almost to herself.

"Yes, imagine all the opportunities in science and research we will have after this," Bianca said.

Lisbeth started, as if she had forgotten that Bianca was there.

There was one minute left before they took off. Bianca's heart began to pound against her chest, and for a moment she was worried it would pound itself to death. Everything around her fell silent as her panic grew.

Lisbeth smiled wide as the shuttle began to lift from the pad.

There was something wrong. Bianca felt it. As the shuttle lifted itself completely from the pad, Bianca felt a wave of nausea come up from her stomach. She looked over at the compartment that stored her bear. If she could just hear her parents one more time…

She could see Lisbeth's mouth moving, but no sound was coming from it. *You're just having a panic attack,* Bianca told herself. *Calm down.*

But Lisbeth's face had changed. Her smile was fading, and all at once Bianca's hearing came back, and she could hear a beeping in the compartment.

There *was* something wrong. Her heart was beating faster than she had ever thought it could beat. *We're going to die,* Bianca thought to herself. She saw Lisbeth unfastening herself and her hands instinctively reached to unbuckle her own restraints. She could hardly lift herself up from the seat, the force pushing down on her was so strong. The shuttle began to tilt and Bianca knew that it would soon be pulled down by the Earth, into the water.

As she headed for the escape pod, she remembered her bear,

turned and rushed back to get it. But when she reached the pod, clutching the bear, Lisbeth turned and started to shut the door.

"I'm coming," Bianca got out. It was a moment before she realized that Lisbeth was smiling at her. "What?" Bianca asked, desperate.

"This is it," Lisbeth said. "I know what they meant. I can see it now. 'Teenager sole survivor of one of the first automated shuttle launches'."

Bianca's eyes widened. She clutched her bear close to her, the weight of everything making her head heavy.

"What are you talking about?" she managed.

"They'll never let two teenagers back on a shuttle launch like this, not after it's failed. But I can still be known by the world as the only one to have survived it." Lisbeth stared at Bianca, not looking away.

Bianca shook her head. "No. No, you can't. They'll know," she said, even as she realized that there had not been any acknowledgment of the problem, no instructions whatsoever, through their headsets. What had happened?

"Why?" Bianca asked.

"I'm supposed to be great, to reach new heights," Lisbeth said. "I have to. I can't go back. I want… I want everything," she said.

Bianca wanted to cry, but what would be the point? She laughed bitterly. "You took it. You took the money those people were missing, on the bus when we first came here. You took my marbles, too," she said.

Lisbeth looked down for a moment. "I'm tired of not having anything. I'm tired," she replied.

Bianca stood straight. She handed her bear to Lisbeth. "For my grandparents." Lisbeth reached over and took it, and the door slid shut. Bianca was alone as the pod was released.

The world looked on as the pod separated, cheering for the two survivors they thought were inside.

The journalists swarmed the beach near the site of the crash. The first images of Lisbeth showed her clutching a small bear, crying. The debris from the shuttle was pulled onshore little by little, but there were no signs of Bianca.

Poor Lisbeth, the world thought. Her friend had suffered an attack and had been unable to move, unable to reach the pod. *At least her attack spared her any suffering she may have felt upon impact,* Lisbeth repeated in interview after interview.

The interview offers, and the money that accompanied them, continued to pour in immediately after the catastrophe. It was only a few days before Lisbeth was scheduled to meet with the President of the United States.

Lisbeth was sure she was set to receive an award, a medal of some kind. A plaque at least. She wore her best suit and was picked up at her aunt's home, from where she would be driven to the space center for a live television appearance with the President.

As she walked in and shook hands with the President, Lisbeth could hear noise outside of the conference room. Her aunt pushed her way in, shoving reporters out of the way. Her eyes were wide and her face looked pale and sick. Her way was blocked by security, but instead of bothering to identify herself, she merely held up Bianca's teddy bear and pushed the button on the back.

The cameras were rolling, the President's smile fading from her face as the conversation between Lisbeth and Bianca in the shuttle played from the teddy bear's recording box.

As Lisbeth was escorted from the room, she realized that the three sisters were never wrong.

Lenna stood with Bianca's grandparents in front of the tomb-stones. Three new ones had been erected: for Lisbeth's grand-parents, whose health could not take the news of Lisbeth's actions; and for Bianca, although there was no body to bury in the soft dirt under her tombstone.

The tents were being erected around them, and soon the cemetery would be filled with people. Bianca's grandparents clutched the teddy bear in their hands as they walked away, and Lenna knew that, though it broke their heart to hear it, they would never record over Bianca's voice.

As darkness filled the world, footsteps approached the tombstones. Lenna looked up to see three women. They stopped under the tree, in front of Bianca's tombstone, and set down a rolled sheet of paper. Then the tall woman in the center spoke.

"My sisters and I, we never got the chance to give this to Bianca. This belonged to her," she said, and the sisters bowed and moved away.

Lenna kneeled down and picked up the piece of paper, the top part torn away.

> *From the keeper of sound*
> *Your mother's voice rings*
> *From the keeper of sound*
> *The Fates shall sing.*

A Midwinter Night's Brainwashing

ALLAN DAVIS

"If we shadows have offended,
Think but this, and all is mended,
That you have but slumber'd here
While these visions did appear.
And this weak and idle theme,
No more yielding but a dream . . ."
- PUCK, *A MIDSUMMER NIGHT'S DREAM*

"**T**uck, I really don't know if this is a good idea…"

"Can it, Mitch. I know what I'm doing." Robin Goodfellow Tucker—"Tuck" to his friends, for the obvious reasons—completed the key combination that would initiate the system bootload, and stepped toward the door.

In the next room, six people were reclining on medical couches. "First," he said, without introduction or preamble, "stretch out on the couches so that we can get them aligned with your bodies. Then we'll hook up your helmets and slip you into the simulation." All six people relaxed back against the couches and waited patiently for Tuck to move down the line, clicking switches on each bed. Once all six had been measured and comfortably arranged, he asked them to sit up again.

Tuck moved back down the row, offering assistance as his friends put on bizarre helmets that looked like something out of Doctor Emmett Brown's wildest dreams… or nightmares.

"Look," he said, "I really appreciate all of you coming out tonight." If anyone noticed that he spent a few extra minutes helping Heather with her own helmet, they gave no sign.

"Glad to help out a friend," Andrew said. "But why are we here at night instead of during the day?"

"Sorry. It was the only chance I had to squeeze in time on the system. I'm just an intern, you know?" Heather's helmet was properly secured, and Tuck moved on down the line, double-checking the rest of the helmet straps and fastenings.

"Once I start the system, the helmet will use nerve induction to feed images into your brains. It will be like dreaming; you won't be able to move at all in here, but you'll be able to explore the virtual world however you like.

"I need for you to explore—and try things out. If you see something interesting, go for it—eat the food, drink the drinks, stuff like that. I'll interview you after the simulation is over and get your full impressions on your experience inside the computer."

"This isn't going to be dangerous or anything, is it?" Andrew asked.

"Not in the least," Tuck replied.

He hoped none of them noticed the very slight hesitation before he answered.

❦

Mitch had the sense to keep his mouth shut until the door sealed. "She is totally and completely out of your league, you realize this. She's never even given her phone number to anyone."

"That's about to change," Tuck said.

"And you think no one is going to notice that the most unreachable girl in the school suddenly falls head over heels for the science geek? Coincidentally, on the one night he invited her over to try out the new virtual reality simulation with deep dark government brainwashing subroutines built into it?"

"I've got that covered," Tuck said. "Now, we just need to get her to drink the potion. Start it up."

Heather opened her eyes, and the lab was gone. She was now surrounded by trees, standing in a small clearing. There was a low table with something sitting on it just ahead of her.

A noise from Holly made her turn around, and she dashed out of the clearing, looking for her friend.

"No!" Tuck shouted. "Don't turn around!"

By the time Heather found Holly, Andrew had found the table. He didn't hesitate in the least; he scooped up the small bottle, downed it in a gulp, and continued exploring in the direction Heather and Holly had gone.

"Mitch, shut it down." Tuck was focused on the screen, trying to track six people simultaneously as they wandered the simulation. "It's a bust. Reset it."

"Working on it," Mitch grumbled under his breath. "I've got three other subroutines to pause, gimme a second."

"You may not have it," Tuck said.

Andrew stepped into the clearing, walking up to the two girls. They stood transfixed, staring in fascination at a crystal clear waterfall, over two hundred feet high. He shouted a greeting over the roar of the water. Holly heard him first, and turned around to meet his gaze.

"Yep. Too late."

As soon as Holly met his eyes, the drink took effect. Andrew dropped to one knee, never taking his eyes off of Holly's, and reaching up to gently take her hand. "Holly, my love," he said.

"Got it," Mitch said.

❦

Holly blinked in confusion at the helmet in her hands. She had the distinct impression she had just been somewhere else. But that couldn't possibly be true, could it? She looked up, scanning her friends around the room, and Andrew's eyes met hers. Why was he staring at her like that?

Tuck moved down the row, helping each of them adjust their helmets. Heather's helmet seemed to give him some trouble, and he spent extra time trying to get it latched into place.

"I really appreciate you coming here tonight," he said. "I'm sorry we're doing this so late at night. Interns can't get prime time on the servers, you know?

"The simulation should seem totally real to you, so you can explore, and you can eat and drink stuff. When you're all done, I'll review things with you, get feedback on the experience, that kind of thing. So, if you'll lie back and relax, I'll start the simulation in just a moment."

❦

Tuck watched the screen as his avatar left the room.

"Do you think they had any clue that the simulation started as soon as their heads touched the sensors?" Mitch asked.

"No," Tuck said. "I don't think they even noticed." He loaded the forest, placed the potion, and watched as the friends appeared in the clearing. The potion, again, was right in front of

Heather, though not so much that anyone would get overly suspicious. In fact, every person had a low table in front of them this time around.

"Wow," Holly said. "This is so totally cool. It's like we're really here." *She picked up the turkey drumstick that had appeared before her.*

Heather held up the soda bottle. "This just seems so out of place here," she said to Holly.

"Oh, I don't mind," Holly said. "Here, I'll trade you? I'm not hungry, but I could definitely use a drink."

Tuck stared at the screen, mouth agape, as Heather handed the potion bottle to her friend. Holly downed it, then swayed dramatically as the potion took hold. Andrew, just a few steps away, leaped to her aid, putting an arm around her waist to keep her from falling. At his touch, she opened her eyes and met his gaze.

"Reset it, Mitch." Tuck pounded on the counter next to his keyboard.

"Tuck," Mitch said, as the simulation cleared out and the six participants returned to their beds, "are you sure you know what you're doing? I mean, this is some serious spook stuff here. You're poking around at secret government subroutines and we don't know all of the ramifications of—"

"Just restart the damn program, Mitch."

Mitch shut up and reactivated the staging area.

❦

Andrew fastened the helmet to his head while Tuck went through his spiel. He noticed that Tuck spent a few extra seconds checking Heather's straps, but barely even glanced at his.

His eyes caught Holly's while Tuck was checking her helmet, and she scrunched up her eyebrows at him for some reason.

I think I need to ask her out one of these days, he thought to himself.

"The simulation should seem totally real to you when it starts," Tuck was saying. Andrew realized he had missed a chunk of his friend's instructions because he'd been too busy staring at Holly. To cover for his inattention, he blurted out, "So, do you want us to do anything while we're in there?"

"Yeah, exactly," Tuck said. "If you see anything you can eat or drink… well… eat or drink it, you know? I'll talk to each of you separately when we're done to get your full impressions.

"Now if you'll relax, we'll get ready to start the simulation."

❦

"Mitch, you know what to do, right?"

"I've told you already this is a really stupid idea, right?"

Tuck glared at him, and he backed down.

"We give each of them a potion, they all drink. The only one that's effective is Heather's, and as soon as they drink it, we replace everyone's avatars with yours."

"Right," Tuck agreed. "No possible freaking way anything can go wrong."

Heather set the empty vial back down on the low table in front of her. Funny, she thought, how drinking something made her a little woozy and wobbly; she reminded herself to mention it to Tuck, in their talk after the simulation.

She looked up at Holly's giggle, and couldn't help laughing herself.

"Tuck," Holly announced, in a very amused voice, "why does Andrew look like he's got a horse's head?"

"That's not a horse," Heather corrected, "it's a mule." And as her eyes met Holly's, she realized that Holly's head looked like a cat's.

The cat-faced Holly brought a hand up, so that no one could see what she was whispering to Heather, and said, "You know, he still looks kinda cute."

"Dammit, Mitch, what the hell happened?"

"Um… minor bug in the avatar routine. It's not designed to change in the middle of the simulation, looks like. It flipped over to some dark mythological symbolism design. I'm trying to clear it up now."

"Might as well end the simulation while you're at it."

"Yeah, doing that too."

Tuck worked his way down the line of beds, double-checking that each helmet was firmly attached. He fought with Andrew's helmet for a moment, and barely even glanced at the straps for Heather's before moving on, Andrew noticed.

"I'll go start the simulation," Tuck said. "Just… wander around, lemme know what you think of it when we're done."

Dude looks like he's working too hard, Andrew thought. This was supposed to be fun, and he was treating it like a damn research paper.

As he stretched out on the table to start the simulation, he realized Holly was staring at him. *Have her eyes always sparkled like that?*

"Tuck, you need to drop it," Mitch said.

"Not until this works," was his reply.

"You say that now," Mitch said, "but you haven't looked at these readings. Andrew's serotonin levels are off the charts, and Heather's not too far from them. One more loop through the sim and they're risking brain damage."

"Brain damage? From a virtual sim? That's not even possible."

"Tuck," Mitch said, "you're using the same nerve pathways. This isn't just a sim, remember? Every time we restart, we run the same signal down the exact same neural path. You can't keep reusing those neurons without risking problems later."

"But we're close! I can feel it!"

"Tuck, do you really want your best friend—and your potential girlfriend—reduced to babbling and drooling?"

Tuck hesitated for a long moment, his back to Mitch, but started the sim again anyway.

Heather found herself walking dreamily through a forest. She could feel the beginning of a migraine building in the back of her head, and there was a red and gray haze surrounding her vision. She would have to tell Tuck that his simulation induced headaches.

Her foot caught on a root, and she tripped; when she put her hands up against a tree to catch herself, they went halfway into the trunk. She blinked several times, trying to clear her vision.

Mitch jumped when the alarm went off. Red lights started blinking all over his console. "That's it, Tuck," he said. "The built-in safeguards are kicking in. If we don't shut down the sim, it's going to start shutting down the whole system—and we have no freaking idea what will happen if the sim crashes with someone still wandering around in it."

Tuck hesitated for a very long moment. Then he sighed, long and loud. "Fine," he said. "We're done."

Heather worked her way to her knees, and realized she was next to a small table, with a bottle on it that said "Drink Me." She reached out, and found the bottle was actually about three inches to the left of where it seemed to be. "Eat and drink," Tuck had said. She lifted the bottle to her lips and drank it down.

Tuck grabbed the microphone. "The simulation is ending," he said. "Everything that happened here tonight will fade from your memory. As you go to sleep tonight, this will feel like it was just a dream, and it will disappear into your subconscious just as easily. You won't remember a thing.

"Okay," he said to Mitch. "Let them out."

When Heather sat up on the exam table, the first face she saw was Tuck's. He stepped through the room, checking on each of them, helping them to their feet.

"I'm sorry the simulation failed," he said. "Maybe we can try again some other time. I'll let you know."

Andrew stepped across the small room to help Holly down off the table. Their eyes locked, and she was leaning quite heavily on him as they left the room. Tuck noticed that Andrew's hand was dangerously low on her hip, and she was leaning her head on his shoulder.

Mitch stepped up next to him. "Wouldn't you like to be a fly on the wall when they wake up together in the morning?"

Tuck frowned at him and said nothing.

"Tuck?" Heather said. He turned, offering a hand as she

staggered a step, and then was surprised when there was something in his hand. "Would you… call me? Sometime?" She offered him a shaky smile, and headed out of the lab.

Tuck looked at the scrap of paper in his hand while Mitch let out a guffaw. "So, it really did work after all? Color me impressed. I take it all back. She's never given her number to anyone at all. You did it."

"Nope." Tuck balled up the paper and pitched it into the farthest corner of the lab. "Tomorrow, when she wakes up, she'll have never given her number to anyone. All forgotten, just like I told her to do. Just like a dream."

Mark Corey

PATRICIA SCOTT

"This, as you say, suggested
At some time when his soaring insolence
Shall teach the people—which time shall not want
If he be put upon't, and that's as easy
As to set dogs on sheep—will be his fire
To kindle their dry stubble, and their blaze
Shall darken him for ever."
- SICINIUS, *CORIOLANUS*

It's a modern day battlefield of carefully tended turf and pristine dirt, with unforgiving paint lines marking the boundaries. You step on that field with eight other guys that you've sweated with, trained with, probably bled with, if you've been working hard enough to be the best. The nine of you take that field and man your stations.

There are people that would tell you it's just a game. It's all chance. Nobody can hit the ball every time. Those people are the ones that have never risen above anything but mediocrity. They settle. They settle for having fun, they settle for the person they think they can get, just like everything else in their lives, they settle for the easy way. Not me. Not my team. We don't settle. We fight. We walk out onto that diamond knowing that we're the best and knowing that it's our game to win. The other team is just there for us to take out while we make ourselves look good.

Baseball isn't just about hitting the ball. It's about playing your averages. You lead your batting lineup with the guy who hits consistently but not far. You don't want to start with an out at the start of the inning. Your second guy, he's better about getting those outfielders to have to chase that ball. Your third and fourth guys, you want them to be your power hitters—these are the guys that are going to get onto the bases and clear them without breaking a sweat. They're fast and strong.

The other team has to strategize. Your first baseman, he's got to have good reflexes and a strong throwing arm, so if that ball flies at him, he'll get that out, then send the ball where it needs to go. He's sharp and accurate when he throws. Your outfielders have to be able to get under that ball and whip it to your basemen, because a slow guy out there who isn't paying attention? He's going to be the death of your team.

Your pitcher, though, your pitcher has to be your strategist. He's been studying the other teams. He knows how to break them apart. This guy can't hit fastballs. This guy, he's short, so his strike zone is practically microscopic. That guy has trouble with curve balls. That one, if you just get it fast and low over the plate, he'll never even realize it passed him until the ump yells "strike". There's no time for the pitcher to get tired or sore. He's got to keep that baseball in play. If you have to sacrifice a hit, you give it to that guy because he can't manage to haul his butt to the plate fast enough to be safe.

I'm this team's leader. I spend hours studying footage of the other teams, cataloging their flaws, because we deliver victories. Nobody celebrates second place. Nobody says that you were good enough. They don't talk about that time you almost go to the State Championships. They don't remember the guys who almost break records. It's the guy whose name gets engraved on that plaque that hangs in the trophy case as you come in the front doors who gets all the glory. I am the one who works for it. I'm the one who deserves that glory. The other teams, they're just stepping stones to my victory.

I've just finished my junior year of high school, and the

baseball season is in full swing. We got started with practices at the end of February, keeping that focus on our own skills. I spend hours, every day, in my backyard throwing baseballs at cans and through a tire. That's what it takes—dedication, practice, that willingness to do whatever it takes to get to the top. That's how I lead my team. That's how we win.

When I'm not practicing my pitching, I'm doing batting practice and reviewing footage from our games and from games of all of our opponents. My mind has become an encyclopedia of area baseball statistics. I can list the rosters, at-bats, RBIs, and anything else you want to know about the guys on my team and the guys on theirs. It's all how I play that game to win. You have to know who and what you're up against in order to defeat them.

Luck happens sometimes in baseball. You get that guy that's had maybe two at-bats all year who steps up to the plate and makes the grand slam. It's the one shining moment of heroism he'll ever have in his life. It may be good, but it won't be good enough—not against solid skills, perfected over an insane amount of practice.

I know who I am on that field. I know the worth of what I do on that pitcher's mound for myself, for my school, and for my team. Without me, our team would have been languishing at the back end of tournaments, barely managing to pick up an extra game or two during the season because they managed to go up against a team worse than they were in the initial round.

Now we're two-time state champions, and we're headed for a third championship with an undefeated record. With me on this team, we've got recruiters coming to every game. I see them out there, wearing their polyester button-down shirts and their smashed fedoras, trying to blend in with everyone else. Except they've got binoculars and cameras and never have any family resemblance to anybody on the field with me.

I know. I've studied my team as intently as my opponents. I know them by their stances, by the way they hold a bat, the differences in their gaits, the nervous tics that show as they anxiously await the next play. Baseball is a reactionary game. The other side does something, you try to make sure that whatever it is they did doesn't work to their advantage.

This is my third year taking the field with my army. They've been mine since I proved my freshman year that I could out-pitch and outlast Danny Keller, who was a senior. He'd get sore about inning seven and never did learn how to ignore the protests and twinging warmth of overused muscles. He'd get slower and more erratic, until the other team could start hitting consistently toward the ninth. It gave them all the opening they needed to storm our gates and lay waste to the lead that we had built.

Any given game, I treat those points as my castle. My job is to protect my fortress and tear down yours, pure and simple. If I can keep you from building at all, even better. It's what I do. It's what I'm good at. Everyone who's ever played with or against me knows it, too.

Today is the first game of the state tournament. There's a recruiter here that I recognize. He's been coming to games since I was a freshman. First it was one game, then two. He's been to three games already this year. This makes the fourth. He's checking me over, trying to see if I'm showing any signs of burning myself out. Not a chance. I'm only getting better from here.

I've still got some growing to do. There's still muscle to be put on. With access to better equipment and better coaches and trainers, there's no doubt that as good as my game is now, it's only going to get better. This isn't arrogance. It's the truth.

There's six other recruiters in the stands and they're all watching me.

We take the field against the Taggert Tigers. They've got a guy who does okay taking first bat. I throw him a slider, dead down the center, and he swings a split second too late, ruining his chances to get a hit. He hesitates. He always hesitates. I know this because I've watched him overthink instead of trusting his instincts. He swings and misses more than he connects and it's easy to pick him off. Three different pitches right in a row and he can't anticipate what I'm doing next. I keep him off balance and he can't manage to recover.

This is all-out, no-holds-barred war. I am playing for my future. Now is not the time to have pity or to show weakness. There is no place for mercy on this diamond. I throw with everything I have. Every point of fracture that I have cataloged becomes another place to exploit, getting me closer to my goals.

I love baseball. I'm good at it and have been for as long as I can remember. Ever since that first time I picked up a glove and played catch with my dad in the backyard, I knew. This game is all I want to do with my life. After high school, I'll play in college for a while, until I can move on, probably to a triple-A team with a solid affiliation with the Big Show. They'll call me up, I know this with certainty. The way my record stands right now, I'll be ready. I'll go in there when the time is right and show those guys what they're missing.

First, though, is the immediate team at hand. They aren't people. They're an obstacle to my calling. I just have to pick them off, one by one. I'm in that particular mindset that I get into when I pitch where I know I'm doing well. My mind automatically brings up the strategy that will bring my team to the win and my body executes it flawlessly.

Coach and our catcher are giving me signals, which I

acknowledge. Then, I give them a few signals of my own. We've played together long enough that they trust me. There aren't any arguments if I indicate that I think we should go in a different direction.

It's hard to explain what it feels like on that field for me. It's higher than knowing I'm the king of this game right now in our area. There's almost a godlike quality to it. I'm infallible here. I know what I'm doing, and what's more, everyone else knows it, too.

Those other teams, they don't want to go up against me. They know it's a losing battle. When they see our name on the other side of that scoreboard, they already know they've lost. I just have to make it official.

One inning passes, then the next. Nine pitches at a time I kill their dreams. It's simple. Throw this guy fastballs. Throw this one curves. That one can't deal with knuckleballs to save his life. There's no tricks here, just simple, honest strategy. One guy manages a hit, but it's low and it bounces across the grass to smack securely into my first baseman's glove.

I didn't pitch a no-hitter, but it was close enough to being one that it sends the other team packing. They'll go home still feeling proud, because they'll get to say that they almost got a hit against me. *Almost* wasn't good enough to advance them in the tournament, but that's all they're going to get from me and from my team.

The rest of the tournament goes pretty much the same way. I make them wish they'd never seen me, one throw at a time, and make sure my other teammates don't have much to do. The thing is, when they have to hit and run, they do it just as well as I pitch. We don't have to climb the rankings—we were first seed. We just have to defend, and we do. I get to bat once a game in the six games we play.

Every time, I get to home plate. I hit one home run, which the recruiter I recognized got to see. I pitch three no-hitters. It's a new state record. I'm going into the local history books on this one, which is a good start toward getting me into the nation's history books, and then to the world's. State championships now, and eventually I'll be on TV screens while fans watch the World Series in breathless anticipation.

The Bradenburg Bombardiers take the state championship for the third year in a row, just like everyone knew we would, and I'm awarded the MVP trophy for my superb performance on the mound. A couple papers interview me. They're simple questions: when I started playing, what do I do in the off-season, do I want to keep playing. These are things I don't even have to hesitate to answer.

It takes a day after the games before the recruiter calls my house and asks Mom and Dad if he can have a meeting with me. We've been expecting this. I've always known that this day would come. It's never too early to start planning out the next stage of the game, especially one that's laid out as neatly and predictably as this one is.

He introduces himself as Wally, and he's from a school in California. Their team's been consistently high-ranked for the last decade, and they've won the College World Series multiple times in that span. They want me. Like, full-ride want me. There's just one little hiccup.

My grades are decent. They aren't too bad, but they aren't fantastic, either. Baseball rules my life; and that's okay, Wally assures me, because the school has great sports medicine and physical therapy majors that would probably be right up my alley, as well as a program to train future coaches. There are abundant opportunities for me to gain all the skills I need to have a career in baseball and beyond. It won't necessarily be a walk in the park—after all, I'm going to have to maintain at least a C-average to compete on the team, and that will have to be on a full course load while I'm attending all required training and practices.

But I'm confident I can do it. It's just college, it's not like I'm going to have to deal with that much difference in what I do now. My grades are the way they are because there's a nerdy kid next door. He fixes my homework, completes it when I don't have time to, and in return, I act like I know him. It's just enough credibility to keep him from getting pummeled every day after school by the rest of the jocks. He lives off our scraps, but to him, they're a feast. There are even some of the girls that want to hang around with us who make the mistake of thinking that if they get in good with Roger, then they'll get in good with us. It doesn't work like that, but it's funny to watch them try; and it makes Roger happy, so we let it go on.

Wally isn't concerned about my grades, though. I keep it to myself that those are really more Roger's Bs on my report card than mine, because that won't look good. I'm a baseball player. That's what I'm going to do with my life. I don't need to worry about anything else. I'm waiting for Wally to get to his point. If the grades aren't the issue, then what is?

I catch something about the university wanting to create "citizens of the world", whatever that means. Just sounds to me like another word for "mediocre". I keep that thought to myself. There are steps you have to take to get where I'm going, and if I miss one, the recovery will be almost impossible.

Finally, Wally says, "To guarantee admission, we want to see our incoming students be more well-rounded when they come in to our program. Your grades aren't quite good enough, and your baseball skills won't make up for that. You'll have to do reasonably well on your SATs and, quite frankly, we'd like to see that you've developed an interest in something other than baseball."

I feel my life skidding to a halt. There's no room for anything in my life other than the game. I know people who claim to eat, breathe, and sleep something, but even they think my level of dedication to this sport that I love is insane. Even Beth, the girl I date off and on, knows that when baseball season starts, she's better off breaking up with me than trying to make dating work.

"Well, uh, what would you suggest?" I say it, even though I don't mean it. I don't care about Wally's opinion. I just want to get signed up and go play for my next team.

"It may seem a bit late to get involved in any other school activities, but you do have your entire senior year to consider. Think about something like, oh, say, student council? You could show a community-minded spirit, perhaps an aptitude toward politics on some level, maybe even demonstrate some team building skills. It will give you that extra little bit of 'oomph' that you might need to get your application through. Our deadline is December. By then, you ought to have been able to establish yourself in another activity well enough."

I have until December to turn this around. It's just a little detour, that's all. I have to take this route to get into college so I can play ball. It's just student council, I shouldn't have any problem getting elected. Everyone in school knows who I am. They're clamoring to say "hi", just to touch a little bit of the glory that follows me off the field. I am a star and all of them know it.

Wally leaves and my parents look at me. I just shrug and say, "Guess I'll run for student council, then. How hard can it be?"

They don't have any doubts. The next day, Mom buys me supplies so I can make posters. She even prints out a bunch of pictures of me playing to put on them. They'll know who they're voting for when they see them. It makes sense to me. It's strategy. I know how to deal with this.

The way our school is set up, the student council holds their elections in September. There isn't much to take care of when it comes to official business until then, I guess. The committees who are in charge of the activities and that stuff are mostly volunteers. I know that because of Beth. She's really into planning and decorating for the dances. That's girl stuff that doesn't interest me much, so I just leave her to it, except when they need a guy tall enough to hang stuff on the walls or whatever.

The first week of school, there's an assembly. That's when you announce you're running. So, on the first day of school, I walk in to Mr. Peretti's office and declare my intention to run, first thing in the morning. He raises his eyebrows at me and stares at me a long time before he says, "Really, Mark? I mean, it's, okay, nice to see you do something besides play ball, but I'm kind of surprised to hear that you've taken a sudden interest in student council."

"Yeah, I talked to a recruiter this summer, from a school I really want to go to. He says I gotta be more well-rounded, so he suggested I do something besides baseball. I've got to December to show 'em that I'm a good candidate for them."

He nods. "It always does come back to baseball with you, doesn't it?"

I just shrug. He acts like I don't know anything else, and maybe I don't. I'm a specialist, but that doesn't mean I can't adapt to a situation. I have to do that all the time on the field. You don't get to assume that the other guys are going to play exactly the same way they did from the beginning of the season to the end of it. They learn, they get better, and if you don't learn and get better, too, you just blow the whole game before you've even started.

"You gonna put my name in as an official candidate or what?"

Mr. Peretti sighs, but he takes out his pen and scribbles a note onto a page of lined paper. He uses the same kind of notebooks most of his students do. It's kind of sad—you'd think he'd get better ones.

"Have a particular office you intend to run for in mind, Mr. Corey?"

"President, Mr. Peretti. I'm going to be president."

"Of course you're going to be student council president. Good luck, Mr. Corey. You can begin posting your campaign materials at two tomorrow afternoon. The speeches will occur at the Friday assembly. You will have five minutes to state your platform and make whatever campaign promises you think you'll manage to push through the council."

"Thanks, Mr. Peretti. Have a good day."

Even though I'm not allowed to put my posters up yet, I start campaigning right away. I tell a few people that I'm running, because I know they'll spread the word. It's a hot topic of gossip, after all—Mark Corey, state champ pitcher, running for student council president. Of course, there are the extra little tidbits they'll throw in there, making sure everyone knows what a cool guy I am. They make sure to point out that I dominate on the diamond, so I'll be sure to see to all of their concerns.

I go through classes just like normal. Roger's got basically the same schedule as I do, except for a couple nerd-bomber extraordinaire classes he takes in the afternoon. It makes it easier to match up homework assignments. He just makes sure he gets my homework done on time, and I make a point of sitting next to him in class.

Everybody knows that I only deal with the best, and since I always sit next to Roger, he earns extra cred as the smartest guy in school. You'd think that since I don't have time for all this classwork crap that means that I bomb every test I ever take. Me and Roger have this system, though. See, the homework, it's just busy work. Everybody knows that. The teachers don't want to have to deal with a bunch of whiny students, so they just give you tons of stuff to do so you're all worried about getting it done and keeping up your grades.

Even Roger thinks half our work is pointless, which is why he's so willing to take care of it for me. About a week out from the test, though, Roger makes some drill cards for me with the major stuff we're going to have to know. This is where Roger turns out to be my equal when it comes to strategy. He can figure out with scary accuracy what kind of stuff any of our teachers are going to put on those tests. I miss a few answers here and there, but my test scores are consistent, and I never run the risk of getting caught. You get caught cheating on a test, you get expelled. If I get expelled, that means that I can't play ball anymore, and I will not let that happen.

I know there are people who would be surprised that I do actually study for the tests. I figure they don't matter. All that matters is that I get through the tests and get that much closer to getting out of here.

As the day wears on, I notice that there are clusters of kids hanging back to talk to each other. They whisper and look my way. At first, I think it's because they're like most of the rest of the student body. A lot of them smile at me and give me nods or looks of approval, because they know what I've done for this school. Most of them don't talk to me, though, because they know it's not going to get them anywhere. I'm a busy guy and I've got important things to do. They can't do anything for me, so they're better off getting out of my way so they don't become obstacles.

It's the way the world works. It's the way the world always works. No matter where you go, there are big fish and there are little fish, and the big fish eat the little fish. I'm a big fish here, and I'm only going to become a bigger fish. The minnows need to swim away.

But when I see a few more of them, I realize that they aren't giving me the usual looks of admiration or envy. They're looking at me like they can't stand me. I have no idea what that's about. I don't even know most of their names. Whatever their problem is, it can't have anything to do with me. I've never done anything to them.

As the week passes, though, the rumor mill keeps churning. The whole school knows I'm a candidate for student council president now, but I've found out that there's a group of kids who are actually trying to keep me from getting elected. They're the ones whispering in the corners to each other, talking about how I'm just a jock and the only thing I care about is myself and baseball. They're sure I'm going to ruin the school. I can't see how that could happen, though. There's only so much power they give the student council.

The day before the speeches, they actually issue a statement, posting it along with all the campaign posters in the halls. It's smear tactics, pure and simple, trying to put doubts in everyone else's heads. They're all about how leadership on a baseball field doesn't equate to leadership in the classroom, and they list off a few things I've done that seem to make their case that I'm arrogant.

And, yeah, maybe I didn't exactly make them all feel welcomed when they first moved to town. Maybe I didn't invite any of them to any parties that I've had. Maybe I don't acknowledge them on a day-to-day basis. But I'm not the only one who treats them like that. They're just trying to make me look like a jerk.

I don't give them much thought. I don't need to. I practice my speech instead, because I'll have to sound impressive. They won't care whether or not I make sense, they'll care that I can talk like I know what I'm doing. That's not hard. I do it all the time in class. There are a lot of teachers here that seem to think you have to participate in class discussion to earn your grade.

I go through my speech twice. I don't want to waste my time on stage stuttering around, not when I have idiots trying to take down my campaign. They don't matter, and neither do their stupid statement posters.

When it's time to give my speech, I point out that all of them know me. They know what I can achieve when I set my mind to it. The Bombardiers are three-time state champions, and that happened with my guidance. I'm the pitcher and the team captain, and I ushered them to victory, even as a freshman, when everyone was sure that we'd end up dead last at the tournament.

They're cheering as I promise that I'll make our school a better place. I don't give any specifics. I don't indicate that this is a little step in a much bigger climb. I just tell them that we'll be cooler than any other school, we'll be admired for the way that we do things, and all they have to do to put us ahead of that game is just elect me.

After the speeches, Mr. Perretti explains how everything is going to work. There are seven candidates for president, so instead of just a straight ballot election, they'll take the top three. Those three will have to get enough support to stay in the race next week, in the form of signatures from the student body. Each of us will have to get at least sixty. Once we hit that magic number, we'll be allowed to give another speech—this one eight minutes long—and there will be a final election.

He keeps talking about things like primary races and a bunch of crap that I think Roger tried to help me memorize for civics class last year. Whatever. It's all democracy, and all I have to do is get sixty students to say they like me enough to sign a petition to keep me on.

I have four days to get my signatures. That's just fifteen signatures a day. I get more high fives than that in an afternoon. It's going to be cake.

Except it isn't. The people that used to cheer me on the field have been listening to those stupid nerds. I get brushed off, smiled at, declined. It feels like I'm losing my mind. All I have to do is get a few lousy signatures on a piece of paper to secure my future. None of them care.

The guys on my team all sign, easily enough, but I'm not sure if it's because they want me to get on student council or if they just feel like they should, for the good of the team. After all, we've still got one more season. We take that championship in the summer, we end up holding a state record. Nobody's ever done that before, and they know they aren't getting anywhere near that title without me.

Beth makes a point of signing where all of her friends can see her. They'll follow her lead. She's always been able to do that, get people to do the stuff she thinks they should. She even manages to get me to do stuff for her, too. As soon as she signs my petition, she smiles up at me. She's beautiful. She knows it, too.

"So, you'll be taking me to the Homecoming Dance."

It's not even a question. Not that I've ever expected Beth to ask me anything. She's like me. We get what we want. Both of us have plans, and neither one of us has ever let anything get in the way of that. She's just lucky that so many of her plans either fit mine or have no real effect on anything I'm trying to do. Beth is like everything else in my life. She either helps me or, as far as I'm concerned, she doesn't exist.

"Guess so. When is it?"

"Next weekend, Mark. You'll have to go anyway, that's when the next speech is."

"Sure. I'll get you at five-thirty."

She nods. That's always the plan when we go to a dance. The dances start at seven. I pick her up at five-thirty, we get something to eat, then we go to the dance. It takes very little preparation on my part to pull it off, and it makes her happy enough that she dates me when she feels like it.

Once Beth is done signing, her friends step up to sign their names, too. High school is a brutal place. You either fit in or you get left in the dust. Some of us figure out how to keep ahead of that game way faster than others.

It still takes me the whole four days to get all the signatures. I get so many stupid questions about what my plans are for my term and how I see myself improving the school. It's like they expect me to fix all their problems. The thing is, not one of them realizes that whatever their little problems are, they aren't mine, and if they want something done about it, they should do the same thing that I've had to and try to fix it themselves first, instead of whining for someone else to do it.

An hour before the deadline, I turn in my sixty signatures. Mr. Peretti frowns when he takes them. I stand there and watch as he checks them against the other signature sheets. Each student was only supposed to sign one petition, and the candidates themselves were to refrain from signing. If a candidate qualified, then they would be added as having voted for themselves, since Mr. Peretti did not anticipate any selfless voting.

One of the other candidates had acquired seventy-four signatures, which would have put her in the race and left me cold, but she was working on homework and had asked her teacher a question. The explanation ran long and she missed the deadline by almost half an hour.

My candidacy is formally cemented. I'll be asking for votes to serve on the student council.

Everything is just a step in a plan—if not yours, then somebody else's. I've figured out that my classmates want me to say something that will make them feel good about voting for me. They'll need a reason to. It takes me a while to think of what to say. This isn't the kind of strategy I'm used to employing. Then, Roger points out that I just need to think of this speech like giving a talk to the guys in the dugout. As soon as I realize that, deciding what I need to tell them to get their votes is easy.

On the night of the Homecoming Dance, I get on that stage and talk about how I want to be part of their team. I'll listen to their concerns and make this student council all about serving their needs. And then I give them my platform: off-campus lunches. We shouldn't be stuck eating cafeteria lunches, when just a few blocks away we could be feasting on burgers and pizza. Right now, we have to deal with a closed campus policy that makes no sense. Tardy is tardy—we all know that—and it shouldn't make any difference if you're late because you were in the cafeteria or late because you were stuck in line at a fast food joint waiting to pay for your soda.

The dance floor erupts in cheering, and I can feel the surge of adrenaline that tells me I'm going to win. It's not even much of a contest. When the votes are tallied, I stand head and shoulders above everyone else in the results. There are congratulations all the way around. I am the new student council president.

The losers of the race just give me sour looks. But if they wanted to win, they should have tried harder. It's their own faults. They didn't want it bad enough. I did.

My first meeting is on Monday. My intent is to go in and just be there, make my presence known, and let the student council stuff that has to happen do its thing. I assume that I'm a figurehead. That's what most of these things are.

But it's not quite that simple. I'm supposed to run the meetings, but it's not like it is when I'm running a pre-game meeting or a meeting at practice. There are these stupid rules that I'm supposed to follow, and something called "points of order". Mr. Peretti actually hands me this thick book and acts like I'm supposed to read it and learn something from it. I guess that I'll have to see what Roger can tell me about it.

Then, people start bugging me about getting the off-campus lunch policy. Since they won't let me get anything else done—and I mean, I'm constantly getting random people coming up to me in the halls pestering me about how I had promised—I start looking into what it's going to take. It turns out, I have to go in front of the school board and argue our case. I can't even ask anyone to pinch hit for me. As student council president, I have got to get up there myself and tell them why making us stay at school the whole day is so lame.

To go before the school board, I have to schedule an appointment. It's like I don't even matter. I have to submit in writing why I want to speak at their next meeting. They can even tell me "no" if they want to, which I think is just ridiculous. If I had to go through all of this just to get to be president, then I think that should count as an automatic that what I say goes.

I just want everyone to shut up about the whole thing. It gets to the point where I officially declare a nerd-free zone in the cafeteria. Some of the football guys help me enforce it. If you want to sit in the cafeteria at lunch, you have to keep the talk strictly limited to outside stuff or homework. Nobody wants to hear about what is or is not getting accomplished by the student council president while they're trying to choke down a greasy slice of floppy hamburger pizza, because our school is too cheap to spring for pepperoni. A couple of the more annoying people resort to eating their lunches in the library, but then things cool down for a while.

I make it known that they're not allowed back in, because they're causing too much drama. The football guys make sure they spread the word that they'll cart anyone out who makes lunch unpleasant for everyone else. I think I've pretty well got it solved.

A month into my term, a cluster of the losers come in, wearing posterboard signs and chanting that lunch is theirs, too, like anyone cares what they think. We try to get them out of the cafeteria before things get out of hand, but then one of the nerds actually takes a swing. Of course, the football player dragging her out by her collar doesn't take very well to it. He doesn't realize, though, that she has some kind of belt in one of those weird fus, and she mops the floor with him. It makes the other nerds brave.

Before I can even yell for everyone to calm down, the cafeteria erupts into a free-for-all. There's not supposed to be fighting on the field in baseball, and there sure as hell isn't supposed to be fighting on school grounds. I wade in to try and break it up, but I just get a couple punches to the face for my trouble. I know it's bad when Mr. Peretti and Principal Munroe have to pull a couple dorks off me.

We spend the next few hours getting grilled by teachers trying to figure out what just happened to their school. I am informed that I will be punished for my role.

"I didn't do anything," I protest. "I was trying to get people to stop!"

"Mr. Corey, you are the reason this became an issue in the first place. It seems that you've been barring other students from entering the cafeteria, which is against our code of conduct. All students have a right to be in public areas of this institution during appropriate hours. They should be in the lunch room at lunch time."

"Really? You're taking their word for it, Mr. Peretti?"

"Yes. I am. You know why? Because I've had you in my classes, Mr. Corey. I know what you're like. You got a little bit of power and you thought you could do whatever you wanted. Doesn't work that way. I've been trying to get those students to tell me why they were skipping lunch, and now I know. Stories are all consistent, Mr. Corey. Your student council career just ended."

I don't believe him. There's no way they'd do that to me, not after everything I've done for them, not after everything I sacrificed to give them their championship baseball team. Peretti doesn't have that much clout, not in this school.

Until he does. As of four-thirty, I'm informed, I no longer serve as student council president. To add insult to injury, I am also being suspended. I will not be allowed to make up any of the work that I miss on the three days I will be required to be absent. My stomach drops as I hear all of my dreams crumbling around me. It's over. For the first time in my life, I'm facing true defeat. School policy states that if you've been suspended, you are ineligible to play any school sports for the remainder of that year. I have been exiled from the baseball team.

My parents are called. Dad has to come and get me, because Mom's still at work. He chews on me all the way home. He's never told me I'm a disappointment before. I get grounded. I'm not even allowed to go over and talk to Roger.

Three days is a long time to sit at home and think. I still can't believe that everyone thinks this is all my fault. They're all treating me like I'm not good enough to be around them. Beth even texts me to tell me she's breaking up with me. She can't be seen with a loser.

Since I can't turn in the work anyway, I don't bother with the stuff that I could do for classes. Whatever I miss is what I miss. I can maybe manage to get my grades up enough next quarter to even them out, so it doesn't look so bad. Just a little hiccup, you know, no big deal. Kids have these things happen to them all the time right? It's normal.

Except I'm not normal. I was born for greatness. Everyone around here knew that for a while, but you sure can't tell it now.

When I go back to school, nobody will even talk to me. You'd think I was some smelly slob who never showers, the way they avoid me. Nobody will sit close to me, not even Roger. Roger used to be like my little sidekick, always trotting at my heels, trying to catch up to my shadow. Even he's too good for me now.

It makes me realize that, at least on some level, I really did think of Roger as my friend.

Other people would probably just curl up in a ball in a corner of their bedroom and whine about how much their life sucks. Me, though, I get angry. Every day, I just feel angrier. They still want to claim the team, still want to tell everyone we're state champs and we're headed for a record next year. The difference is, not one of them bothers to say my name in conjunction with any of it. I was their hero. Now, I'm just their scapegoat.

I get to the point where I don't even care about the record any more. They don't deserve it—not after the way they treated me. There's a way for me to control this. There's something I can do about this. I can show them. They're going to wish they'd never messed with me or made me lose my status in this school.

It's easier than I thought it would be. The Taggert Tigers have been runners-up to my team the last three years. Their pitcher and team captain is Tully Adus. He's a decent enough player, consistent where it matters. His main flaw is that he's had the misfortune to go up against me.

It isn't tough to find him. He and his team go over to Gino's

Pizza to hang out most days. Gino tolerates it because he played for the Tigers. They pretty much have free reign to go sit in there, do their homework, whatever.

I go over on a Thursday night. I'm wearing a hoodie and jeans. It's dark outside, pouring rain, and the last thing on most of the Tigers' minds is baseball. But I think I've got a pretty good gauge on Tully. He's enough like me that I can tell even when he's not thinking about the game, he's thinking about the game. He wants to win as bad as I do, and he's trying to figure out what he can do about it.

He gets up to go over to the soda machine. I go stand beside him, acting like I'm waiting my turn. I don't waste any time. If I'm going to do this, I have to seize the opportunity. I'm not sure I'll have another one.

"You want your championship, Tully?"

He looks at me so fast I hear his neck pop. That's not a good sign. His body's already starting to give in small ways. He pushes himself too hard, he'll be a has-been before he ever even makes it to being an *am*.

"Corey?"

"Yeah. Look, don't make a big deal out of it, okay. Nobody can know I'm here."

"What are you doing?" Tully hisses.

"They screwed me over." My voice rises, even though I don't mean for it to. "They think they're so great. I got kicked outta school. That means I can't play for my team any more. They deserve to go down for that, and I can give you everything you need to make that happen."

I can see Tully thinking. He's not sure whether I'm making him a genuine offer, or if this is some new strategy to mess with his head.

"Just a second," he says.

He turns away from me and pulls out his phone. He pounds out a couple of texts and sends them. While I'm filling my Mountain Dew, his phone beeps. He checks the screen then looks at me again.

"All right. But we're not talking about it here. The rest of my team doesn't need to know about this, and I can't be seen talking to you. "

I agree with him. I want the loss of the Bombardiers' precious championship to come as a shock. If they suspect that I'm talking to Tully, then there's a chance they might try to get something together that could counteract this. That's the last thing that I want to happen.

I deliberately leave a napkin sitting on the counter. It's got my phone number on it. As I go back to my table, I glance back. Tully's shoving the napkin in his jeans pocket.

It still takes him a couple of months before he finally breaks down and calls me. We meet up in one of the city parks in Bradenberg. It has a baseball diamond at one end, and there are little kids playing catch over in the outfield. They're yelling at each other and giving each other pointers. I was like that once. At least, I think I was. Now, though, all that matters is revenge.

I start spilling secrets. All of the weaknesses that I'd strategized over the seasons to hide are coming to the surface. Throwing our best hitter a fastball will get him every time. Our third baseman broke two of his fingers last year and after he catches three or four balls, his hand goes numb. He's never told Coach, but he told me.

It should make me feel bad. I'm betraying them, and part of me knows it, but I can't find any part of me that wants to offer them a chance to recover. My dreams are dead. They died the moment Peretti and all his little cronies got me thrown out of school. That school doesn't deserve to win anymore. Not after they turned on me.

There's a playbook, where I've kept all of our signals. This is the part that will damn me forever. It's the ultimate moment of disloyalty. Coach is too lazy or too unimaginative to change the signals from year to year. Maybe it's just that he recognizes that the majority of the kids he sees out on the field don't see the battlefield. They're just playing baseball for something to do. They don't study it, or live it, or eat it, or breathe it. It's a game.

It's not my game anymore. I know this, as I hand the playbook over to Tully with all of my notes. He's got enough in there to conquer every team he faces—especially mine. It's the keys to the kingdom. His eyes get wide as he flips through the battered notebook. He knows what I've given him.

"There's no coming back from this," Tully says. His voice wavers, like he's feeling a little afraid.

"There was no coming back the moment they told me I was suspended," I answer.

My life feels empty without baseball. It revolved around the game for so long. Nobody talks to me, and no one will take the chance getting caught being decent to me at school. I've got nothing better to do than study. My grades are better than they've ever been. I retake the SAT and get a better score.

I can't stay completely away from the ballfield, though. It haunts me. I watch local news and read the paper to keep up with scores. The Tigers are having an undefeated season. They've become the team to beat. The Bombardiers are floundering. Without me doing all that work and driving them forward, they're lost. They get a couple lucky breaks, but they can't seem to get it back together enough to put together a run for the championships.

They don't even make it to the playoff tournament. They aren't champions this year. There's no record. I go watch Tully play his last game of his senior year. He throws a no-hitter. He's a hero. It should have been me.

Wally tells me that if I play a little community college ball, he'll come check out a game or two, but I can see the lie on his face. It's in the way he won't look at me when he says it.

Maybe I can find a minor league team that will let me walk on, someplace with a community college that thinks my grades are okay. I started out with the world at my feet. I was a monument of greatness. Now, I'm just choking on my own mediocrity, hanged by my own stupid pride.

Angel & Demon

HEATHER DIXON

"Thus from my lips, by thine, my sin is purged."
- ROMEO, *ROMEO AND JULIET*

DENVER, UNITED STATES WEST. DATE: 2075 AD

T he demon was bright, which was not at all how a demon should look. So fiercely, brightly handsome that he was almost brittle. He had bright golden hair with a forelock that curled charmingly over his forehead, and bright blue eyes that were so bright they were ice. When he smiled, his teeth shone perfectly straight and bright. He looked young, around eighteen or so, and was brightly intelligent for his presumed age. Everything about him was *bright*.

Which is why he fit in so well with the League of Government Youth, an establishment that took the brightest and sharpest from across United States West to the capital city, where they were taught debate, rhetoric, and other government workings.

The demon had been on this assignment for the last year. Playing the part with ease. Smiling for the cameras with various senators, shaking hands, kissing babies, and of course, breaking into internet coding and deleting the occasional anti-commune website that somehow managed to ckc through the tightly-regulated electronic ether.

And then, of course, punishing the offender when they were found.

That part was certainly a diversion from classwork, to say the least. The last hunt had ended with the Government Youth chasing the offender through abandoned sewer pipes and, once cornered, kindly informing him he would have a government trial before "accidentally" shooting him instead. The pathetic tripe had gone down reciting the antiquated Constitution.

It was quite delightful—to the Government Youth, anyway. Rubix had remained behind the group, watching them prey like beasts. When he was a younger demon, several millennia ago, he would have taken pleasure in it. Now, it was common and boring and—he dared think it—pointless.

But he had his orders. There was a certain GY (a member of the Government Youth, that is) who would do very good things for The Cause, if he could be persuaded to murder someone. And once he'd killed, there would be no turning back. He'd be theirs.

The demon had made friends with the boy, a fifteen-year-old from Arizona with large, dark eyes and a somber face. He'd been inducted into the Government Youth three years ago, but was being slow to come around to the United States West's (and Purgatory's) ideas. Still, the demon had slowly become friends with the boy. Friends enough, in fact, that the boy had revealed to him his sacred Navajo name: Cloud Hawk. Considering that all GYs were known only by their regulation numbers, it was a sign of ultimate trust.

The assignment, the demon felt, would have been a piece of cake—were it not for a certain other GY. She'd arrived in Denver shortly after the demon. And she had also made friends of Cloud Hawk.

Not that it had been difficult for her to catch the boy's attention. She was beautiful—or, rather, *pieces* of beautiful. She had features that would be stunningly attractive in different places or different times: a nose that would impress Roman emperors, dark eyes with long lashes that Persian princesses would poison for. Her lips were full and dark, the image of a starlet's mouth from the 1940s. Thick, dark, shiny waves of hair reached the middle of her back in cascades. She looked young—perhaps sixteen—and had the delicate figure to match. All this combined made for a rather odd confection of a person that would shine through any period of time. And the demon had seen a lot of periods of time.

She was different in other ways, though. Her eyes had a light in them that the rest of the Government Youth did not. She was smart, but purposely did poorly in her assignments and took absolutely no pleasure in the debate sessions, choosing to bow out instead of argue. Because of this, the other GYs had dismissed her as "weak." They knew it wouldn't be long before she was weeded out and expelled north. (Or shot. You never knew, with the Government Youth.)

She was an angel. The demon could tell. And if he'd had any doubts about it, she'd come right out and confirmed it last week, during US-W New Economics 406.

"Student three-oh-seven-five," said the professor at the front of the auditorium classroom, and the angel, down the row from the demon, stood up, shaking so much she nearly dropped her tablet. The professor continued without a pause, holding up the electronic screen that displayed her written words. "You certainly took a *unique* approach to our assignment on eugenic abortions."

The angel stubbornly lifted her chin and said nothing.

"It's very well-written, however illogical," said the professor, eyeing her warily. "Perhaps you were being a devil's advocate?"

"No," the angel said firmly, her trembling hand clutching the chair back in front of her. "Heaven's advocate."

The demon had nearly choked to keep from laughing. She'd come right out and said it. The professor looked as though he didn't know what to think of her.

Still, having an angel around threw a clog in the gears. The demon was used to angels trying to meddle in his assignments, but he usually got rid of them fairly quickly. He was good at what he did. It annoyed him, though, how persistent this angel was. She was... sticky.

But it wouldn't be long until he was rid of her, too. The apex of his assignment was drawing near. After this, it would be back to Purgatory, where he'd report to his supervisor, hobnob, as it were, with his other demon friends, and wait for another assignment.

The night the moment came was hot and dry, but storm clouds fizzed in the distance, the kind that were taller than they were wide.

"Monsoon season," Cloud Hawk said solemnly, looking at the sky from their dorm room window.

"Monsoons are only in Arizona and India, genius," said the demon. "Not on this forsaken rock called Denver."

Cloud Hawk smirked.

His smile faded, though, when a GY burst into their dorm room, positively hopping. The demon recognized her as a rather stupid—yet feral and eager—second-year, number 8321.

"We saw a resistance member!" she crowed, waving the pistol in her hand about. "Posting—not lying—*papers*! On the main thoroughfare buildings! *Papers!*"

"How delightfully old-school," said the demon, rising from his cot in the corner. "Next thing you know, they'll be dropping pamphlets from the sky, RAF-style."

Both Cloud Hawk and GY-8321 stared at him blankly. The demon sighed. One of the downsides of making jokes among the Government Youth was that they'd never been taught history. Not the real version, anyway.

"Right," he said. "We going to chase him down, or what?"

The hot wind whipped the group as they prowled the street. Thunder boomed in the distance. They'd barricaded the trains and traffic in the name of US-W, and their raw excitement grew even wilder when they found a stack of papers that had been dropped by the rebel: "*You are Being Lied To!*" He couldn't be far.

It was decided they would split up and head the rebel off around City Center East. Tonight was the night, the demon knew.

"Seven-four-eight-four," he said, tossing his pistol to Cloud Hawk. "You stick with me.

Cloud Hawk nodded.

The GYs split into groups of ten, running through streets crammed with halted vehicles, alongside trains full of weary passengers. The onlookers stared glassily as the demon's group threaded their way through to a dimly-lit sector of the city.

The resistance member was just a short distance ahead. The demon could see him, weaving between the cars of the immobile trains—a glimpse of a foot, a flash of tweed jacket. He ran with a limp.

The GYs were on his trail like coyotes, dead-ending him in an alley that was lined with rotting garbage and stank of it, too. The rebel clutched the pile of posters to his chest. He was a mousy-looking accountant of maybe forty, wearing threadbare clothing and a wedding ring. So he was a traditionalist as well. The demon almost laughed. No one hated traditionalists as much as the Government Youth. This would be easy.

"Cornered," said the demon, crossing his arms and smiling at the man. The rebel remained strangely calm for someone who had at least five pistols pointed at him—one of which was Cloud Hawk's.

"Any last words?" said the demon.

The man somehow found his voice. "I feel sorry for you," he said. "For all of you."

"Oh, spare us," said the demon, rolling his eyes. The rest of the group behind him laughed and echoed nastily, "Yes, spare us." "Please." "*Honestly.*" "Play a violin."

"Don't shoot him," came a voice from the back of the group. "Take him into custody. He doesn't deserve murder."

The demon nearly swore. He whipped around sharply to see the angel, huddled at the back of the group. She had somehow arrived without him noticing, and she was shivering, even though the night was hot and muggy.

"Of course he deserves murder, he's spreading lies," screeched GY-8321, brandishing her pistol at the accountant, who winced. "He's a resistance member!"

"Shoot him," said the demon in a low voice to Cloud Hawk. Cloud Hawk's pistol hadn't moved from its target, but his dark eyes remained fixed on the angel. The wind whistled through the alley, whipping dust and papers between the abandoned buildings.

"Cloud Hawk," she whispered. "Don't. Don't do it."

The pistol began to shake in Cloud Hawk's grip.

"What, are you actually letting a *girl* tell you what to do?" the demon drawled.

The pistol's shot was drowned out by the thunder that boomed over them. As though it had split the sky, rain burst from the clouds and poured over them in sheets.

The rain seemed to drench the GYs' feral excitement. Cloud Hawk stared at the resistance member with wide eyes as the red-splattered posters fell from his hands and he slid to the ground.

At the back of the group, droplets coursed down the angel's face. But the demon knew it wasn't just rain.

Assignment over with, he disappeared from the group,

avoiding any last eye contact with either Cloud Hawk or the angel.

Perhaps it had been the thunder. Or perhaps it had been the look in the angel's large eyes. But for the first time in his existence, the demon was shaken.

HERCULANEUM, ROMAN EMPIRE. DATE: 79 AD

The sky rained ash. Light flashed, too, electric snaps in the great clouds of sulfur and gas; it illuminated the ash-brine sea, filled with Roman ships slogging through the night to evacuate the people of Herculaneum before the volcano erupted. The mountain in the distance was alight in patches of fire. In but an hour, the pyroclastic flows would bury the city.

The angel coughed, because everyone else was. She didn't need to cough, and she didn't need to hold a rag against her mouth. But if she didn't, it would arouse suspicion among the masses of people pressed around her. They all held bundles of their belongings, and covered their mouths with cloths in order to breathe. Panic was thick in the air—thicker than the ash. A crowd huddled under massive stone arches by the pier, waiting to load the ships. They were so packed together it seemed like everyone in the city was there. The sweltering heat was unbearable.

Among the pack and panic, a young boy streaked with soot hobbled on a crutch, coughing tiny coughs. He held a ragged little bundle under his free arm. The angel immediately recognized him, and she pushed away from the crowd to follow after him. He was part of her assignment.

She followed his slow progress—he often stumbled, or was shoved away, and he fell to his hands and knees. Her heart broke for him. In spite of all this, every time he pulled himself back into a three-legged gait and pressed onward.

Away from the throngs of the main evacuations, the angel could see where the boy was headed: a small fisherman's boat, bobbing alongside a derelict pier of rotting wood. The boy must have known this poorer area of the docks well, for he navigated across the fallen beams and broken planks with skill.

Already the fisherman's boat was packed to the brim with wealthy citizens of Herculaneum. Still more were boarding. A flash of light caught a glimmer of coin crossing into the fisherman's palm; he was charging exorbitant fees to take the people to safety up north.

The boy deftly slipped among the last group boarding. The angel joined him, the rag still pressed over her mouth and nose.

He almost boarded without being noticed, but little seemed to slip past the fisherman's beady, narrow eyes. In a blurred movement, he caught the boy's wrist in a tight grip. The crutch clattered down the plank. The angel quickly picked it up.

"See 'ere, boy!" the fisherman said to the struggling boy. "This ship is for paying folk! I don't reckon you have any *denarii* for passage, do ye?"

The boy struggled against his grip, coughing weakly. "Please, sir," he stammered.

From behind him, the angel spoke up firmly. "Let him come," she urged. "Look at him, he's awfully slight. He won't add a bit of weight to your ship."

The boy nodded eagerly. The ash on his face was streaked with his tears.

The fisherman hesitated, still holding the boy in his vice grip. The boat was filled with twenty citizens, and there wasn't room for even one more person. But the angel was right: he was a starved little thing and wouldn't add enough to make a difference.

"He's just a child," the angel pleaded. "Your mother taught you such kindness. It would do her memory good."

The fisherman did not release the boy at the invocation of his mother, but he looked at the angel oddly, as though she had stirred up forgotten memories buried long ago.

"*I* need passage," came a rather cool, unconcerned voice from behind them. "And *I* can pay."

The angel paled. She turned quickly to see who stood at the end of the loading plank, richly dressed in Roman clothes.

She recognized him immediately. The bright gold hair, the ice-blue eyes, the overconfident air of someone who thought they knew the secrets of life. The demon. She hadn't seen him since that particular assignment, eons ago. But she remembered everything about him.

Like her, he was coated gray with ash. But he was smiling slightly, showing a sliver of very white, straight teeth. In his hand he held a drawstring bag full of coins. He shook it, the coins jangling together.

The angel turned on him. "Rubix Grosvenor Saulus Jarhnam, don't you *dare*," she whispered angrily.

The demon Rubix nearly dropped the bag in surprise. She knew his name. *All* of his name. How did she know his name?

Quickly, the angel turned back to the fisherman. "Surely your heart isn't made of coin," she said.

The dredged emotions within the fisherman lined his ashen face. He looked at the boy, then at the demon Rubix, expecting him to say something.

And Rubix hesitated.

There was a taut moment of utter silence. Then the fisherman grabbed the boy's arm and yanked him into the boat.

"Get in," he growled, throwing the boy into the group on the ship. "An' don't tip the load, or you'll be the first thrown into this sooty brine."

The boy nodded eagerly. The angel managed to hand the crutch to him through the knotted tangle of people before the fisherman cast off, and the boat sludged across the ocean. The boy's grateful face shone in the darkness.

In the distance, the volcano flared.

The angel turned to face the demon Rubix, who surveyed her with an unreadable expression.

"You win," he said, in an equally unreadable voice.

"It's not a game," the angel replied.

"You care so much about the boy?"

"I care about the fisherman," said the angel.

And that was that.

"Thank you," she added quietly, "for giving him a chance."

And then she was gone. Rubix was left alone on the pier with a bag of coins and the memory of a smile. The volcano erupted behind him, sending blasts of heat through the city, followed by fast-moving volcanic offal. It would incinerate those huddled under the arches and bury the city.

But it didn't bother Rubix. He was used to this kind of heat. He lived with it every day.

ROTTERDAM, NETHERLANDS. DATE: 1941 AD

The outdoor café was close to the industrial part of the city—or what *had* been the industrial part of the city. It had been bombed flat less than a year ago, and there were still piles of debris in the alleyways and pockmarks in the buildings from the shards.

Life continued, however, just with more soldiers. They stood on street corners and in doorways. There were even a few eating at a small bistro table near the angel and her friend, talking in German and laughing loudly.

The angel kept her voice low as she spoke with Hilda, the girl of seventeen sitting across from her, who was frowning and pushing her spaetzle around on her plate.

"Think of how many lives it could save," the angel said quietly. "And all it would take is getting them to the resistance."

"I don't know," the girl muttered.

"You could do it tonight. If it gets past curfew, I bet you could stay the night in their home. You wouldn't be caught. I'm sure of it."

"I don't know," the girl muttered again.

"Well, you'd better know soon!" said the angel rather fiercely. "All *you* have to worry about is losing your German boyfriend! *They're* going to lose their lives if you don't help!"

Hilda stood sharply, threw her napkin down on her plate, and stormed off. The angel watched as she crossed the street, skirts swishing haughtily, adjusting her hair and refusing to look back at the small café. She disappeared around the corner. The angel sighed.

She hadn't been the only one watching. From the shadows of the café, Rubix the demon watched as the German soldiers—still laughing loudly—paid the waiter and left, leaving the angel alone on the sidewalk, glaring at her plate.

Rubix slung his coat over his arm and strode to her table. He was dressed smartly in a well-fitted suit and fedora, and even wore a pair of perfectly round glasses. He looked no more conspicuous than a Dutch university student who'd decided to take his lunch outside.

"Bad day?" he asked.

The angel looked up, startled. The *startled* transformed into *wary* as Rubix took a chair.

"Mind if I sit with you? Thanks," he said, without waiting for a response. He half expected her to disappear right then, even though the waiter might have seen her. But she didn't, though she watched him a like a cornered animal.

"You," she said.

"Me," replied Rubix, still smiling cockily. "Relax, angel. I'm not on your assignment. How is it going, though? Rubbing shoulders with the daughter of the diplomat in charge of issuing visas? What *could* you be saying to her?"

The angel's lips had become razor-thin.

"You have a temper," he said. "I didn't realize angels had tempers."

"Why are you here?" asked the angel.

"I've been doing some work nearby."

"I hope it's going poorly," said the angel feistily.

"Temper, temper," Rubix said with a grin. The truth was, his assignment was going very well. He had nearly convinced the Dutch woman down the street to turn in her Jewish stowaway.

"I hope they see how awful you are and they don't listen to a word you say," snapped the angel.

"We'll see, won't we?" said Rubix genially. "It's not like we can force people to choose."

"Then I hope they choose good."

"Well. You hope they choose *well*," Rubix corrected.

"No," she said stubbornly. "I hope they choose Good."

Rubix rolled his eyes, but smiled in spite of himself. A waiter came to take his order, and he ordered the exact plate the angel had: a dish of potatoes, a sausage, and some kind of sauce. When the waiter returned with the plate, the angel and the demon still sat in stony silence. Rubix made a show of cutting the sausage into little pieces. Then he launched into a new topic.

"I've been dying to ask—figuratively, of course, but it's been on my mind for an epoch or so now—how did you know my name?"

The angel lowered her eyes, but, to his surprise, she answered him.

"I looked you up in the Life and Death Department files," she admitted. "They keep a record of all the demons there, too. I couldn't help myself. I was so angry with what you did to poor Cloud Hawk."

"Who?"

"Cloud Hawk!" she repeated, affronted.

"Oh. Right. Him," said Rubix. His mind pulled together the vague memory of a young Navajo. He'd not given Cloud Hawk a thought since the assignment had ended. "Wait—you remember the names of your assignments?"

"First of all, they're people," she said, her temper flaring. "And second of all, of *course* I remember them. Every single one. Don't you?"

Rubix avoided her question by parrying with a new one. "And do you remember all the demons? You remember me, obviously."

The angel turned her fork between her fingers.

"Yes," she finally said. "I remember you. On the docks near Herculaneum. You let the fisherman save the boy."

"Did I?" said Rubix. "I recall almost convincing him to take *me* on his ship."

"But you paused."

"Maybe I was just shocked you knew my name."

"I can see when a demon's heart isn't in his work."

"I don't have a heart."

"Oh... says *you*." The angel smiled teasingly.

The demon remained stone-faced. The idea that he might have actually have a heart was a new one to him. He didn't know how he felt about it.

But he knew he didn't want her to go. Angels often avoided

demons at all costs; having a conversation with one was unheard of. And yet here was one who remembered him, who knew his name, and—of all things—thought he had some good in him. Highly irregular.

Because he didn't want the encounter to end, Rubix changed the subject.

"Ever wonder what it tastes like?" he said, nudging the pieces of sausage around his plate. "Food?"

The angel smiled sheepishly. *A-ha*, Rubix thought. It was a smile that said, *All the time*.

Rubix speared a sausage piece with his fork and dared a bite, chewing slowly and thoughtfully. As with every time he'd eaten before, he couldn't taste it. It was like chewing rubber that fell apart in one's mouth. He could barely swallow it.

"Did you taste anything?" asked the angel hopefully.

"Not a thing. Mortals swear by this stuff. I don't understand it."

"Some of the angels have actually lived," said the angel, "and they tell me they'd give anything to taste a potato again. Oh! And salt. They really miss salt."

"I hear chocolate is very good, too," said Rubix, smiling.

"Chocolate!" the angel exulted, then blushed. The waiter nearby looked up from cleaning the tables, then went back to work. From the corner beyond the café, a smartly-dressed Nazi officer glanced at them, his hands firmly clasped behind his back. His eyes were so bright blue, they pierced. They lingered on Rubix and the angel, then he turned his attention back to the street.

"Jonah's our choir leader," she said, in a quieter tone, so only Rubix could hear. "He's a once-lived, too. He's written a song about chocolate. It's a lovely song. I could almost taste it."

Rubix smiled.

"I'm—going to be born soon," the angel went on, with the excitement of someone who had thought about the prospect for half an eternity. "I plan on eating all the chocolate bars I can stuff in my mouth!" She laughed, a sound like bells.

Rubix did not laugh. Normally it would infuriate him, talking about becoming mortal. The way angels rubbed that advantage into the demons' faces—it was maddening. Rubix was a never-born, which meant he hadn't been born yet, and, since he was a demon... he never would be. Every time he thought about it, he became fumingly angry. It was absolutely unfair.

But now, he couldn't be upset. Not around this angel. He folded his arms and kept his face solemn, but he did not feel anger.

At his expression, the angel quickly sobered.

"I'm—sorry," she stammered. "I know I shouldn't talk about that in front of demons. The archangels tell us not to, anyway. I'm sorry. I'm just... excited."

Rubix waved it away. "Do you get to choose when you're born? What era, I mean?" he asked.

The angel jumped on the question eagerly. "No," she said. "But, if I had a choice, it would be here. Assignments in this era—the Second World War—I think they're my favorite."

"What? Now?" Rubix looked around at the faces of the passersby, taut with worry. As the war progressed, he knew those faces would become taut with hunger as well. He frowned. "The nineteen-hundred forties? When there's so much evil? Granted, angel, that's merely a professional opinion."

"Julianne," said the angel quickly. She suddenly became very interested in adjusting her jacket and hat, but the furious blush on her cheeks betrayed her.

Julianne, thought Rubix. She'd given him her name.

"It's—because—there's so much *good* in spite of it," she stammered on quietly. "I think, deep down, everyone wants to do good. Even demons."

Rubix stood.

Julianne stood, too, her chin stubbornly lifted.

"Cinderella time, I'm afraid," said Rubix, forcing a smile. "I daresay you'll catch trouble talking to me."

"I'm still glad I did," Julianne replied.

Rubix gave a half-shrug and slung his coat over his arm. He left without paying for his meal.

Half a block away, in an alleyway still shattered from the bombing, he leaned against the jagged brick wall, pulled off his glasses, and rubbed his face, hard. She was most definitely getting under his skin—and into his heartless heart.

And this could be a problem.

SATAN'S QUARTERS, PURGATORY. DATE: NULL

Satan had a wicked sense of style, and Purgatory had plenty of fashion designers who'd cared more about clothes than about who wore them. As such, Satan was attired in a striking three-piece suit, immaculately fitted to every angle of his form.

It also fit who he was. Devilishly handsome, shamelessly chiseled, brilliantly sinful, fiendishly rogue. A lock of his dark hair hung mischievously over his forehead; he had such perfectly straight, white teeth that when he smiled it almost cast a spell. To look at him was to be cut by his sharpness. He carried an aura of darkness wherever he went.

His quarters were sparsely decorated: hard floors; ceilings as tall as a cathedral, but with no paintings; strange-colored lights that cast strange-colored shadows. A tessellated wood screen along the wall added an oddly 1960s aura.

And mirrors. They were everywhere. All shapes and sizes, all frameless, all reflecting pieces of Satan as he stood on the dais in the middle of the three largest, like a bride at a wedding shop.

He stepped down from the platform as Rubix entered the room. Rubix kept the folded-up paper clasped in his hand as he drew near. It was a summons. Rubix had only ever seen Satan standing at the stage podium at the Purgatory-wide company meetings, so far away he was a speck. He'd never actually been summoned by Satan before. He wasn't an important enough demon for that.

Or so he had thought.

Rubix spoke before Satan had a chance. "You summoned me?"

Satan corrected him just as quickly. "'You summoned me, *Master*'."

"You summoned me, *Master*?" Rubix repeated, so innocently it was offensive.

Satan paused, then returned to straightening his tie in front of one of his numerous reflections. "It's come to our attention that you haven't been quite, ah, as *zealous* with your assignments as you once were."

Rubix didn't have anything to say to this, so he kept quiet.

"You used to be very good. Your supervisor tells me you always met the quota. And it is thanks to you we have Zedick in our ranks."

Cloud Hawk. Rubix didn't react, but Julianne's words echoed within him.

"Tell me... ah..." Satan paused with that prompt, his dark eyes searching Rubix.

Rubix rolled his eyes. *I've been working in Purgatory since the dawn of time, and he still doesn't care to remember my name.*

A quieter, sweeter voice whispered in his mind: *"Of course I remember them... every single one..."*

Julianne had remembered his name.

After a long pause under Satan's cold, bright stare, Rubix gave in and offered his name: "Rubix."

"Ah, that's *right*," said Satan warmly. "Rubix. Tell me, Rubix. Your supervisor has shown me your charts, and it seems there's recently been a steady downgrowth in your salesmanship. It's almost like your *heart* isn't in your work anymore."

Rubix folded the paper in his hands yet another time before answering.

"Well, that's a faulty accusation," he said lightly. "I don't have a heart."

"Oddly, your job performance has dropped significantly since your little café chat with a certain angel."

Rubix froze. Satan had seen. How had Satan seen? As far as he knew, he'd been the only demon on the assignment.

"Ever since then, your work simply hasn't been acceptable," said Satan. He smiled, a sickly sincere smile.

"That was ages ago," said Rubix carefully, as Satan straightened his tie in the mirror. "I'd almost forgotten it myself. Anyway, it wasn't really a *chat*. You know how angels don't stick around."

"Hm," said Satan. "Nedock?"

Rubix turned as a figure stepped out from the shadows near the tessellated screen. He was dressed smartly in a Nazi uniform, boots to the knees, hands clasped behind his back. He had piercing blue eyes. Rubix immediately recognized the Nazi officer who'd stood on the corner near the Rotterdam café. He trained his face into an impassive stare.

"I didn't realize you had another agent on my assignment," he said coolly.

"Nedock was on the Gruber assignment," said Satan, "but he saw you 'in conversation'."

"It *was* a 'chat'," said Nedock, the curl of his lip revealing pointed teeth. "He was talking to *her*. And it was *disgusting*."

"The Gruber assignment?" Rubix repeated. "The *Hilda* Gruber assignment? So, tell me—did she take the visas to the Dutch resistance after all?" He chuckled at the other demon's expression. "She did, didn't she? That means the angel won... and *you* lost, Nedock."

Nedock lunged at him with an angry hiss. The world was a blur and a tangle as Nedock and Rubix fought and clawed and hit the floor.

"*Calm* yourselves, *please*," said Satan.

Nedock gave Rubix one last kick, extracted himself and slithered over to Satan. Rubix had the last laugh, however. Nedock had lost to Julianne. *Well done, angel.*

Satan turned back to his mirror and began to straighten the lining of his suit at the cuffs. "We expect better things from you, Reuben. If you don't show any growth in your sales, you will be transferred to the BKD again. You *do* have so much experience there."

BKD. The Brimstone Kindling Department. Rubix had spent nigh unto eternity trying to get promoted out of that department. Shoveling, shoveling, shoveling... some days he would report to work, and they'd have him shoveling what he'd shoveled the day before into where it had previously been. The smell of sulfur still burned in his nostrils, long after the visions of piles of molten rock had faded.

"Of course... *Master*," said Rubix, bowing so Satan could not see how anger had turned his face red. He whipped around quickly and strode past Nedock—who smugly raised his chin—and out of the room.

"*'Reuben'*," he fumed.

Julianne hadn't been to this area of Heaven in quite a long time, even though it was her favorite sector. She'd gone here all the time when she was younger, excitedly thinking about all the things she'd do when she was a mortal. But since she'd gotten her clearance to be born, she'd tried to focus on her work until the time came.

As she neared the Department of Life and Death building, a grand, stately structure with pillars that disappeared into the misty sky, she felt the familiar sensation of excitement fluttering inside of her—like the feeling of having swallowed a hummingbird. Clouds drifted over her feet and the fog curled with each step as she climbed the stairs, took a deep breath, and clanged the knocker of the massive wood door three times.

It wasn't long before the door creaked open with a cavernous echo. The man at the door wore a long white robe, his wings tucked behind his back. His face was wrinkled from thousands of years of smiling; his back was stooped from sitting at a desk for almost as long.

His face brightened into a warm grin when he saw Julianne standing timidly on the portico.

"Miss Julianne," he said. "I certainly haven't seen you here in a while. Do come in, won't you?"

She didn't need to be asked twice, positively leaping through the doorway after Bob, the Archangel of Life. His name was actually Robert, but he insisted everyone call him Bob, because— in spite of being one of the most ancient beings in Heaven— "Robert is an aged, stuffy name."

Julianne followed him into The Hall of the Living. Millions of hourglasses stood on every available surface—desks, tables, chairs, thousands of cabinets. They even hung from the ceiling. The hall was so vast that the distant hourglasses were only pinpricks of glitter.

And each hourglass was unique: some were trimmed with braided wood, some were glimmering white, some were carved ebony. Some even had colored glass. But all of them had the same attribute: the Sand of Life—the white, translucent dust that stars were made of—flowed inside them. These were the hourglasses of the living.

Julianne reverently walked among them, admiring the craftsmanship of each.

"I haven't been here in a while," she admitted to Bob, who was dusting the nearby hourglasses. "Not since I got clearance. I wanted to focus on the Work."

"Good girl, good girl," he said airily, but then added, "Did you see? While you've been out working like a zephyr, they've brought your sand to cabinet forty-seven. What do you think of that, eh?"

"Forty-seven!" Julianne echoed, positively beaming. She cast a glance back toward the entranceway. To the right of it was the Hall of Files, a room which she had visited often. Its walls were lined with never-ending drawers, each holding its own hourglass, labeled with a name and designated Life Sand. Every cabinet numbered according to the wait to be born.

The fluttering in Julianne's chest could have caused a tornado. Soon it would be cabinet forty-six, then forty-five, then forty-four, all the way down to one... and then...!

Julianne's smile faded as she remembered her conversation with Rubix at the Rotterdam café.

"What is on your mind, Miss Julianne?" asked Bob, polishing a glass with the large sleeve of his robe.

It took a moment for Julianne to voice the words. "Hourglasses of the never-borns... where are they?"

Bob slowly set the hourglass he was polishing down.

"Well. Let's see, here," he said.

A short time later, Julianne found herself in the basement of the Hall of the Living, a dark, cavernous room that was lit only by one hanging lamp. It smelled thickly of must; the air here had not been stirred in a long time. Julianne gazed at the mess and tangle of hourglasses before her.

If there were spiders in Heaven (and there weren't), the room would have been thick with cobwebs and the empty shells of dead insects. Instead, everything was covered in the glitter-dust that was found in Heaven. It sparkled with each step Julianne took forward into the mess.

And mess it was, for although the dust improved the look of things, the hourglasses themselves were horrible, twisted creatures of different shapes and sizes. They reminded Julianne of skeletons, devoid of life and hope. These were the hourglasses of those who had chosen to become demons, and who had forfeited their birthright. They lay unused in a dissolute state on the tables and the floor, in large piles that extended as far as the eye could see.

"Do you know where Rubix Jarnham's hourglass might be?" she asked Bob.

"The demon?" Bob's cheery, wrinkled smile faded a little. He had helped Julianne find Rubix's file, epochs ago. "I—don't know, Miss Julianne. I'm afraid it makes little difference whose hourglass is whose down here."

"Then I will find it," said Julianne firmly, and she stepped into the tangle of hourglasses.

Bob's faded smile now turned to a frown, one with the power to fully remind Julianne that he was *Master Archangel Robert*, not just *Bob*. She lowered her gaze to her feet.

"He has good in him, Master Robert," she said meekly. "I've felt it."

Bob's frown remained stolid. "I've seen angels fall from keeping company with demons. But I have never seen a demon rise from keeping company with angels," he said. "You be careful, Miss Julianne."

Julianne nodded, still looking down at her feet. Bob seemed to fade away, back to his work upstairs, and she turned her attention to the hourglasses, picking her way through each pile, reading the dusty plaques at the base of each one. *Zebulon Keller,* read one in etched letters. *Charlotte Brandywine. Dedicor Hollow.*

There was no concept of time in Heaven, but it seemed years before Julianne found it. Buried underneath a pile of twisted black hourglasses with starved-looking glass. Carved from fine, deep walnut, with thorny posts and dusty bowls. *Rubix Grosvenor Saulus Jarhnam.*

And it was empty. No Life Sand would ever fill this glass.

Julianne held the hourglass to her chest for a long, long time.

LONDON, ENGLAND. DATE: 1666 AD

Night had fallen, but it had been dark all day with smoke from the raging London fire. Now it had billowed into a storm of its own, and burning hot embers rained over the panicked Londoners who clogged the streets, carrying what belongings they could to escape the fire. It reminded Rubix of the Vesuvian eruption, when he and Julianne had met the second time—the sky ablaze, hot wind almost whipping the bundle he carried out of his arms.

Granted, everything reminded him of Julianne these days. She was in his mind and in his heart—he was convinced, now, that he had one—constantly. Satan's reprimand, ages ago, had not changed that. He'd tried to make a decent effort of it, convincing his assignments to choose darkness, but it hadn't lasted long. He'd realized what a heel he was being.

The BKD wasn't far off, and he knew it. There'd be nether-world eyes watching him on this assignment. He'd have to do everything in lockstep if he wanted to keep his feet in the mortal world.

Rubix pushed through the crowds of people, searching for his assignment.

"See here, you're off the wrong way!" someone yelled at him above the roar of the fire. "You'll be no better'n coal in less than a mile!"

"One less person in the streets!" another Londoner yelled back.

If this elicited any laughter, Rubix didn't hear it. He threaded his way through, and the further he got from the old Roman gate that led to the outer city, the thinner the crowd became. The smoke grew oppressive; heat burned his face. The last of the stragglers, the ones who had hoped the fire would not jump streets (it did) were hurriedly gathering their valuables and trundling out of their wood-and-brick houses. The fire was so close now, flames licked the roofs of houses nearby. A brigade added to the cacophony and noise, tearing down houses with thunderous crashes to form a fire break.

Rubix spotted his assignment here, a portly man of about fifty, stumbling down the front stairs of an old tenement. He coughed as he dragged a worn writing desk along with him. His eyes were small and watery, and his red tomato of a nose showed too much drink. Thomas Morland: butcher, terrible poet, and infamous drunkard. Rubix noted he was carting off his writing desk and a grubby collection of quills, yet was purposely neglecting—

"Your wife! She's still inside!" came a soft voice that pierced Rubix to his center.

No.

Rubix warily stepped into the shadows beneath the eaves as Julianne—clutching two children with soot-streaked faces and bright red hair—pleaded with the man.

She was more beautiful than Rubix remembered, even with tangled hair and sweat dripping down her face. She wore a simple dress, the white sleeves gray with ash. And yet, she shone. Rubix couldn't move.

"I—I think she already got out," Morland stuttered, motioning vaguely to the stragglers dragging furniture toward the city gates. But this was a lie. Rubix had read about Morland in the assignment background. He knew that he did not particularly care for his wife, hadn't for years, and wished fervently that divorces were legal.

"I haven't seen her," Julianne urged, as the child in her arms fussed. "Surely she's still sleeping!"

The man pretended not to hear her and coughed into his sleeve.

"Oh, *my*," a silky-smooth voice murmured in Rubix's ear.

Rubix jolted away to see a very calm, very handsome man standing in the shadows next to him. Satan himself.

He was quite as stylish in Old English garb as he was in twenty-first century suits: a perfectly-stitched crimson jacket and carved-gold buttons; high-heeled, shiny black boots; a broad, white collar that showed absolutely no signs of soot. The look was topped off by a long, curly wig and a small pointed beard. But the dead, cold eyes were as dead and cold as always.

"The poor man is *quite* undecided," said Satan with a little smile. "I daresay he needs some… *convincing*."

Rubix remained silent as stone.

"Apparently he's not the only one," Satan went on, the smile gone. "You know, it's really not shoveling the coals that is so unbearable. Five minutes of shoveling is hardly even memorable. One hour? Well, even *that* would garner volunteers. No—it's the *eternity* of it. More than the eternity. It is the lack of *hope*. Hope that you will ever be able to extract yourself from the blackened fire, or even that you could *die*, end the torment by throwing yourself into its blazing depths. But no. It is only, singularly, an eternity of agony and burning forever, and ever, and ever. Get *out* there, *Reuben*."

Rubix whipped away from Satan and strode toward Morland, who was waving Julianne away, coughing and grasping at his writing desk.

Julianne covered her mouth, her dark eyes glistening as the firelight poured orange over Rubix's advancing form. She breathed his name, but he paid her no mind. He merely grabbed Thomas Morland by the throat of his lacy collar, lifted him off his feet, and throttled him.

"Get in there and be a *man*," Rubix snarled. "If you don't, the guilt will eat you *alive*—and trust me, I *know* what that feels like. Brave the fire or you will regret it for all eternity!"

He threw Morland forward, and the man hit the steps with an *oof*. Immediately he was on his feet and through the old tenement door without a moment's hesitation.

The world held its breath.

The thunderous roar of the fire; the yells of the brigade nearby; the cries of lost children: all hushed.

Rubix turned. Julianne still had that wide-eyed *look* on her face.

"Hello, Julianne," Rubix said casually. He nodded to the two children clinging to her. "What lovely children you have."

Julianne set the red-haired child down on the cobbles next to his brother, stepped to Rubix, and, with tears glistening in her eyes, wrapped her arms around his shoulders. She stood on her toes, and touched her lips to Rubix's.

White fireworks exploded in his vision. The kiss was unlike anything he had experienced before. It was distilled sunlight, concentrate. It was the peace of a thousand celestial years condensed into one moment. It filled Rubix's center and overflowed into his limbs.

When Julianne withdrew, Rubix's sensibilities had fallen to pieces.

"When I spend the next eternity shoveling brimstone," he said softly to her dark, sweet eyes, "the memory of that kiss will have been worth it."

And then reality came crashing back in. The yelling, the destruction, the roaring crescendoed as the rubble and smoke around them suddenly burst upward.

The children at Julianne's side screamed and clutched her skirts. Julianne wrapped her arms around them as walls of fire encircled their small group, blazingly brimstone-hot.

Rubix could see the silhouettes of demons form from the red walls, horns of fire and claws dripping molten silver. Satan stepped forward at the head of them, now dressed impeccably in a suit and tie.

"How disappointing, Remus," he said, breathing smoke. "You really did show so much promise."

"*Rubix!*" Rubix snarled. "It's *Rubix!*"

The walls of fire crashed down over them. It smothered and suffocated the world. And then it ebbed, back to the distant yells and crashes.

Julianne remained, clutching the two children, shaking, until another angel was sent to retrieve her.

❦

"Master Robert, *please!*" Julianne begged.

The archangel Robert frowned at the empty hourglass, adorned with pricks of wooden thorns, that Julianne had placed among the piles of records books on his desk. She had positively thrown herself into the Department of Life and Death, without even knocking, and in an instant was before Bob, the demon's hourglass in hand, pleading with fervency.

"He's good," she said. "I *know* he is. He fought for our side!"

Bob frowned. "Then he would be paying for it, indeed," he said.

Julianne rubbed her fingers along one of the carved thorns on the hourglass's post. In the same files she had found Rubix's name, she'd also dared to look up "Demonic Punishments." The tortuous sentences of unending futility were simply unbearable. And Rubix would be spending the rest of eternity enduring them, because of her.

"All he needs is a *chance*," Julianne said, sliding the hourglass to Bob. "I know—I know you can do something. You're the Archangel of Life!"

"Miss Julianne," Robert said, closing a tome full of names, "even if he had not forfeited his choice eons ago, there is nothing I can do. He has no Life Sand. Even I cannot change that."

The emptiness of the hourglass shone mockingly at Julianne. She thought of her own hourglass—now in cabinet twenty-three—with the small bag of sand tied to it in a neat little bow.

I have sand, she thought.

"Give him mine," she said.

"Miss Julianne?"

"My sand. It's mine, isn't it? I choose to give it to Rubix. You fill the hourglasses, you can do this!"

Bob stood and drew a hand through his silver hair.

"You can't give up your sand," he said. "You're already cleared for mortality. You'll be forever in stasis if you don't have it—not unlike your friend Rubix."

"Then we'll split it," said Julianne firmly, following him as he shelved the book of names. "We'll both have sand that way, won't we?"

This made Robert frown.

"I—suppose," he said slowly. "Though such a thing has never been done before."

"But *can* it be done?"

Master Robert was silent for a long moment.

"It can," he finally said.

Julianne nearly leapt into the air.

"But it means that neither of you will live very long," Bob warned. "You will only live half of your designated years."

"But Rubix will have a chance, won't he?" said Julianne. "It will get him out of Purgatory, won't it? And it will give him another chance, just like all of us. I know he'll choose Good," she said emphatically, handing Rubix Jarhnam's hourglass to Bob. "I know it."

BKD, PURGATORY. DATE: NULL

In the sweltering, choking pits of molten lava, a black ocean cracked with red, a solitary demon shoveled. He'd lost count of the days, weeks, years, millennia he'd spent in the same repetitive motion of jabbing the shovel into the kindling— wrenching upward, carrying the stuff for a mile or so, dumping, returning to the original spot, and beginning again. Satan had been right. It wasn't the task that was so harrowing, it was the fact that it would never end. Ever.

Rubix lacked hope, but he did have one thing: the memory of

Julianne's kiss on his lips. He could still feel it. With every step he took, each pile he shoveled, the idea that someone could love him in spite of who he was… he would shovel forever and never regret his decision.

"You're slowing down, Rubix Cube," jibed the taskmaster, rising up behind him. He laughed at the nickname like it was the funniest thing in the world. Rubix did not laugh, because it wasn't funny and it wasn't clever. A child living in the twentieth century could have come up with it.

The taskmaster himself was a man who wore old jeans and a grubby t-shirt. He was a once-lived who had earned his sentence with each boxing he'd given his wife. Now he continued his actions in life with his actions in Purgatory.

Rubix ignored him and dug his shovel into the coal—then stopped. The strangest sensation swept over him, like being showered in a million little sparks. Rubix removed his hands from the shovel and looked at them. They pulsed and glowed, as though silver blood was suddenly being pumped into them.

"Rubix!" came the taskmaster's hoarse cry.

Rubix disintegrated into a thousand embers of Light.

LITZMANNSTADT, POLAND. DATE: 1942 AD

The Polish factory smelled thickly of fabric and sewing machine oil. When the sun beamed through the grubby windows, its rays of light illuminated air heavy with fabric lint. Since the Wehrmacht had invaded several years ago, their ranks had grown ever larger, and the soldiers needed uniforms.

At one of the long factory tables, a girl—sixteen years old, with dark eyes, long, black hair, and a nose that she had inherited from her mother, grandmother, and generations all down to Abraham—wore an armband bearing a Jewish star as she cut yet another bolt of fabric. Her fingers had become calloused from forever holding scissors, cutting, cutting, cutting, and she had to wrap her wrist with a rag, it hurt so at night. Her face was drawn from lack of food, and she knew she had nothing to return to that night in the Ghetto, except an empty cupboard and a blanket made out of burlap.

But she had not yet been taken to the other factories in distant cities, as her parents had been. She was still in Lodz, and she was deeply grateful for that. It was here in Lodz that she had met *him*.

The girl pinned the last pieces of the cut fabric together and went to get another bolt of the thick uniform material. As she passed, a fellow worker—Karin, a girl of fifteen—slipped a note into her hand.

Butterflies fluttered inside her as she tucked herself away behind the tall bolts of fabric leaning against the wall, and opened the note to reveal the German soldier's handwriting. The girl knew German, and read with ease:

I need to have my uniform fitted—I'll whistle for you.

Whistle. That meant he'd meet her at the usual place and time, as the factories' whistles ended the day and the Lodz people plodded back to the Ghetto. They'd had to come up with their own code, in case the notes were intercepted. It made her feel quite daring! The girl quickly tore up the note, but the words fluttered inside her for the rest of the day.

When the whistle blew, the girl had packed up her scissors, signed her card, and nearly took off running into the press of people, all wearing armbands. As they neared the barbed wire entrance, however, she deftly made a sharp turn and hurried down an old alleyway, down a few stairs that submerged below the street, and into a tiny basement coal room. There was only room enough for the large stove and two people: her, and him.

He was a German soldier, with golden hair and eyes so bright blue they were ice, and he stood tall above her. His uniform fitted him to perfection, a picture of what a Nazi soldier ought to look like. Yet, unlike a German soldier, he grinned and opened his arms when he saw her, and the girl flew into them. They held each other tight for a long moment.

"Missed you, *Liebling*," he said softly.

She kissed him in reply. As though just remembering, he retrieved something from his knapsack on the floor and gave it to her. It was an English chocolate bar.

"You'll need this," he said.

"Chocolate!" she exulted, clasping it between her hands like a treasure. "Where did you get it?"

"Black market. Traded my cigarettes for it."

"Oh, no!" the girl said, trying to push the chocolate bar back into his hands. "You shouldn't have traded your cigarettes away. They're good for you!"

"I like chocolate better," he lied. "Anyway, you'll need the chocolate. We're leaving the city. Tonight. Right now. That's why I've been gone so long. I had to get everything sorted out for our escape."

The girl looked at him with wide eyes. It struck the soldier to his center with a sudden familiarity. He'd only known the girl for a few months, but those eyes—it was almost like he'd seen them long before.

"I've—packed," he said, trying to get his bearings. "I've got enough in this knapsack for both of us. For a few days. Cheese, bread, that kind of thing. Money, too. And train tickets and fake visas, see?" He unfolded his wallet and showed her the forged papers. "I told you about my Swedish friend, right? Well, he has a friend who works in the shipyard in Hamburg. They can secure us a place in the hull of an old ship headed to Stockholm. Then north we go, until this stupid war is over."

"Hamburg!" the girl cried. "Back into Germany! We'll both be killed!"

"No, we won't. You'll have to wear a scarf to cover your lovely nose, but it's winter. No one will think twice. Take off that ridiculous armband, though. You're *Leisl* for now. And me? I'm going to pretend to be a wounded soldier headed home. We'll give them the slip and head for Sweden. Then we see what we can do to get your parents to Sweden, too. Look, J—*Leisl*," he said, noting that the girl was trembling, "I'd die a million times over if it meant I could save you."

The girl's eyes glistened. "You'd do that for me?" she said.

"I would, and I will," said the soldier. "You'd do the same for me. I know it in my heart."

The girl opened the chocolate bar and split it into two equal pieces, and for a long moment they savored the taste. Then he took a small knife from his pocket, cut the stitching from her armband, slid it off and threw it into the stove.

They left the tiny basement room, the girl wrapped in a scarf and the soldier with his knapsack slung over his shoulder, and dared step out into the deepening sky.

In the reflected light of Julianne's hourglass, Bob watched them as they hurried into the night.

"What do you know," he said. "She was right."

Onyx

ALICIA MICHAELS

"O, beware, my lord, of jealousy;
It is the green-ey'd monster, which doth mock
The meat it feeds on. That cuckold lives in bliss,
Who, certain of his fate, loves not his wronger:
But O, what damnèd minutes tells he o'er
Who dotes, yet doubts, suspects, yet strongly loves!"
- IAGO, *OTHELLO*

-1-

Napet Space Station
Laro Pub
3015

The low buzz of conversation filled the crowded taproom, mixing with the obnoxious electronica music blasting from the speaker system. Scantily-clad waitresses in metallic miniskirts served neon-colored mixed drinks and foaming brews. The majority of the bar's patrons consisted of men in uniform—soldiers of Earth's army dressed in plain black-and-gray uniforms with their ranks denoted by pins attached to starched collars.

The atmosphere felt jovial, despite the many problems plaguing the human race as a whole. As Isaias Royce hunched over his foaming mug, he eyed them all with undisguised disdain. They acted as if their planet hadn't been destroyed by their own negligence and waste, as if they didn't float, homeless, on a space station, just waiting until a new planet could be found and prepared for them. They acted as if they'd forgotten the countless lives lost, decimating the population to less than a million. No, all they cared about was their liquor and their half-naked waitresses.

Meanwhile, he had problems of his own.

Sighing, he tipped the mug back and drained it to the dregs, throat bobbing as the cold brew made its way down.

"What's eating you?"

The voice of Reid Blackford, a specialist from his unit, snapped him out of his reverie. Isaias frowned. As a captain, Isaias outranked him, yet Reid seemed to have forgotten that. The fact that they were distant cousins had made Reid overly familiar and downright annoying.

"Nothing," he snapped, signaling the bartender for a refill. "Sit."

Reid obeyed, ordering his own beer as Isaias' was delivered.

"Nothing, hm?" Reid mumbled, drumming his fingers against the bar top in the most bothersome way. "Less than twenty-four hours after Cronius March makes first lieutenant, and I find you sulking in a bar. And you say it's nothing."

Isaias' scowl deepened. Reaching across the space separating them, he grabbed Reid's wrist in a tight hold, dragging the young man toward him until the legs of his stool scraped against the floor and they sat almost nose to nose.

"Watch yourself," he growled.

Shoving Reid back into his seat, he hunched back over his fresh mug.

Straightening his rumpled uniform, Reid frowned. "Geez, relax! I just thought..."

"That's your problem. You don't think. It's just so... it's unfair," he muttered. "Several recommendations from his fellow officers, added to my list of achievements, should have been enough. I should have known he would give it to someone else.

That black bastard and his damned superiority, thinking he's better than everyone else just because—"

"Would you keep your voice down?" Reid hissed, glancing around nervously. His gaze landed on a black couple laughing and talking nearby.

Isaias laughed. "God, you really are an idiot. The major isn't black like *them*. It's unnatural, that black skin and those eyes."

"It's why they gave him the name Onyx," Reid remarked, "because his Ethelene name was too hard to pronounce."

"That's another thing," Isaias scoffed. "He isn't even one of us, how can they promote him to lead?"

Reid shrugged. "I don't like it any more than you do, but what can we do about it? Nineteen years old and already a major. I can't stand the prick, but you have to at least admit he's accomplished a lot, considering how he came to be here. The last of his kind, I heard."

"I don't have to admit anything," Isaias countered. "All I have to do is bide my time."

"I hear you were offered a position as his ensign. A cushy job with more money, and you get to be his right hand."

"His right hand, huh? Maybe that idea has some merit. As his right hand, I could kill him and make it seem like he did it to himself."

Reid's eyebrows furrowed in confusion. "Huh?"

"Nothing," Isaias replied, brushing him off with an absent wave of his hand. "You wouldn't have understood anyway."

Reid had always been incredibly dense.

"Won't last long anyway," Reid said between gulps of beer. "When the general finds out what he's done, he'll discharge him faster than you can blink."

This got his attention. He straightened on his stool, eyebrows raising toward his hairline. "You have dirt on the major? Spill."

Reid gazed left to right, ensuring no one could overhear them. "Word has it, he's been screwing the colonel's daughter."

A wide grin spread across Isaias' face, and glee filled him so quickly he almost couldn't contain the chuckle welling in his chest.

"My God, that's insane. And he has no idea?"

"He's clueless."

Isaias frowned. "Didn't you have a thing with her once?"

Reid lowered his eyes, seemingly embarrassed by the reminder. Twin spots of red appeared on his cheeks. "Yeah, but it wasn't a big deal."

Isaias snorted. "Right, and I'm sure seeing them together has no effect on you. Thinking about him touching her with those alien hands—"

"All right!" Reid snapped, his entire face red now. "Maybe it does bother me. Whatever. It's not like there's anything I can do about it."

Isaias paused, his mug lifted halfway to his lips. "Or, is there?"

Reid set his mug down and perked up, turning to face him. "I'm listening."

"Well, I see this sort of thing all the time. Just because Colonel Tian likes Onyx as a soldier, doesn't mean he wants the Ethelene sniffing around his daughter. Why do you think they're keeping it a secret?"

"You're not thinking…"

Isaias stood and signaled the bartender to close out his tab.

"Yes," he declared. "I'm thinking it's high time the colonel learned what his precious little girl's been up to."

Dia Tian stared through the panoramic window of the cramped hotel room, giving her a picture-perfect view of deep space. In the days of the apocalypse, when mankind faced certain death if they did not evacuate their home planet, the galaxy had seemed like such an intimidating place—a yawning, endless sea of blackness filled with the unknown.

Now that she'd lived on various space stations, though, she'd discovered comfort in being so close to the stars. They twinkled much closer now, interspersed with clouds dyed various colors by naturally-occurring gases. No manmade thing could compete.

"Daydreaming again?"

The deep voice intruding on her solitude brought a smile to her face. Turning, she locked gazes with the soldier who'd stolen her heart.

"Am I, Onyx?" she asked, walking to join him in the center of the room. It didn't feel so cramped with him here. Everything—the entire world—seemed far vaster with him in it. "If I'm dreaming, then I never want to wake up."

He smiled, something he rarely did. When they'd first met, Dia had thought his hard face intimidating and harsh. Now that she knew the secrets his lips concealed, she appreciated his usually placid expression. It made his rare smiles all the more enchanting—a perfect display of white teeth against his black-as-night skin.

They called him an alien, which she supposed he was, being from another planet and all. Yet to her he seemed to possess more humanity than most people she knew. They called him odd, and believed him to be inherently evil just because of where he'd been born. But she knew better. With her, he'd never been anything but good—open, honest, loving. She couldn't have asked for better if she'd tried.

He wrapped his arms around her, leaning down from his towering height to kiss her forehead. "I'm afraid the dream has to end sometime. We can't go on like this."

Sighing, she leaned into him, resting her face against his chest. Instead of a heartbeat, the inside of his chest emitted a low, steady hum—like machinery. Yet, his skin felt warm and he drew in air just like she did. They really weren't so different. If she could see that, why were others so blind?

"I know," she replied. "Not like it matters anymore. No one can break us up. We won't let them."

Hiding their relationship had been her idea, not his. Lying wasn't programmed into the DNA of the Ethelene, who had been a highly intelligent species. They believed in knowledge and truth, and shunned deceit. Onyx was the last of his kind, and she'd corrupted him by making him more human. However, she'd known her dad would never understand. If he'd known for a moment that she cared anything for Onyx, he'd have sent her clear across the galaxy to another space station. He'd have kept moving her around to keep her out of the major's reach, until one or both of them lost interest, or until she could be married off to someone more 'suitable'.

"I don't like lying to the colonel," he said, taking her shoulders and pulling her back so he could look into her eyes. "I want everyone to know we belong to each other."

She smiled up at him and reached up to caress his strong, dark jaw. "They will. Let's go tell him now, together. The sooner it ends, the sooner he'll get over it and we can get on with our lives."

His fathomless eyes, as dark as his skin, glittered like precious gems and he smiled again. "I like the sound of that."

Lifting her to meet his height, he kissed her, taking her breath away. Everything that existed outside the door of their tiny hotel room faded away, and for that moment, there remained only the two of them.

A knock sounded at the door, and Onyx reluctantly released

her. His hawkish gaze darted to the door.

"It's probably room service or housekeeping," he reassured her. "No one knows we're here."

That proved untrue when he crossed the room to open the door. The major's personal ensign, Captain Isaias Royce, stood on the other side, an expression of shock on his face as he glanced past Onyx and saw her standing there.

Her cheeks grew hot, but she refused to act like she was embarrassed. They hadn't done anything wrong.

Snapping to attention, Isaias saluted Onyx with a swift, sharp motion.

"I apologize for disturbing you, Major, but when I went to your first lieutenant and told him it was an emergency, he told me where you were. I understand that you're off today, but—"

"It's all right, Royce," he replied. "What is it?"

"The council has gathered and you're being summoned. Now."

Onyx turned back into the room, crossing toward the garment bag draped across the bed. "Go back and tell them I'll be there shortly. I just need to change into my dress uniform."

"Of course, sir."

Saluting again, the ensign backed out of the room, leaving them alone once more.

"What do you think that was all about?" Dia asked, wringing her hands as she watched him change. "You don't think they're sending you out again, do you? You just got back."

He shrugged, reaching for his shirt. Dark, Ethelene tattoos covered his chest and back in an intricate pattern, etched over rippling muscles. Despite his serene expression, she noticed his darting eyes. He was thinking.

"It's possible," he replied. "It doesn't matter to them that I just got back. My unit has the best success rate, and the Matsai have been stirring up trouble all over the galaxy. If I'm needed, they'll call me and there's nothing I can do. It's my duty, Dia."

Feeling bad for making him think she'd want him to do otherwise, she came forward and began helping him with his buttons.

"I'm a colonel's daughter," she reminded him. "I've watched my father leave for explorations and battles since I was a little girl. I'm proud to watch you do the same."

He grasped her hands, stilling them when she reached for his tie. "Don't be afraid."

She forced a smile. It was too late for that. The Earth Army had been exploring for almost a decade in search of an inhabitable planet. Along the way they'd encountered many hostile alien species, most of whom saw humans as inferior beings and wanted nothing more than to exterminate them. War had decimated their numbers, leaving them vulnerable to attack. The Matsai took that to mean one thing: open season on humans and their space stations.

"I'm not," she assured him. "So long as you come back to me."

Grasping her chin, he tipped her head back and kissed her as if stealing her last breath. "Always," he whispered. "I will always come back to you."

- 2 -

Napet Space Station
Earth Army—Space Flight Corps, Division III Headquarters

Onyx entered one of several officers' conference rooms contained within the building housing his division. The third division of Earth Army's Space Flight Corps was nestled right at the heart of Napet's gleaming city. Steel and glass reflected the light of billions of stars inward, lighting his way along the long corridor.

The building was mostly empty, as it neared midnight. His commanding officers had summoned him in the dead of night for something they'd cited as 'an emergency'. While Dia had feared his being sent out on a mission, he knew it had to be more than that. Assignments were never given in this haphazard manner. Officers were called in and given orders, which also got transmitted to them via email. The tablet he always kept nearby would have alerted him to any incoming orders or messages.

There had been none.

Which could only mean he'd been accused of some form of treachery. Again.

He sighed, ensuring his posture remained erect as he marched into the room and to the center of the circle of tables where his superiors sat. Five years hadn't been enough to prove him a good soldier, or a decent human being.

Of course, he wasn't human, but that didn't seem to matter when he was killing off the Matsai for them. It didn't matter when he took his orders like a good boy, and went the extra mile to ensure that he excelled at a level far beyond his peers. Sometimes, he thought perhaps he'd done it. Why else would they promote him to major if he hadn't earned it—if they didn't trust him?

Yet, someone always feared him, or saw him as a foreigner infringing upon their privilege. It wasn't enough that he'd lost his family and home—that his home planet had been destroyed in a war *they* had started. It didn't matter that he'd spent most of his childhood in a prison, working to earn enough money to buy his freedom, or that as a soldier he had an impeccable record. After all, having an army full of young men—most of whom were no older than twenty-one—meant someone always found trouble. Drunkenness, lasciviousness, bad conduct: all were offenses his fellow soldiers, both enlisted and officers, had been found guilty of at one time or another.

But not him. He'd always done everything he could to fit in, short of altering his dark, Ethelenian skin. He wouldn't have even if he could.

Standing at attention, he met the eyes of each of his superiors with confidence. Cowering had never been his style, and he didn't intend to start now.

"Major," said General Watrous from his place dead center. "Thank you for making haste to arrive promptly."

He inclined his head. "Of course. It's late, and I'm certain you all wish to have this done with so you can all return home."

To his left, Lieutenant General Wycke raised his bushy gray eyebrows at him. "Do you know why we've asked you here tonight?"

"No, sir," he replied quickly. Rapid responses made them feel respected.

"I want you to know that I think its bull," the lieutenant general said, shaking his head, his expression reading as one of annoyance. "But once the colonel brought the matter to our attention, I'm sure you realized it became our responsibility to investigate."

Onyx's blood ran cold as his worst fear became reality. They knew about Dia and him.

"Of course," he said aloud, determined that they would never see him sweat. "You're only doing your duty, like any good officer."

Wycke nodded in agreement. "Precisely." Turning to his left, he got the attention of the private standing at attention near the closed door. "Show Tian in."

The door swung open and Colonel Tian entered, his face a mottled shade of red, a murderous glint in his eyes. He bared clenched teeth as he neared, marring his otherwise handsome features. He had the same swarthy skin, dark hair, and hazel eyes as his daughter, though at the moment it became hard to see the resemblance.

"I'll see you decommissioned for this, you piece of alien trash," he growled, so low only the two of them could hear.

Anger boiled his blood, just beneath the surface of his skin, but Onyx ignored him, refusing to even acknowledge that the other man had spoken. If he showed anger, they would say they'd always expected him to act in such a way. He wouldn't give them the satisfaction.

"Colonel," General Watrous said, folding his hands in front of him. "You have entreated us to decommission Major Onyx under the rules of Article 246—behavior unfitting a commissioned officer. Under what grounds?"

"The son of a whore has been... he..." The colonel could hardly get the words out, he'd grown so angry. He sputtered and stuttered for a while before finally getting it out. "I have been informed, just tonight, that he has been consorting with my daughter behind my back. In secret, in seedy *hotel rooms*, no less."

Wycke hardly looked concerned, though a few of the other officers stared at Onyx with disgust. Many of them trusted him with an entire fleet of ships, but they wouldn't leave him alone in a room with their daughters for more than five minutes.

"Is this true, Major?"

Squaring his shoulders, Onyx did what he'd always done: he told the truth.

"It's true, I have been seeing Dia Tian for the last six months," he admitted. "But I never took her to a hotel room until—"

"Until you talked her into doing whatever sick sexual acts your kind indulges in against my wishes, you sadistic—"

"Until after I'd married her," Onyx interjected, swiveling his head to meet the colonel's narrow glare. "Dia and I are married. She is my wife."

A low hum filled the room as the other officers leaned toward each other, whispering among themselves. If at all possible, the colonel turned even redder.

"No! That can't be true! I know my daughter. She would never do something like that without telling me."

"It's true," Onyx insisted. "I have the documents to prove it. We've been married for a month now. We had our reasons for keeping it a secret, but had intended to tell Colonel Tian together in private."

He could feel the censure being directed at the colonel for openly airing out his family's dirty laundry. The army frowned on the personal lives of their officers spilling over into their duty. It made things far too messy.

"There you have it, Colonel," said Wycke. "The boy's gone and married her. This is cause for celebration, not reprimands and secret meetings."

"My daughter's marriage to a dishonest, filthy alien?" the colonel hissed, his chest heaving with rage. "Tell me, sir. Would you want him married to *your* daughter?"

"Half the enlisted have been in trouble for drinking too much and disorderly conduct. The other half can't keep it in their pants and practically live in the infirmary complaining about the burning sensation when they take a leak. Major Onyx has served the army with honor and distinction. If I had a daughter, I could think of no better man for her."

Onyx fought back a smile. He could always count on Wycke to have his back, even when the others failed him.

"But... but he *lied* to me! He encouraged my daughter to keep secrets from me. I know Dia, sir. She would never willingly lie to me. He's practiced some kind of alien sorcery on her. I know he has!"

Onyx cleared his throat. "With all due respect, Dia is seventeen. I do believe that is the age humans are encouraged to find a mate to begin procreating. Earth's population is severely diminished, and every young girl must do her part. Dia and I just so happen to have fallen in love, making the decision of choosing a mate easy for us both. We kept it a secret only because we wanted privacy and time to be together before I come down on orders."

"You wanted her to yourself so you could influence her," Tian accused. "That way, no one could stop her from making such a horrible decision!"

"Enough!" Watrous thundered, pounding one fist on the table. "I have heard quite enough. Colonel, if the marriage is legal—which I'm sure it is—then there is little that can be done about this. Dia has reached the age of consent, and Onyx has done the right thing, marrying her instead of continuing to carry on with her behind your back. You should be grateful she's chosen so well."

The Colonel seethed, lowering his eyes to the floor. His jaw tightened and loosened spasmodically, his hands clenched tight behind his back.

"We will hear no more of this," Wycke agreed. "This matter hardly constitutes a decommissioning. You are lucky we don't bring *you* up on charges for dragging us all from our homes this late over nothing. You are dismissed."

Tian faltered, glancing from their commanding officers to Onyx with fire in his stare. Onyx had never felt so hated in his life. Yet, relief flooded him now that it had all been dragged out into the open. No more secrets. He and Dia were free to be together in public, something he'd always wanted.

"I said, you are dismissed, Colonel," Wycke repeated, his

tone indicating he wouldn't tolerate defiance.

Snapping to attention, Tian saluted the other officers. "Good night, sirs."

They saluted him back, and the room fell silent as he exited. Onyx remained at attention, as he hadn't been dismissed yet.

"Major, first allow us to congratulate you on your marriage," Wycke continued. "You hardly needed to keep it a secret. We all must do our duty in the repopulation effort, and well... you aren't human, but you look like one, and you have proven yourself to be honorable. Your son will likely be as good an officer as you someday."

Will you all scorn him behind his back like you do me? Will you call him a half-breed?

It was one of his greatest fears—one of the reasons it had taken him so long to marry Dia. Even though he'd known from the first time they'd kissed that she was the one, he'd waited. He'd never wanted to ruin her life by sentencing her to an existence like his—one where she would be shunned because of him. Yet, she'd insisted that all that mattered was their love. She didn't care about such things.

Even now that it had been done, he wasn't so sure. Still, he possessed just enough selfishness that having her outweighed it all. One shard of happiness among the ruin that the rest of his life had become.

"Thank you, sir," he replied.

"Now that we are all here, you may as well know that you'll be coming down on orders first thing in the morning," Watrous chimed in. "The Matsai were spotted in Quadrant Four, near the Avaron Space Station. We believe they mean to attack."

"When do I leave?" Onyx asked without hesitation. Despite the way he'd been treated, nothing excited him more than engaging in battle and putting his knack for strategy to work.

"As soon as your fleet can be readied," Wycke said. "You'll have fifty airships in your charge. They're expecting you."

He nodded. "A request, sir?"

"Yes, Major?"

"May I be allowed to bring my wife along?" he asked. "Under the circumstances, I do not believe it's wise to leave her behind."

The moment I'm gone her father will start poisoning her against me.

The last thing he needed was the colonel sticking his nose into their new marriage. Besides, he knew she would only worry once he was gone, despite her insistence that she could handle it.

"Request granted," Watrous replied with a decisive nod. "We could hardly expect to keep a man away from his bride."

He forced a smile—but not a real one, not the one he showed Dia. One that put them at ease and made them see him as servile and non-threatening. It worked. They smiled back.

"Thank you, sir."

"You are dismissed, Major."

Turning on his heels, he marched from the room, his hands curling into fists at his sides. If he were anyone else, the bogus charges would never have been entertained. It didn't matter that he'd been dealing with their prejudice his entire life. It still stung after all he'd done to prove himself to them.

Dia. I still have her. She would never…

That thought gave him hope, along with the reminder that he would get to take her along when he left. For so long he'd been a stranger in a strange world.

With Dia, he was home.

Earth Army Barracks
Napet Space Station

Isaias stood near the open doorway of the major's barracks room, hands clasped tightly behind his back. He fought to keep his face impassive, when all he really wanted to do was lunge across the room, take the alien imposter by his throat and squeeze the life out of him. He'd been disgusted to learn that the daughter of such a prestigious family would choose to marry Ethelene scum instead of one of her kind. Not that he could have had her—he'd been married for a year already. After all, it was his duty as a young male of Earth to participate in the repopulation effort. Still, Dia should have been with someone *like* him. Just the thought of the half-alien offspring they would make turned his stomach.

No, throttling the major wasn't good enough for him. He would destroy the man in his own way. The *smart* way.

"I need you to deliver this to General Watrous," Onyx said, turning and extending a large manila envelope to him. "It's Dia's and my marriage certificate. I don't want there to be any question that the marriage is legitimate."

Isaias accepted the parcel and tucked it under one arm. "Right away, sir," he said in his most subservient tone.

"After you've done that, I need you to prepare to leave."

"Did we come under orders, sir?"

The major nodded and turned back to the open trunk on the bed. Inside were several uniforms and a few changes of civilian clothing.

"Yes. The Matsai were spotted in Quadrant Four in large numbers. I'm taking a fleet to Avaron on a scouting mission. I want you to come along, but on a separate ship. I need you to escort Dia there to meet me."

Great, now I'm stuck babysitting your whore of a wife.

"I want her to have as much time as she needs to prepare for the journey, so there's no rush," Onyx continued. "Maybe you should bring your wife along, too. They can have each other for company."

Isaias rebelled inwardly at the idea. One of the main reasons he hadn't been reluctant to marry at such a young age was because being a soldier meant he hardly ever had to see her. Ellena was pretty—the main reason he'd married her—but she was also an idiot he couldn't bear to be in the same room with for very long.

Biting back the refusal, he nodded. "Good idea. I'll start getting everything ready for the trip."

Onyx nodded back, though his face remained impassive. "Thank you, Captain. I've found you to be a valuable asset. Choosing you for my ensign was a good decision, I think."

Because I'm only good enough to babysit your wife and carry around your mail? I should have been first lieutenant!

Saluting, Isaias turned to leave, anger clogging his throat and making his chest heave with rapid breath. He relaxed his hand, which had clenched into a fist, wrinkling the envelope containing the marriage license. Fixing his face into a mask of bored indifference, he went about completing his tasks for the major.

He encountered Reid right after delivering the major's parcel to General Watrous. The young man stood slumped against the wall, staring off into space as other soldiers breezed past him, some casting him curious glances. His eyes were bloodshot with dark circles underneath.

Isaias crossed the hall and approached him, taking in his disheveled hair and rumpled uniform.

"You look like crap," he said. "If one of your superiors sees you like this—"

"I don't care," Reid whined, running his hands through his hair and ruining it even more.

"You're overreacting."

"No, I'm not," Reid snapped. "I wasn't honest when I said the thing I had with Dia wasn't a big deal. I... well, I was going to ask her to marry me."

"Now she's married to the Ethelene."

He lowered his head. "I want to die."

Isaias snorted. "Don't be a dumbass."

"I love her! I don't think I can bear to see them together."

Grasping Reid's arm, Isaias dragged him toward the nearest men's restroom and propelled him inside. Finding it empty, he slammed the door behind them and locked it.

"Okay, enough! Just because you want to screw her doesn't mean you love her. And just because she picked another guy, doesn't mean you go and off yourself. No girl is worth killing yourself over."

Reid sniffed, turning to peer at his reflection. "Every time I think about it, I just want to throw that Ethelene through the nearest window and watch him float off into deep space. How do I get over her?"

"You don't," Isaias replied with a shrug. "If you want her, go after her. Who cares about a stupid piece of paper? All you have to do is make her see how wrong she was to choose him. And if it means that much to you, I'll help you."

Reid frowned, glancing up to meet his gaze. "You will? Why?"

Isaias forced a smile. "Because we're friends, that's why. Besides, nothing would bring me more satisfaction than sticking it to the major. If you do everything I tell you, I guarantee you can have her. After being with him, she's no good as anyone's wife anyway."

"Hey, don't talk about her like that! It's not her fault. She doesn't know what she's doing."

Isaias shrugged. "Prove it. Show her she's made a mistake. I'm telling you, it'll work."

Reid turned on the faucet, splashing his face with water. Wiping it clean on his sleeve, he took a deep breath. Then he turned to face Isaias and sighed.

"Tell me what to do."

- 4 -

Avaron Fleet Command Center
Avaron Space Station

First Lieutenant Cronius March scanned the bustling hangar, searching the crowd for the familiar face of Major Onyx. Taking a quick count of the airships flanking his left and right, he cursed.

"Only fifteen," he murmured to himself.

He couldn't know what had happened to the other thirty-five, though he tried to keep himself from imagining the worst—a difficult thing, considering the circumstances.

A young corporal approached him, wearing a shoulder patch marking him as being stationed here in Avaron.

"Lieutenant, glad to see you've arrived safely." The corporal paused, snapping his heels together and saluting him with a crisp motion.

"First Lieutenant March," Cronius introduced himself. "And this is less than half my fleet. I was separated from the rest of my unit in a nasty storm out in Quadrant Three. Have First Lieutenant Bryson or Major Onyx arrived yet? Any other airships from Napet?"

The boy shook his head, eyes wide. "No, sir."

"Get me your commanding officer, now," Cronius ordered. "We need to organize a scout mission to explore Quadrant Three for any sign of the missing ships."

The corporal saluted again and turned to carry out the order. "Right away, sir."

"Incoming!" shouted one of the hangar's mechanics, alerting the others to the approaching ship.

Breath held, Cronius dashed toward the nearest window, staring out into space. He grunted in frustration when he realized the ship wasn't Onyx's. However, it was a Napet ship, which could mean news concerning the rest of the fleet.

He waited impatiently for the ship to land and its occupants to emerge. The major's ensign, Captain Royce, strode down the gangplank, followed by Dia Tian, and Isaias' wife, Ellena. Cronius rushed forward to meet them.

"You made it safe," he said as the ensign saluted him. "Did you encounter the storm as well?"

"We left a day after you did," Captain Royce replied. "We received word of the storm and were able to skirt it. Are you just now getting here?"

Cronius nodded, shooting the major's wife a nervous glance. The last thing he wanted to do was worry her over her husband.

"Yes, and with less than half the fleet. The major and about thirty-five of our ships are still out there."

Dia gasped, her wide eyes darting around the hangar. "Onyx is still out there? Has anyone heard from him at all?"

He placed a hand on her shoulder, squeezing gently. The poor girl was shaking. "Not yet, but I'm already working on a plan to find him. I'm waiting for one of Avaron's commanding officers, and we're going to send out a search party. Don't worry, we'll find him."

She nodded, but he could see tears brimming in her eyes. He

turned to Ellena.

"Maybe you should help her find their quarters and get her settled. I'll report any news right away."

Ellena took Dia's hand and led her off after waving goodbye to her husband, who hardly spared her a glance.

"You were good with her," Isaias remarked.

Cronius shrugged. "I've been married before. I know how worried my Della would have been if she were in the same situation."

The ensign rubbed his chin. "I didn't know you'd been married. What happened, divorce?"

He sighed. "No. I lost her to the Virus X outbreak."

He turned away from Isaias to go in search of that officer. Not that he disliked the man. He just didn't like talking about Della with anyone. The memories were still too painful.

- 5 -

Avaron Banquet Hall
Avaron Space Station

"I don't know why the Ethelene's return is worthy of so much celebration," Reid slurred, sloshing beer over the sides of his glass. "The only party I want to throw that man is a funeral."

"Would you keep your voice down?" Isaias hissed, leaning toward his dinner companion across the table.

The major had arrived a few short hours ago, with twenty of the missing airships, putting to rest many fears that they'd been taken down in the storm. Isaias had watched with revulsion in his gut as Dia had run to the hangar to meet him. Crying hysterically, she'd thrown herself into his arms and sobbed, clinging to the front of his uniform jacket.

Unlike Reid, Isaias was good at hiding his true feelings. He'd simply welcomed his commanding officer home and shown him to the quarters he'd be sharing with Dia.

A lavish banquet had been thrown together to celebrate the major's return, as well as a fortunate occurrence due to the storm—the Matsai ships that had been spotted near Avaron had been caught up in the tempest as well. Almost the entire approaching fleet had been destroyed.

Reid turned his watery eyes on Isaias and scowled. "Since when do you tell me what to do?"

"Since I decided to help you get Dia away from that alien bastard," Isaias muttered. "Besides, I outrank you. So shut up, and drink your beer. Remember the plan."

He'd be surprised if Reid remembered his last name after the amount he'd had to drink, but there was no going back now. His need to destroy the major had only increased by the day—and was further exacerbated by the sight of the alien seated at the place of honor, wearing his dress uniform and smiling with the beautiful Dia at his side.

All around them the banquet commenced, with a lavish mean, and toasts shouted out across the long table. After the dessert course had been served, the music began and the dance floor started to fill. Declining to join the fun, Isaias crossed the room to where Cronius stood, sipping a glass of water. He gazed across the room at Onyx and Dia, swaying against each other to the music.

"They look happy," Isaias murmured.

Cronius nodded. "He's a lucky man. Seeing them together reminds me of what I had with Della. I miss that."

Isaias reached up and slapped the lieutenant on the shoulder. "Chin up, Lieutenant! This is a night for celebration. How about a drink?"

Cronius shook his head, a look of determination crossing his face. Everyone knew he'd struggled with alcohol addiction in the past. Now that Isaias knew the man's wife had died, he understood the reason. It could be exploited quite easily.

"I don't drink," Cronius said. "But thank you."

"Oh, come on!" Isaias urged. "One drink won't hurt. Just a little something to lift your spirits. Seeing them together so happy must hurt for a man who has lost his wife. I cannot imagine that sort of pain."

Cronius sighed. "I think I'll just go back to my quarters."

Isaias wrapped an arm around his shoulders, propelling him toward the crowded bar where drinks were being served. "The party's just getting started! Don't go to your room. You'll only get depressed and mope alone." He raised his hand to catch the bartender's attention. "Two scotches on the rocks."

Cronius leaned against the bar, lowering his head. When the drinks were delivered, he reached out and accepted his without argument.

Two hours later, Cronius was red-faced and swaggering, lifting his glass along with the other men at the bar, singing at the top of his lungs. Isaias stood back, nursing his second drink, watching the lieutenant come unraveled before his eyes.

From his left Reid approached, flushed and glassy-eyed, clearly drunk. He made a beeline for Cronius, who had his backed turned and didn't notice the other soldier's approach.

Isaias merely stood back and watched as Reid slammed into Cronius from behind, cursing and swaying on his feet. His face dark as a thundercloud, Cronius turned, his mood suddenly changed as he confronted Reid. The two began arguing, and while Isaias couldn't hear a word, he knew Reid threw insults at the lieutenant—because he'd urged him to do so. It was common knowledge that one of the reasons Cronius avoided alcohol was because he couldn't control himself when he drank. He got angrier by the second, and before Isaias knew it, the two had moved from trading words to trading blows.

Reid swung first, wildly, missing by a mile and careening into his target. Cronius gripped the front of Reid's uniform and shook him like a rag doll before delivering a perfect left hook. From there, everything exploded into chaos as Reid countered by shoving Cronius against the bar and attempting to crack a bottle upside his head. Cronius blocked the blow, sending the bottle flying and causing it to shatter against another soldier's temple. The man went down like a lead weight and his companions converged on the fighting pair, turning a simple fistfight into a riot.

Bottles flew, stools overturned, and curses rang out to mingle with the music as the men fell into a frenzy of bloodlust.

Isaias found one of the enlisted men from his brigade and took him by the collar. Fixing his face into an appropriate mask of concern, he steered him away from the fight.

"You need to go find Major Onyx!" he bellowed to be heard over the commotion. "Tell him to come now. Most of the men here are ours, and he is the only one who can get them to fall in line. Hurry up!"

As the specialist ran off to carry out the request, Isaias took a seat at the banquet table and crossed one leg over the other. Finding a half-empty glass of wine, he lifted it to his lips and took a swallow. It tasted sweet—as sweet as watching the beginning of his plot fall perfectly into place.

- 6 -

Onyx was startled out of sleep by pounding on his door. He jolted upright, temporarily disoriented as he fought to reconcile reality from dream. In his sleep, he'd been back home, on Ethelene. He hadn't seen its beautiful desert landscape since he was six years old, yet he still remembered it vividly—the golden sand dunes and clear, cloudless sky; the caverns filled with Ethelene's precious gems and minerals; its gleaming glass buildings reaching up toward the sky like searching fingers; its people, tall, slender and dark like the onyx he'd been named for.

For a moment, he realized his eyes had filled with tears, and homesickness had become a pain deep in his chest. Glancing left, he found Dia beside him and sighed. She looked like the purest, most innocent of creatures in her sleep, eyes closed, lips slightly parted. She stirred as the pounding came again and his name was shouted from the other side.

"What is it?" she mumbled, eyes still closed.

He stroked her hair and made to leave the bed. "I don't know. I'll find out. You go back to sleep."

He knew the last couple of days had to have exhausted her. She'd been worried about him, and had confessed to hardly sleeping at all while he'd been out in deep space, unheard from. He'd tried to transmit several messages to Avaron letting them know he and most of the fleet had survived, but signals were weak because of the storm. He felt guilty for causing her to worry, and made up his mind to do something to make it up to her soon.

He opened the door, ignoring the shocked expression of the specialist standing on the other side. Undoubtedly, he'd heard of the infamous Major Onyx and was stunned at having his first look at the Ethelene up close. He'd been sleeping without a shirt, and knew the markings and Ethelene tattoos etched into his skin were foreign and strange. Still, he refused to cover himself up to put someone else at ease. His markings were a part of him.

"Yes?" he said, breaking the man out of his stunned trance.

"Major," he replied, blinking and meeting his gaze. "There's a riot taking place in the banquet hall, started by two of your soldiers."

Onyx cursed and turned away from the door, searching the dark room for his uniform.

"Close the door," he commanded. "Wait for me. I'll only be a moment."

He dressed quickly. Next to his uniform, Dia's evening gown lay on the floor, shimmering in the meager light of the moon filtering through their window. He sighed. The night had been spectacular. He'd enjoyed it, mainly because Dia had been with him, looking like an angel in her silver gown, charming generals and influential men and their wives, a perfect complement to his more reserved demeanor. For once he hadn't felt like an outcast at a social gathering. He'd been less focused on others, and spent his evening enjoying her company. It made the entire thing more bearable.

Now, some idiot from his platoon had gone and ruined the night, dragging him from his warm bed with his wife.

He met the captain in the hall and followed him silently to the banquet hall.

He heard the riot before he saw it—the sound of breaking glass and splintering wood, curses and the thud of fists against flesh. Clenching his teeth, Onyx approached the horde of drunken, brawling soldiers.

Filling his lungs with air, he allowed his voice to carry in a way he never had before.

"Enough!"

It bellowed across the room, louder than even the music, bringing all activity to an almost instant halt. It was a skill he'd never needed before—a necessity for the Ethelenians, who often had to speak loudly to be heard over the whipping winds whistling over the sand dunes of their planet. It was yet another one of those things that made him 'unnatural' to them. It had come in handy, though.

The crowd of guilty-looking men all turned toward him. Most of them were his men, as the specialist had reported, and seemed to realize how much trouble they were in the moment they laid eyes on him.

In their midst was his newly-promoted first lieutenant, Cronius March. The sight of him, so drunk he could barely stand, his face and knuckles bruised, filled Onyx with fury.

And they call me a barbarian.

"Have you all gone insane?" he said, more quietly this time. "We are guests in Avaron, and this is how you behave? I am ashamed to claim you as part of my squadron."

Heads hung in embarrassment; not one of them responded. Turning, he found his ensign coming toward him from across the room. Unlike the others, he was untouched, and didn't appear drunk.

"Captain," he said as the man reached his side. "Tell me what happened here."

Isaias cleared his throat, hands clasped behind his back. "I wouldn't want to speak against my fellow soldiers, sir. Please don't ask me to do that."

Onyx understood the camaraderie that existed between his soldiers. To ask his ensign to snitch on them would only make him a pariah. They'd never let him live it down.

He sighed. "Very well. I want you to oversee the men as they clean up this mess they made." He turned to glance at the bedraggled bunch. "No one leaves until every piece of glass and broken furniture has been picked up. My ensign will be responsible for ensuring the job is done." He turned back to Isaias. "Take the day off tomorrow, you've earned it. Thank you."

"For what, sir?"

"For not following the crowd," he replied. "I appreciate that."

Glaring at his first lieutenant, who looked as if he wished the floor would open up and swallow him, Onyx scowled. Having his sleep interrupted had him in a foul mood.

"Lieutenant March!"

Cronius stepped forward and saluted. "Sir?"

"I want to see you first thing in the morning. Come in uniform."

Several pairs of eyes fixed on Cronius, many in pity. His conduct had put him in a world of trouble, and almost everyone there knew what would come next.

The lieutenant would be decommissioned.

Isaias watched the last of the men trickle from the banquet hall just before sunrise. They made a pitiful sight, but he couldn't feel sorry for them. Things had happened just the way he'd planned, and now he had an opening to influence events further.

He stood and stretched, crossing the room toward Lieutenant March, the last man in the room apart from him.

"Are you all right, sir?" he asked, putting on his 'concerned' mask again.

Cronius sighed, running a hand through his disheveled hair. "I'm ruined," he murmured, not meeting Isaias' gaze. "My career is over."

He clapped the officer on the shoulder. "Don't think that way. Maybe the major has gotten some sleep and will be in a better mood this morning. It's not too late to fix this."

Cronius shook his head. "Everyone knows that once he makes his mind up about something, there is no changing it. Besides, I have no right to make demands of him after what I did. I shouldn't have let that guy get me all riled up. I don't even *know* him! The whole thing was my fault. Drinking... it does things to me, and I knew better."

"Don't be so hard on yourself," Isaias encouraged. "You're a man, and men make mistakes. That might be hard for an Ethelene to understand, but… hmmm…"

"What?" Cronius asked when he trailed off.

Isaias tapped his chin with his index finger and pretended to think it over. "Well, I was just thinking… the major is stubborn, but there is one person he listens to. His wife."

"Dia? I don't think involving her is a good idea."

"Why not? I heard her telling my wife how grateful she was that you comforted her when the major was missing. I'm sure she'd be happy to speak to him on your behalf. If you can make an ally of her, it will go better for you."

Cronius frowned, considering. "Maybe you're right."

"Just think about it, okay? In the meantime, you'd better go get cleaned up before your meeting with the major."

Cronius grasped his shoulder before he could walk off, and gave it a squeeze. "Thank you. I appreciate your kindness. The major is lucky to have you as his ensign."

Isaias forced a smile and fought the urge to drive his fist through the face of the man occupying a job that should have been his.

"Anytime."

He and the lieutenant exited the hall together, parting ways at the door. He ran into Reid on his way to his own chamber.

"There you are," Reid mumbled, obviously still drunk. "What the hell is the point of your little plan if I'm going to get in trouble and possibly lose my rank?"

Isaias scowled at him, a reminder to lower his voice. "Don't be an idiot. You may have a few weeks of extra duty, but nothing worse. You're enlisted, not an officer, so no one expects much from you, anyway. The point was to get Lieutenant March decommissioned, and from the looks of things, he will be. Look, I haven't steered you wrong yet, have I? Just trust me."

Reid blinked at him, eyes unfocused. "Yeah… yeah, I guess you're right."

"Now go take a shower and sleep it off," Isaias grumbled. "You smell like a brewery and you look like crap."

Reid stumbled off to do his bidding, just another puppet on the strings Isaias manipulated masterfully. Honestly, they all made it so easy.

Dia pushed her rationed breakfast around on her plate, staring down at the cold food listlessly. After waking up that morning to find her husband in a foul mood, she didn't have much of an appetite.

After telling her about the incident that had taken him away from bed last night, Onyx had informed her that he intended to strip Lieutenant March of his commission—a revelation that had horrified her. Cronius March had been a longtime friend of her family, and he wasn't much older than her brother had been. Aside from that, she'd lost said brother in the same Virus X outbreak he'd lost his wife to. All the families of the dead had gone through dark times, but none darker than Cronius. His wife had been pregnant when the virus took her, and Dia had always admired him for carrying on so bravely after losing his entire family.

She'd tried to talk Onyx out of his rash decision, but he hadn't been in the mood to argue with her. He'd dressed quickly in his uniform and left to meet with Cronius. Even though the decision had been made, she still hoped there was something she could do to help.

"Are you all right?" Ellena appeared at her side, a look of concern on her face.

Dia shrugged, pushing her plate aside. "Didn't sleep well last night, and Onyx is in a nasty mood today."

Ellena took the chair next to her, her eyes glittering with excitement at the prospect of gossip. "Did it have anything to do with what happened last night after we left the party? I heard there was a *riot*."

Dia sighed. "I heard the same thing. Onyx says the whole thing was started by Lieutenant March, of all people."

Ellena shrugged. "Well, that explains it."

"Explains what?"

"The lieutenant came to me just half an hour ago asking me to bring you to him. He wanted to talk to you. Maybe he thinks you can help him get in good with the major."

Dia ran a hand through her hair and rested her elbow against the table, then her head on her hand. "I don't know if I can do much."

"Well, maybe you should see him anyway. He seems really messed up over it."

Dia stood and carried her tray to the closest trashcan. She felt a certain responsibility to Cronius for some reason—maybe because the plague of Virus X had intertwined their lives in a way. She understood his loss, and realized it must have something to do with his bizarre behavior the night before. Starting a fight just seemed so unlike him.

"Where is he?"

"Hanging out in my chambers," Ellena answered. "Isaias is gone for the day, so he's there alone. Now's the perfect time to talk to him."

"Let's go, then," Dia replied.

The two navigated the winding halls of Avaron's main hub until they reached the officers' quarters. Ellena and Isaias' chamber was just across the hall from the quarters she shared with Onyx. They entered the room to find the glass door leading out to the small balcony open. Cronius stood leaning against the rail, his head lowered and his shoulders slumped.

"I'll stay in here and give you two a moment," Ellena offered.

Dia left her in the small common area of the little apartment and stepped out onto the balcony behind Cronius.

"Lieutenant," she said.

He turned to face her, his face haggard and pinched. He looked as if he hadn't slept a wink since the night before.

"Dia," he answered, forcing a smile. "I'm glad you could come. I hope I'm not getting in the way of any plans you might have had today."

Shutting the balcony door behind her, she joined him against the rail. "Of course not. I had hoped I'd run into you anyway. How are you holding up?"

Cronius exhaled on a heavy sigh and shook his head. "Major Onyx is still very angry with me, as well he should be. I made a real mess of things last night."

"Nonsense," she countered. "My husband might have a temper and a no-nonsense approach to leading, but he's smart enough to know that people make mistakes. I think that in time, he'll come to his senses and forgive you."

Cronius shook his head. "I don't know about that. During our meeting he informed me that he is going to approach his C.O.s about stripping me of my command when we return to Napet. I'll be lucky if they don't bust me all the way down to warrant officer."

Dia reached out to touch his shoulder in a comforting gesture. "I won't let that happen. Try to stay out of his way while we're here, and I'll work on him a bit. I know Onyx, Cronius, and he's… well, sometimes I think the anger gets to him."

Cronius nodded. "That's understandable. He's a foreigner in

a foreign place, and has been treated with far less respect than he deserves. I made him look bad last night, and that is unforgivable. He has a hard enough time fitting in as it is."

"Nothing is unforgivable," she declared. "He will understand once I explain the circumstances."

"You don't have to do that."

"Of course I do. Virus X took a toll on us all. You can't be the only man who took comfort in alcohol after losing family members."

He shook his head. "That's why I'd sworn off drinking. I don't know what I could have been thinking last night. I haven't had a drop of alcohol in over a year."

"If you promise me that it won't happen again, I will do everything I can to make him go easy on you," she offered.

"Oh, I swore off drinking again last night. That man who started the riot isn't the kind I ever want to be."

Dia took both his hands in hers and gave them a squeeze. "You aren't that man. I have known you since I was a little girl. You're a good man, and I think you're a great officer."

"You've grown into a kind, beautiful young woman. Your father must be so proud."

Thinking of his anger over her hasty marriage, Dia bit her lip and stifled a laugh.

- 7 -

"Is everything ready for the meeting with Avaron's captains tomorrow evening?"

Onyx posed the question while distractedly rifling through a stack of files. Even though he'd given Isaias the day off, the ensign had still reported to the office he'd been appointed to while in Avaron to assist him with his tasks for the day—insisting that he had nothing better to do than help Onyx. It was one of the many reasons he'd chosen him for the post of ensign. He had proven to be a valuable asset.

"Yes, sir," Isaias replied, giving the checklist on his clipboard a cursory glance. "If you don't need me at the meeting, I plan to spend tomorrow preparing for our journey back to Napet."

Onyx nodded, rising from his place at the desk and stretching his cramped muscles. They'd been at it for hours. "Is there anything you don't think of? That would be great." Glancing down at his watch, he frowned. "I'm sorry, I've kept you through lunch. Maybe we should have something sent up."

Isaias smiled. "Already done."

"Good, because I'm starving. Let's take a break while we wait for the food to come."

Striding toward one of the large floor-to-ceiling windows offering a panoramic view of the citadel around them, Onyx stared out into the bright afternoon. Encased in a massive dome, the space-station was a jumble of buildings practically standing on top of each other, with the main hub at the center. The hub stood in a tall cylinder, with various wings branching off like the tentacles of an octopus. Each tentacle was visible to the ones on either side because of the windows. From here, they had a bird's eye view of their living quarters.

"How is Ellena liking Avaron?" he asked.

Isaias joined him at the window, hands clasped behind his back. "She seems to be enjoying it with Dia along for company. It was a good idea, bringing them. If Ellena is left on her own for too long, she's liable to get into trouble. I like to keep an eye on her." He squinted and cocked his head to the side, seeming to spot something across the arcade below them. "Oh, there she is right there, standing out on the balcony... and with some random guy, too. See what I mean?"

Onyx squinted, following Isaias' pointing finger to the part of the building directly across from them. The windows of the officers' quarters faced them, their balconies jutting out in neat little rows. He found a male and female standing on the balcony he'd indicated, but frowned when he took a closer look.

"That's not Ellena, that's Dia… and Lieutenant March. And what kind of trouble?"

Isaias cleared his throat. "My bad, I thought it was Ellena. That *is* our room. Anyway, don't worry about it. Dia probably came over to hang out and March might have already been there. Ellena is always… entertaining… when I'm not around."

Onyx's stomach turned at Isaias' insinuation. Was that the sort of behavior an officer should expect from his wife? He knew that most marriages these days were made for the purpose of repopulation, but he and Dia were in love. Just because Ellena fooled around behind Isaias' back didn't mean Dia would follow the same pattern.

"I should talk to Dia about it," he murmured. "No offense, but I don't want Dia 'entertaining' anyone when I'm not around."

"None taken. It's not as if I've been entirely faithful, I have to admit. But everyone can see you and Dia are crazy about each other. It's just… well, Cronius March… ah, I shouldn't say anything."

Onyx felt a premonition creeping up his spine as he turned to face his ensign. "Anytime a man has something to say, but neglects to say it, it is usually because he fears the outcome. Trust me, you don't have to fear my reaction to anything you have to say. You've always been honest with me, and I appreciate that. What do you know about Lieutenant March that I don't?"

"He is a fine officer, well qualified for his post," Isaias replied, as if reading from a script.

"And as a man?" he prodded.

Isaias shrugged. "As I said last night, sir, it wouldn't be right for me to snitch on a fellow officer. I think his actions last night spoke for themselves."

Onyx glanced back across to the balcony, his heart slamming against his ribs as Dia reached out to grasp both of Cronius' hands. She smiled up at him and laughed, and he imagined the sound, clear and high like the chiming of a bell.

"So you're saying…"

Isaias' hand came up to his shoulder and squeezed. "Well, a man who lets alcohol rule his life is unstable and unpredictable. One day he's starting fights, the next he's sneaking around to visit the wives of other officers. But, hey, don't listen to me. I tend to be naturally suspicious of people."

"That's because people aren't always what they appear to be. There's nothing wrong with being cautious."

"No, sir, there is not. Maybe you should just watch and see what happens. Don't say anything, just observe their behavior. It's what I would do."

A knock sounded on the office door, indicating their lunch had arrived. Isaias gave him another pat on the shoulder, then went to answer it, leaving Onyx standing at the window alone. Despite his best attempt at ignoring the foreboding feeling burning low in his gut, he couldn't push it away as he watched his wife smile and laugh with another man.

When Isaias returned to his quarters that evening, Ellena waited for him alone. Dressed for dinner, she paced the living room, glancing at her watch.

"There you are!" she exclaimed when he entered their room. "We're going to be late for dinner! Hurry up and change."

His upper lip curled as he took in her revealing dress and red lips. "You look like a prostitute."

Ellena gasped, picking up a pillow from the nearby couch and throwing it at him. "Don't be a jackass."

He shrugged, tossing aside the pillow and sinking into an armchair. "It's the truth. Did you do what I asked you to?"

With a snort, she lifted a silver bracelet from the small counter separating their living area from the kitchenette.

"I don't know why I bother to do anything for you when you treat me like crap all the time, but here it is."

Isaias extended his hand and accepted the bracelet. "Because you know better than to cross me," he murmured, not bothering to thank or even acknowledge her for the item. "Are you sure it's the right one?"

She rolled her eyes. "Dia never shuts up about the thing. It's the bracelet Onyx gave her the night he told her he loved her. She's going to throw a fit when she realizes it's missing. What do you want it for, anyway?"

"Don't worry about that. You just go change your clothes. I'm not taking you anywhere looking like that."

Ellena stomped off to change, leaving Isaias alone to stare at the stolen bracelet.

"It's funny how such a small thing can cause so much chaos," he mused aloud, watching the light glitter on the surface of the piece of jewelry.

Dia glanced at the clock as Onyx swept into their quarters, an hour late for dinner. She stood, relieved to see that he was all right. When he hadn't come or sent word, she'd been worried. Besides, she was anxious to talk to him about Cronius and get it over with. Seeing how distraught the lieutenant was over the whole situation had made her even more determined to help him.

"Hey," she said, smiling as she stood to greet him. "How was your day?"

Onyx avoided her gaze and brushed past her, going into the small bedroom off the sitting area. "You didn't have to miss dinner," he said, his voice muffled by the wall between them. "I got held up, but you should have gone without me."

She frowned at his cold, even tone. Maybe now wasn't the best time; obviously, he'd had a bad day at work. Following him into the bedroom, she found him changing out of his uniform.

"That's okay, I didn't mind," she said. "Besides, I thought maybe we could have dinner sent up and spend the night alone."

She came up behind him and wrapped her arms around his waist, resting her cheek against his bare back. He stiffened, but didn't pull away.

"Did you, now?"

"Mm-hmm," she murmured, inhaling his distinct scent. Her fingers traced his Ethelene tattoos. "I missed you today."

"I'm sure you did," he snorted, pulling away from her and jerking on a t-shirt.

She blinked, stunned as he continued changing, still avoiding looking at her.

"Is everything all right? Did you have a bad day or something?"

He shrugged. "Just a long one. Maybe you should go ahead and get dinner sent up. I'm starving."

She nodded, toying with the hem of her shirt and studying him intently. His behavior was unusual, to say the least. "Sure," she whispered.

Leaving the room, she put a call down to the kitchen, then set about prepping the little dining table in the kitchenette. By the time he emerged from the bedroom, dinner had arrived. She laid it out on the little table and portioned everything out. He took the seat across from her and finally looked at her. His gaze was intense, his fingers tight around his fork when he lifted it.

"How was *your* day? What did you do?"

Why did his scrutiny make her feel like she'd done something wrong?

"Just hung out with Ellena," she replied.

"Just Ellena?" he asked.

She nodded. "Yeah. I tend to stay away from the other wives. Most of them only wanted to be my friend before because I was General Tian's daughter. Now that I'm your wife it'll be even worse. I'm not interested in being used."

He didn't reply. For another moment, he simply watched her, as if waiting for her to say something else. After a while, he turned his attention to his plate and started eating. Dia followed suit.

"Everyone's talking about what happened last night," she said between bites.

"Men who drink too much can always be counted on to act like idiots," he replied. "Nothing new about that. The situation's being handled."

"Oh, I'm sure. It's just… well, I hate that Lieutenant March is being decommissioned over it."

Onyx paused, his fork halfway to his mouth. "You and Ellena discussed that today?"

"Yeah," she replied. "I'm sure the punishment is the status quo when officers get out of line, but—"

"But what?" he snapped, dropping his fork onto his plate. "You want to tell me how to do my job now?"

Dia started, rearing against the back of her chair. Even when he was in a bad mood because of work, he never took it out on her.

"N-no," she stammered. "Of course not. It's just that I've known Cronius March since I was a kid. He was friends with my father. He's a good man."

"Is he? How do you know?"

Her heart began to race, and her palms broke out into a sweat. She had always hated confrontation, and arguing always turned her stomach and made her jittery. They'd never fought before.

"Well… I… I just do. He's served in the army with honor, and he was a family man before… before Virus X took out half of Napet."

"Yes, I know all about his wife and child," Onyx said, his expression softening a bit. "He wasn't the only person who lost someone."

"I know that better than most," she reminded him. "But I still had my dad, and I have you. Cronius has no one. Did you know he had a drinking problem after they died? He fought his way back from that, and hadn't had a drink in a year before last night. He had a little slip-up, but it was just a mistake. People make mistakes."

His jaw clenched and he glanced away from her. His dark eyes became even more inscrutable, if such a thing were possible. She'd always been drawn to the mystery in their depths, but now she found it frustrating not to be able to guess at his thoughts.

"Yes, people do make mistakes," he replied. "I suppose you think I should forgive him for making me look like a fool as his commanding officer?"

She reached across the table and took his hand. "Would it be so hard? You told me that he was the best candidate for the job when you promoted him. Has that changed because of one mistake?"

He sighed, running his free hand over his short hair. He gave her fingers a squeeze with the other.

"I love how you care about people," he said. "I'm sorry for

being a jerk. I've had a long day and I didn't sleep well last night. I'm… I don't know what's gotten into me."

She stood and rounded the table toward him. Grasping his face, she tilted his head back and smiled down at him. "No need to apologize. We all get grumpy from time to time. Why don't we finish dinner and go to bed early?"

He turned in his chair and reached for her, pulling her down onto his lap. "What do you say we go to bed right now?" he murmured.

He leaned into her and she met his searching lips with her own. "I say that's the best idea I've heard all day."

- 8 -

Cronius had just finished donning his uniform and was preparing to leave his quarters for breakfast when a knock sounded at the door. Crossing his living area quickly, he opened it to find Major Onyx standing on the other side, with Isaias flanking him. His throat constricted as he quickly snapped to attention and saluted.

"Major," he said, trying to control his voice. It came out shaky and breathless. "Is there something I can do for you?"

"We need to talk."

He backed away from the door. "Of course. Come on in."

The two entered his quarters and Isaias closed the door behind them. Onyx took a seat in the armchair, and Cronius sat across from him on the small loveseat.

"Mind if I use your bathroom?" Isaias asked.

Cronius shot to his feet, remembering his little houseguest. He'd left her sleeping in his bed, as he hadn't wanted to wake her. In his state of loneliness and distress over the incident that might have cost him his career, he'd slept with a fellow soldier—a woman he'd caught staring at him enough times to know she

220

was attracted.

"Um…" He paused, scratching the back of his neck. "Use the outer door here, not the bedroom door. I have… company."

Isaias gave him a grin that clearly said 'you dog, you', before finding the hallway door giving access to the bathroom, which also connected to his bedroom.

"Sorry about that," Cronius said, his face flushing in embarrassment as he turned back to the major.

Onyx shrugged. "I shouldn't have intruded on your personal space. I just… I wanted to talk in private."

Cronius leaned forward, resting his elbows on his knees. "It's okay."

Onyx cleared his throat. "I've been doing a lot of thinking about things. Maybe I was a bit hasty to jump straight to decommissioning. While your actions were reprehensible and irresponsible, I do believe you are sorry for what you did. It was out of character for you, and I'm certain it won't happen again."

Cronius sat up straighter, hope causing him to smile. "No, sir!" he insisted. "I had a one-time break in my sobriety, and I'm ashamed to say I let anger get the best of me. It will *never* happen again, in or out of uniform."

The major nodded, his sharp eyes assessing him. "I've heard stories of what happened to your family, Lieutenant. I know that Virus X affected many families, so I can understand how grief can lead someone to lose themselves."

"Losing my wife was the darkest moment of my life," he admitted.

"I can only imagine. I will admit, it took putting myself in your shoes to understand. I don't have a family anymore, Lieutenant. I have my wife, and that's it. If I lost her…" He trailed off, a hard look transforming his face for a split second. He shook his head, as if to shake the thought away. "Anyway, my C.O.s will want a full report when we return, and I can't lie to them. Too many witnesses. But, instead of recommending that you be decommissioned, I plan to have you placed on a probationary behavioral monitoring program. For ninety days you'll have to adhere to a pretty strict protocol, then go before the board for a review and evaluation, but I think you can do it."

Cronius breathed a sigh of relief. "I'd do it for twice that long if I had to. Thank you, sir."

He stood and extended his hand to the major. Onyx stood as well, placing his own hand in Cronius'.

"Don't make me regret this," he warned.

"I won't, sir."

By then, Isaias had emerged from the bathroom, though he could still hear the sound of running water indicating that Cronius' companion had entered in his place.

"Perfect timing," Onyx said to his ensign. "We're done here. Lieutenant, I expect to see you at the meeting with Avaron's captains this evening. We'll be having dinner with them and discussing Avaron's security in light of the Matsai sighting nearby."

"Of course. I'll see you then."

He straightened and saluted the major, who returned the salute before turning to leave. When they were gone, Cronius fell onto the sofa, throwing his head back and laughing hysterically. Just the day before, things had seemed so hopeless. He'd been about to lose his career in addition to his wife and family. He told himself to find Dia Tian and thank her at the earliest opportunity.

Onyx gritted his teeth and tried not to stare at the woman sitting across from him. One of the six Avaron captains present for the meetings, she'd caught his eye the moment she entered the room. Not because he found her attractive or because anything about her struck him as remarkable, but because of the piece of jewelry she wore around her wrist. The sight of it robbed him of his concentration, causing him to lose track of the conversation taking place around him. To his left and right, his first and second lieutenants watched him in confusion, though neither remarked on his state of distraction.

"Which is why I think an increased military presence in and around Avaron is the wisest course of action, considering the circumstances."

Onyx blinked, realizing he'd missed almost everything Captain O'Ryan had just said. He leaned back in his chair and pretended to consider a course of action he hadn't even heard. His eyes continued flitting back to the female captain and the bit of silver hanging from her wrist. It just didn't make sense.

What was a stranger doing with his wife's bracelet?

"I'll need time to confer with my lieutenants on the matter," he said finally. "We'll reconvene in the morning after breakfast to discuss the matter further. I may have to put in a call to my superiors at Napet."

"Very well," Captain O'Ryan replied, seeming satisfied with his answer. "Until tomorrow."

The room began to empty as the Avaron officers stood and took up their files, folders, and notepads before trickling out of the conference room.

Onyx stood as well and located Isaias on the other side of the room. He took his time making his way toward the ensign, careful not to show any outward sign of urgency.

"Isaias."

The ensign saluted. "Sir?"

"That female captain... what do you know about her?"

Isaias followed his gaze across the room to where she stood smiling up at Cronius. The two were talking in hushed tones.

"That's Captain Moore. I believe her first name is Vivian."

"I need to speak with her alone. Arrange that for me, please."

"Right away, sir."

Onyx resumed his place at the conference table and waited, hands folded in front of him. He fought to keep them from shaking as anger gripped him. Two things he'd never been able to abide were liars and thieves.

A few moments later, he sat alone in the room with Isaias and Captain Moore. "Should I leave, sir?" Isaias asked, glancing awkwardly between him and the captain.

"No," he answered. "Sit. I need a witness."

Isaias obeyed silently, and Onyx turned to the woman sitting across from him. "Captain Moore, I hope you don't mind if I cut right to the chase."

The captain shifted uncomfortably in her seat and cleared her throat. "Of course not," she replied. "Is something wrong?"

He shrugged. "That all depends. I need to know where you got that bracelet."

Her eyes widened, and she glanced down at the piece of jewelry. Just the sight of it touching someone else's skin filled him with rage. The woman didn't even know she played with fire by parading it around in front of him.

"Captain, when I give a command, I expect swift obedience," he snapped when no answer was forthcoming.

She jumped, her face not unlike that of a deer caught in headlights. "I don't want anyone to get in trouble," she replied.

Onyx frowned. "Whoever you're protecting, I suggest you think of yourself and your own career. If I report you for wearing stolen property, you could lose your rank."

Vivian gasped. "Stolen? I think there's been some kind of mistake. This bracelet was a gift."

He raised one eyebrow dubiously. "From?"

"Look, our personal lives are our business. It was giving to me by the man I've been seeing, and he's a fellow officer—one of yours. I don't know what you're talking about, but it's not stolen. He's not that kind of guy."

Onyx stood, bracing his fists against the table. He was quickly losing his battle for composure.

"I can assure you, the bracelet is stolen. You see, it belongs to my wife. I know, because I gave it to her. The inside bears an Ethelene inscription. Seeing as I am the last remaining Ethelene in the universe, I think it's safe to say it's the same one."

"An Ethelene..." She trailed off, reaching down with one hand to unclasp the bracelet.

It fell onto the table with a *clink*, and she turned it over, revealing the markings etched onto the inside—not unlike the tattoos he bore on his chest and back. He had committed the inscription to memory: *I'll always come back to you*. It had been his father's promise to his mother, just as it was his to Dia's.

"Oh my God," she whispered. She looked up at him, her mouth hanging ajar. "I'm so sorry, sir. I didn't know, I swear. He gave it to me and... oh, I feel so *stupid*! What kind of guy gives someone another woman's bracelet?"

"That's what I aim to find out," he said, reaching across the table to take up the bracelet. She didn't resist. "I want a name."

She sighed, lowering her head. "To think I tried to protect the bastard."

"He could have gotten you in trouble, so there's no need to shield him," Isaias cut in. "Sorry, sir, for interrupting. Captain, whoever it is, you'd be better off letting the major handle him."

Running a hand through her short hair, she snorted in disgust. "Lieutenant March. Do your worst with him, I don't give a rat's ass."

Onyx felt his fingers close tight around the bracelet, and his lungs began to burn. He'd forgotten how to breathe. He was drowning, suspended in this moment and dying a slow, painful death. He hardly recognized his own voice when he spoke. "Cronius? *You* were the woman in his apartment this morning?"

She nodded. "Yes, and don't go spreading that around. We didn't want to get in trouble for fraternization, but now I don't want anyone to know I had anything to do with that scumbag."

"Cronius *March* gave you *this* bracelet?" he asked, needing confirmation.

It made no sense. Why would his lieutenant have his wife's bracelet? Had he been right to suspect him based on Isaias' information? It seemed like evidence, yet he couldn't fathom how it had come to be.

"He left it in the bathroom for me," she confirmed. "He'd already left when I finished getting dressed and came out to thank him. We made dinner plans, and I was going to thank him for it then." She made another sound of disgust. "I'll thank him with my foot up his—"

"Leave," Onyx choked out, no longer able to endure her presence.

She frowned. "I'm sorry?"

"You're dismissed. Don't tell anyone we had this conversation. Especially not the lieutenant. I'll deal with him."

"You're welcome to him," she muttered, standing and making a quick getaway.

Onyx slammed the bracelet down onto the table once she'd gone. His entire body trembled, and he clenched his hands into fists in an attempt to keep from breaking something. A long silence stretched on, during which he felt the sympathetic eyes of his ensign on him.

After a while, Isaias spoke. "Sir…"

"Don't," Onyx snapped, shaking his head. "You have done

enough."

"Me, sir?"

"You planted doubts in my mind about Dia," he murmured. "You opened my eyes to… hell, I don't know what. I think a man whose wife cheats on him is happier not knowing."

"You don't mean that," Isaias countered, taking the seat beside him. "A man who walks around blind is weak. Knowing makes you strong. It strengthens you to deal with betrayal."

"You don't understand," he whispered, lowering his head. "I am an outcast here. No one understands me. I'm not one of you and I never will be. But Dia…"

"She loved you anyway."

"A lie, apparently."

"Maybe not, sir," Isaias offered. "It all seems like a big misunderstanding to me. I'm sure there's a reasonable explanation for all of it. Just talk to her. Everyone knows she loves you."

Onyx wanted to believe that. Up until now he had.

"After the Earth Army took out what remained of my people and captured me, I was imprisoned and studied. The government wanted to know everything they could about me and my kind. Once they determined a lone Ethelene wasn't a danger to them, I was let go. I was twelve. Do you know what I wanted?"

"No, sir," Isaias replied.

"To belong," he said. "I wanted it so badly that I did everything I could to be like the other boys. And for a while I thought it was working. A group of kids in the orphanage I lived in seemed to take me under their wing, inviting me places with them and letting me join their games."

"That's good, isn't it? It worked."

Onyx laughed, shaking his head. "That's what I thought before they led me down a dark alley and beat me until I was blue as well as black." He laughed again, bitterly. "They reminded me that I wasn't one of them, and had no chance of becoming like them. From then on I was shunned."

"But things have changed now. You're one of the most powerful men in the army. You've come a long way."

"Do you think for a moment that my position is secure? As secure as, say, Lieutenant March's? After what he did, he should be discharged, but because of me he is going to keep his rank and stay in the army. Do you think if I behaved in the same way I would be given the same mercy by my C.O.s?"

Silence was his answer.

"Exactly," he continued. "It's why I've always striven for excellence. If I couldn't be like everyone, then I would be better. I have to prove myself to everyone just to cling to the edge of their good graces."

Isaias nodded in understanding. "You didn't have to do that with Dia."

He stood, pocketing the bracelet. "I *thought* I didn't."

"Do you think she's playing with you, like those boys did all those years ago? She doesn't seem like the type."

Onyx paused on his way to the door and glanced at Isaias over his shoulder. He shrugged.

"Neither did those boys, until the very end."

With that, he turned and left, his mind in turmoil over the evidence seeming to burn a hole in his pocket.

- 9 -

When Dia returned from visiting Ellena across the hall, Onyx was waiting for her. He startled her, his voice reaching out from the dark bedroom where he sat in a chair in the corner, face shadowed. She faltered on the threshold, uncertainty causing her stomach to flip. He'd been acting so unusual lately, she hardly knew how to approach him.

"Hey," she said, reaching to turn on the light. "How was your meeting? Why are you sitting in the dark?"

He glanced up at her, jaw clenched, eyes wide. None of the familiar warmth and kindness was on his face, and she felt as if she was looking at a stranger.

"I have a headache," he replied, shrugging like it was no big deal. "Where have you been?"

"Oh," she replied, crossing the room and flopping down on the bed. "Across the hall with Ellena."

Instead of pacifying him, her answer seemed to irritate him. She knew Ellena could be annoying, but she hadn't realized how much Onyx disliked her.

"Across the hall," he murmured, not exactly addressing her. He stared off into space as if thinking that over—as if her words presented some mystery that needed solving.

She folded her hands in her lap and sighed. "Is something wrong? Did you have another bad day?"

No response. Staring at his profile, Dia fumbled for the right words to say to help him snap out of this funk. Usually, she could make things better for him, soothe him when the outside world treated him badly. Lately, it seemed she'd lost her touch.

"Onyx," she ventured. "What's going on? I wish you'd talk to me. I don't like to see you like this."

He emitted a short, dry bark of laughter, his eyes snapping up to meet hers. "Is that so?"

She wrinkled her brow. "Of course not. Please talk to me."

His nostrils flared as he took a deep breath and released it on a sigh. "I have a question."

"Okay," she said, hoping they were now getting somewhere.

"Did you bring your bracelet? The one I gave you… my mother's bracelet?"

She nodded. "Of course. I always have it with me."

He raised his eyebrows. "I haven't seen you wearing it."

She stood, crossing the room to the small chest holding their meager belongings. "That's because I only wear it for special occasions—you know that. It's right…"

She gasped, trailing off as she opened the little box she kept her bracelet in to find it empty. Her heart began to pound, and she rifled through her clothes, searching for even the slightest flash of silver.

"It's gone!" she whispered, her voice strangled. "But I always keep it in this box!"

Onyx stood, crossing the room. Looming over her, he gazed down, his face hard and brutal. "Did you lose it? Misplace it somewhere, maybe?"

Her heart pounded in her chest as she continued searching, panic bringing tears to her eyes. She'd always loved that bracelet. Onyx had given it to her before telling her he loved her—a night she always thought of as the greatest in her life. It had belonged to his mother once, so she knew it was special to him. She'd been honored that he wanted her to have it.

"I don't know how that could have happened," she insisted. "I wore it the night of the banquet and then… I swear, I put it back in here."

One of his hands tensed into a fist at his side. "Are you sure you didn't wear it again after that? Maybe it fell off."

She stood, running a shaky hand through her hair. "I must have without realizing it. I'm so sorry, honey. I'll… I'll find it. I will search this entire station if I have to."

His upper lip curled as he stepped closer, reaching into his uniform's breast pocket. "There's no need. It found its way to me."

Confusion and hurt tore through her, and her eyes widened when she recognized the piece of gleaming silver in his hand.

Why would he torture her like that? She lifted her hands and shoved hard against his chest, anger brimming over and spilling out of her in a rush.

"Damn it, Onyx! Why would you screw with me like that? It's not like I lost it on purpose."

"Of course not," he countered. "I'm sure you would have expected your boyfriend to return it to you the next time you visited him, right?"

"My… my *what*?"

"Don't play stupid, Dia. This was found in Lieutenant March's quarters… in his *bathroom*. So, what happened? Did you leave it in there while showering after screwing him?"

Before she could stop it, her hand shot out toward his face. His head whipped to the side when her palm made contact, cracking across his cheek with a loud and resounding *smack*. She trembled from head to toe as the tears she'd been holding back finally began to fall.

"Have you lost your mind?" she asked, her voice rising a few octaves. "How could you accuse me of cheating on you?"

His jaw hardened, and it seemed the slap had hardly fazed him. "Then explain how your bracelet got in his chambers. Explain why I *saw* you on Isaias and Ellena's balcony the other day, *holding his hands*."

Her throat constricted and went dry. "It's not what you think. I only went over there because he asked for my help. He didn't want to lose his commission—"

"And screwing the major's wife ensures he gets whatever he wants, right?"

"No!" she cried. "It wasn't like that!"

He threw the bracelet across the room and reached for her, his fingers biting into her shoulders. She cried out in pain, but he only held her tighter.

"Don't tell me how things are," he whispered, his voice far more ominous in its quiet. She would have preferred it if he'd screamed at her. "I know how the world is. People smile to my face, and scorn me behind my back. I never thought you'd be one of them."

She shook her head, choking back sobs. "You're wrong," she murmured. "I love you. I would never—"

"Stop lying to me! Let's just be honest with each other for once, Dia. It was fun while it lasted, but maybe you realized marrying me was a mistake. And who can blame you? I'm not even human."

"How can you say that? Don't you know me at all?"

He shook his head, letting her go. "I thought I did. But now I'm starting to realize that you're just like the rest of them. I don't know you."

She swiped at her eyes with the back of her hand and backed away from him. "I don't know how Lieutenant March got my bracelet, but I swear nothing happened. Please, you have to believe me."

"I want to," he said, turning his back on her. "But you've been sneaking around behind my back doing God knows what and I... I can't."

Shaking her head, she turned to leave the room. "Then you can sleep alone tonight. I'm not going to stand here and let you accuse me of something I didn't do. I love you, but if you can't trust me, then..."

She trailed off, leaving it at that. What else was there to say?

Grabbing a sweater and throwing it on over her pajamas, she stormed from the apartment, forgetting shoes. But she couldn't turn back. Going back inside to face him now would be too hard. She paused just outside Isaias and Ellena's chambers, fist poised to knock. At the last second she decided against it.

Unsure of where she was going, she took off down the hall, blinking back blinding tears.

Everything was so messed up, but somehow she had to fix it. She'd defied her father to marry Onyx, because she'd known their love was real. It was worth fighting for. Maybe the lieutenant could help her talk some sense into her husband. But first, he had some explaining to do about her bracelet.

Starting off toward his quarters across the main hub, she hardly noticed the dark shadow trailing her until it was too late. It followed her to the end of the hall and the high glass walkway leading from one side of the hub to the other. Caught off guard, she gasped when a pair of hands reached out at her from the dark and spun her around to face their owner.

Her jaw dropped when she found herself face to face with her ex-boyfriend.

"Reid?"

"Dia," he slurred. The smell of alcohol was so powerful on his breath, it caused her to gag. Despite his drunkenness, he was strong, clinging to her and trying to wrap his arms around her. "Baby, we need to talk."

"Don't call me that. Let go!"

She pushed against his chest, writhing in his arms. Their breakup hadn't been mutual, but she'd thought he'd gotten over it. It had been two years.

"Please, just hear me out. I know your feelings for me can't be completely gone. We had something special."

She shook her head. "We dated for, like, three months, and it wasn't even that serious. I'm happily married now, Reid. You need to let the past go."

"'Happily'? You don't look so happy to me. You've been crying."

"That's none of your business. Now let go of me!"

"I can make you happy," he mumbled as if he hadn't heard her. He held her closer, pressing her up against the railing lining the side of the catwalk. "Just give me another chance."

Trapped and helpless against him, she couldn't do much to stop him when he lowered his head and kissed her. She squirmed against him even more, kicking and flailing, but he only pressed her harder against the rail, choking her with his writhing tongue and putrid breath.

Then, just as suddenly as he'd kissed her, he was gone, his body weight removed from her as if it had been snatched away. Falling to her knees and fighting for breath, she glanced up to realize that he actually *had* been snatched away—by her husband, who grabbed him by the collar and planted his fist in the middle of Reid's face, resulting in a gory spray of blood.

- 10 -

Isaias dashed across the glass catwalk toward the scene rapidly developing—the moment he'd finally get to watch unfold just as he'd planned. It took everything within him not to laugh hysterically at the sight of Major Onyx pummeling Reid, who was helpless to defend himself in his drunken state.

"Isaias!" Dia cried, running at him with wide, tear-filled eyes. "Please, help me stop him! He's going to kill him!"

Sure enough, the major seemed oblivious to his own actions, let alone the fact that two people witnessed his brutal assault. His dark fist was coated in blood as he drew it back and slammed it into Reid's face over and over. Blood stained the glass beneath them, and the front of Reid's shirt.

"Major!" Isaias cried, running forward and grasping Onyx's flying fist. "Sir, you have to stop!"

"Get off of me!" Onyx bellowed, his strength beyond any-thing Isaias had ever encountered as he threw him off. He grasped Reid by the collar and lifted him to his feet. "Which of you had her first, hm? You or Cronius?"

Reid couldn't have answered if he'd tried. He swayed on his feet, his face a bloody, unrecognizable mess.

"Onyx, stop it!" Dia screamed, throwing herself at him and attempting to pry him off of Reid. "It isn't what you think! None of this is what you think!"

He threw her off, sending her reeling into the silver railing.

"Don't touch me," he growled, narrowing his eyes at her. "One man, I might have forgiven you for. But two? You're a slut, Dia. You're a dirty little whore, and I wish I'd never met you."

Isaias watched as her chin trembled and her chest heaved as sobs welled in her throat. Fixing his face into that practiced look of concern, he stepped forward.

"Sir, maybe you should go back to your quarters. This has gotten out of hand. We can work this out after a good night's sleep. No one has to know what happened here."

"Mind your business," Onyx snapped, turning his attention back to Reid. "If you want to help someone, get Cronius as far away from me as possible, because he's next."

"No!" Dia cried, standing up and approaching him again. She reached out to grab his wrist just before he could deliver another blow to Reid.

"I said, don't *touch* me!" he bellowed, pushing her away again, harder this time.

Dia cried out as she lost her footing, careening back against the rail, arms flailing wildly. This time, her momentum took her up and over the silver beam, and with an inhuman scream of terror, she fell out of sight. A moment later came the sound of breaking glass, another mewl of agony, and then the sickening thud and crunch of impact.

Onyx's answering cry was even louder, even more

inhuman… even more terrifying as he dropped Reid to the ground and ran to the rail.

Leaning over it, he reached out as if to catch her—far too late.

His voice echoed, its agony like music to Isaias' ears as he screamed out, "Dia!"

Isaias stepped over Reid's prone body and glanced over the railing, his eyes locking on the broken, limp form of Dia Tian below. If at all possible, things had worked out even better than he could have ever planned. What could a man do that was worse than taking a man's life?

Taking the one thing he loved most in the world.

Eyes wide, he turned to meet the major's gaze. Summoning his most accusatory tone, he narrowed his gaze and shook his head.

"You killed her."

She wasn't dead yet.

As Onyx knelt beside Dia's mangled body, he detected the rise and fall of her chest and heavy, wheezing breathing. Sobs tore through him so powerful he could hardly breathe, and tears robbed him of his vision as he gingerly slid one hand beneath her head and lifted it. Blood soaked her hair, wetting his fingers. It trickled from her ears and the corners of her mouth. Her limbs were twisted like a rag doll's, and her breathing told him she'd probably broken several ribs. She wasn't dead, but there was no way she'd survive.

"Dia," he whispered, his voice ragged and hoarse from screaming. Watching her go over the side of the railing had been the single most devastating moment of his life. He'd thought losing his family and home planet had been the worst, but nothing could compare to this pain. "Dia… I'm so sorry. I did this to you, I… I'm so sorry."

She whimpered, turning her face in toward his chest. He held her tight, kissing her forehead.

"Onyx, I… I never…"

"It's okay," he whispered. "I don't care about any of it. I'd forgive you anything if I could change this. If you could live, I would forget about all of it. Despite everything, you are the love of my life. You gave me hope in humanity, in the world. When I didn't have anything or anyone else, I had you. I love you. I would never have stopped loving you."

She nodded, tears streaming down her face and mixing with the blood. She tried to smile, but it turned into a painful grimace, stained red by her blood.

"You didn't mean to," she whispered between labored breaths. "It's not your fault."

He shook his head, his own tears dripping from the line of his jaw and splashing on her cheeks, mingling with hers.

"I can't do this," he groaned, his emotional pain manifesting as a physical ache in his gut. "I can't survive… I can't live without you."

"Yes, you can," she whispered. "You will."

Glancing around him, he found shattered shards of glass all around them. Looking up, he realized she'd slammed into a light fixture on her way down, causing it to shatter. That had been the sound he'd heard. Reaching out, he closed his fingers around the largest shard he could find.

"I don't want to," he whispered, his eyes fixated upon the shard. It was the only way. He could never be the same without her. She had been his reason for living. He'd had nothing before her, and he'd have nothing after… not even a life.

"Onyx, no," she whispered. "Don't."

"If you're not in this world, there's no place for me in it," he declared, lifting the shard to his throat. "Wherever you go, I go.

My people believe that souls destined to be together will find each other after death. Do you believe that?"

She nodded, squeezing her eyes shut as more tears squeezed from their corners. "Yes," she whispered. "I do."

He nodded. "Open your eyes. Look at me."

She did so, her lower lip trembling. "Onyx, I'm afraid."

He forced a smile. "Don't be. It's almost over. Soon, you won't feel any more pain. You'll close your eyes and wake up someplace else. When you do, I'll be there. I promise."

She nodded. "I'll be waiting."

He waited until her breathing had slowed and stilled, and her chest ceased moving. Her head slumped and he knew she was gone. Sniffling, he lowered his head to kiss her one last time, heedless of the blood. The shard of glass had sliced his fingers, causing him to bleed, but he hardly felt the pain. He felt nothing as he brought it up to his throat, and sank it into his flesh. He remained numb as he dragged it from one side to the other, barely registering the hot gush of blood that followed.

- Epilogue -

Napet Space Station
Three months later

Lieutenant Cronius March waited until the sound of running water had ceased before stepping from his bathroom stall. He fixed his eyes on the man standing in front of him, head lowered as he dried his hands. A quick glance around him revealed that they were alone. Ensuring it stayed that way, he crossed the bathroom and locked the door.

Isaias Royce straightened, lifting his head at the sound of the lock sliding shut.

"Lieutenant," he said coolly.

"I suppose I have to call *you* 'Lieutenant' now, too," Cronius replied, walking across the bathroom toward him slowly. "Congratulations are in order on your promotion."

Isaias turned to face him, his expression smug. "You just can't stand it, can you? All the superiority you felt at being promoted over me, and where has it gotten you? In another few years I'll outrank you, and maybe *you* can be *my* ensign."

Cronius sneered, his nostrils flaring in disgust. "Careful, Lieutenant. A man can never have too many friends in the army. He can, however, accumulate too many enemies. I am not a man you want for your enemy."

As he'd expected, the idiot grinned, crossing his arms over his chest.

"Is that supposed to scare me? Do you have any idea who you're messing with? I could destroy you."

Cronius raised one eyebrow. "Like you destroyed Major Onyx?"

Isaias frowned. "What the hell are you talking about? The man got jealous because his wife was sleeping around, and he killed her. Then he felt guilty for what he'd done and killed himself, too. And good riddance, I say. He never belonged here, anyway."

Cronius' hands shook as he continued on toward Isaias, his fingers closing into fists.

"Major Onyx was a good and honorable man," he said, voice quivering with rage. "He loved his wife, and she was all he had in the world. That, and a position that he worked hard to get and keep. And you, who has had everything handed to him his entire life, just couldn't be happy with what you had. You had to envy him, and for what? Because a pretty girl chose him instead of you? Because he had the nerve to pass you over for promotion? Because a man from another planet earned more respect in his life than you ever will?"

Isaias grabbed him by his lapels and shoved him backward. "You're the one who needs to watch himself. I told you, I don't know what you're talking about."

Shrugging out of his hold, Cronius reversed their positions, grasping Isaias' throat and slamming him back against the tile wall.

"You can play stupid all you want, but we both know you drove Onyx to do what he did. Did you think I wouldn't find out that you manipulated your friend Reid into kissing her on the catwalk that night? Or that you were the one that planted Dia's bracelet in my bathroom for Vivian to find?"

"You can't prove a thing," he hissed, his breath growing rapid and shallow as he fought to breathe.

Cronius smiled. "Oh, really? Tell that to your wife, who told me that you explicitly asked her to steal the bracelet, or to Reid, who ratted you out for almost getting him killed."

Isaias' cocky expression melted away, and for the first time he looked genuinely afraid. And Cronius March, a man who had lost everything, found strength and pride in his moment of triumph.

"You think you've won," he whispered, leaning closer and tightening his fist around Isaias' throat. "Now that he's out of the way, you've been promoted, and all is right in the world of Lieutenant Isaias Royce."

Drawing in a ragged breath, Isaias raised his chin in one last moment of defiance. "It's your word against mine, and we both know how convincing I can be. I won't do a day of jail time for any of it. Even if I did manipulate him, he did it all himself in the end. Dia's blood is on his hands."

Cronius nodded. "You're right." Moving swiftly, he retrieved the knife from his pants pocket and flicked it open. Isaias gasped, legs buckling as Cronius jammed it into his side, right between his ribs. "And now your blood is on mine. I'll bear the burden gladly to see a great man avenged."

Cronius stabbed him again, twisting this time, rewarded with a fresh spurt of blood. Isaias' legs buckled, and Cronius stepped away from him. Standing over him, he watched as the newly-promoted lieutenant fought for his last breath, falling over onto his side. Taking up a handful of paper towels, he cleaned Isaias' blood from his knife and closed it, sliding it back into his pocket.

By the time he turned to leave the bathroom, Isaias had gone still. His eyes stared after Cronius, fixed in the shock he'd experienced in death.

Unlocking the door, Cronius made a quick exit, putting as much distance between himself and the bathroom as possible before he reached into his other pocket to retrieve the item he always kept there. Smiling, he opened the pocket watch that carried a picture of his Della inside. With his fingertip, he traced the lines of her beautiful face. And in that moment he understood that he hadn't just done it for Dia and Onyx—he'd done it for Della, too. Because no love so pure and real should have been cut short so tragically, the way his and Della's had been. The way Dia and Onyx's had been.

As he made his way home for the night, he took comfort in the thought that two lost souls now rested easier.

The Taming of the Dudebro

JANE WATSON

"Thus have I politicly begun my reign
And 'tis my hope to end successfully.
My falcon now is sharp and passing empty,
And 'til she stoop she must not be full-gorged,
For then she never looks upon her lure.
. . . And thus I'll curb her mad and headstrong humour."
- PETRUCHIO, *THE TAMING OF THE SHREW*

"Is the broccoli ready?"

Patricia Verona reached for the measuring cup, gently sweeping the vegetable pieces she'd just chopped from the cutting board into the glass container. "Ready!" she declared with a grin, passing the cup to her best friend and cooking class partner, Grizz Sheridan.

"Perfect," Grizz muttered, gently shaking the chopped broccoli into the wok. "So, like I was saying, we need something really spooky and dramatic for when the ghosts appear." Her brown eyes widened as she waved the spoon in the air, exclaiming, "Smoke bombs!"

Patricia reached for the green onion and snorted. "C'mon, you know the rules. No fire hazards."

Grizz sighed, pouting her lips. "Yeah, you're right." Then she glanced at Patricia and murmured, "Sorry, I know that *you're* supposed to be coming up with all of the creative elements, and I just wrote it. I'm just *so excited* to see my story come to life!" She squealed, bouncing up and down.

Patricia laughed and nudged her, reminding Grizz to stir the pork fried rice. She tapped her chin thoughtfully. "Hey, I know:

we could do stuff with the lights when the ghosts appear! Like, a different color spotlight for each one, and then dim the rest of the lights so that the stage is super dark. And—"

"Mm, I smell pork! Pork fried rice!"

Patricia groaned at the sound of the new voice. She glanced up to see fellow senior Kurt Minola standing in front of their station, rubbing his hands together eagerly as he admired their handiwork. She shouldn't have been surprised by his sudden appearance, since he showed up in her cooking class so often he might as well have been taking it himself. But that would have involved work. Instead, he always managed to appear at just the right moment to eat the food that he'd had no part in making.

Unfair, she thought, tucking a strand of dark blonde hair behind her ear as she took in the teen who stood before them. A stereotypical surfer dude, he sported cargo shorts, water shoes, and a black hoodie with a "Santa Cruz" emblem on the left lapel. *Because he clearly wants to look like a tourist in his hometown,* Patricia thought with a snicker.

As he reached for the sizzling wok, Grizz swiftly whacked his hand with the spoon. "Hands off, idiot. Are you *trying* to burn yourself?"

Kurt frowned, looking wounded. "But it smells so good. C'mon, Trixie, you'll let me have it when it's done, right?"

Patricia bristled. She absolutely *detested* being called anything other than Patricia, but 'Trixie' had to be her least favorite nickname. It made her sound like a dog. "It's Patricia," she corrected him for what was probably the thousandth time. "Go mooch off someone else."

"But your guys's smells the best!" Kurt protested.

"'Your guys's,' huh?" Patricia sighed, passing the chopped green onion to Grizz when her partner held her hand out. "Aren't you supposed to be in class right now? How is it that you waltz in here to steal the fruits of our labor practically *every single day*? Doesn't your teacher care?"

"Nah, babe, Mr. Baxter is super chill," Kurt said in his usual relaxed tone, absentmindedly picking a red pepper up from the work station.

Patricia rolled her eyes and gritted her teeth, focusing her attention once more on the recipe. She hated being called 'babe' even more than she hated being called 'Trixie.' Why couldn't Kurt go bother someone else?

"Well, you're looking at our lunch," Grizz practically growled, narrowing her heavily lined eyes at the tall, muscular teen. "So none for you."

"Aww, man," Kurt pouted, his shoulders sagging. "But I love pork fried rice."

"Kurt! Kurt!" a girl's voice called from the far corner of the room.

Patricia and Grizz both looked up to see Sophie Sinclair and her partner, Hannah Diaz, waving. "You can have some of ours, Kurt!" Sophie told him with a giggle.

Kurt grinned. "Hey, thanks, babe!"

Patricia and Grizz shared a look of disgust. The way girls flung themselves at him was revolting. Kurt *was* pretty good looking, Patricia had to admit, being six-foot-five and very well-built, with dark brown hair and hazel eyes. But as Patricia had learned years ago, he—like most of the members of the Vista High water polo team—was also an insufferable jerk who couldn't get enough of himself. A sizable portion of the girls at their school had yet to learn that, though, or else just didn't care, throwing themselves at the team every chance they got.

As he left their station to join Hannah and Sophie, Patricia stuck out her tongue slightly and made a noise of distaste. "Ech, thank goodness he's gone."

Grizz nodded and gave the ingredients in the wok another stir. "I think we're about ready for the soy sauce."

"Coming right up," Patricia said with a grin, reaching across the counter for the bottle.

As she passed it to Grizz, she overheard their cooking teacher, Ms. Hunt, snap, "Kurt Minola! How many times have I told you, you don't get to eat anything if you didn't make it! Go back to your own class!"

"But Ms. Hunt," Kurt whined with an endearing smile, causing both Hannah and Sophie to giggle, "I can't help it if I'm hungry all the time. I'm an athlete. I have to keep up my strength."

"Then pack a banana," Ms. Hunt quipped, but she turned away from Kurt and the girls to check on the rest of the students.

Grizz clucked her tongue as she watched the scene. "Ms. Hunt is way too nice to that loafer," she commented as she stirred in the soy sauce.

"Yep," Patricia agreed, turning her attention back to the task at hand. "Okay, I think we just need to add in the ginger and minced garlic, and we are done!" She reached for the small piece of ginger that Ms. Hunt had instructed them to finely chop.

Just then, there was a crackle over the intercom, and the disembodied voice of the secretary, Mrs. Blair, said, "Ms. Hunt, is Kurt Minola in your classroom? I checked with Mr. Baxter's class and he told me to try yours."

Ms. Hunt lifted her eyes to the ceiling, as if asking for strength. "Yes," she said with a sigh. She turned her head toward the subject in question, who was leaning over on Hannah and Sophie's table and whispering, eliciting giggles from the pair. "He's here."

"Tell him the principal needs to see him," Mrs. Blair's voice said.

Patricia raised her eyebrows at Grizz, intrigued by this news. A quick glance around the room showed that she was not the only one paying attention to the intercom. Many of the other students had stopped their activities and were gazing at Kurt with interest.

Ms. Hunt nodded as the intercom clicked off. "Kurt," she called. Kurt didn't appear to hear her—he just kept whispering to Sophie and Hannah. Patricia snickered as Ms. Hunt rolled her eyes and, looking absolutely exasperated, marched over to him. "Kurt!" she snapped as she reached him.

Kurt whipped his head up, looking confused. "Wha—?"

"The principal needs to see you," Ms. Hunt told him, turning on her heel and expecting him to follow. "Come on, I'll get you a hall pass."

"Bummer," Kurt muttered. He put a hand on both Hannah and Sophie's shoulders. "Catch ya later, babes. Save me some of that rice?"

Patricia raised her eyebrows at Grizz as the two abandoned girls giggled in reply.

As soon as he'd left the room, Grizz whirled on Patricia and whispered in a singsong voice, "Oo-ooh, Mr. Water Polo Champ is in *trou*ble. I wonder what he did?"

Patricia shook her head slowly, eyes widening as she thought of the possibilities. Was it because he'd been ditching his own class for cooking? Or was it more serious? She picked up her knife to resume chopping the ginger. "Maybe he left campus during the day to go surfing again."

"Or maybe he was caught smoking in the boys' bathroom or something," Grizz suggested eagerly.

Patricia considered his cut physique and obsession with water polo. "Maybe he's been using steroids."

Caught off-guard, Grizz let out a boisterous laugh and had to cover her mouth. Quickly recovering, she paused, deep in thought. "They probably just want his parents to make another donation to the Dean's Fund," she mused glumly, adding the ginger to the wok with little enthusiasm.

Patricia wiped her hands on her apron. The Minolas were definitely one of the richer families in town. They often made large donations to the school and other establishments in the area. "But they probably just could've asked Ben to tell them that," she reasoned. Kurt's twin brother, Ben, was responsible and beloved by the faculty—the total opposite of Kurt. "I mean, Kurt would probably forget to even *mention* it to his parents, but Ben wouldn't."

Grizz thought about this, taking the minced garlic from Patricia. "Good point. Which means," she continued with a slow grin, "that our boy Kurt probably *is* in trouble." She inhaled deeply and sighed, satisfied. "That would be almost as good as this pork fried rice."

After lunch, Patricia sat beside Grizz in their drama class. She was carefully taking notes as Mr. Gardner lectured on *The Taming of the Shrew* when she felt a sharp poke in her right arm. She turned curiously to see Grizz brandishing her pencil, motioning for her to look at something. Patricia rolled her eyes at what she saw. Kurt appeared to be holding a four-way note-passing session with the three girls surrounding him. Each giggled shyly as their hands touched his.

Grizz shook her head in disgust. "It's like witnessing an orgy," she whispered to Patricia.

Glancing back at the foursome, Patricia had to agree. It was surprising to see Kurt in class, actually, since he skipped drama almost as much as he turned up in her cooking class. *At least he's awake for once,* she thought. Then, wrinkling her nose in annoyance, she turned her attention back to copying notes from the whiteboard.

"Well," Mr. Gardner said a few minutes later, glancing at the clock on the wall, "your homework is on the board. Take these last few minutes of class to break up into your individual groups to talk about your projects. For those not participating in the theater festival, please gather to discuss the thematic elements in Act I of *The Taming of the Shrew.*"

Quickly scribbling the homework into her day planner, Patricia stood with the rest of the class as they migrated into their groups; but she paused as she noticed Mr. Gardner approach Kurt, who was still hunched over a note, laughing.

"Mr. Minola! May I have a word with you?"

Kurt jumped at the sound of the teacher's voice. "Uh, sure," he replied, looking confused as he followed Mr. Gardner.

Ha! In trouble twice in one day! Patricia stared after them for a moment before shouldering her bag and joining Grizz, who had already chosen a spot in the corner.

"Okay, so I guess we can go over the script and I can write down what props we're going to want, and maybe how the stage should look?" Patricia suggested as she slid her backpack off and sat down.

Grizz nodded, pulling a notebook out of her messenger bag. "I had some ideas for finishing the script, too, lemme write them down real quick."

Patricia dug through her backpack and pulled out the binder where she kept all of her notes and sketches for their one-act play. While she waited for Grizz, she began to doodle ideas for how the props should be laid out on the stage. According to Mr. Gardner, how much or how little they used in their production was completely up to the director; even if it was a period piece, the cast could wear modern clothing so long as it fit the theme.

However, being a known overachiever, Patricia wanted her production to look as professional as possible. She'd dreamed up costumes, props and sets that probably went above and beyond the theater festival's expectations.

"Grizelda? Patricia?"

Patricia's reverie was interrupted by Mr. Gardner's appearance. Grizz grunted and rose to her feet, her brow furrowed, but she kept her annoyance at being called "Grizelda" to herself. Patricia knew Grizz loathed her full name—it was too stuffy and old-fashioned for her taste. From a very young age, she'd declared that everyone should call her Grizz with two 'z's, and immediately shot down any other (albeit more conventional) nicknames that people had tried to stick her with. Given her fiery and sometimes quirky personality, Patricia could not imagine a more fitting name for her best friend.

"I'd like to talk to you about your project," Mr. Gardner began, folding his arms over his chest.

Patricia shared a worried look with Grizz before replying, "Oh, okay…" *Did we do something wrong?*

Their drama teacher sighed. "Well, I was looking over your outline, Patricia," he began, referring to the preliminary ideas that Patricia had turned in a few days prior, "and I saw that you had ideas for costumes and props. You were also talking about doing some actual set work, right?"

Patricia nodded, clutching her binder to her chest. "Yeah, I really want to showcase the fact that Mrs. Winchester is trapped because of the earthquake. I thought there could be a lot of debris, and maybe have a cutout that's like her door that the cast can come in through."

Mr. Gardner pursed his lips thoughtfully, which made Patricia nervous. Were her plans too over the top?

"I think it's great, but with all the ideas you have, I just don't see how you are going to be able to do this all on your own. It's quite a bit more extensive than some of the other plays, and there are only two of you." Taking a deep breath, Mr. Gardner continued, "That's why I'm assigning Kurt Minola to the project."

Patricia felt as if the wind had been knocked out of her. She looked over at Grizz. Her friend's eyes were bugged out and her mouth was agape, a sure reflection of the horror that must be showing on Patricia's own face. "Wait, what?"

Mr. Gardner held up his hands as if to calm them. "Now, I know it seems odd, but I spoke with the principal this afternoon, and it seems Kurt's parents were not happy with his quarter report card. Since college acceptances are already out, they want to make sure that he pulls his grades up so he doesn't lose his spot."

Patricia frowned. "What does that have to do with our play, though?"

"He is currently flunking this class," Mr. Gardner stated flatly, "and will have no hope of passing unless he puts in some serious extra credit. Now, I know you girls are receiving some extra credit for participating in the theater festival, but Kurt is going to have to do a *lot* more than that. Aside from redoing some assignments—and actually turning them *in*," he added wryly, "I want him to dive fully into this project. I think if he clocks in so many hours with you, I will be able to raise his grade in good conscience. I will also, of course, expect him to write a paper on his experience of working firsthand on a production. So, assign him whatever you need him to do. Building props, stage managing, running errands…"

"Mr. Gardner," Grizz interrupted, planting a sickening sweet smile on her face that Patricia knew was completely phony, "we really don't need his help. We're fine. This play is kind of like

Patricia's baby, and I think she'd rather have full control."

"Oh, but she will," Mr. Gardner replied, nipping Grizz's strategy in the bud. "Patricia, you will be completely in charge. After school, on weekends, whenever you are working on the one-act, Kurt is expected to be there. You will be supervising this portion of his grade. If he doesn't put in the work, he doesn't get the extra credit." Seeing Patricia's sour expression, he added, "Don't worry, Patricia. If he goofs off, *his* grade will suffer, not yours."

"Mr. Gardner, can't he work on someone else's?" Patricia pleaded. She didn't want to sound desperate, but she felt backed into a corner.

"You two need a lot of help if you want your production to be anywhere near your expectations," Mr. Gardner replied seriously, though not unkindly.

"Then assign us someone else!" Grizz exclaimed, tugging on a red-tipped lock of her hair in agitation.

Mr. Gardner shook his head. "I'm sorry. I'm sure Kurt is not your favorite person, but I think it is in everyone's best interest that he works on this play. You are two of my best students. You are both responsible and dedicated, and I am *confident* that you will judge his contribution to your play fairly and honestly."

Patricia sighed, closing her eyes for a moment. What he was saying was true; neither she nor Grizz were part of Kurt's little fan club. They didn't even consider themselves his friends, so there was no way that he could sweet-talk them into letting him do no work while still getting credit. And, though Patricia didn't want to admit it, she would be fair with him, and not try to spike his attempts to pass. If he was willing to put in the effort, she'd be willing to put up with him.

She glanced over at Grizz, who nodded glumly, knowing that there would be no way out of it. Finally, she said, "Sure, Mr.

Gardner. We'd be happy to have him in our group."

Mr. Gardner's face broke into a relieved smile. "Wonderful. I'll call Kurt over to give you a few minutes to discuss the project."

Patricia blew a stray bang out of her eye in frustration as Mr. Gardner went to fetch Kurt.

"'Sup, Patty, Zel," Kurt greeted them when he reached their corner.

While Patricia merely grit her teeth at the nickname, Grizz inhaled sharply and spat, "You know damn well that it is *Grizz*, you—"

Patricia quickly held out her arm to stop her, widening her eyes to send a warning message to her friend. "Hey, Kurt," she greeted him, a forced smile plastered on her face.

"So, Mr. Gardner said that if I'm in your play I'll get extra credit," Kurt began in his usual relaxed tone. "I'll take a small part."

Patricia cocked a brow, shocked by his gall. *Lazy and presumptuous as always.*

Before she could respond, Mr. Gardner cleared his throat, having crept up behind Kurt without him noticing. "As usual, Mr. Minola, you appear to have selective hearing. You must participate in this production, but that does not mean you will be acting in it. And if you are, it will most certainly not be the only contribution you make. As I understand it, carpentry is a hobby of yours, is it not?"

Kurt looked taken aback by this question, slowly scratching his ear as he replied, "Well, like, I've made a couple boards." Patricia could only assume he meant for surfing. "Oh, and, like, this really sick stand for my stereo system."

Mr. Gardner turned to Patricia and Grizz and lifted his eyebrows, appearing pleased. "There, see? He can work on the sets and props for you."

Patricia grimaced. She did not at all enjoy the thought of trusting Kurt with any aspect of their play, particularly something that involved power tools.

"Though if you would like to try your hand at acting," Mr. Gardner continued, "maybe you could come to the tryouts and read for their play. If they select you, acting could be a portion of your grade."

Now this was getting ridiculous. Kurt? Act? That was most certainly *not* an option. "Um, Mr. Gardner, I don't think there's any role that…"

"Oh, Patricia," Grizz interrupted her, smiling sweetly at Kurt and Mr. Gardner, "I think Kurt should *definitely* come try out if he wants to." Turning to Patricia, she said seriously, "In fact, I have a character that he'd be *perfect* for."

Patricia stared at her as if she was crazy. *What on Earth are you up to?* she wondered, racking her brain. She'd read Grizz's drafts and could not recall any character that Kurt could pull off. But, seeing the mischievous glint in Grizz's eye, she quickly caught on. "Oh, oh! Right! Yeah, Kurt, you should definitely audition. And of course there will be lots of other things we can have you do."

Kurt nodded with a lazy smile on his face. "Sweet."

Patricia tossed her long hair over her shoulder and nodded to their teacher. "Just leave it to us, Mr. Gardner. We'll go over everything with Kurt."

"Thank you so much, both of you," Mr. Gardner replied. "Kurt, I expect to see you in my office today right after school to go over those assignments." He looked severely at Kurt over his wire-rimmed glasses.

Kurt nodded. "Sure thing, Mr. G."

With an exasperated sigh, Mr. Gardner left the group,

shaking his head.

"Okay, Kurt," Patricia began, "since tryouts are on Friday, Grizz and I have a lot to prepare beforehand. Grizz will have to finish the script, and—"

She was interrupted by the loud buzz of the bell, signaling that class was over. When Kurt stood and reached for his backpack, Patricia held up her hands. "No, no, stay for just a second. Here, let's exchange numbers. We can meet up after school to work it all out, and you can see what we're going to be doing." She pulled her cell out of her pocket and glared expectantly at Kurt, who reluctantly reached into his hoodie and produced his own.

After rattling off numbers to each other, Patricia smiled, satisfied. "Okay, I can't do today, but let's meet here tomorrow, right after school. Can you make it?"

Kurt nodded without hesitation. "Sure thing, Patty."

Rolling her eyes but choosing to ignore the nickname, Patricia smiled thinly. "Great. See you then."

"Can you believe this?" Grizz said as Kurt walked away. "Argh, stuck with Kurt the Jerk for our entire play!"

Patricia wrinkled her nose in commiseration as they filed toward the door and into the hallway. "I know, but there's nothing we can do about it. Dammit," she swore under her breath.

"Why do we have to be so responsible and reliable?" Grizz demanded bitterly, only half-joking.

"No surprise that he's flunking, though," said Patricia as they wove through the throng of students congesting the hallway. "He hardly ever even shows up to drama."

"Probably thought it was gonna be an easy A that would boost his GPA with no effort while he coasted through senior year," Grizz said. "Like all the other tools around here who think that just because they got accepted to a college, their grades can tank and there won't be any consequences."

Patricia shook her head. "How stupid can you be?"

Grizz laughed, then glanced at her watch and realized the bell was going to ring any second. "Gotta run, I'll talk to you later!"

Patricia watched her friend hurry away, her red-tipped hair trailing after her. Stifling a laugh, she turned and entered her own classroom.

"All right, *tous les mondes,* choose a partner and do exercise B numbers one through five, on page two-hundred thirty-three, *s'il vous plait,*" Madame Kelley instructed the next day during Patricia's final period French class.

As Patricia pulled out a clean sheet of binder paper, she felt a tap on her shoulder. Ben Minola had leaned over from his chair next to her, and he asked with a smile, "*Avec moi?*"

Patricia grinned. "*Absolument.*" Clearing her throat, Patricia began to read the directions aloud in French. "Okay, so we're supposed to change the following sentences to use the conditional tense. *Numèro Un. J'irai consulter...*"

After several minutes, Ben finished writing the last answer. Craning his neck to check the clock and seeing that there were a few minutes of class left, he stared down at his textbook. "So, uh, I heard from Kurt that you're stuck with him for your one-act." He glanced up and met Patricia's eyes, his dark brows furrowing in sympathy. "That sucks."

Patricia laughed at his reaction, which pretty much summed up how she felt about it. "Yup, it does." Then she took in a deep breath and smiled at Ben. "But it's what Mr. Gardner wants. Maybe it won't be so bad."

Ben nodded, running a hand through his short black hair. "I

hope not. Our parents were pretty pissed at him the other night. They laid down the law, so he'd *better* put in the effort if he knows what's good for him."

"Yeah, well, I'll find out soon enough," Patricia said with a cluck of her tongue. Seeing Ben's curious look, she explained, "He's meeting me and Grizz in the auditorium right after class."

"Patricia?" Madame Kelley interrupted them, standing at her desk with her eyebrows raised. "If you and Benjamin are done, could you write the answer to *numèro trois* up here, *s'il vous plait?*"

Patricia blinked rapidly, glad that Madame Kelley hadn't reprimanded them for chit-chatting in English. Glancing at Ben, who flashed her an easy grin, she stood. *"Oui, Madame."*

At the end of class, as Patricia sat scribbling the night's homework into her planner, a shadow fell over her. She looked up in surprise to see Ben standing next to her desk again. "Have you started on your paper for English yet?" he asked casually, shouldering his backpack as she stood.

Patricia pulled her hair up and away from her back, adjusting the straps of her bag. Then she let it fall freely down her shoulders once more and nodded. "Yeah, a little bit. All I've got is an outline, though."

"Yeah, same here," Ben said. "It's really hard to pick a theme, too. I don't know if it's senioritis or what, but I feel like my paper-writing… ness is… not good." He scratched the back of his neck awkwardly as Patricia laughed and added, "See? I can't even brain anymore. Words… hard… brain… ow…"

"Okay, that was pretty special," Patricia said with a laugh. "I do the same thing, though! Recently I've been making a ton of stupid spelling mistakes. I'm just going to blame it on being tired, because my brainpower can't have depleted that much, right?"

Ben raised an eyebrow as he surveyed her for a minute. "Nah, you don't *look* like you've gotten stupid," he told her seriously. When she bit her lip and smacked him, he grinned and held his hands up. "Kidding! But seriously, we *are* in the home stretch, and that means that the workload is just way worse. And on top of it all, you're directing your own play for the theater festival. That's got to be taking a lot out of you."

Patricia shrugged. She knew that he was right—she'd done the school play every year since she was a freshman, so she knew how hectic it could be, even when you weren't running the whole thing on your own—but she didn't regret her decision one bit. "Yeah, it'll probably keep me pretty busy, but I'm still excited. I can't wait for the festival!"

They slowed their steps when they reached the auditorium door. Patricia turned, expecting Ben to take his leave. She was surprised he'd even bothered to walk with her all that way. But she was even more surprised when he held the door open for her and followed her into the auditorium.

"Hey!" Grizz said, her eyes widening as she took in Patricia's companion. "Hi, Ben, what's up?"

Ben smiled and lifted his hand in a wave. "Hey, Grizz, how's the playwriting going?"

Grizz lifted her notebook and wiggled it enthusiastically. "Rockin'. I think I had a major breakthrough last night. I was kind of scared that it wouldn't be done in time for auditions, but now I think it'll be a piece of cake."

"Cool! What's it about?" Ben asked.

"So, you know the Winchester Mystery House, right?" At Ben's nod, Grizz went on, "Well, I toured it for the first time over break, and the idea of restless spirits haunting her was, like, way too cool. When we got to the room she'd been trapped in during the 1906 earthquake, I had such a brainstorm." Grizz made an excited gesture with her hands. "Wouldn't it be cool if *ghosts* had caused the quake?" She lifted her eyebrows. "Huh, huh? What do you think?"

"That sounds awesome!" Ben exclaimed. He turned to Patricia. "What do you have planned, Director?"

Patricia folded her arms across her chest. "I haven't fully decided yet. I'm thinking of doing a bunch of cool stuff with the lights and costumes, to give it a haunted feel. And I really want the set to look authentic, with fallen furniture and stuff."

Ben nodded, looking intrigued. "That is going to be so cool. Kurt should be able to help you with the set and props if you need stuff built. He's pretty good with carpentry."

"Yeah, that's what Mr. Gardner said," Patricia replied, though she was relieved to hear Ben confirm it.

"Speaking of which," Grizz said, "where *is* that brother of yours?"

Ben looked at his watch and frowned. "I have no idea. He was supposed to meet you right after class, right? His last class isn't far from here. He should've been here by now."

Patricia heaved a sigh and dug out her phone. "Okay, I'll text him to light a fire under it."

Several more minutes passed, producing no reply, and no Kurt.

"I'll run over to his locker and see if he's still there. He probably got distracted by some girl. You try calling him," Ben told Patricia before breaking into a jog and heading out the door.

Grizz rolled her eyes and sank into a nearby chair. "Ugh, what a pain in the ass he's already being. It's twelve after three, where *is* he?"

Patricia pursed her lips and began to dial Kurt. She bounced on her heels in annoyance as it rang several times. "Come *on*, Kurt, we don't have all day," she muttered.

Finally she heard a click and realized it was going to voicemail. "Hi, you've reached Lucy," a recorded voice that was most definitely *not* Kurt's said. "I can't get to my phone right now, leave a message after the beep!"

Patricia pulled the phone away from her ear and stared at it incredulously. "Why that stupid, good for nothing…"

"What? What happened?" Grizz asked, glancing first at the phone, then Patricia, expectantly.

"That moron gave me the wrong number! It was some girl named Lucy! Luckily I just got her voicemail."

Grizz threw her head back in frustration, looking toward the ceiling as if asking for strength. "Argh! Now what do we do?"

Before Patricia could answer, Ben returned. "He's not by his locker or his last class," he reported, panting a little from running.

"Oh, you missed the best part," Grizz called sarcastically from her chair. She pointed at Patricia. "He gave her the wrong phone number!"

"What?" Ben asked in exasperation. Patricia handed him her phone. "That sneaky bastard," he muttered under his breath as he stared at the screen. He shook his head and handed the phone back to Patricia. "That's not his number. That's not even *close* to his number."

"He deliberately gave me a fake number?"

Grizz began to mutter undecipherable curses under her breath from where she sat.

Patricia set her jaw and said to Ben, "Here, give me his real number so I can call him."

"No," Ben replied, shaking his head as he pulled his phone from his pocket. "*I* am going to call him." He held the cell to his ear, and the girls soon heard the phone pick up and noise on the other end of the line. "Hey, man, how ya doing?" Ben said. "Um, so I just have a quick question for you... WHERE THE HELL ARE YOU?"

Patricia jumped, startled. She'd never heard Ben yell like that—he was usually so calm. She raised her eyebrows and looked over at Grizz, who mouthed, "Rock *on*, Ben."

Ben stood still for a moment, frowning as he listened to Kurt. "Wha—you're on a *date*? At the *Boardwalk*? Dude, no, you're supposed to be here in the auditorium with Patricia and Grizz!" He fell silent again, letting Kurt speak. Then he rolled his eyes and said, "No, how could you forget? ...Yeah, uh-huh. Just like you *forgot* your own number, and gave Patricia a totally fake one? Yeah, smooth move there, moron."

Ben looked over at Patricia with an apologetic smile before gritting his teeth and hissing into the phone, "You'd better wrap it up real quick or I'm telling Mom. And don't play the 'bro' card on *me*, Kurt. You're the one flunking, and when the teach is nice enough to offer this to you—yeah, well Grizz and Patricia have been waiting for you for *half an hour!*"

It was obvious that Ben wasn't getting through to his twin, so Patricia marched over to him and snatched the phone out of his hand with lightning-fast agility. "Kurt Minola!" she snapped into the phone, hand on hip. "Get your *butt* back to school this minute or you can kiss your extra credit goodbye!"

"Oh—uh... okay, sure thing, Patty," she heard Kurt say on the other end of the line.

"And for the *last* time, it's P-A-T-R-I-C-I-A!" Patricia shouted, pressing the 'end' button before he could reply. She took a deep breath to calm herself and handed the phone back to Ben. "Sorry about that."

Ben took the phone back, a slow grin forming on his face. "No, that was awesome. Is he coming?"

Patricia smiled in spite of the frustrating situation. "I think so."

Grizz rose to her feet and flipped a lock of hair over her shoulder. "He'd better, if he knows what's good for him."

"Thanks for calling him," Patricia told Ben.

Ben shrugged, hands in his pockets. "No problem. Sorry he's such a pain."

"It's not your fault the cosmos cursed you with him for a twin," Grizz laughed.

Ben sighed. "He has gotten so *lazy* these past few months—worse than usual! He was actually not *too* bad with doing homework and stuff 'til this year. His grades were decent enough to get into college. Now that he's *in*, he thinks high school doesn't matter anymore. His grades were worse last semester than they'd ever been, but I think my parents chocked it up to the stress of applications, so they let it slide."

"Stress, my eye," Patricia commented, folding her arms across her chest.

"Yup. But when they saw his quarter report card?" Ben lifted his hands, making an explosive sound. "There was a lot of yelling."

Grizz lifted an eyebrow. "Ouch. I would say I feel bad for the guy, except, hah, I don't."

"Well, if it makes you feel better, you aren't the only one saddled with helping Kurt. Guess who got roped into tutoring him in math and physics?" Ben lifted two thumbs and pointed them toward himself. "This guy."

"That's rough," Grizz muttered, tugging at the hem of her short-sleeved plaid shirt.

"Yeah, well, what can you do?" Ben remarked, shrugging. "Oh, here, let me give you his real number," he said to Patricia, pulling out his phone once more.

"Score. Thank you Ben," said Patricia, swiftly texting the

contact information to Grizz as well.

"Great, like I really want that idiot's number contaminating my phone," Grizz grumbled, rolling her eyes. Then she cocked her head to the side. "Hang on, I hear something…"

Patricia craned her neck toward the door. She heard it, too. It sounded like… wheels?

Sure enough, Kurt soon rode into the auditorium, hopping off of his skateboard and hoisting it over his shoulder. *Really? He rode his skateboard in the hallway?*

"Hey, bro," Kurt said when he walked up to Ben. Glancing at Patricia and Grizz, he added, "'Sup, girls."

Grizz threw her hands up in annoyance, turning her back on Kurt without a word.

Ben merely shook his head and lifted his backpack from the floor. "I'll go over your homework with you after dinner," he told his brother in a flat tone, before turning toward Patricia. "See you, Patricia, Grizz." Looking into Patricia's eyes steadily, he raised his eyebrows and mouthed, "Good luck."

Patricia smiled in reply, lifting her hand in a wave. "Later, Ben." As she watched him leave the room, shaking his head and muttering something, she thought to herself, *Thank goodness he was here.* At least now they could get *some* work done.

"Okay, Kurt," Patricia said, pulling her drama binder from her bag, "how about Grizz tells you a little about the script. Then I can show you my sketches outlining what the visuals are going to look like."

Kurt had sunk to the floor, hunching over his phone and smirking as he texted. Patricia sighed heavily, pinching the bridge of her nose. "Kurt!" she shouted.

Kurt's head jerked up. "Uh, what?"

Patricia put her hands on her hips. "Put away your phone. We have work to do."

"Oh," Kurt replied lazily, sliding the phone back into the pocket of his hoodie and following Patricia up the steps to the stage, where a table and chairs had been set up.

Grizz slid into her seat and opened her notebook. "All right, so my play is about Mrs. Winchester and—"

"Who?" Kurt interrupted, leaning back in his chair, stretching his long legs under the table. Patricia scrunched her nose and scooted away when his foot brushed hers.

Grizz stared at him. "Um, Sarah Winchester. As in the Winchester Mystery House?"

"The what house?"

Patricia shared a look with Grizz. "You know, that big, weird house in San Jose that has windows in the floor and doors leading to nowhere? There's billboards all along Highway 17 advertising it?"

Kurt shook his head. "Nope, no idea what you're talking about."

Good grief! Ben *knew about the house…* "Well, anyway," Patricia said, "it's pretty cool. I'd always heard about it, but I didn't go myself 'til a couple years ago. You should tour it sometime."

Grizz flipped through her notebook. "Moving on. Sarah Winchester was a lady whose husband was a gun manufacturer. Her misfortunes in life led her to believe she was cursed, so she visited a medium who told her she was being haunted, and that she must never cease construction on her house…or *else*." Grizz hissed as she leaned forward in her seat, widening her eyes dramatically.

Kurt didn't react. He looked utterly bored. "So, what is your play about?"

"Well," Grizz went on, looking quite pleased with herself, "there was a huge earthquake in 1906, and it caused a ton of damage to her house. She actually was trapped in one of the bedrooms for several hours afterward. When her servants finally found her and freed her, she was in a frenzy. Boom!" Grizz slammed down her hands on the table, startling Patricia. "She stopped fixing up the front of her house. It was in shambles due to the damage from the quake, but she just left it and started gung-ho working on other parts of the house. So, *I* thought it would be cool if the cause of the quake was the vengeful ghosts, trying to exact their revenge on Mrs. Winchester because of how she got all this money from a company that ruined their lives. I wrote about three different ghosts who come to her, gave them each a little backstory, y'know."

Kurt snorted. "Dude, ghosts aren't real."

Patricia grimaced. He really shouldn't have said that to Grizz, who was a firm believer in the supernatural.

Sure enough, Grizz's eyes widened in fury, face reddening as her nostrils flared. "Listen, you—"

Patricia held up her hands, knowing that Grizz's tirades could take hours. "Kurt, it is *fiction*. Your opinion on ghosts does not matter. So, this is what we are thinking for the production..."

As she explained their ideas for the props and set, she watched carefully while Kurt blankly stared at his fingers, tracing them across the tabletop. It was obvious he wasn't listening. Sighing, she finished, "Tryouts are Friday at five-thirty here in the auditorium. We'll have short sections for both of the male roles for you to read."

Kurt nodded, finally looking up. "Okay."

"Even if you don't end up wanting to try out, I'd like you to come anyway," Patricia told him, clasping her hands on the table in front of her. "It'll be good for you to see how the process works, since you've never auditioned for a play before. You can write about it in your paper."

"Sure thing, babe," Kurt said with an easy smile, reaching for his skateboard. "So, are we done here?"

Patricia looked at Grizz in annoyance. Grizz rolled her eyes and shrugged.

"Yeah, sure," Patricia said. There wasn't much left to do right then, but she hated letting Kurt off the hook that easily. "We'll do more this weekend. Remember, Friday, five-thirty—sharp."

Untangling his tall legs from underneath the table, he stood and shouldered his skateboard. "Got it. Catch ya later."

Patricia sighed as he disappeared, keys jangling from his belt loop. Then she turned to Grizz. "I say we go get smoothies."

Grizz nodded emphatically, hoisting her messenger bag off of the floor.

Friday night in the auditorium, Patricia checked the time on her cell phone yet again. Six o'clock, and Kurt was nowhere to be seen. No calls or texts from him, either. She didn't really *want* him to be a cast member, but if he was going to be *this* unreliable so early into the process, how was she supposed to trust him with *anything*?

"Patricia?" Mr. Gardner called from his seat in the chair against the wall. "It's your turn."

Patricia took in a deep breath and planted a smile on her face. She needed to stop worrying about that screw-off. It was time to cast her play!

Hurrying to the center of the stage, she faced the sea of students waiting to audition and cleared her throat. "Good evening. For those of you who don't know me, I'm Patricia Verona. I'm a senior, and I'm directing a one-act written by fellow senior Grizz Sheridan. It's kind of a ghost story that takes place in the Winchester Mystery House. There are four parts we're holding auditions for, two guys, two girls. One will be

Mrs. Winchester herself, and then the other female role will be a young woman whose beloved was killed—and who was then murdered herself—seeking revenge for their deaths. Then there will be two male ghosts: the sweetheart who'd been shot, and a soldier who had tried to stop the war." Glancing at her clipboard to make sure she hadn't left anything out, she said, "Okay, so, everyone interested, please form a line right there by the stage steps!"

Hopping off of the steps and joining Grizz, Patricia clicked her pen nervously a few times as she slid into the theater seat. She watched each performance carefully and took quick notes. Whenever Grizz made a comment about a certain actor, she made sure to write it down alongside her own thoughts.

The process was over all too soon. As the last person auditioning for their one-act thanked them and left the stage, Patricia glanced at her phone once more and sighed. Still no messages from Kurt. "Of course he wasn't going to show," she muttered in annoyance.

She locked her phone and slid it back in her backpack. She could deal with it later—the other drama students were holding their own auditions next, and she and Grizz were supposed to stay for the entire session.

Twenty minutes later, she felt a large hand tap her shoulder. She glanced up in shock to see Kurt standing there, pulling one earbud out as he said, "Hey, made it."

"What—" Patricia began to screech, before remembering the auditions were still going on. "What *took* you so long?" she hissed, barely above a whisper.

"I had stuff to do," he replied casually at regular volume, causing Grizz to frown and shush him with a finger to her lips.

Patricia made a noise of disgust and reached up to drag him down into the seat next to her—which was no small feat, considering how tall he was.

"Ouch!" he exclaimed as he landed half-in, half-out of the theater seat.

"Shh!" Patricia commanded, nervously looking around to see if anyone had noticed all the ruckus. "And what do you mean you had 'stuff' to do?!" she demanded quietly. "You were supposed to be here over an hour ago!"

Kurt shrugged. "Sorry, but I'm ready to audition now."

Patricia's nostrils flared in anger. "Ex*cuse* me? It's too late! The auditions for my play are over!"

"But I'm here!" Kurt exclaimed, confused.

Patricia held a finger to her mouth and whispered harshly, "For the last time, please be quiet! It's rude enough for you to come so late, but someone else is picking out people for their play now! You're being very disrespectful."

To Patricia's surprise, Kurt actually looked chagrined. "Oops," he replied in a much quieter voice, "my bad." Then he glanced around. "Well, if it's too late, I guess I'll take off." He started to stand up.

Patricia held out her arm to stop him. *Oh, no. You are so not getting off the hook that easy. You made us wait, so you can wait.* "You know what, Kurt? When everyone else is done, you can try out. I'll stay late just for you," she whispered sweetly, looking over to Grizz and winking.

"Aw, thanks, babe," Kurt smiled, leaning back in his seat and putting his earbuds back in.

Patricia quickly reached over and ripped them from his ears. "No music. And no sleeping, either. You are gonna sit right there and pay close attention."

Kurt stared at her vacantly for a second, as if not sure how to reply. Finally, he turned toward the stage and watched in bewilderment as each student took their turn and auditioned.

Patricia glanced at Grizz and grinned. Grizz held out her hand in reply to quickly high-five her.

Finally, when the last audition was through, Mr. Gardner ran out to the center of the stage. "Wonderful, everyone, just wonderful," he said. "This room is filled with so much talent and excitement, it brings joy to my heart. Now, casting will be posted Monday morning on the bulletin board right outside the auditorium, so make sure and check it first thing. Good luck to you all, and have a great weekend!"

As everyone in the auditorium rose to their feet and started milling around, Patricia stood and motioned for Grizz to follow her to talk to Mr. Gardner. They had to shove past Kurt, who was still seated, legs sprawled in front of him, blocking their path. "C'mon, Kurt." She nudged him with her foot. "Time for you to show us your stuff."

Mr. Gardner looked up from his notes as the three approached him. "Oh, Grizelda, Patricia… Kurt," he greeted them. "How can I help you?"

"Kurt wants to try out for our play," Patricia explained. "But he was late, so…"

Mr. Gardner stared at Kurt disapprovingly over the top of his glasses. "Kurt, you should know better than that. You cannot expect to be allowed to participate if you do not respect scheduled times and deadlines."

Kurt shrugged. "Sorry, Mr. G."

Mr. Gardner stared at Kurt silently for a moment. "However, since this is Patricia's time and her play, it is up to her whether you are still allowed to audition." He looked at Patricia and Grizz in turn. "What is your decision?"

"Oh, we totally think he should try out," Grizz said enthusiastically, an innocent expression on her face.

Seeing Patricia nod demurely, Mr. Gardner eyed them both

suspiciously. Patricia was sure he was on to their little scheme, and was relieved when he simply sighed and said, "Very well. I will be in my office catching up on grading. Please stop by when you are finished so that I can lock up."

"Thank you, sir," Patricia said sweetly. When Mr. Gardner walked away, she was pretty sure she heard him chuckle under his breath.

Turning to Kurt, she pulled a sheet of paper from her binder. "All right, get up on the stage and read for these two parts," she instructed, highlighting the sections featuring the two male ghosts. "Grizz, will you read with him?"

"Sure thing," Grizz replied, taking the audition sheet when Patricia offered it.

Patricia made herself comfortable, propping her feet on top of the seat in front of her. She wouldn't have dared to do that if Mr. Gardner had been there, but since he had left them to their own devices… *Time to have some fun.*

Grizz started off, reading the lines of Mrs. Winchester very dramatically, bugging out her eyes in terror. "'Please, spirits! What do you want with me?'"

Kurt froze, staring at the script for a few seconds. Patricia cleared her throat loudly. When he didn't reply, she rolled her eyes and snapped, "Kurt, it's your line. The one that starts with 'We have come…'"

Kurt read the lines out loud woodenly. "'We have come to take revenge for the blood the Winchester men spilled through the creation of their firearms. Blood in exchange for blood…' Whoa, man, sounds brutal."

Grizz stamped her foot and crossed her arms. "Really?"

"Stick to the script, please!" Patricia called up to the stage.

"But, Trixie, I can't help it if I speak from my heart," Kurt told her sincerely, grasping his puka shell necklace and gazing at her with wide hazel eyes.

Patricia slumped forward and covered her face with her hands. "Okay, *Kirk*, just try it again."

Kurt stared at her blankly. "Uh, my name's *Kurt*," he replied, clearly missing the point.

Grizz shrugged and nodded. "Yeah, let's get back to work, Kirk."

Before he could argue, Grizz repeated, dramatically holding a hand to her forehead, "'*Please*, spirits! What do you *want* with me?'"

"Uh," Kurt began, blinking as he stared at the script, "'We… we have come to take revenge for the blood the Winchester men spilled through the creation of their firearms! Bl-blood in exchange for—blood…'"

They ran through that scene many more times; Patricia knew full well that there was no way that he would get better, but she wanted him to see that having a part in the play was a lot harder than he thought—not to mention punish him for being over an hour late. Besides, how could she, in good conscience, sign off that he'd participated if she let him slack off?

After they'd done the scene to death, Patricia stood, clapping her hands. "All right, then."

"Sweet. Are we done, Patsy?" Kurt asked, hopping off of the stage.

"No, Burt, now you need to read the part of James," Patricia told him.

Kurt blinked at her in confusion—though whether it was because she'd called him "Burt," or the fact that he had to go through that all over again, she wasn't sure.

Patricia lifted a hand and waved him back up the steps. He took center stage again, staring at the script. "'It was your family that, uh, tore me apart from my beloved…'"

"Say it with *passion!*" Patricia commanded, pointing her pen at him.

"O-okay," Kurt mumbled, then heaved a sigh of frustration. "Ugh, I just—this is so lame. How can I even sound like I mean it? I mean, he's being so sappy. Ghost needs to get laid."

Grizz inhaled sharply, nostrils flaring. "Just because *you* are an insensitive jerk doesn't mean that someone wouldn't be heartbroken dying in the *arms of his one true love!*"

"Uh…" Kurt began to back away from Grizz slowly, his dark eyebrows raising in surprise.

"And to top it all *off*," Grizz continued, charging forward, her eyes narrowed dangerously, "Adeline *then* gets caught in the war, trying to seek justice, and is killed herself, *by the same rifle that slew her beloved.*" She closed her eyes dramatically, her glittery eye shadow dancing in the stage lights. "How could you live with yourself for all eternity knowing that?" she asked in a hushed whisper.

"Er… okay," Kurt replied, frozen with fear at Grizz's reaction. He held up his hands as if to defend himself. "Um, calm down…"

"Okay, I've seen enough," Patricia intervened. "You can see the results on Monday. I'll talk to you in drama class to let you know when we'll meet up next."

"Cool," Kurt replied with a shrug, taking the stage steps two at a time before grabbing his bag and skateboard on his way out the door. "Catch ya on the flip side."

As soon as he was out of earshot, Patricia raced up the stairs and met Grizz in the center of the stage. Holding out a hand to her arm, she asked sympathetically, "Are you okay? Sorry he was trashing on your script."

Eyes still closed, Grizz took a deep, cleansing breath, lifting her hand and then bringing it down in front of her face as she exhaled. "I will not scream," she whispered to herself. "I will not sabotage his surfboard. Murder is bad."

"C'mon," Patricia coaxed. "Let's go binge on pizza. My treat!" Grizz opened one eye with interest.

As they left the auditorium, Patricia commented, "Either way, his acting sucks *way* more than I expected, so that's out. The play would be ruined."

"Oh, I don't know," Grizz began loftily as they walked toward Mr. Gardner's office, "I think he could really add some pizzazz to the play."

Patricia stopped dead in her tracks. "Doing what?"

Seeing Grizz's devilish smile, Patricia knew it was going to be good.

The following Wednesday, Patricia stood in the auditorium and directed the cast members as they read their lines. "That's good, Phillip. Just remember, you should stand right about here"—Patricia came over and marked his spot on the stage—"so that the audience will really be able to see your expression."

Phillip Dizon nodded, assuming the proper place. He had been chosen to play the ghost James. "Got it, Patricia."

"Okay, could you guys take it from the top, please?" Patricia asked, holding her clipboard and walking to the side of the stage.

Grizz came up beside her. "Forty minutes and he's still a no-show," she grumbled.

"I know," Patricia said with a sigh. Grizz had described the back story of the characters to the actors while Patricia explained a little about what she wanted them to convey. She'd really wanted Kurt there so that she could show him the ropes of how the play worked, but since he still hadn't arrived, she'd decided to have everyone start reading their lines. "I think we have to talk to Mr. Gardner. Nicole, can you talk just a little louder? I'm having trouble hearing you."

"No problem," Nicole Baker, who had been chosen to play Mrs. Winchester, agreed. She smiled and flipped amber bangs out of her eyes with a toss of her head.

"Maybe he didn't like the part we chose for him," Grizz suggested with a sly grin once the actors had started reading again.

"No!" Patricia pretended to gasp, holding a hand to her chest. "We gave him the most *important* role of all!"

Grizz pulled out her cell phone. "Well, I'm sick of waiting. I'm not keeping everyone here late just because of him." She snickered as she typed out a rather menacing text. Patricia watched gleefully over her shoulder.

Just as Grizz was about to hit send, the echoing sound of wheels rolling in the hall reached Patricia's ears. She turned and saw Kurt roll into the auditorium just as he had the week before, bringing the board to a stop with his foot and kicking it up into his hands. "Hey," he greeted Patricia and Grizz with a lift of his chin.

Patricia set her jaw. Facing Natalia, Peter, Nicole and Phillip, she clapped her hands for their attention. "Okay, take five everyone."

Descending the stage steps, Patricia marched swiftly over to Kurt, who was balancing his skateboard on top of a closed theater seat. "Listen up," she snarled, all her patience gone. "You were supposed to be here forty-five minutes ago. You *do* realize that showing up late just means you have to *stay* late, don't you?"

Kurt ignored her, rummaging through his bag and producing his mp3 player and earbuds.

"Um, no!" Patricia snatched them from his hands.

"Why?" Kurt demanded, looking confused as usual. "You

told us to take five!"

Patricia rolled her eyes. "I told *them* to take five so I could talk to you!"

Kurt ran a hand through his short thatch of brown hair. "About what?"

"About—" Patricia stopped herself, noticing the other actors watching with interest. She sighed and grabbed Kurt by the elbow. "C'mon back here with me."

As soon as they were behind the curtain, Patricia said, "If you expect to get a good grade in this class—heck, if you expect to even *pass*—then you need to stop doing this!"

Kurt leaned against one of the many wooden crates that were backstage. "Doing *what*, babe?"

Patricia gritted her teeth. "Well, apart from calling me 'babe'," she muttered, "you keep showing up late—*ridiculously* late! Where have you been? And don't say water polo practice, I know that the season is over."

Kurt shrugged with a lazy smile. "There were some really great waves, and I thought, 'oh, hey, it's cool, it'll be flat soon,' but they, like, kept coming, you know? And I just had to ride them out."

Rolling her eyes, Patricia snarled, "Your grade point average *cannot* handle an F, which is what you are going to get if you don't start taking this seriously. You can kiss going to college goodbye."

Kurt snorted, shoving his hands in the pockets of his baggy jeans. "Man, will you chill out? I already got into college. And my primo choice, too—ASU!"

Patricia looked him straight in the eyes. "Okay, I cannot be the first one to explain this to you: your acceptance is contingent on your grades staying the same or improving from the time you were accepted." She folded her arms. "If you do worse, you're out."

Kurt stared back at her silently, and for a minute Patricia actually thought he was taking what she'd said seriously. Then he broke his gaze, turning his head with a chuckle. "Yeah, whatever, Penelope. I'm the captain of the Vista water polo team. The ASU team is hella competitive, and the coach really wants me. I took a tour and stayed overnight with a couple of the guys—the team loves me! They're awesome. They won't revoke my acceptance when they need me."

Patricia took a step closer to him, unable to believe his sheer ignorance to the gravity of his situation. Did he think that the admissions board honestly cared about *the water polo team*?

"Um, yes, *jerk*. Yes, they will. This isn't the olden days with football where your grades can be in the toilet and no one will care. If you don't clean up your act, you can kiss Arizona State *and* their 'awesome'"—she made air quotations with her fingers—"water polo team goodbye."

Suddenly Kurt straightened, taking his hands out of his pockets and stepping closer to Patricia. She stood frozen on the spot, only able to stare quizzically into his hazel eyes as he leaned in toward her. "Well, then, you could really help me out," he said in a low voice, taking yet another step closer. "Just say I've been doing a bunch of work and it'll be all good."

She stuck out a hand to his chest to stop him from moving any closer—a bad move on her part, since she could now feel his well-defined pecs. He was dangerously close, because when she breathed in she could tell how *good* he smelled, like the ocean mixed with really nice aftershave. She felt lightheaded for a moment, and could hear her heart hammering in her chest. No wonder so many girls were crazy about Kurt. He was so tall, so cut, so *manly*. She inhaled sharply, only making it worse.

"I'll make it up to you." Kurt reached out and lightly touched her arm just above the elbow. "We could do dinner or a movie… Or I could take you to my secret spot on the beach," he told her in a husky whisper.

All at once, Patricia snapped to her senses. Taking a firm step back in her knee-high boots, she screeched, "Not gonna *work, Kirk!*" as she lifted a hand and smacked him away.

She had no idea *what* had come over her. How could any girl *actually* like him? He was hot and he knew it, and he thought that he could *bribe* her into lying and letting him get the extra credit while he never even showed up. In his mind, girls were nothing more than his tools.

Well, Patricia was just going to have to prove who was the *real* tool here, wasn't she?

"I'm not one of your little fangirls, desperate for your attention," she hissed, folding her arms across her chest. "If you keep coming late and don't do what I ask, I'll tell Mr. Gardner, and you will flunk. Your choice."

"But—"

"Uh-uh, don't wanna hear it," Patricia said firmly, holding up a hand to silence him.

Kurt simply stared at her for a moment, his jaw slackening a little bit. Then he grumbled, "Fine, what do you want me to do?"

Patricia smiled to herself, knowing that she'd won for now.

"So, he comes over an *hour late* to the auditions—which really ticked me off—then he mocked Grizz's script when we stayed late to let him audition, and *then* he was late to rehearsal last night!" Patricia whispered to Ben the following day at the end of their French class. When they'd finished the assignment on the board, he'd casually asked her how the one-act was going, and received a play-by-play of Kurt's shenanigans over the past week. "And then he tried to seduce me into just letting him slide."

Ben shook his head in disgust. "Of course he did. That creep."

They were interrupted by the bell. *"Ah, c'est l'heure!"* said Madame Kelley with an exaggerated sigh, earning a laugh from the class. *"Au revoir!"*

As Patricia rose to her feet and began packing away her books, Ben said, "He can't keep doing this. If Mr. Gardner expects you to help him out—"

"I talked to Kurt," Patricia informed him as they left the classroom together, "and he *seemed* to hear me. It's hard to read behind that vacant expression," she added with a sly smile.

Ben laughed, his eyes crinkling. Then his expression sobered. "I'm telling my parents."

Patricia frowned. "You don't have to, Ben. I don't want your brother to be mad at you."

But Ben shook his head, one hand tightening on the strap of his backpack. "I know he's not been doing his work. He's been B.S.ing his way through our tutoring sessions, trying to get me to give him the answers. He was out practically all weekend, not coming home 'til hella late… I need to at least clue them in."

Patricia nodded. As they walked down the crowded hallway, she smiled and said, "Well, enough of Kurt. How are you?"

Ben grinned. "Good. It's been getting sorta crazy, so I'm glad I didn't do track this year." Ben had been on the track and field team his sophomore and junior years. "I've actually got to get to a science club meeting now. Gonna do some pretty cool experiments."

"Well, don't burn off any eyebrows," Patricia teased with a laugh.

"Will do. Or not do," Ben agreed, chuckling. Lifting his hand in a wave, he turned and headed down the hallway.

Patricia waved back, staring after his tall form for a moment as he walked away.

The next day, at five minutes to seven, Patricia sat in the auditorium flipping through her notes. She was flanked by Grizz and Phillip, who had shown up ten minutes early.

"Hey, guys," Peter greeted them as he came in. Soon he was followed by Natalia and Nicole.

Patricia rose to her feet. "Okay, well that just leaves Kurt."

"Let's just start without him," Grizz said, crossing her arms. "No point in waiting, since—" She paused midsentence as she heard two familiar voices in the hall. "What in the…?"

Patricia turned to the door, eyes widening as Ben entered with Kurt in tow. Glancing at her phone, she saw that it was exactly seven o'clock. "Wow, right on the dot! Good job, Kurt." She stared at Ben quizzically.

Kurt snorted. "If it were up to him, we would've been here half an hour ago."

Grizz lifted her eyebrows at Patricia, clearly intrigued by the situation. "So, Ben, um… what brings you here?"

"I had to drive Kurt," Ben explained with an eye roll. "Mom and Dad took away his car keys and want me to keep an eye on him to make sure he's doing his work."

"Only because *you* ratted me out!" Kurt grumbled. "Gallant here thought that he would make me look bad in front of Mom and Dad."

Ben whipped his head around and glared at Kurt. "Hey, Goofus, I didn't *have* to make you look bad. You did it all on your own. You *still* haven't been doing your homework, and Mr. White told them you were skipping out on your English tutoring sessions, too."

Kurt scoffed. "Like I want to have to spend private time with that nerd Matt."

"Man, whatever! Just because Mr. White was smart enough

not to assign you to work with some girl who was wrapped around your little finger."

"You're just jealous 'cuz you can't get any," Kurt said with a smirk, folding his arms across his chest.

"Jealous? Of *you*?" Ben drew himself up to his full height of six-foot-six and stared at his brother incredulously. "I'm not the one whose grades are so far down the toilet that Mom and Dad threatened to cut me off!"

"Only because *you* snitched! Thanks to *you*, I'm stuck without my Pacific Blue Jeep Wrangler Islander! With my lucky Tiki on the dash!" Kurt cried, looking desperate.

Grizz cocked one eyebrow. "What the hell are you talking about?"

"Oh, get over it!" Ben snapped back, rolling his eyes. "Forget about your stupid car—I'm stuck ferrying you around for the rest of forever! Or until you pass. *Whichever comes first.*"

"Kahuna is *not* stupid!" Kurt exclaimed, looking genuinely hurt by Ben's remark. Patricia had to cover her mouth to hide her laugh.

"He named his car 'Kahuna'?" Grizz whispered.

"And I'm the one whose life is ruined," Kurt continued. "Stuck with my lame little brother day and night, how uncool is that?"

Ben pulled at his hair in exasperation. "I'm only eight minutes younger than you! And do you think I *want* to be stuck spending all my free time babysitting you? I have *things* to do, Kurt!"

Kurt put on a mock pout. "Oh, what things? Nerdy little science club? Mathletics?"

"It's *mathalon*, you idiot."

"Either one sounds *stupid*!" Kurt snapped, giving his brother a shove. Ben frowned in annoyance and shoved him right back, and, as everyone in the room watched with interest, the argument devolved into a shoving match, each of the Minola brothers trying to outdo each other with insults.

"Idiot!"

"Rat!"

"Jerk!"

"Nerd!"

"Moron!"

"Stop it!" Patricia commanded, inserting herself between the two of them and pushing them apart.

Kurt's chest rose and fell quickly from the exertion. "He started it," he grumbled.

Ben glanced down at Patricia in disbelief before glaring at his brother. "Did not!"

"Did too!" Kurt took a step forward, ready to brawl once more.

"*Enough!*" Patricia commanded, still holding them apart. "Go to your separate corners. Grizz, you take Kurt back to the prop closet. I'll be right there."

"My pleasure," Grizz replied gleefully, skipping forward and reaching a hand up to grab Kurt's rather large ear. "Come along, my pet."

"Ow, ow, leggo, *leggo!*" Kurt cried, doubling over as she dragged him away.

Patricia laughed before turning to Nicole, Peter, Phillip and Natalia. "Okay, guys, if you could get on the stage and do some warm-ups real quick, we'll start rehearsing in just a few."

Finally she looked at Ben with a smile. "Sorry about that." He didn't reply, merely looking down, red-faced. She followed his gaze and realized that she was still grasping him firmly around his muscular bicep. "Oh! Sorry." She dropped her hand awkwardly.

After a moment of uncomfortable silence, she told him, "I'm really sorry you got stuck with Kurt. I feel like it's my fault."

Ben shook his head with a smile. "It's not, Patricia. It's Kurt's. Besides, what I told our parents was just icing on the cake. A bunch of his teachers had called them, too."

Patricia folded her arms across her chest and leaned in to whisper, "Did your parents *really* cut him off?"

Ben nodded, shoving his hands in his pockets. "Yep. They *really* want him to go to college. Especially since everyone already knows he got in, so their reputations are on the line, now, too."

Patricia bit her lip. She knew the Minolas were wealthy, and that the family was totally into the country club, charity ball scene. It would definitely be embarrassing if one of their sons got kicked out of college before he'd even started.

"They said if he doesn't buckle down," Ben continued, "they won't pay for college even if by some bizarre chance he *did* still get in. They took away his car and cut off his allowance, and they said he's not getting another cent until he proves he is responsible enough to fix this."

"Wow. Think it will work?" Patricia asked.

Ben shrugged. "Guess we'll see, huh?"

"Yeah, well, thanks for bringing him. Maybe tonight I can actually get him to do some of the stuff on my checklist." Patricia rubbed her hands together and laughed wickedly.

Chuckling, Ben glanced around before asking in a low voice, "Sure you don't want me to stick around to kick his ass if he doesn't do as he's told?"

Patricia grinned and shoved him playfully. "Don't worry. I think we've got this."

Ben seemed hesitant. "...Okay, then. Your rehearsal ends at nine, right?" Seeing Patricia's nod, he replied, "All right, see you then."

"Bye!" Patricia replied, staring after Ben for a moment before mentally going over a checklist.

Oh, yes. Kurt had his work cut out for him.

Several rehearsals later, Patricia was seated in front of the stage, watching carefully as the actors did a run-through. "Kurt!" she called out to the tall teen, who was standing idly by, staring off into space. "Earth to Kurt!"

Natalia, noticing he still wasn't listening, skipped over to Kurt and gently shook his arm. "Kurt," she said, flipping long platinum blonde hair over her shoulder, "I think Patricia is talking to you."

Kurt seemed to snap out of it, turning his attention on Natalia. "Oh, sorry. What'd you say, babe?"

Natalia giggled shyly, pointing offstage. "Patricia needs you."

He turned to Patricia. "'Sup, Persephone?"

Patricia gritted her teeth, gripping her pencil tightly. "Oh, nothing much, Kyle, just the fact that you *missed your cue*, again!"

Kurt stared at her blankly. "Oh, I did? Uh… what's my cue again?" He grinned as this earned yet another tinkle of laughter from Natalia.

Peter and Phillip looked at each other and rolled their eyes. "You're supposed to rattle the chains when I say, 'You, who are living on the vast fortunes of our misery,'" Peter snapped.

"*Oh*, right, right," Kurt said distractedly, still looking at Natalia.

"Okay, places, everyone! Take it from Mrs. Winchester's line, 'What must I do?'" Patricia instructed, leaning back in her chair with a sigh.

Rehearsal went on for a few more minutes, until, once again, when it was Kurt's cue, he stood there and did nothing. "Kurt!"

Patricia cried. "You're supposed to do the ghostly howl right then! You know, like we talked about?"

Kurt looked sheepish. He cleared his throat. "Okay… *awww-rrrroooo…*"

Patricia turned around in her seat when she heard Ben burst into laughter. "Aren't you supposed to be doing your home-work?" she asked, one eyebrow raised. To Patricia's surprise, Ben had stuck around the last couple of rehearsals, claiming he couldn't get anything done, knowing he would have to pick Kurt up in a short amount of time.

Ben lifted a fist to his mouth and pretended like he was coughing. "Um, sorry," he said, unable to hide his grin.

Patricia frowned at Ben and turned back in her seat to face the stage. "No, that sounds like a wolf. It's supposed to be like this: *eeeeeeee-ohhhhh,*" she wailed like a banshee. "Try again."

Kurt heaved a sigh. "*E-I-E-I-O…*"

Ben's laughter that time reached the stage, and Kurt stopped abruptly. "Do I *have* to do this, Patsy? This is *so* lame. Can't you just use a stereo?"

Turning briefly to smack Ben's notebook to silence his laughter, Patricia replied, "No, *Kirk,* we can't. You are *very* essential to this production. You help to demonstrate the fact that the ghosts mean business."

Kurt's shoulders sank. "But I just can't get into this."

Patricia stood and put her hands on her hips. "You have to *try*. Like… think back to when you were little and would pretend you were a pirate, or a cowboy, or something. Could you do it then?"

Kurt shrugged, looking confused. "Yeah, sure, but that was just pretend…"

"That's what acting *is*, genius," Phillip muttered.

Patricia decided to switch tactics. "Lots of girls come to the theater festival, Kurt," she said. "*Lots* of girls. And your name is going to be in the program, so they'll know it's you…"

Raising his eyebrows, Kurt stepped forward. "They will? But"—he suddenly looked doubtful—"won't they laugh at me?"

Patricia shook her head fervently. "Oh, no, not if you do a good job. They'll think you're awesome. Knocking over stuff and making scary sounds with no synthesizer? That's really cool!"

"We came up with this part especially for *you*, Kurt," Grizz added, voice dripping in sweetness.

"And you can do a really good job if you practice. Can't he, Natalia?" Patricia looked at her expectantly.

Natalia grinned and nodded at Kurt enthusiastically. "I believe in you, Kurt," she cooed.

"Really?" Kurt brightened at the thought. "All right!"

Patricia glanced at her cell phone and said, "Okay, guys, we only have a few minutes left to use the stage, so let's just finish this page of the script."

When they were done, the cast descended the stage steps, but Patricia moved to intercept Kurt. "Kurt, you need to stay a little longer. We have a job for you."

"Bummer," he mumbled. Turning to Natalia, he whispered, "See you next time, babe," earning a nod and giggle from her.

"Okay," Grizz said as she stood from where she'd been poring over spare fabric that she'd found for costumes, "I think the storeroom will have all the plywood we'll need."

"This is gonna involve some heavy lifting," Ben, once again eavesdropping, surmised. He rose to his feet and hopped over the row of seats before him. "I'll come help."

"We can't use power tools here on campus, so we're going to need you to saw the wood and do everything else that requires your tools at home," Patricia explained as they walked to the storeroom. "Then you can bring it to rehearsal and paint it here."

Kurt merely shrugged in response.

Once inside, Grizz flipped on the light. "Man, this place is a sty," she muttered, staring at the jumbled mess of poster boards, boxes, crates, and unnamable *junk* that covered the floor. Then her eyes lit up as she noticed the tall pieces of wood leaning against a shelving unit. "Bingo!"

"That would be good for the door," Patricia mused, pointing to a sheet of plywood that was balancing precariously atop the shelving unit.

Grizz noticed a fat beam propped underneath a stack of wooden poles. "Hey, that would work, huh?"

Before anyone could react, Kurt reached his long arm behind the poles and grabbed the beam. When he tugged it forward, it knocked loose the sheet of plywood and sent it soaring toward Patricia.

"Look out!" Ben cried, wrapping his arms protectively around her as he quickly pushed her out of harm's way.

Heart hammering in her chest, Patricia kept her head down, clutching Ben's arms. After a moment or two she dared to straighten up, cheeks growing warm when she realized how close Ben's face was to her own as he peered at her in concern.

"Are you okay?" Ben asked her, his voice still a bit raspy with adrenaline.

Patricia nodded slightly, still not releasing her grip on Ben's rather muscular arms. "Y-yeah, thanks."

Grizz whirled on Kurt. "You moron! You could've killed Patricia!"

Kurt didn't answer at first, staring at Patricia with wide eyes, his face shades paler than normal. "Oh, man," he muttered in a daze. "I-I didn't mean to…"

Ben turned to Kurt, arms still protectively around Patricia. "You've gotta be careful, Kurt! I could've helped you move the wood! That was really dangerous!"

Kurt nodded slowly, still seeming dazed. "Oh, man," he repeated. "I'm really sorry. Are you okay?"

Patricia sighed, finally straightening as Ben released her. She snapped back into director mode as soon as her heart slowed back to a normal pace. "Yeah, I know you didn't mean to. Here, let's just pick out the wood and you can carry it to the car. I'll give you some drawings of how I want the pieces done, okay? Can you please have it done and back here on Tuesday so that we can start painting it?"

Kurt shook his head quickly, then nodded. "Yeah, sure thing."

Once they'd loaded the wood into Ben's car, Patricia gave Kurt detailed instructions on what she wanted done, handing him drawings and written directions so that he couldn't claim he'd forgotten.

As he got into the passenger seat, he rolled down the window and told Patricia, "I… I'm really sorry. I'll be more careful from now on."

Patricia stared into his hazel eyes, which crinkled apologetically, and she knew he meant it. "I know you will," she said with a small smile.

Before Ben got in the car, he turned to Patricia. "You're sure you're okay?" he asked her quietly, placing a hand to her shoulder.

Patricia flushed, folding her arms nervously. "Yeah, I'm sure. Thanks for rescuing me from the board of doom," she said with a laugh.

As the brothers drove away, Grizz turned to Patricia and said, "I can't believe Kurt was so…"

Patricia nodded, knowing exactly what Grizz was getting at. *Maybe there is a human buried deep inside that musclebound brain after all,* she mused with a lopsided smile.

"Okay, now let's work on painting the door and the pillars," Patricia told Grizz the following Tuesday. Turning to Kurt, she asked, "Can you bring over the door you built?"

Kurt glanced at her, shifting uncomfortably. Patricia's stomach knotted. Now that she thought of it, she hadn't seen him bring anything in with him. Ben hadn't been able to drive him to rehearsal that day, so they couldn't be waiting in the car, either.

"Kurt," she began menacingly, "where are the set pieces I asked you to build?"

"Oh, *those*," Kurt replied with a laugh. "I forgot to bring them. Don't worry, I finished them this weekend like you asked me to."

Why do I not believe you? Patricia wondered snidely. Sighing, she said, "Go help Grizz with the costumes."

Groaning, Kurt slowly shuffled over to Grizz, who was sitting on the floor surrounded by patterns, thread, pincushions, and a melee of clothing.

"Come, my pet," Grizz whispered eerily, removing a pin from her mouth and carefully pushing it into the pincushion. "I have a very important task for you. I need you to measure the cast for costumes." She tossed him an electric blue measuring tape.

"Sweet," Kurt replied, starting to move toward Natalia and Nicole, who were running lines together in the corner. "Which lucky girl is first?"

"Oh, no," Grizz called after him teasingly, "not the girls. I need you to measure Peter—around his waist, his chest, then from the nape of his neck to his tail bone, please."

"What?!" Kurt recoiled in horror.

Grizz shrugged innocently. "Well, I'm making his uniform jacket, and I need to be exactly sure of his measurements."

"B-but… can't one of you chicks do it?"

"No," Patricia said harshly before Grizz could respond, "we're busy. And you are supposed to be helping us. So unless you want to be here all night long, you had better do what Grizz tells you."

Kurt looked between Grizz and Patricia for a moment, seeming at a loss. Then he heaved a sigh. "Okay. Man, Zelda, this is cruel." Cupping his hand over his mouth, he shouted, "Yo, Pete!"

Peter looked up from his script. "Yeah?"

"C'mere for a sec. I need to measure you."

Peter's eyes widened as he shook his head fervently. "No."

Kurt turned back to Grizz and shrugged, tossing her the measuring tape. "Aw, too bad. He doesn't want me to."

Grizz swiftly caught the tape and chucked it right back to him. Then she turned to Peter. "Peter," she began coyly, batting her lashes and pouting her lips, "I'm very busy making this jacket, and I need your measurements. Won't you be a sweetheart and let Kurt measure you, just this once?"

Peter stared at Grizz for a moment in silence, mouth agape. Then he slowly nodded. "Okay."

As Kurt clumsily wrapped the tape around Peter's chest, Peter growled, "One false move and I'll punch your lights out."

Kurt rolled his eyes, calling out the number as he took each measurement. "Dude, same goes for you."

When the task was done, he trudged over to Grizz. "Good job," she said. "Now I need you to sew the lace onto these sleeves." Grizz lifted an old dress that she'd found in the prop closet and was currently embellishing to be Adeline's costume. "And then the lace on the bodice as well. It's already all pinned into place, so it should be a snap."

Kurt looked at the offered dress and sneered. "Sewing is for chicks, man. I'm not doing that."

"Well, if that isn't the most sexist comment I've ever heard," Grizz snarled, brandishing her sewing scissors.

Patricia hurried over. "No, he's right, Grizz. Sewing *is* for chicks. We can't ask him to do that."

Kurt nodded. "Yeah, what she said."

"After all," Patricia went on, "he wouldn't know the first thing about sewing. It requires brain cells that he doesn't possess."

Grizz nodded slowly, catching on. "Oh, yeah, definitely. Sorry, Kurt, it's just too much to ask of you. You're not smart enough to sew on a button."

Kurt looked affronted. "Hey—"

"No, no." Patricia held up her hands. "After all, it takes a keen mind and a steady hand to do something so complex. No mere man can do it."

"I bet I could!" Kurt cried out, reaching to grab the pin cushion.

"Oh, no, you couldn't!" Grizz protested, holding the cushion away from him.

Kurt set his jaw. "I can so! Here, I'll prove it. How do you thread the needle?"

Hiding her grin as she shared a look with Patricia, Grizz showed Kurt how to thread the needle and stitch on the lace.

"So, the bellboy asks the photon if he needs help with his luggage, and the photon says, 'Oh, I don't have any. I'm traveling light,'" Ben told Patricia as he was driving the next day, glancing over at her to gauge her reaction.

Patricia threw her head back and laughed, one arm hanging out the window of the passenger seat of Ben's Expedition. "Okay, that was good."

"Really? I haven't driven you to madness yet with my dumb science jokes?" Ben asked with a grin.

Patricia made a disbelieving noise, reaching over to playfully shove him.

"Hey, watch it, I'm driving here!"

Patricia held up her hands in submission. "Whoopsie, my bad."

Glancing quickly at her before turning his attention back to the road, Ben asked, "So, what subject are you doing for your French presentation?"

"I'm thinking *Le Chat Noir.*"

"Oh, yeah, that nightclub with the poster of the cranky looking cat?"

Patricia giggled at his description. "Yes, that one. What about you?"

"I'm gonna do Augustin-Louis Cauchy."

"Ooh," Patricia said in an awed voice, then grinned and asked, "Who's that?"

Ben laughed. "He was a physicist and mathematician in the 1800s."

"Cool. A subject that definitely appeals to you."

"Yep," Ben agreed. "I plan to be a physics major. Maybe even a physics and math double major."

Patricia pumped a fist in the air. "If you did both that would be so hardcore. Do it, do it!"

Ben chuckled at her enthusiasm. "The college I'm going to has an awesome program—really great resources and labs. It's gonna *rock.* But what about you? Do you think you'll do any other major besides theater?"

"Hm…" Patricia mulled that one over. "Maybe a French minor. Or something super cool, like classics!"

"Classics would be *awesome,*" Ben enthused. "You could learn

Latin! Man, I've always wanted to know Latin."

"Definitely."

Ben pulled into a cul-de-sac and approached a large beautiful Colonial two-story home—the Minolas' house. Patricia had voiced her suspicions to Ben about Kurt not making the set after French, and, since Kurt was going to be at tutoring for a while, Ben had offered to bring Patricia by their house to see if he had indeed been fibbing.

"Wow," Patricia breathed as she undid her seatbelt. "You guys have a *nice* house."

Ben ducked his head shyly. "Thanks. His shed's out back, but it's easier to get to it through the house."

As they walked through the entryway, living room and kitchen, Patricia took in the cozy decorations and beautiful furniture. Ben pulled open a sliding door and led her through the nicely landscaped, fenced backyard to a large shed that looked like a miniature version of their house. "Here's where he does all of his stuff," Ben told her as he opened the door.

Once inside, Patricia could see how much Kurt really did like carpentry. There were all sorts of tools hanging from pegs on the walls, plus a table saw and a large workbench. As she passed by a surfboard propped against the wall, she ran a hand along the sanded texture. "This is really cool."

"Aw, man," Ben groaned, lifting a bunch of materials from the ground and placing them onto the workbench. "He hasn't even *started*!" Sighing, he ran both his hands through his hair in a frustrated motion. "I'm sorry, Patricia. I should have known. I'll make sure he does it in the next couple days."

Patricia shook her head, crossing her arms as she replied firmly, "Nope. *I'm* going to make sure he does it."

"No, Kurt, you have to make it wider than that," Patricia scolded the next day as she sat with Kurt in his shed, watching his work like a hawk. He'd been pretty ticked that they had sneaked into his workshop to find out that he'd lied, but there was nothing he could do about it now.

Except complain.

"But Trixie, it looks fine this way," Kurt whined, setting the piece of plywood back down.

"No, it doesn't! The door in the Winchester Mystery House has a glass panel in the center. The cutout has to be wide enough so that the actors can walk through it and not snag their costumes or trip and knock it over. Do you want our play to look bad? Cut it wider!"

Kurt heaved a sigh, lowering his safety goggles over his eyes once again and carefully lining up the wood to the blade. Patricia grimaced and covered her ears as the saw went off. *The things I do for my play,* she thought, hating how the sound of the saw made her skin crawl.

When he was done, he slid it off the table and held it up for Patricia to test. Carefully she lifted her foot and stepped through the rectangular section that Kurt had cut out of the center of the "door." She shook her head. "About an inch and a half wider, please."

"Listen, Pam," Kurt began, pulling his goggles off and sitting down on a stool.

"I'm listening, Kyle."

Looking confused for a moment, Kurt continued, "I don't know why you are being so obsessive about this. Most people probably aren't even going to have props and sets and stuff. No one is gonna care."

"Do you really take such little pride in your own work?"

Patricia asked him, standing to touch the surfboard he'd made. "You wouldn't want to make a crappy surfboard and have people see it, would you?"

Kurt scoffed, stretching out his long legs. "Yeah, but that's surfing! Something important! This play is boring. Theater is boring. I wish I'd never taken this class. I just can't get into it."

"Maybe if you *tried* to be interested in it—read the script, did *something*—it wouldn't seem like such a waste of time." When he rolled his eyes, she pulled her hair away from her face in frustration. Finally, she said, in a much calmer tone, "Okay, Kurt, what *are* you into? Besides girls and surfing," she added wryly.

"Cool things, like music, and sports, carpentry, car shows… oh, and history!" Kurt added, putting his hands in the pockets of his hooded sweatshirt as he leaned back slightly.

Patricia was taken aback. "Wait—*history*?" She was shocked that he found something so academic "cool."

"Yeah, dude, especially military history," Kurt went on, eyes shining with excitement. "Ever see a Civil War reenactment? They're radical."

Patricia couldn't believe her ears. The military history thing made sense in a strange way, but he liked Civil War reenactments? "But Kurt, that's theater!"

Kurt looked at her incredulously. "Nah, babe, it's *history*."

"But it's acting! Someone had to put together the production build the sets, do the lighting, the makeup, the costumes, even the script. And our play is historical, too."

Kurt looked at her and laughed. "But it's about ghosts! That's not history!"

Patricia tucked a strand of hair behind her ear and replied, "But Mrs. Winchester was a real woman, and her house is a historical landmark. Grizz worked hard to add a supernatural element to a real event—the 1906 earthquake."

Kurt watched her carefully for a moment, slowly nodding. "Yeah, I guess it *is* history, huh?"

Seeing that she'd made a breakthrough, Patricia continued, "And theater can be really cool if you give it a chance. Like, there's a ton of historical plays."

Kurt looked interested. "Whoa, really?"

Patricia nodded enthusiastically. "Yeah! In fact, Shakespeare wrote several—*Henry V, Antony and Cleopatra, Julius Caesar...*"

"Sweet," Kurt muttered, running his hand absently over the plywood door. Then he sighed. "Argh—it's just, this is all so *much* work. The play, tutoring, all the homework..." He slumped forward on the work table, burying his head in his hands.

It's your own fault, you big crybaby, Patricia thought with an eye roll. But aloud she said, "Okay, just think of it this way: you just have to work hard until the end of the year to achieve your goal."

Head still on the table, Kurt turned slightly to look at her. "My goal?"

"Getting into ASU?" Patricia prodded.

"But I'm already *in.*" Kurt lifted his head slightly. "It doesn't matter if Mom and Dad cut me off. I'm getting an athletic scholarship—"

"But for how much?" Patricia interrupted. She knew it couldn't be a substantial amount. When he told her, she threw her head back and laughed. "That's not even going to cover your dorm! And since your parents are loaded, I can guarantee you aren't getting any other financial aid, right?"

Kurt furrowed his brow. "Uh, yeah, I guess..."

"So you have to do this, for your goal!" Patricia balled her hand into a fist to cheer him on. "Tell me, why do you want to go to ASU?"

Sitting up straighter, Kurt said, "For everything, dude!

Tempe is awesome, there's sorority babes galore, and their water polo team is the best around! The guys and coach were so cool. I did an overnight with a couple of the team members. They were even talking about doing a *theme house* next year. And did you know, with the summer Olympics just a few years away, they scout out of college? I want to play in the Olympics!"

Wow. The Olympics? Patricia blinked, surveying him for a moment or two. "Think of it this way: everything you have to do now is just work to achieve that goal," she said. "Sure, it's hard now, but it's only until the end of the year. In the fall you can apply yourself right off the bat in all your classes, and get help right away if you need it. If you play it smart, you'll never have to do something like this again."

Kurt sat up fully, turning on the stool to face her. "Whoa," he breathed. "I guess I never thought about it that way before, but you're right. I gotta do this—for water polo." Then he sighed and scratched the side of his head. "No matter how much it sucks."

Patricia put a hand to his arm. "I know it's a lot of work, and it can seem overwhelming, but it's the same for me. I want to be a theater major when I get to college—I want to be a director someday. This is my chance to get up in front of everyone and show them that I can do it. Maybe if we work together, we can make both of our dreams come true."

Kurt smiled slightly. "Sounds good to me."

"Um, am I interrupting something?"

Patricia turned quickly to see that Ben had entered the shed, holding a tray laden with snacks. "Oh, how sweet! Brownies!"

"And lemonade," Ben added with a smile, coming over to set the tray down on the workbench. "Thought you guys might need some nourishment. Mom baked these last night."

Patricia took a brownie and put a hand to her mouth as she bit into it. "They're delicious!"

"Yeah, thanks, bro," Kurt said, grabbing two at once.

Ben laughed, though Patricia noticed that it sounded a little strained. He poured a glass and handed it to Patricia. "No problem," he said. "So, how goes it?"

Before Patricia could reply, Kurt said enthusiastically, "Great! Just need to make this section a little wider, right, Patty?"

Patricia looked at Kurt in surprise. Then, with a nod, she replied, "Right!" Seeing Ben's curious look, she smiled and shrugged.

Grizz's eyes widened as Kurt and Ben carried in the set pieces at their next rehearsal. "Wow, he actually did it," she said to Patricia under her breath.

Patricia nodded happily. "Yeah, don't they look nice?"

Grizz stared at the pieces as they went by. "Our play is gonna be *so* badass."

"Yo, Zelda!" Kurt called as he set down the door. "I got the stuff you wanted."

"For the last time, it's *Grizz!*" Her annoyed expression faded as he held a plastic bag out to her. Peering into it suspiciously, she saw that he'd gotten all of the paint and supplies she'd asked him to. "Wow. Um, this is great, thanks. Okay, why don't you help me paint this door, and then you can stitch some more embellishments onto Phillip's uniform."

"Sure thing," Kurt agreed easily, pulling out the paint and brushes.

"Wow, Kurt, it looks so good," Natalia cooed as she came over to admire his handiwork.

Kurt flashed a grin, twisting the cap off of a paint tube. "Thanks, babe."

"One second, Kurt!" Patricia called. "We need to lay down newspaper or something so we don't get paint on the floor.

There's some in the back, I'll get it."

"I'll help," Ben offered, hurrying after her.

As they gathered old newspaper from the storeroom, Patricia commented, "Kurt sure is a lot more eager to help."

Ben nodded, holding out his arms to let her place more paper atop the stack he was carrying. "I know. He actually seems excited about the play now."

"Maybe he actually listened to me," Patricia mused as she closed the door behind them.

Ben turned to her curiously.

Seeing his look, Patricia quickly said, "I gave him a pep talk the other day. Well, it was kind of more like a smackdown. I think he may actually realize now that he *will* be screwed if he doesn't do his work."

Ben broke into a surprised grin. "I hope so. That'll be better for everybody."

Patricia let out a breath with a laugh. "Don't I know it."

As Grizz and Kurt delved into painting, Patricia set the stage with the props that were ready to go, helping the actors to mark out their places and rehearse.

"Okay, remember, reach for the candlestick and hold it just so"—Patricia demonstrated to Nicole—"so that the audience can still see your reaction. Okay?"

Nicole nodded, taking hold of the candlestick. "Got it."

"Okay, let's give this part a run-through, then." Patricia skipped down the steps and took a seat.

After the actors had finished, Ben turned to her. "That was great. It's really coming along."

Patricia smiled proudly. "You think so?"

Ben grinned in return. "Definitely."

"Ben!" Kurt suddenly called from where he was busily painting. "Do me a favor, bro!"

Ben looked over to him suspiciously. "And do what?"

"I've got a Spanish test this week, can you grab my flash cards from my backpack and quiz me?"

Ben looked over at Patricia, impressed. He stood and retrieved the flash cards from Kurt's backpack. "All right, I'm gonna give you the Spanish first and you give me the English. Ready?"

"Hit me," Kurt replied, not looking up from his work.

Ben cleared his throat. "*La corbata.*"

"Tie," Kurt replied without hesitating, furiously swiping his paintbrush.

"Good." Ben flipped to the next card. "*Los zapatos.*"

"Uh… shoes?" Kurt asked, head cocked to the side.

"Ding ding ding!" Ben called out with a grin. "Okay, *el estante.*"

Kurt was silent, tapping his paintbrush thoughtfully. "Um… uh…"

"C'mon," Ben encouraged, flipping the card over to look at the English answer, "you can do it. It's found in a store, kind of important…"

Kurt suddenly threw his hands up in the air. "Rack!"

"Woot!" Ben cheered. "You got it!"

Patricia watched the scene and smiled, glad to see Ben so excited about Kurt doing well. Kurt really seemed to want to make a change to his life.

"Wow, Kurt," Natalia called from her spot on the stage, "you really are *maravilloso!*"

Kurt turned toward her and grinned. "*Gracias, chica!*"

Patricia rolled her eyes and returned to her notes. *Then again, the more things change, the more they stay the same.*

❦

A couple weeks later, Patricia and Grizz were looking over the costumes, which were just about finished, except for Peter's jacket and Phillip's uniform.

"If someone had some really nice dress pants," Grizz mused, "we wouldn't have to buy or make anything."

"I'm sure one of the guys or their dads will have something like that," Patricia told her, patting her on the back. "Don't worry!"

"Hey, guys," Ben greeted everyone as he walked in the room with Kurt. "Wow, the costumes are looking great," he commented, crouching to look at them closer. "What do you think, Kurt?"

"Sweet," Kurt agreed, seeming distracted. "Oh, hey, Trixie, I checked out the Winchester Mystery House this weekend, and you were right, it *is* history. That place is off the hook, man!"

Patricia lifted her eyebrows at Grizz, who looked equally shocked. He actually went there? Because of her play? And he liked it? Patricia felt herself smile at the thought. "Well, I'm glad you enjoyed it."

Kurt grinned, lifting his hands enthusiastically. "Totally! Staircases leading to nowhere, doors that open to a straight drop down, a room with that many fireplaces? So trippy." Then he lowered his hands and looked at Grizz with furrowed brows. "Oh, but Rizzo, there's, like, a problem with your script."

Grizz bristled at the nickname. "What problem?" she scoffed incredulously.

Kurt stuck his hands in his pockets. "Well, the Winchester rifle wasn't used during the Civil War. That was the Henry rifle. Oliver Winchester didn't buy the rifle company until after the war—1866. His most famous gun model came out in 1873 and was called 'the gun that won the West.' So the ghosts wouldn't be from the Civil War. They'd be, like, Rangers, or cowboys and outlaws, or something."

Patricia inhaled sharply. She couldn't believe her ears. If that was true, then poor Grizz's script...

Patricia turned to gauge Grizz's reaction. She was just sitting there, jaw set and eyes narrowed. "What?" she finally said with a disbelieving laugh. "That can't be right." She pulled her phone out of her pocket to do an online search.

"Wait." Her hand shot out to seize Patricia's arm in a death grip. "He—he's right. No, no, no, he can't be right..."

Patricia looked at him suspiciously, all the while trying to wiggle her arm free. "How did you know that?"

Kurt grinned, oblivious to the chaos he had wrought. "History is my *jam,* man! Especially stuff about firearms and battles and all that."

Grizz rose to her feet, her heavily lined eyes bugging out with rage. "If you *knew* that, then *why didn't you say anything?!*" she screamed, balling her hands into fists that shook. "You had to keep your mouth shut until my costumes are almost finished, until the theater festival is *almost here*?! What, did you think it was *funny?!*"

Kurt scratched his ear nonchalantly. "Oh, I didn't know 'til I went to the house, and then I did some reading on it. Dad has tons of books on local stuff."

Grizz stood there on the spot, quaking for a moment. Then, suddenly, she lunged, brandishing her long, hot-pink fingernails at Kurt. "*DIE!*"

Ben and Patricia leapt to intervene, Patricia holding Grizz from behind as she kicked and screamed. "Death is too good for him," Grizz screeched, her red-tipped hair flailing about. "Tar and feather him! Give him the rack!"

Suddenly her head whipped around, her attention now focused on the costumes that lay a few feet away. "Ruined! All ruined!" Ripping herself from Patricia's grasp, she flung herself onto her knees and snatched the half-finished jacket, pulling furiously at it to rend it in two. "All this time—*wasted*! I'm gonna be a laughingstock! I'll have to work night and day—no sleep for me—to fix this idiotic mistake!"

"No, Grizz, stop!" Patricia cried, diving to grab the jacket from Grizz's hands.

Grizz held on stubbornly, tugging violently on the fabric as she whimpered, "How could *Kurt Minola* be smarter than me?!"

"Grizz, stop, stop!" Ben pleaded, forcibly lifting her to her feet by hoisting her by the underarms. "It's okay, you didn't know!"

Patricia stood and put her hands to Grizz's shoulders. "Grizz, I didn't know, either! And neither did Peter, or any of the others!"

Ben nodded and shrugged. "Me, neither. I think one of the times I went the tour guide even said something about the Civil War."

"Yeah!" Patricia nodded encouragingly. "And the tour guides talk so fast, and the house is so big! I don't think the rifles actually came up that much."

Grizz's shoulders heaved as she slowed down her breathing. Then her eyes filled with tears. "It probably was on one of those information signs out front," she said with a sniffle. "Why didn't I do more research? What kind of a writer *am* I?" Gazing at Patricia, she whispered, "I've ruined the play."

"No, you haven't," Patricia said soothingly. "Look at the gorgeous costumes you made—Mrs. Winchester's dress can stay the same!"

Grizz nodded slowly, her makeup running down her cheeks. "That's true…"

"And the guys' clothes are pretty similar," Ben told her. "I mean, we can look it up to be extra sure, but I don't think they would need much altering."

"Yeah." Then Grizz's face fell again. "But the script… my characters…"

"Well, Kurt says that history is his 'jam', right?" Turning to Kurt, who'd been standing there looking quite uncomfortable, Patricia lifted her eyebrows expectantly.

He nodded. "Yeah, and I love Westerns."

Patricia smiled. "There, see? Kurt will look stuff up and help you adapt your script."

Grizz eyed Kurt suspiciously. "You will?"

Kurt shrugged and nodded. "Yeah, sure thing. My dad has tons of books, and we can also look online. I can help with the costumes too," he surprised them all by volunteering. "I have a ton of cowboy hats and boots and stuff."

Grizz furiously wiped her face with her sleeve, taking a deep breath and returning to normal. "Well, what are we waiting for?" she declared, reaching into her bag for her keys. "Let's get a move on! To Casa Minola! Away!"

As Grizz gathered the costumes and prodded Kurt out of the auditorium, Patricia smiled and turned to Ben. "Well, hopefully that will work out."

Nodding, Ben said, "He really listens to you."

Patricia looked surprised. "Huh? No, he doesn't," she said, laughing uncomfortably.

"No, really," Ben insisted, putting his hands in his pockets. "He just agreed to helping Grizz, he's been buckling down and applying himself like you encouraged him to, and when he had me take him to the Winchester Mystery House this weekend, he wouldn't stop talking about you."

Patricia's eyebrow crinkled in surprise. "Really?"

Ben nodded and dropped his gaze to the floor, suddenly

looking uncomfortable. "Um, Patricia, I…"

Patricia stared at him, holding her breath as she waited for him to finish his sentence.

Luckily for Grizz, they only had to make minor changes to the script and costumes. Grizz ended up turning the jacket she was making for Peter's character into a vest and gave him a button-down shirt, and it turned out that the dress for Natalia's character, Adeline, didn't need any changes. With the addition of Kurt's cowboy hats and boots, the costumes were finished and looked great.

In fact, as time went on, everyone in the play noticed that Kurt had begun to actually make an effort. During a dress rehearsal, Patricia kept a close eye on Kurt, who was getting better and better at his role. His ghostly moans sounded truly bone-chilling, and he was now competent at waving the chains around without causing bodily harm.

As he roamed across the stage in his costume, a long black hooded cloak so that the audience would only catch a glimpse of his ghostly presence, he seemed very into his part. "*Ohhhhh-ohhhhhhhhh,*" he wailed, knocking over a table on cue.

Patricia grinned to herself. *This is going to look so good when it's all done,* she thought in excitement.

Just then, Kurt dropped his chain and it fell on the stage with a clatter. "Whoops, my bad," he called out.

"Kurt," Patricia reminded him, "remember, never, ever, ever break character. If that happens during the actual show, do not say anything, just quietly pick it up and go back to haunting. People are less likely to notice mistakes if you act like nothing happened. The show must go on!"

Kurt's eyes looked a bit glazed as she was talking, but then he nodded and grinned. "You got it, chief."

After they were done rehearsing, Patricia held up her hands. "Okay, now we're going to try that with lighting, so I'm going up to the light booth for this next run-through. Grizz, can you come with me?"

Once in the light booth, Grizz clapped her hands together enthusiastically. "This is looking *so awesome*."

Patricia grinned, turning a control. "Yeah, your costumes look so good."

Grizz gazed off into the distance, looking embarrassed but pleased. "Why, thank you." Then she sighed. "I hate to say it, but I'm glad Kurt is in our play." Seeing Patricia's horrified look, Grizz held up her hands. "No, no, he's still a tool, but if it hadn't been for him, people at the festival would've seen the big mistake I'd made."

Patricia nodded slowly. "Yeah, that's true. And the sets do look really good." She looked down and saw Ben walk in with a couple pizza boxes. "I guess everything's working out, huh?" she said with a smile.

When the rehearsal was over, Grizz and Patricia descended the precarious spiral staircase that led from the lighting booth. Kurt leapt off the stage and rushed over to Patricia. "Dude, Trixie, the lights made it choka!"

Patricia cocked an eyebrow, emitting a small laugh. "What?"

Kurt smiled. "Choka. Surf-speak for 'awesome'."

"Ohh." Patricia nodded, tucking a strand of hair behind her ear. "Well, thank you."

"Hey, everybody!"

Patricia turned her head to see Ben standing nearby, brandishing the pizza boxes. "Dinner is served," he said with a grin.

"Actors, please change out of your costumes before you eat, lest you risk my wrath!" Grizz called with an innocent smile on her face. Then she skipped over to Ben, plucking a pepperoni slice from the top box he was holding and taking a large bite. "Mm, delish! Thanks!"

"Yeah, thanks so much, Ben," Patricia told him as she joined them.

"No problem," Ben said. "There's pepperoni and," he shifted the boxes, moving the bottom one to the top of the stack and opening it, "ta-da! Hawaiian."

Patricia could feel her mouth water at the sight of the ham and pineapple pizza. "Oh, my favorite! You rock."

"The play is looking good. I think you guys are there," Ben told them, setting down the pizza boxes on a table.

"I hope so," Grizz replied, wiping the corner of her mouth with a napkin from the pack Ben had brought with the pizza, plates, and soda.

Patricia laughed, setting down her slice. "No, we *are* good. It's gonna be choka!" she said with a laugh, making a "hang loose" sign with her left hand.

"Thank you so much, I'm so glad you liked it," Patricia told her English teacher as he congratulated her after the theater festival. The play had been a success, the applause afterward causing her face to hurt from grinning so much. Now all of those who had participated were lining the hallway, exchanging hugs and congratulations.

Turning to Grizz, she sighed with relief and said, "I can't believe it's over."

Grizz grinned and leaned against the wall, folding her hands behind her. "I can't believe Kurt didn't trip and knock over the set."

Laughing, Patricia smoothed the skirt of her coral-colored dress. "I know! He was actually…"

"Pretty good?" Grizz supplied grudgingly.

Patricia nodded, combing her hair with her fingers. "Yeah. I'm glad, though. Could you imagine if he'd—"

"Don't say it," Grizz warned with wide eyes.

"Ladies!" Mr. Gardner greeted them as he appeared. "Excellent one-act, truly a masterpiece. I must say, you seemed to use Mr. Minola's time well—the props were superb, and his role..."—Grizz and Patricia side-eyed each other, trying not to snicker—"What an excellent use of the stage. Well done. I think working together has worked out in everyone's favor," he surmised, peering keenly at Patricia over his glasses. "Well, I won't keep you. This is a time to celebrate!"

"Thank you, Mr. Gardner," Grizz and Patricia said in unison as their teacher walked away.

"He's right, things really *have* worked out," Grizz said slyly, elbowing Patricia in the ribs.

Flushing, Patricia bit her lip and elbowed her back.

"Hey! Watch the sash!" Grizz admonished, referring to the short purple dress with black sash that she'd chosen to wear for the festival, complete with a matching black shrug and clutch.

"Um, hey."

Patricia lifted her head as Kurt approached them. He'd already changed out of his costume and was back in his street clothes of jeans and a polo shirt. *I guess this is his way of dressing up*, she thought with an eye roll. "Hey, Kurt."

Taking in Grizz and Patricia, he said, "You both look amazing."

Grizz grinned, putting a hand to her hip and striking a pose. "Don't we, though?"

"Um, Patricia?" he began, looking nervous as he shuffled in his sneakers. "Can I talk to you for a second?"

Patricia's eyes widened, feeling as if the wind had been

knocked out of her. In all the time she'd known him, he had never *once* called her by her proper name. "Um, sure."

"I'm gonna congratulate Chase on his play," Grizz said, winking dramatically and trying to conceal her snicker as she passed Patricia.

Kurt shifted his weight from side to side before saying, "So, I just talked to Mr. Gardner, and he was really impressed with what you've told him. He says that this will help my grade *a lot*. I mean, I still have to finish that paper, but that'll be a cinch. Um," he mumbled, scratching his scalp and looking nervous, "what I'm trying to say is, I owe it all to you. Sorry I was being so lame before. You showed me that theater can be really cool. So... how about we go out?"

Patricia stared at him. "What, like a date?" Was that what Ben had been hinting at that time they were working on the costumes? Did Kurt... did Kurt *like* her?

Kurt nodded with a smile. "Yeah, babe. I really want to make it up to you for how much trouble I caused at first."

Patricia broke into a smile. "Aw, Kurt, that's so sweet of you! I accept your apology, but I'm afraid I can't go out with you. My boyfriend wouldn't like that."

Kurt looked dumbfounded, his jaw dropping slightly. "Your... boyfriend? Dude, I didn't know you had a boyfriend."

Patricia nodded, craning her neck to look around. "Yeah, actually, he should be..."

"Ready to go?" Ben asked as he walked up to her with a bouquet of flowers, dressed in black pants and a gray button-down shirt.

"Oh," Patricia breathed, taking the offered bouquet and cradling it in her arms, "Ben, that's so sweet!"

Ben grinned, then turned to Kurt and clapped him on the shoulder. "Good job in the play, bro."

Taking Ben's offered arm, Patricia turned and told Kurt, "Yeah, you did a really great job. We've got dinner reservations, so we have to get going, but have a good night!"

Kurt's eyes widened in sheer shock. "Wait… what…?"

"You know, I feel pretty bad for him," Ben commented as they made their way through the parking lot toward his car. "He seemed so depressed when we left. I guess he must be into you now."

As he held open the passenger door for her, Patricia shrugged. "Well, I *do* feel bad about that, but there's nothing I can do. Don't worry, he'll find someone new soon."

Ben laughed and nodded. "Yeah, I guess you're right."

Patricia grinned. "Why, there's a lad. Come on and kiss me, Ben."

Ben's face lit up happily, and he did just that.

Star Walker

ALEX IRWIN

"The spirit that I have seen
May be the devil: and the devil hath power
To assume a pleasing shape; yea, and perhaps
Out of my weakness and my melancholy,
As he is very potent with such spirits,
Abuses me to damn me."
- HAMLET, *THE TRAGEDY OF HAMLET*

The outer doors of the spaceship slide open, and for one blinding moment all Letta can see is an enveloping blackness that drinks everything in and leaves nothing behind. She can feel herself being drawn toward it, wanting to slip into that void and float with the stars. Instead, she presses her forehead to the glass separating the main body of the ship from the evacuation chamber. Her gaze is fixed on the small metal box on the floor of the chamber. As she watches, it tips over, and the ashes inside spiral out, sucked into the blackness.

Her mother's ashes are stardust now.

The doors slide together again and the hushed awe that had spread over the funeral party finally cracks. Quiet words slither through as the attendees, mostly first class residents, begin to trickle from the gate toward the main deck for refreshments.

Someone clears his throat behind Letta and she quickly wipes her eyes on the back of her hand before turning around. The Council of Six waits behind her, all dressed in the white uniform that signifies prestige. The same white uniform that her mother used to wear. Councilperson Pol, an old man with barely-there gray hair and a greenish tinge to his cheeks, steps forward awkwardly. So, the other five have put Pol up to speaking with her, then.

She lets her eyes slowly rove over each of them, daring them to meet her eyes. They all look at the floor with their hands pressed together as if in prayer. Even C.p. Pol, the mouthpiece of the group, refuses to meet her glare. Letta grimaces with revulsion. All these people, these adults, trying to lord authority over her when they can't even get up the courage to look her in the eyes.

"C.p. Pol, what can I do for you?" she asks, standing briskly at attention. She needs to appear steady and reliable, but she flinches as her voice comes out foggy, squeezed out of a swollen throat and saturated with tears.

Pol clears his throat again. It's a sound that grates on Letta's nerves.

"Well, firstly, the council—no, the council and *I*—would like to offer our sincere condolences about your mother. Captain Leticia Hamilton was truly one of the greatest people on board this fine ship—"

"'One of'?" Letta raises an eyebrow and tries not to smirk as Pol tugs nervously on his jacket and glances back at the rest of the council with awkward, stilted movements.

"Yes, well, there are plenty of great people on board with us here on the *Elsinore*. Your mother was just one of many, and, uh, one of the best..."

"The best," Letta corrects him through clenched teeth. She itches to relax her muscles, but she remains still, keeping her face passive despite the waves of anger and grief that crash within her.

"In any case, the other matter," Pol continues, choosing to ignore Letta's comments, "is that we are afraid we cannot grant your request to take your mother's place as the captain of the

Elsinore."

They said no. How could they say no? Formality seems unimportant now. Letta falls back against the glass, her hands curling into fists. She is filled with the hot urge to punch something; but just as suddenly as that need appears, her energy drains from her, and all she wants is to sink to the floor and never get up again.

"What?" she whispers. She refuses to believe that she was rejected. Her mother had been *training* her for this, training her to take over once they landed on New Earth. It was all she had done from the day she started school until now. They cannot take this one thing she had left of her mother's legacy away from her.

"The council believes that you are just far too young at this point in time. You *are* only seventeen, Leticia. We just don't think you have the mental capabilities to care for the ship or prepare the people for landing. Ultimately, at this stage in your life, you do not possess the necessary leadership qualities. Maybe in ten years, once we've landed…"

He trails off, and then adds something that Letta has to strain to hear. She can barely make out the words, but she is sure he whispers, *"Or not at all."* It's these words that propel her forward, jamming her finger into C.p. Pol's chest.

"Who?" she shouts at him, but he just stares at her, his mouth opening and closing like a bug-eyed fish. She's so close she can see the strings of spit in his mouth and smell his acrid breath. She whirls on the other council members and they all step back, holding their hands up like she's going to attack them. Like she's uncontrollable.

"Who?" she screams, slamming her hand against her forehead. "Who is replacing my mother? Answer me!"

"I am," a voice says loudly and clearly. It's a voice that Letta recognizes. She looks up to see her aunt Claudia standing in the gateway, dressed in prestige white with the captain's badge pinned proudly to her chest. The garish red of the badge is like a blood stain against the white.

"You?" Letta is breathless. She steps forward. Pol places a clammy hand on her shoulder, but she shrugs him off easily. She looks back at the council, her eyes no longer filled with rage, but pleading now. Pleading with them to reconsider, even though the tantrum she has just thrown has guaranteed she will never be fit to lead.

"But she killed my mother," Letta says, and falls to her knees, unable to muster the energy to stand any longer. She can feel the shocked stares of the council boring into her back, but their voices melt together. Through the haze, she hears murmuring. It's Pol's voice, but it sounds so far away, like sound waves radiating off a distant planet.

"Someone send for the Law Officers."

The words register deep inside her and her brain clicks into drive once more. Accusations made against the captain always result in one thing—the accuser being relocated to a lower-level jail cell. Then they are given one of two choices: work as a laborer in the Agriculture Center, or be released to the infinite hands of space. Neither option seems appealing to her. She has no desire to shovel up animal droppings or harvest the modified crops, and even less to relinquish her life. She curses herself silently. She should have kept quiet, maybe investigated more. As it stands, the only evidence she has comes from a source no one else would ever believe.

She looks up at Claudia, expecting to see a frown of worry or anger at being outed. However, Claudia merely looks bored, as if she were accused of murder every other weekend and finds the whole affair tedious. She is flanked, now, by four guards. Each guard is a low-ranking cadet, dressed in the customary Law Office black uniform, standing two-by-two at her side. They hold their e-batons loosely in their hands, the hard sticks humming with electricity. Their eyes dart around the room, on high alert for danger. Letta recognizes one of them: Tess Pol, C.p. Pol's eldest child. Her tightly-bound red hair is unmistakable, as very few people have red hair on board. The only other that Letta can think of is C.p. Pol's son.

The sight of the guards sets a flare of anger rushing through Letta. The very fact that Claudia brought protection to what was supposed to be a simple funeral only further proves Claudia's guilt.

Claudia shifts her hand slightly, brushing the arm of Tess Pol. Tess gestures to the other three guards, and they descend upon Letta like a flock of vultures swooping on their prey. Only after a delayed gesture from Claudia do the hands, hungry for violence, release her.

Claudia smiles that wide, toothy grin of hers. "It's all right, Leticia. Grief makes strangers of us all, as I'm sure you would agree." Though she speaks to Letta, it is clear she's addressing the whole room. Letta can almost feel the tension ease out of the others with each word of poison that spills from Claudia's lips. She scrambles to her feet, pushing away the hands that try to help her up. Unlike everyone else on this ship, she is not one to so easily forgive and forget. Claudia holds her hand out for Letta to take, but she ignores it. Claudia shrugs and clasps her hands together, holding them close to her chest, that suspicious smile never fading from her face.

A figure emerges in the doorway behind Claudia and moves to her left. It is Letta's father. Letta feels herself relax slightly. This is the first Letta has seen of him all day.

Well, that's not strictly true, she corrects herself. He'd been at the funeral, but he was more of a stoic, impregnable presence Letta could only sense behind her. From the whispers of the crowd she knew her father was there, felt him standing close, but she never saw him. Now his face looks vacant, his eyes raw and his lip bloody where he's gnawed it out of stress. It's a shock to see him wear his grief so plainly. Never once has Letta known him be anything but the strong, enduring pillar of the community that she and every other resident aboard can depend on.

In his hands is an instantly-recognizable purple card. Letta has one herself, slotted into her identification band, buried deep in the smooth, dark skin of her forearm. It gives you the name of your Genetic Partner, the only person on board whose DNA is distinct enough from your own as to prevent inbreeding. Her father's should still be inserted into his arm. It should say her mother's name.

Her father only glances at her briefly as he passes the chip to Claudia. Claudia grins, so wide that Letta hopes her cheeks rip apart.

"Ah, thank you, Grant!" Claudia rolls up her sleeve and pushes the chip into the micro slot on her arm. It is such a quick and fluid motion that for a moment Letta does not register what it means. She only stares at Claudia's arm as she rolls down her sleeve.

"Tell me if I'm right, Leticia. Sisters share similar DNA structures, do they not?" It's like Claudia has gouged open Letta's skull. But Letta ignores the obvious question. A child in preschool could answer that. It is not an answer Claudia wants— she wants acknowledgment of what that tiny, innocuous movement actually means. Letta can only combine every bit of rage and grief boiling within her and direct it toward her father in the form of what she hopes is a chilling glare.

"Don't look at me like that, Letta. We have so little time left before we land, and it is our duty to reproduce. You would do better to start thinking of your own Genetic Partner than of mine," her father says in defense, but it sounds as if he is reading off of a cue card, like they are not his words. He's just Claudia's parrot now. Letta has never felt such disgust for her own family before.

Her father has the gall to look indignant as he places his hand on Claudia's shoulder and squeezes it gently. In return Claudia places her own hand on top of his. Letta suddenly has the urge to rip their hands apart, hopefully injuring one of them—preferably Claudia—in the process.

"In this time of strife, we must present a united front to the residents of the *Elsinore*," her father continues, oblivious. "Letta, trust me, this is what your mother would have wanted." Letta almost wants to laugh. Her mother wouldn't have wanted this. She wouldn't have wanted it to seem like she'd never existed. She wouldn't have wanted to see her husband, Letta's father, so desperate to move on that he clings to the next person who can give him any sort of power on board.

Letta is reluctant to admit it, but her father and Claudia do present a united front. Now all they're missing is the grieving daughter who looks to her aunt like a mother. But Letta refuses to play that role. She doesn't understand how they could even expect her to, or how two people could be so obtuse.

"You have no idea what my mother would have wanted," Letta accuses, her skin burning.

"And you do?" Claudia asks. Her question hangs in the air, as sharp as jagged glass. Letta is at once aware of the council behind her and what's left of her family in front of her. She realizes she wants no part of either.

There is a shimmer behind Claudia, like heat rising. Letta's gaze fixes rigidly on the spot. Her surroundings slip away as her eyes focus on the doorway.

Her mother emerges from behind Claudia like a cloud. Her hazy body solidifies and she stands very still. She looks immaculate in her captain's uniform and badge, her curly black hair combed to the side and braided tight in the exact same knot Letta tied her own hair in that morning. Her mother places her index finger on her lips, shushing Letta. Then she floats backward into the hall, beckoning her to follow.

Letta lurches forward, desperate to not lose her view of her mother. She shoves her way between her father and her aunt, pushing their cloying grip away with her hands. There is a small *oof* from her father, but Letta ignores it. If he's injured, he has Claudia to look after him now.

In the hallway she sees her mother disappear into corridor B-6, just around the far corner. Letta picks up the pace running after her. Behind her, Claudia shouts, and then Letta hears the thumping footfalls of the guards following close behind. She speeds up, her own feet slapping the ground loudly.

She passes a group of maintenance workers, but they barely glance at her, so focused are they on their task. She rounds another corner and sees her mother slip into a room just ahead. The Recording Room. Letta's passed by the door with its silver sign often enough. It's locked. It's always locked.

She begins to roll up her sleeve, the noise of the guards growing louder and louder behind her. She presses her bare forearm against the scanner. Nothing happens. She wiggles her arm left to right, and finally the machine beeps.

NEGATIVE ENTRY

She curses. Of course Claudia would have recalibrated the scanners for her own ID band, but how she managed it so quickly is beyond her. Letta's own band used to give her access. Her mother made sure of it. Letta slams her fist against the door in frustration. In a fit of desperation, she tries to pry the door open herself, rolling her shoulders and attempting to jam her fingernails into the plastic sliver between door and wall. Her fingers slip and she bangs her head.

Rubbing the tender spot on her forehead gingerly, she turns around and leans against the cold metal. She can hear the guards clearly now, their breathless chatter as they draw closer. They appear at the end of the hall and shout into their comms.

"We have sights on her, Captain."

"Orders to approach and detain."

Letta notices a slim red box jutting from the wall opposite her. A small window on its front protects a lever. The words printed across the glass spark an idea in Letta: the fire alarm. All doors on this level would automatically unlock, and any open doors would shut immediately. All oxygen on this level would also be sucked out by the vents. She hesitates, her hand poised over the box.

Another shout from the guards spurs her. She punches through the safety glass, yanking the lever down. The vents judder into action, working swiftly to remove oxygen from the nonexistent fire. The light changes from the white glare of the overheads to a slow, beating red as the emergency lights click on and the alarm blares a wailing cry. The fire doors further down the hall slide shut in the guards' faces. Letta grins at her success before pushing open the Recording Room door and locking it swiftly behind her.

Once inside, she relaxes slightly. Her head is throbbing, but she can't tell if it's because she's hurt it or because of the lack of oxygen. She goes to the small slot on the wall present in every room on board and takes out the oxygen mask. There's enough there to last two hours, but she's willing to bet that Claudia will get to her long before the mask runs out.

She briefly considers whether or not the guards got masks, not to mention the maintenance workers down the hall; but she pushes the thought to the back of her head. She can't dwell on that now. She pulls the mask on and activates it, the sudden rush of pure oxygen making her dizzy.

Her hands sting from trying to pry her way in and she shakes them, as if the pain will simply fall out. Blank screens stare down at her from all four walls, looming over her, poised to peck at her the way she has seen birds do to worms on the Earth documentaries.

The main screen is in the center of the far wall. Letta runs her hand under its control panel, searching for the switch. She's been here before, she knows what to do. The familiar hot plastic smell as she turns the monitors on reminds her of the times she visited the place with her mother. Her mother always said that a captain didn't have to know how to fix everything on board the ship herself, but she did have to know how it all worked together. Letta can't help but smile as she remembers the hours she spent here, with nothing but the quiet whir of the machines and the slow rattle of the broken air vent.

The sound is comforting to Letta now, a familiar mechanical chuckle coming from the vent in the ceiling as it sucks the oxygen out. The screen in front of Letta flickers to life and opens onto the control panel. She quickly scans it for anything from her mother.

Reflected against the screen, she sees her mother's apparition point to a folder labeled *Captain's Log*. She opens it and sees that her mother's methodical organizational skills were also present in her filing system. There are hundreds, if not thousands, of dated folders, all rolling back to when her mother was first appointed captain by the Council twenty years ago.

The most recent entry was dated for two nights past. The

night her mother died.

Murdered, Letta corrects herself. The night her mother was murdered. She opens the file and her mother's face fills the screen, alive and full of color. A stark contrast from the specter she's seen wandering the halls.

"Captain's Log. Date: the sixteenth day of the eighth month of the year two thousand five hundred and fifty two. Tenth Captain Leticia Hamilton." Her mother rattles out the list of facts quickly and without emotion. "Today's tasks were completed in full. The nutritional vaccinations were distributed among the general populace efficiently and with little discomfort. The Med Center wishes to improve on the formula, but I am reluctant to give the go-ahead until I have seen further tests. However, the doctors have assured me that certain confidential experiments have been run, and they are just waiting on the follow-up results." Her mother stops suddenly and looks up to the camera. She sighs.

"Are you paying attention?" she says in the voice she usually reserved for when Letta came home with a bad grade from the Education Center. Letta moves closer to the screen. *This is it*, she thinks, *this is the proof I need*. Her mother taps on the glass and Letta lurches back in surprise.

"Letta, are you paying attention? There is something you need to know."

How did her mother know Letta was going to view these recordings?

"This is not a recording, my Letta," her mother says, more kindly this time. Letta pushes away from the control panel and her chair rolls back, toward the door. She grips the arms of the chair tightly in her hands, gaping at the screen. Behind her there is a scrabbling sound as the guards unwittingly replicate Letta's own attempts at breaking into the Recording Room. She doesn't worry about them, though. There is no way they will be able to get in.

The fire alarm stops suddenly and everything is still. Even Letta's mother on the monitor seems to be watching, waiting, listening.

"Letta, let me in," a voice outside says.

Claudia. That creeping sense of dread anchors itself. Claudia can get inside. She only has to scan her arm and the door will unlock. Letta's only chance is to hope it will take another minute for them to reset the alarm and bring the system back to normalcy. There's no time to watch the video. She grabs one of the transfer wires hanging limply from the screen and attaches it to the slot in her arm. She wants to download all of the logs, but she knows she won't have enough time. She can only hope she gets the most recent, at least.

"Letta, you know that I can easily open the door," Claudia says as Letta begins the download, "but I am giving you the chance to open it yourself. Prove to me you are responsible."

1% complete.

The automated intercom crackles to life. "Attention, all *Elsinore* residents. The fire drill has ended. All functions will return shortly. Please be patient as we test our systems. Our safety concerns are your safety concerns."

12% complete.

Letta grips the arms of the chair tightly once more. She longs to bring the log back up again, but she can't risk Claudia walking in and seeing it playing. The door will only hold for so long.

22% complete.

The intercom bell rings again. "Attention, residents. Sections C to E of Upper Deck 1 are now functional."

Letta breathes a sigh of relief. She's in Section B. Safe for another minute. The loading bar jerks forward, and Letta begins to chant in her head, *please finish, please finish.*

65% complete.

What will she say when the guards and Claudia burst in through the door?

74% complete.

What lie will they all buy?

82% complete.

There is only one thing that will work. The one thing that both Claudia and Letta's father want. The one thing Letta wholeheartedly cannot bear to agree to. But she can't see any other way. She has to play the part designed for her, whether she likes it or not. It's the only way to find the truth.

"Attention, all residents. Sections A, B and F on Upper Deck 1 are now functional. This brings us to the end of our emergency test. Thank you for your cooperation. Remember, our safety concerns are your safety concerns."

93% complete.

The door behind Letta crashes open with a thundering boom. Guards flood the area and Letta jumps to attention, keeping her back to the screen, trying to conceal it. There are even more guards now, older ones she vaguely recognizes from patrols of the Law Office quarters during her captain training. She holds her arms behind her and squeezes the cable with one hand, ready to pull it out. It just needs a few more seconds to complete the download.

The guards part like the Red Sea, and Claudia marches through. She raises her hand as if to jab Letta in the chest, but restrains herself; although, Letta notes, considering the pinched look on Claudia's face, it is with much difficulty.

"Your behavior," she rages, "leaves a lot to be desired."

Letta yanks the cable out of her arm quickly and surreptitiously pushes it back under the control panel where

Claudia might not see it.

"What were you doing in here?" Claudia says, her manner heavy with new suspicion. The monitor is still on, all the Captain's Log folders laid out in plain view.

Letta pinches herself, digging her nails into the soft flesh of her stomach hard enough to make her eyes water. She turns to face her aunt, her eyes spilling over, water coursing down her cheeks like genuine tears bred of sadness. She hunches over slightly, looking up at Claudia through her lashes, and sniffs.

"I just wanted to hear her voice again," she whimpers, rubbing her hands over her face to wipe the fake tears away. The guards shift awkwardly in their places, looking anywhere but at Letta. It's similar to the scene that unfolded outside the evacuation chamber only a short while ago, and Letta must control her urge to smirk at their obvious discomfort. Let them squirm. For all intents and purposes, they just spent the last half hour chasing down a grieving daughter.

But you are *a grieving daughter.*

The thought emerges loud and unbidden in Letta's head. She pushes it down almost immediately. Right now she is a thief and a liar, and that is what she needs to focus on. It will have to do.

Letta takes a hesitant step toward Claudia, and she takes the bait. She wraps her arms around Letta, bringing her in close and squeezing her tightly. Letta presses her face into the crook between Claudia's neck and shoulder and shakes her body as if racked by sobs.

"It's okay, it's okay," Claudia murmurs into Letta's hair. "I miss her too."

There's a tug deep between her ribs and her eyes begin to sting. She buries her face in closer. To Letta's surprise, it's actually comforting. She squeezes her eyes shut and gasps like she's drowning. She shouldn't feel this way, but she can't help it.

She can't tell, now, if she's playing a part or if this is reality. All she wants is for someone to scoop her up and tell her what to do. What is she supposed to do?

She pulls apart from Claudia, scrubbing her face viciously, and looks around for her mother. She would know what to do. She told her what to do before, and she can do it again.

Her father appears behind Claudia. He reaches out for Letta. She flinches as he strokes her cheek, and a flash of something like disappointment crosses his face. But it disappears as quickly as it came.

"Letta, I want you to visit the Med Center," Claudia says in her most gentle voice, the one reserved for speaking with children or the elderly. "You don't have to do it now—or even tomorrow—but I really think you could benefit from talking to someone, okay?"

"Unless, of course, you would prefer to talk to me...?" Her father trails off as Letta nods her head. She takes his hand and he squeezes it. She's reminded of all the times she walked to the Education Center, hand in hand, with her father. They would pass by the observation deck and take a moment to look out the wide, clear windows at the universe beyond. Galaxies unfurling, being created and destroyed—it was all happening out there. The universe is infinite and ever-expanding, so why not imagine the inevitable?

Even at that age, she knew she was but one of thousands on board a tin can in a galaxy that did not care whether or not the human race survived. When Letta got too scared by these thoughts, when the black emptiness right outside seemed only to be the yawning maw of an unseen beast, he would take the time to squeeze her hand and tell her that everything would be okay. That he would protect her.

The gesture now brings up these same old feelings, but Letta can't make herself trust them anymore. She just keeps nodding her head and hoping she won't be punished.

"I'd like that," she says, wondering if they can tell that every word is a lie.

"I don't want your life to change, Letta," Claudia continues as though neither Letta nor her father had spoken at all. "You and your father may both still live in the captain's quarters."

Letta can almost hear her father's sigh of relief. She struggles to not recoil. He's so desperate to remain in the best housing he'd sell himself out to Claudia. But Letta smiles broadly, because she knows that is what Claudia wants to see.

"Thank you so much, Claudia," she replies in as sincere a voice as she can muster.

"I will, however, also be moving into the quarters. You understand, of course, Letta. One must live with their Genetic Partner, no? Eventually you'll be given new rooms, but for now, we shall be together." She runs a hand across Letta's cheek, wiping away a tear that was not there.

"I agree," her father says. "Families should be together in times like these."

A knot tightens in the pit of Letta's gut, and she feels nausea rear its ugly head inside her. She smiles brightly despite her sick stomach. If the price of staying in the rooms she grew up in is having to live with her mother's murderer, Letta would rather live on Deck J by the recyclable sewage waste.

"Now, unfortunately, come the terms of your punishment," Claudia goes on. "I'm afraid I cannot, in good conscience, let someone—even my own niece—get away with such insubordination."

"Well, surely it's understandable, Claudia," her father interjects. "Everything that has happened in the last two days… It must have clouded her judgment."

"Oh, relax, Grant." Claudia smiles and pats Letta's father on the arm like they're old partners, like they've been together for years. Everything Claudia does seems to jab into Letta sharply, gouging like a knife with every gesture, however slight. "Letta, I'm confining you to our quarters until such time as you can compose yourself adequately in public."

Letta's face burns. The last time she was reprimanded like this was when she was fourteen years old and her mother caught her skipping class and goofing off in the halls with friends during inspection. She's not a giggling schoolgirl now, but Claudia's punishment has reduced her to one in an instant. She doesn't even need to look at the guards' faces to know that they are all smirking to one another. Not two days ago, she was performing troop inspections on them with her mother, and now she's getting a dressing-down in front of them.

"Now, Officer Tess Pol will accompany you back to our floor and guard you once inside."

Letta's jaw clenches involuntarily. Of course it would be Tess to escort her. Just another way for Claudia to spy on her, sending her right-hand-man's daughter to follow her around. She realizes that her hands have curled into fists, and she relaxes them quickly, smoothing them against her trouser legs. She grips the material to stop her hands from clenching into fists again and gives Claudia a curt nod.

Claudia smiles and it's like she's painted a target on her face, just begging Letta to punch it. She brushes past Claudia before her body does something she will only regret. Her father touches her arm softly as she leaves, but she can't look at him right now. Even his touch makes her nausea worse.

Behind her she feels Tess' presence, and, as if on cue, the girl marches up alongside Letta.

The two move toward the elevator on Deck B, Letta shuffling

along at a snail's pace so that Tess' marching looks even more ridiculous. The pairing makes Letta bristle, and she knows it's the same for Tess. The only difference is that Tess masks her emotions quickly, and Letta no longer cares how she appears. There is no point in remaining passive in the face of annoyance any longer. Only a captain needs to do that, and Letta has no chance of ever becoming that anymore.

She has no idea what she *is* anymore.

They ascend the elevator to the private Council floors on Deck A. Tess knows this place well; she used to live here with her father and brother before requesting cadet duty.

Tess exits the lift first, still playing the role of guard even though this floor is one of the most well-monitored on the ship. Letta tries to pass her, but Tess stops suddenly and her baton hums to life once again.

"State your name, profession and access level," she says clearly and slowly. Letta sidesteps around her and spots Tia leaning against the door to the captain's quarters. She's unmistakable in that navy jumpsuit that she never seems to want to take off, even though it's spotted with oil marks. When Tia sees Letta she lifts her arm to her forehead in mock salute.

"I said, state your name, profession and access level," Tess demands again. She steps forward, brandishing her baton as if she's planning to beat the information out of Tia. Letta rolls her eyes and walks in front of Tess.

"It's all right. I know her. Stand down, cadet." She waves her down, but Tess doesn't move.

"Ms. Hamilton, please stand behind me. It's protocol. I need this information to verify your guest."

Sensing Letta's impending diatribe, Tia interjects, "It doesn't matter, Lett. Honestly, it's fine, really." She shrugs her shoulders in a nonchalant manner, but Letta knows she's embarrassed even if her face doesn't turn red. She stands awkwardly in her dirty clothes, fidgeting, her hands anxiously tugging at her buttons, twisting them in and out of their holes. "My name is Tia Hilario—"

"I *said*, stand down, cadet," Letta repeats, ignoring both Tess and Tia. She crosses her arms and positions herself between the two. Tia shifts restlessly behind her, and for a split second, a look of uncertainty flickers across Tess' face; but it is swiftly replaced by that familiar expression of smug superiority that Letta recognizes even from when they were children in class.

"With all due respect, Ms. Hamilton, you are not the captain, and I do not take orders from you," Tess asserts herself.

"With all due respect, *Tess*," Letta says, forgoing the girl's title on purpose and eliciting a dirty look from her, "I am still related to the captain, and you will do as I say or I'll make sure you do nothing more than guarding the junior bathroom in the Education Center until you die. How does that sound? Do you want to be a bathroom attendant for the rest of your pathetic life?"

Tess hesitates. The hand holding the baton lowers just a tiny fraction, but it's enough for Letta to feel safe enough to turn. She stomps to the door and scans her arm against the lock panel. The door glides open and she marches in, grabbing Tia by the arm and dragging her in after her.

"At least let me scan her ID band."

"No chance. And you can wait out here. Maybe you'll see your father! Now *that* would be an interesting conversation that I wouldn't want to miss." Letta scans her arm against the door again and it glides closed on the satisfying scowl on Tess' face. Letta laughs gleefully and lets go of Tia.

"That was a bit harsh, Lett. Everyone knows she doesn't get on with her dad," Tia says, rubbing her arm.

"Everyone but her father, actually," Letta says. "I wonder what he'd say if he saw her waiting outside. Maybe I should call him up…"

"If you did, he'd probably think it was a great honor bestowed upon his kid. He's not going to know you refused to let her in."

"Ugh, you're right," Letta groans, rolling her eyes.

"As per usual," Tia says, laughing, and Letta smacks her playfully on the shoulder.

"Careful! Someone's getting a big head now they're in engineer core."

"You can thank your mom for that!" Tia beams and Letta freezes. It dawns on Tia what she has said, and she clasps a hand over her mouth as if to catch the words. But they're already out now, floating and twisting around Letta tightly.

"Oh, Lett, I'm so sorry. I didn't mean to."

Letta shrugs and pastes another mechanical smile on her face. She knows it probably looks rigid and uncomfortable, but she needs it there anyway. It's like it's protecting her.

"It's fine. I know what you meant," she says, brushing off Tia's comments.

"I came up to apologize for not being at the funeral. They only allowed Decks A and B to attend…"

"I know, Tia. Look, it's absolutely fine. I'm fine, everything's fine."

"You're saying 'fine' a lot," Tia points out. "Usually people who are fine don't feel the need to say it over and over."

Letta rolls her eyes again and throws her hands up in exasperation. "Well, how else am I going to convince you? If I say I'm not fine, will you believe I'm fine?" she shouts, and regrets the outburst almost immediately. Tia just raises an eyebrow and purses her lips, crossing her arms firmly across her chest like a pouting child.

"I guess 'fine' is the word of the day," she surmises, her lips twitching. The right side tugs up, and in return Letta feels her own lips turn up. Letta half-grins at Tia and in response Tia smiles back. It's the only smile today that Letta has been glad to see. Letta leans over to Tia and pinches her oil-stained clothes.

"Not sure this is the most appropriate outfit to wear in your captain's quarters. You are so covered in oil, it's even on your face." She giggles and points to a streak of black over Tia's olive-colored cheek. Tia licks her hand and rubs it across her face, which only spreads the oil streak around.

"Did I get it?" she says, her entire right cheek now just a smudge of oil. Letta laughs and shakes her head.

"Not quite."

Tia laughs, too, but there is something odd in her eyes. "You sure you're 'you-know-what'?"

Letta half-grins and nods. "I am. Really. Anyway," she says, swiftly changing the subject, "I have something incredibly important to show you."

"Oh, well, seeing as it's *incredibly* important. If it was just important, I might not bother."

Letta rolls up her sleeve. She turns to the comm-screen on the wall behind her, almost tripping over a small box as she does so.

"What the—" She looks around the room, seeing a few more boxes strewn across the floor. Two perch on the side of the dining table and another is shoved under the couch in front of the comm-screen. She sighs. These must be Claudia's. Considering how fast she'd changed the access codes, Letta is surprised Claudia hadn't moved in an hour before she'd even murdered her sister.

Letta breathes in sharply. Even thinking those words makes her angry.

She bends over the one nearest to her and presses the button on the side to open it. The lid unfurls, revealing a suction bag filled with material. Claudia's clothes, she presumes. The box beside it, meanwhile, is packed with old-fashioned paper books. The titles mean nothing to her, but she picks one of them up anyway. There's a name scrawled on the first page that's difficult to read. Letta's never been very good at reading handwriting. Not much cause to learn it. Very few people use anything other than the comm-screen keyboards, or the communication system in the ID bands, to write.

Despite this, Letta is sure the wide script is a name. She drags her finger underneath, trying to sound out each letter in her head as she goes. When she makes the name out, she almost drops the book.

It's her mother's.

She drops hard onto her knees and rips open the bag of fabric. They're all her mother's clothes. She opens another box and sees all the small velvet snap-lids containing her mother's awards.

So this is what a life boils down to. All your achievements, all your accomplishments, fitting neatly in little boxes to be stored away and forgotten about.

"Are you okay?" Tia asks hesitantly. The constant questioning annoys Letta, but she reminds herself that Tia is just worried about her. She nods her head in affirmation and steps over the boxes, picking her way to the screen. She flicks it on and scans her arm, inputting the information wirelessly. The screen wavers and a box with Letta's most recently downloaded files appears. She accesses the logs, and the playback function opens onscreen.

If she only had a comm-screen in her room. As it is, Claudia could walk in at any moment and there'd be no warning, since the housing chambers on this level are all soundproofed. But there's no helping it. Letta opens the video she watched earlier, and pauses it just as her mother opens her mouth to speak. She feels Tia move behind her and nudge her in the back.

"What is this?"

"The Captain's Log. I, uh, borrowed it earlier," Letta says sheepishly. She turns the volume up on the screen, her finger hovering over the play button.

"Hmm, 'borrowed'—sure. Maybe I am rubbing off on you."

"Something like that. Anyway, you won't believe what I found," Letta says. "Actually, you definitely won't believe what I've been seeing for the past two days."

Tia's eyebrows knit together in confusion, reminding Letta of an image of a furry caterpillar. Tia would not appreciate this insight, though, so she keeps it to herself and presses play. The video starts just like before. Her mother states her name and speaks briefly of the nutritional vaccinations all residents are required to take, since there are only so many nutrients the human body can gather from modified crops and water that's been recycled so many times that people joke that their glass of water is probably the same their great-great-great-grandmother drank.

"…However, the doctors have assured me that certain confidential experiments have been run and they are just waiting on the follow-up results." Her mother stops suddenly once again and looks up at the camera.

"Watch this now," Letta whispers, pointing to the screen. Her mother sighs and pinches the bridge of her nose. This is where she spoke to Letta before. She waits for her mother to address her once more, eager to include Tia in the discovery. Her mother clears her throat.

"I have decided to include myself in the human trials. As captain, I cannot in good conscience request others to volunteer when I refuse to do so." Her mother looks down, presumably at her desk, and Letta hears the rustle of papers and the clink of glass on glass. This is not what happened in the video before. This is not what's supposed to happen.

Her mother finally finds what she was looking for and holds up a small vial filled with a thick orange liquid. There is something printed on the side of the vial, but it's too small for the camera to pick up.

"This is the first of the new doses." Her mother twists the vial over in her hands and in the background Letta hears the hiss of the doors gliding open. Her mother looks up over the camera and laughs lightly. Letta's fingernails dig into her forearm. It doesn't hurt, but it helps to distract her from the brightness in her mother's face. How can someone go from this—laughing and working, completely normal—to the pile of ash Letta saw disappear into space?

How can anything matter, when we all end up the same way?

"Claudia," her mother says, still smiling, "what are you doing here?"

Letta squeezes her eyes shut. She can't do this. She can't watch this anymore. This is it. This is the proof she needs. She feels a cold chill spread throughout her body, like clammy hands running over her skin, even though she's sweating buckets. The knot in her stomach tightens; her breath comes in short little bursts through her teeth.

There's mumbling in the back of the video, the microphone only picking up pieces of her mother's speech, and Letta's eyes shoot open. Her mother is cut off by the screen wavering. The sound turns to static and the image warps, turning her mother into some kind of grotesque monster, her face swirling into a blurry, black hole.

"Letta! Letta!" her mother wails from the twisting screen, her voice just as mangled as the image is. And just as sudden as it started, it stops, like calm waters after a storm in the documentaries she spent hours watching as a kid. Her mother stares, unblinking, out of the screen, locking steady eyes with Letta. Letta presses her hand so tightly against the edge of the screen that it cramps.

"She did this to me, Letta. To us. You are the rightful captain of the *Elsinore* and I should no more be dead than you. Don't take anything she gives you. Stop her, Letta. Swear to me you'll stop her!"

"I swear!"

Letta presses her forehead against the screen. The sensor recognizes the touch, and the image freezes before fading to black. There's a lull where both Letta and Tia stare at the blank screen in silence before the video judders and loops back to the start. Letta raises a shaking hand and shuts off the screen. She blinks, her eyes pricking with hot tears.

"I don't understand, Lett. What—what is this?"

"That's not what it was like when I saw it earlier. It was… different." Letta's voice falters and she wipes her eyes quickly. It was harder to watch the video than she had thought. There has to be more to the video than that. Letta steps away from the screen, her hand aching, and collapses backward onto the couch, sinking deep into the pillows. She closes her eyes. Her brain throbs with exhaustion even though her heart is racing.

Tia sits at the edge of the couch by Letta's feet and pulls Letta's legs onto her lap, resting her arms on top of them. They sit like that for a few minutes, with no sound but their breathing and the generic whir and hum of the electronics in the room.

"I keep seeing her. Everywhere I go, she's there. Watching me. Waiting for me to do something," Letta admits, the quiet crumbling around her. She lays her arm across her face, blocking out the overheads.

"Your mother? Are you sure you're okay?"

"Stop asking me if I'm okay. My answer's not gonna change." Letta lifts her head up to glare at Tia. "I'm not making this up. It's her. I know it's her. You watched the same video as me." She props herself up on her elbows. "You saw her, right? You saw her talking to me?"

Tia sucks on her cheeks, nodding quickly. "When did this start?" she asks, her face fraught with uneasiness.

"Two days ago."

It was late at night when she first saw her. Letta was just drifting off to sleep when her mother came into her bedroom. She was dressed for work, although it was well past midnight, and the lights in Letta's room had dimmed to mimic the night on Earth. Her mother had sat at the end of Letta's bed, and that's when she noticed it: the blood leaking out from her mother's ears, eyes, nose and mouth, blooming on the white uniform like flowers as it rolled down and dripped off her face. She remembers asking her mother what was wrong, and the long silence that followed as her mother did nothing but stare at her. No reaction, not even so much as gagging as the blood dripped from her mouth.

Letta had tried to help, but each time she moved toward her mother, she was always just that little bit out of reach, a millimeter out of her grasp. She had tried to access the comm system on her ID band but it—and the lights in the room—were disabled. She tried the door but that, too, was not working. She was locked inside.

It was only then that her mother opened her mouth, the blood pooled inside dripping out like syrup as she spoke. She told Letta that she'd been murdered, and that the killer was Claudia.

It had to have been real. How could she have dreamed

something like that up before she even knew that her mother had, in fact, died? As reluctant as Letta was to believe it, her mother had to have been a ghost.

She saw her two more times after that. Trailing down empty corridors, the lights flickering as she passed them. What else could she do but follow?

"I think my mother's ghost has been visiting me." She waits, holding her breath, for Tia to burst out laughing. To tell Letta that she is insane. Instead, Tia places a firm hand on Letta's leg. It feels like a tether connecting Letta to reality.

"If you say you saw your mother's ghost, then I believe you."

"You 'believe' me?" Letta repeats, incredulous. "Do you not believe yourself? Your own eyes? What did you see on the screen?"

Tia gulps and opens her mouth to speak, but Letta's ID band vibrates, distracting her. She presses one of the buttons embedded just underneath her skin, opening the holo-screen. A new message. Letta groans as she reads it.

"Look," she says, showing the screen to Tia. "Claudia made me an appointment with the Med Center tomorrow."

"Well, maybe that's a good thing," Tia suggests. Letta scoffs.

"I think it's time you left, Tia. If you see Claudia on your way out, you can tell her from me that I am not, under any circumstances, going to some useless doctor's appointment."

"I cannot believe Claudia is making me go to this appointment," Letta growls under her breath as she leaves the captain's quarters, flanked by two guards. Claudia has upped the security detail since last night. Apparently she didn't appreciate that little episode with Tess yesterday, because Tess is nowhere to be found now. Letta smirks at the thought. Maybe Tess really did get demoted.

She sees the elevator doors ahead closing and darts away from the guards."Hey, hold the door!" She slips into the elevator and presses the button to close the door. The guards react slowly. By the time they've rushed after her, the door is sliding closed in their faces.

Letta laughs out loud, and the other person in the elevator laughs, too. She turns to thank him, but the smile fades from her face when she sees that familiar shock of red hair on top of a scrawny boy no older than she.

"Phell," she says by way of greeting, shifting uncomfortably from foot to foot. Phell starts to wave at her and a thin book slips from his fingers. On impulse Letta jerks forward to catch it. She hands it back to him, reading the printed title. The words are instantly familiar.

"Hey, is that mine?" she asks, taking the small volume back and flipping it open to the first page. Her name is stamped on the inside, as well as the age she was when she first read it. A boring educational book filled with words she couldn't understand and romantic poetry she couldn't care less about. She'd probably donated it to the library years ago and forgot.

"Uh, yes. It was in that box of books you gave me. Remember? It was at the Genetic Partner Ceremony. You said it was your favorite book," he adds, his cheeks slowly turning pink.

"No, I didn't," she says sharply. She opens the book to the first poem. "Why would this be my favorite book? Listen." She begins to read aloud, *"How doth I describe the impossibly sweet perfumes of my love?"* She pretends to vomit.

"You did give that to me," Phell says firmly. "It was a good book. You can have it back now, though, if you want it."

"I don't want it, and I did not give this to you." She pinches the first page between her index finger and thumb and rips it out, crumpling it up and throwing it at Phell. "I did not give this to you either." She tears out another page and throws it at him. "Or this." Another page ripped out, crumpled and thrown.

Phell flinches as it bounces off his head. He moves to press the button to open the doors and escape, but Letta jumps ahead of him, running her hand along all the buttons. The elevator begins its descent as Letta rips out another page. Phell is so close that she can smell him, a mixture of the scent of library books and the pungent stench that clings to everyone in his family. She grabs his sweater and shoves the crumpled paper down his top.

"Do not lie to me again, Genetic Partner," she hisses, then loosens her grip. He twists out of her hands and backs away, smoothing his sweater. "What's the point of Genetic Partnerships, anyway, if we're breeding the likes of you? There's no point at all. We should just get rid of them." She thinks of her father and that purple card in his hands. "Most of them, anyway."

The elevator dings and the doors open on Deck B. Letta marches out, the ruined book still in her hands, and walks straight into C.p. Pol.

"Oh, my—Leticia! Apologies. I did not see you there," he booms, straightening his white uniform. "I see you and Phell have been chatting! What's that in your hands, Leticia? Are you reading? It's wonderful to see you indulging in old pleasures, right, Phell? I remember when Leticia gave you that book—"

"Stop. Just stop." Letta cannot take any more of his senseless prattle. His voice is hammering out a new headache for her.

C.p. Pol looks taken aback. "Ah, yes, well, all right then. In any case, what is the book about, Leticia, dear?" he lumbers on, undaunted. Letta's anger radiates off of her like a supernova about to explode.

"Why don't you just read it yourself?" she retorts, and throws the book at his chest. Before it even hits the floor, she's disappeared down the hall.

Before she realizes it, she's arrived at the Med Center on the main deck. A med worker ushers her in quickly, and she's made to undress in one of the small examination pods. The worker seals her clothes into a suction bag and slips it into the honeycomb of recesses along the lower part of the wall.

The white ceiling curves overhead, giving Letta the sensation that she is trapped inside a bubble. She's never liked these rooms. The circular walls always feel like they're closing in around her, squeezing her into a tiny ball. It doesn't help that the room smells faintly of vomit and bleach.

She changes into the thin white shift the med worker left for her and sits on the examination table, scowling.

The swollen belly of the apprentice doctor, a heavily pregnant woman named Rosa, precedes her as she waddles into the pod. Her lab coat no longer closes over her, so she lets it hang open, exposing her rotund stomach in all its globe-like glory. She greets Letta cheerily and Letta grunts in response. Before, when Letta was training to be captain, she would have asked Rosa about her pregnancy; but why bother with niceties now?

"How have you been, hon?" Rosa says, opening one of the glass cabinets along the wall. "Claudia tells me you've been having trouble adjusting to the new order of things." She roots around and pulls out a pack of slender syringes.

"It's only been three days," Letta reminds her. Rosa pauses, the syringe poised in midair. She squints at Letta, then slips on her glasses, which had been swinging on a metal chain around her neck.

"Are you sure? I could have sworn it was four… Oh, well, never mind. That's just pregnancy-brain for you!" She laughs. "Now hold out your arm, please." Letta obliges immediately, her body used to obeying orders. Rosa flicks the skin hard to make a vein rise and Letta winces.

"Now, that didn't really hurt," Rosa coos. She pushes the needle in, drawing the blood out. Then she removes the vial and places it into the Body Anomaly Detector. Letta recognizes it from one of her mother's detailed tours. The blood pools on the floor of the small machine and begins to spin, the red liquid separating as the device tests it. It stops just as quickly as it began. Rosa reads the small bright screen, tutting and tapping her nails against it.

"Well, this explains your outburst yesterday."

"How do you know about that? You weren't even there."

"Everyone's heard about the girl who would be captain," Rosa says, peering at Letta over her glasses. "Now, Letta. It appears you have a severe vitamin-D deficiency. This would explain your irritability, as well as any feelings of depression you may be experiencing. It's standard on a ship with no natural sunlight for something like this to happen. That's why we take the nutritional vaccinations, to combat deficiencies like yours. Though I've never seen levels so low before. When was your last inoculation?"

Letta shrugs sheepishly. She knows it was months ago. Rosa simply opens her patient records and quickly inputs Letta's name.

"I have been taking oral supplements, though. My mom gave me some of hers," Letta points out, though this is not strictly true. She only just started taking the pill about a week ago, after a bout of lightheadedness.

Rosa frowns and purses her lips. "They're not really meant for sharing—four months?! You've not had a vaccination in four months?" she exclaims, reading the onscreen info. Letta's face grows hot. She's always managed to find a way to avoid the Med Center. There's always something important to do on the days when Deck A residents have their assigned appointments. No one questions the captain's daughter.

"Lida! Come in here, you have to see these vitamin-D levels! They're unbelievable!" Rosa sticks her head out of the pod door, then turns backs to Letta. "She always turns the volume off her comm when she's with patients, and she forgets to turn it back up."

There's a muffled reply and then Letta hears the slap of feet in the corridor. Closer now, Letta can make out the low, gravelly voice of Lida, an official doctor and Rosa's Genetic Partner.

"What did you say, Lida? I can't hear you though the walls."

"I said, what are they like?" Lida replies, walking into the room. She is tying her dark hair back, and her lab coat is zipped up tightly on her straight-lined body. "Letta! Haven't seen you for a while!"

Letta just nods and gives her a quick grin. Rosa gestures to the results and Lida leans in close to inspect them.

"My God, how are you not dead?" she gasps, then cringes, laughing awkwardly as Rosa jams a finger into her back. "Oh, poor choice of words. Sorry."

"It's fine," Letta replies. If there is one thing she's looking forward to, it's people not apologizing to her anymore. Or asking if she's okay. Or forcing her to go to ridiculous medical examinations…

"Are you paying attention, Letta?" The voice is not the high-pitched squeak of Rosa, nor Lida's deep tone. If anything, it sounds like her mother.

Letta jerks alert, her eyes darting around the room, searching for any reflective surface. If her mother appeared to her through a comm-screen, she could probably appear to her in the sheen of a scalpel, too. She could even be in the room right now. Letta swears under her breath. It couldn't come at a worse possible time. There's no way she can just run out of the pod after her mother if she chooses to lead her somewhere else. Her shift would be left flapping open at the back for all the ship to see.

"Ship to Letta! Are you awake, hon?" Rosa snaps her fingers in front of Letta's face and Letta blinks, her eyes stinging. "Jeez, thought we lost you there for a sec!" Rosa says and elbows Lida in the chest. Lida nods solemnly, but she can't hide that smirk on her lips. Everything is funny to these two when they get together.

"I'm going to give you a nutritional vaccination now. It's a new treatment, stronger than the usual ones, but I think it's the best course of action considering your particular vitamin levels."

"Oh, yeah," Letta says, "I've heard about those new vaccs."

Rosa and Lida exchange a furtive glance.

"You have?" Rosa asks, pushing her glasses further up the bridge of her nose. "I didn't think Claudia had told anyone but the med workers. She only approved it for certain members of the general public yesterday."

"Claudia? No, I heard it from my mother. It was in her logs." Letta supposes it doesn't matter who knows she accessed the Recording Room, now. If Rosa has heard about yesterday's events, she'll have heard about that, too; and if Rosa knows, then Lida certainly knows.

Rosa and Lida exchange another look and Letta clicks her tongue against her teeth, growing more irritated by the second.

"Will you stop looking at each other like that?" she snaps, then pauses briefly, considering. "Isn't Claudia moving forward on these vaccines a bit… fast? I only heard about them from the Captain's Log, and it wasn't recorded all that long ago."

"She just wants to move things along as quickly as she can. Get the ship back to normal." Rosa grabs Letta's arm, holding it straight.

"That's what I keep hearing," Letta mutters. Lida pulls out a new syringe, filling it with a thick, orange-colored liquid from a vial from her pocket. It looks just like it did in the video.

Rosa flicks the vein on Letta's arm and Lida inserts the syringe, pushing the liquid in. It hurts at first, but as the syringe empties, the pain subsides. Rosa tapes a piece of cotton wool over the prick of blood.

"All done!" she says brightly as Lida disposes of the syringe, along with her gloves, down the chute to the incinerator. Rosa pulls off her gloves, too, throwing them into the chute before it closes.

"Now, then, would you like to talk about anything?" Rosa eases herself into the office chair and folds her hands over her baby bump. "Such as not getting chosen to be captain? I know that was something you'd wanted for a long time."

"No. I don't care about that anymore. I've just been having bad dreams." That's the easiest way to explain what she has been seeing. But her mother's ghost is more than a bad dream. Dreams, like shadows, disappear come morning. What Letta has been seeing is more like a demon. A demon that will not leave her alone.

But part of her does not want it to.

"Bad dreams," Rosa says. "Well, we have sleeping pills for that. You can pick them up on your way out." Letta's not sure, but she thinks she can detect a note of disappointment in her tone. But she moves on. "So, tell me, how are your dates with your Genetic Partner?"

Letta thinks about her encounter with Phell in alarm, but relaxes when she remembers that even they couldn't have heard about what happened in the elevator yet.

"They're not exactly 'dates,' are they?" she scoffs. Calling them "dates" was just the pathetic attempt of a Councilperson, long since dead, to replicate the mating rituals on Earth. Dates had been useful there, since you could pick and choose who you went out with. But here? There's no choice. You just have to go along with it.

Rosa laughs. "They were dates for Lida and I! Do you remember our first one?" She nudges Lida.

"Ha, yeah. It was during my transition. You were the first person I told my new name to."

"And now we've got this lovely coming along!" Rosa rubs her stomach fondly and Lida smiles, reaching over to place a hand on Rosa's.

"Yeah, well, you two actually like each other. Phell couldn't be more different than me."

"That's just Phell. He's shy. And you don't have to *like* your Partner anyway. You just have to reproduce with them. Just get your breeding out of the way early, and then you can spend your time with whomever you want. That's what most people do, anyway."

"True. You could be with Tia, if you wanted."

"What do you mean? Tia and I are not—I'm not interested in her. Though I can tell by your smirks you don't believe me. I'm not interested in anyone. I don't want to be with anyone."

Lida holds her hands up. "All right, no need to jump down our throats." She chuckles. "Though I think someone needs to do a different kind of jumping down a certain someone's throat."

Letta clenches and unclenches her fist. Why does everyone think she's going to attack them? You poke a guy *one time* and suddenly you're labeled violent.

Rosa says, "Okay, hon, but the library is holding a film screening tonight, and that would be a really fantastic place to go with Phell. Why not give him a chance? You might find you actually like him. We're going, aren't we, Lida?"

"Yes, and I know for a fact your father and aunt are going too, Letta. She said as much when she dropped off the vaccines yesterday."

That catches Letta's attention. "Are there many going?" she asks.

"Well, it's in the upper library, so only Decks A to C are permitted, thankfully." Lida muses. "Why do you ask?"

An idea creeps along inside Letta's mind. Decks A to C hold a lot of people. If Letta exposes what Claudia has done in front of all those people, they will have to pay attention. Claudia can't order *everyone* into confinement.

Letta slides off the edge of the table and runs a hand through her hair, her fingers getting tangled in the knots. If Claudia is there, it will be the perfect time to out her. She has the proof. She has the video. She just needs to show it to everyone. Tia will help her.

"Can I leave now?" she asks.

The two women shrug in unison. It's always so strange when they do things like that. They are so in tune with each other, it is sometimes like they are just one person.

"I don't see why not. But if you are going tonight, ask your G.P. You know it is our duty to—"

"Yeah, yeah, 'our duty to reproduce'. Can I have my clothes back now?"

Rosa purses her lips. "Fine, go. Lida, will you get her clothes for her? I can't reach down, not with this belly."

Lida pulls out the suction bag with Letta's uniform folded neatly inside.

"Oh, and don't worry, Letta. We won't repeat any of this to your family," Lida says as she hands the bag over.

"Fine, great." Letta wrestles her clothes out of the bag, no longer paying attention to either Rosa or Lida. The two women dip out of the pod and Letta tugs her clothes on. Then she opens her contacts on her comm and scrolls down to Tia's name. Her finger hovers over the call button, unsure, but she ultimately presses forward.

"What do you want? I'm working." Tia's voice is tetchy, and Letta knows instantly that she's not been forgiven for her outburst last night.

"I know how we can out Claudia," Letta explains eagerly. "You have to meet me in the library tonight."

"You don't have any proof. If a ghost's testimony is all you're going on, then you've got nothing. I mean, you don't even know how she died."

"I have an idea. And I also have the Captain's Log. That's all I need right now."

"That doesn't prove anything. The video cuts off before anything useful happens."

"But Claudia doesn't know that." Letta lets this idea wash over Tia, dousing her in its brilliance. Claudia will corner herself with minimal help. "Let's see her escape the truth then."

For once, the library floor is buzzing with activity. The shelves, with their multitude of organic books, are pushed to the far walls to make room for the stools dragged here from the canteen by the overworked servers. The Main Deck would have been better equipped to deal with such a large influx of people, but the library is in possession of a far superior projector.

Letta leans over the railings from the topmost level of the library. Behind her, Tia is setting up the projector. The log has already been swapped in for whatever movie was to be shown. All that's left now is for Letta to be on the lookout for Claudia's arrival.

"I still don't see how this is going to work," Tia says, her voice muffled. She's hoisted the projector up just high enough to see underneath, and is busy fitting cables into their spots.

"Just trust me. And remember to shut off the video before it loops around again. Claudia'll give herself away. I know she will."

"But what if she doesn't?"

"She will. She has to."

Tia gives no reply to Letta's unwavering determination. Out of the corner of her eye, Letta sees the gray head of C.p. Pol bent low in conversation with Claudia. Letta's father follows behind them as the three walk through the crowd toward the elevated seats just underneath Letta. She leans even further out over the railing.

"Claudia! Oh, Claudia!" she calls in a singsong voice. Several people in the crowd strain their necks to see her, and Letta waves at each in turn. Claudia skims the room and Letta laughs, a barking sort of sound. "Up here, Claud!"

Her father, Pol and Claudia all lean back to see her. Her father claps his hands together and calls her down. Letta swings around the railing and dashes down the slim spiral staircase, taking the steps two at a time. She stops, breathless, inches from Claudia.

"It's wonderful to see you in such high spirits, love," her father beams, "isn't it, Claudia?"

"Indeed it is, Grant." She, too, smiles then. "I take it your appointment earlier went well? No more bad dreams, I hope."

Letta clenches her jaw. "Oh, it went very well indeed. It's where I got the idea to come here!" She sweeps her arms out, smacking Pol squarely in the chest. He grunts and moves to sit down. Taking his cue, both Claudia and Letta's father go to take their seats.

"Come sit by me, Letta," her father says, patting the empty

stool beside him. It's only two away from Claudia, and if she sits there, she won't be able to see Claudia's reaction when the log is shown instead of the film. She scans the room, looking for somewhere else to sit. She spots Lida helping Rosa. Rosa catches her eye, waving maniacally and gesturing to the right. Letta turns her head in that direction and spies Phell entering the library all by himself.

"I can't," Letta grins. "I've already promised Phell I'd join him." She skips through the crowd, excitement bubbling up inside her the closer and closer it gets to the time for the movie to start. She sidles up to Phell, looping her arm though his. He jolts with surprise, but she grips him even tighter.

"Phell! There you are! I was beginning to think I would have no one to watch this with." She rests against him. "Shall we get a private booth?"

"Uh, there are no private booths. Those are just kitchen chairs."

"Good eye, Phell. I was only joking." She leads him to the row of seats closest to one of the bookshelves. "Let's sit here." She sits down and looks at her aunt and father. Her father nods in their direction and leans toward Pol whispering conspiratorially.

It's a good view, but not quite right. Letta leaps to her feet and moves two chairs down, dragging Phell so forcefully he nearly falls into her lap. She barks another laugh, a strange, manic sound that is becoming as familiar as breathing to her.

"You're very happy this evening," Phell notes, positioning himself beside her. He wriggles in her vice-like grip, then resigns himself to the fact she is not letting go of him any time soon.

"Well, why wouldn't I be?" she proclaims, just loud enough for Claudia and her father to overhear. "Just look how happy my family is! And my mother's corpse hardly cold!"

Those that overhear her halt in their conversations, straining their ears to pick up any gossip. A fixed smile is plastered on Claudia's face, but she tics her head to the side like a dog listening to an inaudible sound.

Pol stands up abruptly, drawing everyone's attention to him. "Perhaps we should roll the film now."

"Yes!" Letta shouts. She leans back, cupping her mouth with her hands to make her voice carry farther. "Tia! Put the movie on for these lovely people!"

Tia's head pops over the railings and she gives a big thumbs up to a scattering of applause. The hum of conversation dims as the overheads do and a square of blue light appears on the bleached far wall. There's a low rustle as people settle where they sit. Letta clutches Phell's arm even tighter, leaning against him, constantly flicking her eyes from the wall to Claudia and back again.

Without warning, the face of Letta's mother fills the screen. Letta watches with gleeful abandon as Claudia freezes to her spot, one of her legs poised in midair to cross over the other.

"Captain's Log. Date: the sixteenth day of the eighth month of the year two thousand five hundred and fifty two. Tenth Captain Leticia Hamilton," her mother rattles off. Letta mouths along with every word, fixing a steady glare on Claudia.

Claudia springs to her feet just as Letta's mother looks up to greet the Claudia in the video. Tia stops it just before it loops around again. Everyone in the audience is whispering in confusion. Letta raises her voice to be easily heard above the hushed mutterings.

"What's wrong, Claudia? You have something you want to get off your chest?"

Claudia glares at Letta with such anger that a twinge of fear rises within her.

"I merely feel lightheaded, niece. You are not the only one affected by Leticia's death. Did you not think that perhaps we would not want to see this? That your father would not be ready to see his late Partner?" Claudia scrambles for Letta's father's hand and holds it tightly. Her father's head is turned away, but she can see his free hand is pressed to his face. In a flash, a flood of guilt ripples throughout her body.

"Can someone please turn the lights back on?" Claudia asks.

"The lights! Someone turn on the godforsaken lights!" Pol booms. The room brightens immediately, dazing the audience with its intensity. When Letta's eyes have adjusted, she sees her father gliding out the doors nearest the Deck A elevator, pursued by C.p. Pol.

Letta pushes Phell away. He stumbles, looking hurt. She ignores him. Focusing on the floor, Letta spots an e-baton. It must have fallen from the hand of one of the Law Officers in their race to leave the library. She bends down and picks it up. It feels heavy and powerful in Letta's hand. It sparks and buzzes when she turns it on. She scans the room and sees Claudia leaving via another door, the crowd spilling out after her.

This is Letta's chance. She can follow Claudia, corner her, and finally get her to admit to what she has done.

She starts toward the doors, anger burning like fire in her veins. She wants to wrap her hands around Claudia's throat and hear her aunt's last breath leave her lungs in a choked sigh. Or press the electric baton against her skull and watch her brain boil and melt. But people will have seen Letta follow Claudia into the corridor. They already all think badly of her, disrupting the first good event since the funeral. She kills Claudia and then what? Claudia is the victim. Letta becomes the murderer. Claudia's memory will usurp Letta's mother. She'll be commemorated forever as the shortest-reigning captain, whose career was cruelly cut short by a wicked, selfish girl.

As Letta hesitates, Claudia disappears into the surge. It would take too long to find her now. Letta's decision is made for her. She turns the baton off and lets it hang by her side.

Lida emerges from the crowd beside Letta and tugs her sleeve. "Your father is incredibly disappointed in you. He wants to talk to you in his quarters."

Letta pulls away from Lida's grasping hands. "What about these people? They all came to see a movie."

"I think you've ruined that for everyone, don't you?"

"I don't know—maybe you and Rosa could get up and tell a story for us all. You're very good at making up stories, aren't you? Not so much at keeping secrets, though. At least not if there's nothing in it for you."

Lida gapes at her. "Don't speak to me like that!"

"I'll speak to liars however I see fit," Letta spits. "I know you're been talking to Claudia about me. How else would she have known about my nightmares?"

Lida's face drains of color as she sputters out some excuse. Letta brushes off her arm, as if she could rub away the taint of Lida's touch the way she would a piece of lint. Then, ignoring Lida, she picks her way through the abandoned chairs.

Letta half-jogs, half-walks down the corridor back to her family's quarters. When she scans herself in, the first thing she notices is that the main room is dark. The only light is a sliver shining through the seal on her parents' bedroom door. Murmurs of hushed conversation drift out from inside.

"Dad!" she tips her head back and yells. "Dad! Who are you talking to?"

Her hand tightens around the baton, and her finger slides the switch on once again. The low buzzing sounds like a blue-bottle fly. She knocks on the bedroom door.

"Dad? You wanted to speak to me?"

There's movement inside and then her father opens the door. "I'm about to go to bed," he says, though he's still fully dressed. "I can't talk to you right now. Even looking at you is making me angry."

"Is there someone in there with you? I'm sure I heard someone."

"Why would there be someone in here?" her father questions. But Letta notices the door to the bathroom is open, and then Letta hears the shower start, followed by vibrant cursing.

"I knew someone was in here!" she crows triumphantly. "Is it Claudia?" She brandishes the baton and her father leaps out of her way. There's a large, dark figure behind the opaque shower glass. The shower is still running, the sound of water masking Letta's footsteps.

It could be Claudia. The more Letta stares at the shadow, the more convinced she becomes that it *is* Claudia. She grabs the edge of the shower glass and yanks it back. Pol is slumped against the shower wall, soaking wet but completely dressed. He gapes at her as pathetic as a drowned kitten. She stumbles back in surprise, and the baton flings from her hand, colliding with his chest. The baton emits a frighteningly loud screech, and Pol shakes violently. He slips, banging his head against the temperature gauge before collapsing in a heap on the floor.

"What did you do?" her father whispers behind her.

"I didn't mean to! I thought he was Claudia," she whimpers, trembling. "Why was he hiding in the shower?!"

"We didn't want you to see him. I didn't think you'd go into the bathroom. I told him to hide there. He must have leaned against the on-button by mistake." Her father speaks quietly and with little inflection. "We were discussing you. We didn't want you to know." He presses his palm to his cheek. "Oh, God. This is all my fault."

Suddenly, her father seizes her by the shoulder and yanks her back, away from the body. He pulls her into the bedroom and shuts the bathroom door, but it doesn't matter. All Letta can see is that heap of skin and clothes lying there, not moving. The screech of the baton echoing and echoing inside her ears like a macabre soundtrack. He didn't even make a human sound as he fell.

"Letta, I don't know where you got this idea that your aunt somehow hurt your mother, but it's ridiculous. Do you think so little of me that you believe I would let her killer go free?" Her father shakes her vigorously. "She killed herself, Letta. No matter how many people you accuse, that fact will never change."

"She didn't leave a note. If she had killed herself, she would have left a note," Letta whispers, biting her lip. Her father sighs and tries to wrap his arms around his daughter, but she wriggles out from under him.

"I know how she died, Dad. It *was* Claudia. Didn't you see the video? That was the last time anyone saw her. She looked happy."

"You don't have to appear visibly sad to be depressed. It's not a cartoon emotion."

"Don't you see?" Letta goes on, barely even paying attention to her father now. "She was the first person to get the new nutritional vaccination. That wasn't a vaccine, it was poison! It had to be! Why else would Mom, the first person to take it, die? Why don't you believe me?" Her voice hitches as she reaches a hysterical pitch and a sob catches in her throat like a swollen lump.

"We don't have time for this," he says. "You need to go. Now. Find Tia. Stay out of sight until I comm you."

"But what about Pol? Shouldn't we get him some help?"

Her father pushes her to the front door and waves his scanner in front of the lock panel. "Don't worry about that. I'll handle it. Just go. Find Tia."

Her father runs a hand across his face just as the door slides closed. Letta has never seen him so tired. She wonders if it will dawn on him, as it has on her, that she was also given the new nutritional vaccine.

She wonders where she should go now. But there's only one place she feels like she needs to be.

She stands in the exact spot her mother's ashes stood when they tipped over and spiraled into space. Now she sits, laying her hands flat on the surface, as if she might feel her mother's presence, or at least see her ghost one last time.

It had been easy to get into the evacuation chamber. Easier than Letta had thought it would be. For some reason her ID band still had authorization for this chamber. She even had the authorization to open the outer doors if that was what she wanted. She'd checked, scanning her arm against the metal frame inside the room. The override button had flashed bright red. It was blinking, still, by the doors behind her. That particular button was usually reserved for people who were accidentally trapped where she stood now, with no protective gear and a countdown slowly ticking down to when the doors would slide open and they would suffocate.

The doors to the main body of the ship hiss open. Letta doesn't even bother to turn around to see who it is. She is thrown forward suddenly, pain radiating out from between her shoulder blades like she's been stabbed.

"I saw you!" Tess spits at her. "I saw you on the cams. You killed my father. Do not try to deny it."

Letta feels another sharp pain, this time on her thigh. She

cries out and rolls onto her back. Tess stands over her, her hair loose around her head like a red mane. She looks feral, her face pale and her lips curled up in a snarl. She jabs her baton into Letta's stomach and Letta curls in on herself, screaming. This was what Pol felt. This was the last thing he was aware of before he died.

Letta opens her eyes and sees Claudia, as regal and poised as ever, standing in the corridor looking over the scene unfolding in the evacuation chamber.

"You coward!" Letta screams at her. "Are you just going to let your guard fight your battles?"

Tess jabs the baton into Letta again and her words are lost in a tortured howl.

"Enough, Officer Pol." Claudia is firm and commanding, every bit the captain she desired to be.

Tess lurches up, her legs spread wide in her earnest need to bend low and hurt Letta. She stands straighter, and in her moment of distraction, Letta kicks her feet from under her. Tess topples to the ground, her own baton stinging her as she falls.

The baton rolls away from Tess' groaning body and Letta scrambles to her feet, gripping the handle carefully. In one quick motion, she brings the full force of the baton onto Tess' chest. The thud is oddly satisfying to her.

Tess starts to shake and fear wraps its icy fingers around Letta, the memory of Pol's empty body playing in her mind. She drops the baton, rubbing her eyes. When Tess finally moves again, Letta has never known such relief.

"You don't understand," Tess says. "Phell will not be able to handle this. He's too fragile." She tries to get to her knees, but she flops forward, her arms weak.

"I said, enough, Officer Pol."

Tess rolls back. Letta sees a faint grin on her face.

"I can tell you that being ordered around by Hamiltons gets old real fast," Tess chuckles, though her laughter sounds forced.

"What's going on here?"

All three whip around to the doorway where Letta's father now stands, his hand holding the door open. Tia hovers behind him, wringing her hands.

"I thought you'd be with Tia, Letta, but she thought you'd be with me," her father continues. He shoves his hand into the pocket of his coat. "I brought something with me. To prove that Claudia didn't kill my Leticia." He pulls out the box Letta saw in the Med pod earlier, the one with the vials. He unzips it, taking out an empty vial, and holds it up for everyone to see. Then he sets the box with the rest, still filled with the orange liquid, on the floor just inside the door.

"I know you think this killed your mother, Letta. But it can't have. I injected some before coming down here, and I'm perfectly fine."

Claudia balks. "That wasn't for you."

"What do you mean? You said it was approved for the general public." His smile wavers. "Right? Please tell me I'm right."

"Approved to specific members of the general public," Letta says, repeating the same words Rosa had said earlier. "You were only going to give it to certain people. Who were you going to give it to? Who else did you *give* it to?"

"Me." Tess' voice is so quiet it is almost impossible to hear. "She gave it to me when we watched the video. When she showed me you... hurting my dad. She said it would make me stronger."

Letta goes to her father, who is leaning against the door frame now, breathing heavily. He drops to the floor and curls in on himself, his breathing becoming more labored by the second.

"Is it happening? Am I dying?" he gasps.

"Don't be ridiculous," Claudia snaps. "You only just took it. It takes longer than that to take effect."

"So you admit it. It's not a nutritional vaccine after all." Letta is relieved, but it is bittersweet. She walks over to her father, touching him lightly on the hip, before picking up the case of vials he discarded. Tia is still standing out in the hall.

"Did you take any?" she asks, but Tia just stares, silent. "Tia! Did you take any?" she repeats more loudly, and Tia shakes her head. Letta breathes a sigh of relief. At least there's that.

Quickly, she shuts the door and locks it from the inside. Tia mouths something to her, and Letta turns on the comm on her ID band.

"What are you doing?" Tia sounds panicked. She tries to open the door, tries scanning her arm against it, but it won't open now unless Letta opens it. She turns her back on Tia and throws the case to Claudia.

"Catch," she says. It hits Claudia hard on the shoulder before falling. Claudia grabs it before it hits the ground and holds it tightly in her hands.

"You're going to open that, now, Claudia, and you're going to take some of your own medicine."

"Or I could just wait until it kills all of you and every single other person I deem unfit to breed upon this ship."

"You could do that. But I imagine I will have pressed the emergency release before then." Letta points to the blinking red light beside the door. "Take it and I won't. We can all go inside and you can find some way to get this stuff out of our system."

"There is no way," Claudia says.

"I'm still not budging until you take it."

The comm crackles in Letta's arm. "You would have been a better captain than her, Lett," Tia says. Letta laughs, loudly, the kind of laughter that starts out forced, but eventually grows more real until you ache with it.

Claudia unzips the pack. "There's no needle. How am I supposed to inject it?"

Letta shrugs. "I don't care. Drink it," she says. "Drink it or I push the button."

"I don't think you will. I don't think you'll force your friend to watch you die."

Letta can feel Tia's eyes boring holes in her back, and she knows Tia can hear every word that's being said in here through the comm.

"Do you think I can do it, Tia?" she says, choking out another laugh.

"Don't burn yourself out," Tia begs. "Just come back inside. Please."

"Stars burn out all the time," Letta reminds her. She likes the sound of that. Stars die in a spectacular eruption of light. She knows this, but she's never seen it.

"You are not a star, Letta."

"But I want to be." She wants it so badly. To be outside with the stars, with her mother.

"I can see her," she whispers. "She's right in front of me."

Her mother floats in front of the outer doors, her arms stretched out, waiting for the doors to open so she can go home.

Letta lifts up the case protecting the button and slams her hand down on it before Tia can try to convince her not to, or before Claudia can try to stop her. The doors slide open and her mother floats out on the ebb of invisible solar waves. Then Letta is sucked out into the vacuum of space, the infinite hands holding her so tightly she feels her body crushing under their touch. She's tumbling, over and over, alongside the suffocating bodies of the others.

She catches a glimpse of Tia banging and banging on the glass, but Letta hears nothing. She walks among the stars now, and there is only blissful silence.

The Desperate Warrior and the Beast
Who Walks Without Sound

T. DAMON

"The painful warrior famoused for fight,
After a thousand victories once foiled,
Is from the book of honour razed quite,
And all the rest forgot for which he toiled:
Then happy I, that love and am beloved,
Where I may not remove nor be removed."
- SONNET 25

Wakiza crouched low, hiding his body behind a thick bramble bush deep in the deciduous forest he lived in with his tribe. He heard a branch crunch behind him, and whipped around to quiet his father, Siwili, who was creeping close on his heels. A short distance ahead, a lone buck grazed in a grassy clearing, unaware of the men who stalked him, though the recent crack of the branch under Siwili's foot seemed to put the creature on edge.

As the buck froze, gazing around at the foliage surrounding him, Wakiza took the opportunity to tiptoe closer, readying his bow with a sharp, obsidian-bladed arrow. He motioned to his father to do the same.

"I've almost got the perfect shot," he whispered, to which his father fervently nodded. "If I miss, fire before it figures out what's going on."

"I doubt I'll need to. Take the shot, son," Siwili replied, unconsciously holding his breath as he waited for Wakiza to release his arrow.

Wakiza took one more swift step forward, pulled his bow back, and shot his arrow in the buck's direction. At first, it looked as though the arrow had not hit, as the buck flailed back and swung its head around to run in the opposite direction, but as it darted away began to falter, slowed significantly, then finally fell to the ground.

Wakiza jumped out of his hiding spot and rushed toward the deer, taking care to approach the buck from the back so as to avoid a potential stab from a swing of its antlers. But as the warrior grew closer, he found that his shot had been precisely true, as it normally was, and one mere arrow shot to the heart was all it took to bring down the enormous stag. Siwili cheered, and the two men dropped to their knees to pay their respects for the life of the animal who would now provide their ailing tribe with food for the next few days.

"I'm proud of you, son," Siwili, whose name meant 'long tail of fox', said as the men trekked back to their village, each lugging a large half of the deer on their backs. "This will help take some of the pressure off of Chief Taima. He's been worrying for days over when the tribe was going to eat next."

"Glad I could help," Wakiza beamed. "This war has been difficult on everyone. If I had one wish, just one wish at all, I'd want the fighting to stop. The Sun tribe should understand that resources are tough to come by these days, and we need to share this land so we can all reap the benefits of it."

"Unfortunately, it's not that simple, my son. The Sun tribe is coming from a place of greed. We can't allow them to step all over us this way. It's bad enough that the Beast has begun to terrorize our tribe. We can't do anything about that, but we do have the ability to fight against our human foes."

"I don't think they're enemies," Wakiza said softly. "And I'm not sure I even believe in the Beast. Seems like a bunch of old folklore to me."

"Perhaps the Beast is unable to be defeated," Siwili replied, ignoring Wakiza's comment, "because he is being prayed to by the Sun tribe. That's where he's getting his strength."

"We'd know for sure if Muraco were here. He is the tribe's shaman, after all. Wouldn't he be able to tell us if the Beast is a spirit, or a monster of flesh and blood? And couldn't he sense if the Sun tribe was controlling him and sending his wrath upon us?"

"Indeed he could. But he is not here, and no one knows where he went, or when he'll be back, if ever."

"He probably left to escape the war," Wakiza said. "I wouldn't blame him. Even I have lost my taste for battle, and it has been my dream to become a warrior since I was a little boy."

"That I know," Siwili replied, glancing at his son with sympathetic eyes. "But you are a great warrior, Wakiza, and an equally exceptional hunter. Though you may not agree with this war, you still have a duty to your people."

Wakiza watched his large feet take turns stepping across the pebble-riddled dirt, only able to look up for a glance at a time due to the oversized carcass draped across his back. He was tall, though not lanky in the least, and every muscle was visibly apparent on his tanned frame. His hair was coarse, dark, and long, and his eyes were a nearly-black brown to match. His name, meaning 'desperate warrior', had been given to him after the exceedingly long and difficult labor he gave to his mother, Bena, while being born. It had been a surprise to everyone in the tribe that she had survived that ordeal fairly unscathed. The chief declared that for a baby to put up such a fight, he must be destined to become a great warrior, desperate to assert his will in any given situation—an extremely auspicious prediction for such a new life. Thus the name stuck, and seemed to grow more and more fitting as each year of his life passed. He became revered among his tribe for his warrior and hunter accomplishments, the perfect son destined for chiefdom in a tribe where the reigning chief only had daughters, and whose wife was too old to produce any more children.

Perhaps Wakiza was a desperate warrior, but he lacked the desperation many had for power, and rather maintained his desperation for a life beyond what anybody in his tribe—even his parents—could understand.

The sun was setting behind the great mountain in the distance. By now, Wakiza and his father had nearly reached their home, the village of the Thunder tribe. He breathed a sigh of relief as the deer carcass was growing heavy upon his back, and quickened his pace to reach the commune before the sun dropped behind the mountain completely and darkness overtook the forest.

As the men approached their village, cheers rang out as everyone noticed the fresh meat being carried toward the chief's house. Upon hearing the ruckus, Chief Taima, whose name meant 'thunder', stepped out of his home and greeted the father and son, thanking them for their contribution to the tribe.

"You have done us a great service, Siwili and Wakiza," Taima said. "And for that, the two of you will get the first bites!"

"It was Wakiza who slew the animal," Siwili admitted. "I just provided moral support."

"Then it is Wakiza we will celebrate tonight," the chief acquiesced. "And he will have his pick of any of my three daughters to spend the night with. Hopefully," he winked, "it will end in a marriage!"

Wakiza shifted his weight uncomfortably, but managed to muster a smile at Taima. "Thank you, Chief," he said humbly. "It is a great honor."

"You bring honor to this tribe, great warrior," Taima replied. "Now, everyone," he called out to the gathering that had formed around his home, "we feast!"

The tribe gathered around the roaring fire after all had eaten their fill of venison, and the chief's wife, Ituha, indicated that it was time for storytelling, a favorite activity amongst the members of the tribe. Wakiza sat alone; that is, until the chief's three daughters emerged from their house after their meal, and upon seeing him swarmed around his body like a pack of ravenous wolves. Their names were Elu, Eyota, and Etenia.

The eldest, Elu, meant 'beautiful', and she was clearly so, and knew it well, always using it to her advantage—as if her status as the chief's favorite daughter weren't advantage enough. She always managed to avoid the tasks of everyday life in the village, spending most of her time doting on her father while her sisters did her share of the work.

The chief's second daughter, Eyota, which meant 'great', was known for her intelligence, though she rarely had an opportunity to use her keen wits, since her father kept her busy weaving intricate baskets and forming delicate pottery for the tribe to use.

Taima's youngest daughter was Etenia, whose name meant 'rich'. She was neither pretty nor smart, but didn't seem to understand that she lacked both brains and beauty. She was known as a spoiled brat within the tribe, and many wondered if she would ever take a husband—or, rather, if one would ever be willing to take her.

"Wakiza! Stay with me tonight," Elu whispered in his ear, taking care to lean forward enough to allow him a glimpse down her dress. He blushed, and looked the other way, which left him eye to eye with Eyota.

"No! He's staying with me. We're going to have deep

conversations." Eyota sat next to Wakiza and scooted as close to him as she could. "A man as intelligent as Wakiza deserves nothing less than an equally smart wife."

"Wakiza is handsome! He needs a wife as attractive as he!" Elu remarked.

"Ha! He doesn't want either of you," Etenia shouted, nearly rupturing Wakiza's eardrum with her screeching voice. She had firmly planted her rear on the other side of him and leaned as close to him as possible. "He wants me!"

"No, he doesn't!" Elu argued. "He wants a wife that wouldn't pain him to look upon each day, with beauty as deep as the raging river, but as soft as the wings of a butterfly."

"Such a woman's looks will fade like the falling star, leaving Wakiza with nothing but a fool for a wife!" Eyota retorted.

"He doesn't want either of you!" Etenia screamed. "He wants the woman who has a little bit of everything—ME!"

"Now, now," a gentle voice interrupted, much to Wakiza's relief. "This will all be decided later on. It's story time now." Ituha smiled at Wakiza, who grinned and let out an exasperated sigh. "I know what you mean," she laughed, then motioned for everyone to gather around her.

"What story is it tonight, Mama?" Etenia asked, sitting cross-legged in front of Wakiza and leaning her back against his knees, as if trying to ensure that he would be unable to get up and leave without her noticing.

"In light of recent events, I've decided to tell you all the tale of Kajika, the Beast Who Walks Without Sound."

"Now, Ituha, are you sure you want to..." Chief Taima interrupted.

"Yes, my dear. I think it's time our people knew about the creature that's been tormenting us. Now, Kajika lives deep in the forest, beyond the areas where we all know well not to venture, slumbering in his lair as he awaits his perfect opportunity to strike the innocent. He lived in this forest long before we came along, and will reside here long after we are all gone. Nobody knows if he is a being of flesh and blood, like us, or an entity, sent here from the underworld to torture the living for all their wrongdoing upon this earth. Some say he may even be an elemental, a creature once good but turned away from the positive to live an existence of evil.

"Kajika resembles a lizard, though he is far more enormous than any other animal that we know of within this forest. He has sharp, jagged teeth and pointed horns upon his wretched head. His claws are massive, and able to slice through skin and flesh with ease. All those who have dared to face Kajika never lived to tell of his wicked glory, and I urge you—all of you—to avoid looking into the Beast's eyes if you are ever unfortunate enough to come upon him while walking in the forest."

"Why?" Etenia asked inquisitively.

"Why, because his eyes will freeze you in place, of course," Ituha, whose name meant 'sturdy oak', replied, her eyes wide. "And then it will be all the easier for him to feast upon your body while you're still alive. He starts at your legs, and works his way up, munching on every bone and muscle as if it were a delicacy. Then once you're at the brink of consciousness, he finishes you off, slicing off your head and saving it for his last bite."

"Oh, come on," Wakiza groaned, rolling his eyes. "Surely you can't believe that's true."

"Then what about all the people who have gone missing?" Eyota argued. "No trace of them has ever been found."

"We're at war with the Sun tribe," Wakiza reasoned. "Isn't it more logical to assume that they were taken as prisoners of war, or possibly killed?"

"The Sun tribe has made no secret of their attacks on us in the past," Eyota remarked. "And wouldn't they use the hostages as a bargaining tool? Seems more logical to me that the Sun tribe allied with the Beast in an attempt to destroy our tribe."

Wakiza sighed loudly. "You're probably right, Eyota," he replied, standing up abruptly and nearly knocking the chief's three daughters over in the process. "Now, if you'll excuse me. Nature calls."

"Watch out for the Kajika!" Taima's three daughters taunted in unison, but Wakiza ignored them and sauntered off into the forest.

Wakiza walked a good distance away from his village, close enough that he could still see the glow of the fire and hear the muffled chatter of his people, but still far enough that the silence of the forest, occasionally disrupted by an owl's hoot or a cricket's chirp, overpowered the human sounds. When he reached a towering oak tree drooped over a cluster of blackberry brambles, he stopped, and waited. He cleared his mind of all the matters of the day—the stress of the hunt, his aching feet from his travels, the incessant attention from the chief's three daughters. He then ran his fingers delicately over a carving in the trunk of the tree, and closed his eyes until a serene and pleasant sound glided through his ears.

"Wakiza?"

He opened his eyes, and felt his heart begin to race. His whole body flushed pink, and his hands started to tremble. "Aiyana…" he whispered. "I've missed you."

A stunning woman stepped into a glimmer of moonlight, and graced forward to embrace Wakiza. His lips found hers, and the two grasped on to each other as tightly as they could. Aiyana's tongue melted into his mouth, her lips soft and smooth. Wakiza had waited so long for this moment, had dreamed of those perfect lips for days, maybe weeks, since he'd last seen her. Now he wanted nothing more than for this tight hold upon her to never come to an end.

Finally, she pulled away from him. Strands of her long black hair had fallen loose from her braid and drifted across her face, as her bewitching copper-colored eyes met his.

"Wakiza," she said, "I didn't know if you'd come. I saw the fire in the distance, I thought it might be hard for you to escape."

"Of course I'd come," the warrior replied. "I'd never miss a chance to see you." He paused. "But what about you? Aren't you afraid to venture out of your village alone like this, with that Beast lurking in the shadows?" He growled, and grabbed around Aiyana's waist playfully.

"I wouldn't joke about that if I were you," Aiyana scolded. "You're asking for trouble."

"My only trouble is you, my love!" Wakiza beamed, and stole another kiss before she teasingly pulled away from him once again.

Aiyana looked up longingly at Wakiza, her eyes dilating as she focused on his chiseled face illuminated by the moonlight. She was a petite woman, lean and athletic, but curved in all the right places. Her name, meaning 'eternal blossom', was, like Wakiza, a nomination that seemed to perfectly suit her in the present despite it being given at birth. Though, as a child, her name didn't always suit her so well. Like the budding flowers of the spring, it had taken many seasons before Aiyana looked the way she did currently. She often wondered if Wakiza would have noticed her in the way he did now if he'd known her in her youth.

"Oh, Aiyana," Wakiza scoffed, "don't tell me you believe all those ridiculous tales about the Kajika. You're smarter than that. The biggest danger to the forest is the war between our tribes."

"I know. It's horrible. I just wish this could be resolved so we could finally be together."

"If only it were that simple."

"Wakiza?"

"Yes?"

"I... I should probably tell you something. But if I do, you have to promise me that you'll keep it to yourself and not tell anybody. Because if you do, everyone will wonder how you knew, and it might give us away."

"Of course I'll keep it a secret. Why, what is it?"

Aiyana paused, and took a deep breath. "My tribe is planning an attack on yours. Tomorrow. Just before dawn. My father is hoping to catch Taima off guard."

"Are you serious? I must warn my people, Aiyana!"

"You can't! Please, Wakiza, you said you wouldn't tell anyone!"

Wakiza sighed, then grabbed Aiyana's hand and squeezed it tightly. "Well, maybe I can try to 'accidentally' make some noise tomorrow morning and at least ensure that everyone is awake."

"I think that's all you can do," Aiyana replied softly. "I just keep praying to the Raven that you're protected, and nobody from my tribe can harm you."

"I'll ask the Mountain Lion for help tonight before I go to sleep as well."

Aiyana smiled. "I should go. You should get some sleep, so you will be well-rested in the morning." She tried to hide her face so as not to show Wakiza the tears that were now welling up in her eyes, but he noticed and embraced her tightly. "I guess this is goodbye then."

"It's never 'goodbye'. It's 'until the next time we meet'," Wakiza whispered softly in her ear. "I will dream of you every night until then."

"As will I," Aiyana replied, and the two kissed one more time before reluctantly turning away from each other and walking off in opposite directions.

As Wakiza ventured back to his village, his mind was preoccupied with thoughts of Aiyana, the impending attack, and the pointless war with the Sun tribe. He wished more than anything that the situation between the two tribes were different. He longed for time spent with his love that could span beyond just a few brief moments.

He was so distracted by his internal fantasies that he didn't even notice a large, dark shadow looming behind a cluster of trees in the short distance. It was only when he heard a raspy groan, followed by what sounded like a deep growl, that Wakiza's senses perked up.

Out of the corner of his eye, he caught a slight yellowish reflection of the moonlight. He froze and squinted, desperately trying to discern the sounds and shadow, but even the most practical of thoughts could not shake the chills his body now felt, and the hopeless, taunting feeling of being watched. The small hairs on the back of his arms stood upright. Just when it appeared as though the shadow was beginning to slowly—yet menacingly—grow larger, rising further above him, Wakiza took off running. He didn't stop until he had safely reached his home.

Wakiza had difficulty sleeping that night. Whether it be because of the impending attack on his tribe, the strange, shadow-like anomaly that loomed toward him on his walk home, or the aching desire for Aiyana that welled up in his heart every time he was forced to leave her side, he could not say. But for whatever reason, he found himself wide awake well before dawn, and took that time as an opportunity to plan his defense against the inevitable battle he was soon to face.

Just before sunrise, Wakiza took a deep breath and prayed to his spirit animal totem, the Mountain Lion, before stepping out of his house and gazing around the camp. He noticed several large clay pots outside of some neighboring homes, and—though he knew he might have to face the wrath of Eyota—began picking them up and violently slamming them down upon the ground, one by one. With each pot that shattered as loudly as a thundering storm, more and more people emerged from their houses, rubbing their eyes and scolding Wakiza for making such a ruckus so early in the morning.

"Oh, no! Sorry, it was an accident," Wakiza said nonchalantly, prompting his people to look at him strangely and mutter that they were going back to bed. But before they could return to the warmth and safety of their homes, a harrowing war cry rang out and echoed through the trees. The sound of pounding drums and darting footsteps thrummed, quickly drawing nearer.

Chief Taima burst out of his house and briefly glanced at Wakiza, confused. "Women and children get into my house, quick! Men, ready your weapons and prepare to fight!"

Just over the peak of the small hill on the brink of the Thunder tribe's camp, intricately painted warriors of the Sun tribe started to emerge and impose upon the village, tearing through homes and breaking everything they could within. The sounds of gasps, then screams, mixed with war cries, echoed through the village and imprinted the pain and desperation of the people deeply into the Thunder tribe's land.

Wakiza drew his bow and positioned himself behind a large rock, peering around at the men who were quickly approaching his hiding spot. When one grew close, Wakiza wasted no time whizzing an arrow his way, slicing through several breastbones and causing quite a few warriors to fall to their knees in pain. Some perished from their wounds, while others desperately tried to drag their ailing bodies away before Wakiza could strike again. But since so many were coming at a time, Wakiza only had an opportunity to shoot each adversary once before another noticed him and headed his way.

Wakiza had knocked down at least ten warriors of the Sun tribe when, out of the corner of his eye, he noticed his father in a hand to hand combat with a man he vaguely recognized. He assumed both his father and the Sun warrior had run out of arrows, and as he ventured closer he was able to make out the familiarity of Siwili's opponent.

Wakiza had only seen him once—and, granted, it was from afar—but he was sure he knew the man to be Aiyana's older brother, Akano. Akano, whose name meant 'worthy of trust', surely had much to prove in this battle, as he was set to become the Sun tribe's next chief, and as Wakiza pondered this thought he realized that because of this, under no circumstances would Akano allow Siwili to walk away from their fight alive. Without thinking, Wakiza rushed to his father's side and threw a swift punch to Akano's face. Dazed, Akano staggered backward, stumbling to the ground.

"Run, Father! I've got this!" Wakiza shouted, only to find his father hesitate and stare back at him blankly.

"This is not your fight, son," Siwili replied, out of breath.

"If you continue fighting him, he will kill you," Wakiza hissed. "Please, Father. He's stronger than you!"

Siwili paused for a moment, eying his son carefully. Then he reluctantly nodded his head, and, though he appeared somewhat defeated, rushed away to find an opponent to fight who was more suited for his age. Though exhausted, he could not stop fighting altogether, as it would bring a horrible dishonor upon his family, and it would be more appropriate for him to have died in battle than given up completely.

Wakiza glanced at his father as he darted away, but was quickly brought back to reality when he felt a tremendous blow to the back of his head. He turned around and was quickly punched again by Akano. Wakiza gathered himself and vigorously swung at Aiyana's brother, landing a forcible jab across his cheek. Akano struck again, this time missing Wakiza and slightly losing his footing, offering Wakiza the opportunity to swiftly thrust his leg under his, forcefully knocking him to the ground. But Akano was quick to stand up again and sprinted at Wakiza, tackling him in his midsection, and the two warriors plummeted to the ground.

Wakiza and Akano rolled around in the dirt, landing blows here and there, but mainly wearing each other out as they continued their fight. Then, out of nowhere, Akano pulled a long, razor-sharp piece of obsidian from the strap of his loin cloth, previously hidden by a perfectly sized pouch that Aiyana had no doubt sewn for him. Wakiza and Akano rose to their feet once more, and Akano loomed over the warrior, wielding the obsidian around as if it were a blade. Wakiza stared at Akano in disbelief, but though he kept his own blade tightly secured to his waist, he did not draw it.

Wakiza felt his heart nearly pounding out of his chest. *This is it,* he thought to himself. *This is how I will die. At the hands of the brother of the woman I love. Seems oddly fitting, I suppose, for a desperate warrior like myself.*

Akano shot forward, swinging the blade across Wakiza's stomach. Luckily, Wakiza leaped backward, narrowly avoiding the slash of the blade and sparing himself the sight of his own entrails being spilled across his feet. Akano struck again, this time aiming for his throat, but a quick movement again from Wakiza resulted only in a slight graze through his left bicep. Wakiza winced in pain, but readied himself for another attack.

Akano lurched forward, and took a quick step in his direction. Wakiza thought fast, and leaned backward while thrusting his arm forward, causing a severe blow to Akano's head. As Akano recovered from the hit, Wakiza swung his other arm around, swiftly chopping his wrist into Akano's arm, and successfully knocking the blade from his hands and away onto the forest floor.

Akano tried to hurdle over Wakiza in an attempt to retrieve the blade, but Wakiza thrust his body upward and tossed him to the ground once more. Then Wakiza bounded over to the blade and hurriedly picked it up, pointing it in his adversary's direction. Akano put his hands up, then lowered his eyes and fell to his knees, admitting his defeat. Wakiza stepped forward, hovering over him, but he did not make the final strike.

Akano knelt, tense, and waited for the blow. When it did not come, he looked up into Wakiza's eyes.

"Aren't you going to kill me?" Akano asked, breathing heavily, his voice shaking slightly.

Wakiza took a deep breath, and looked around to his right and left. Then his eyes met Akano's once more, and he noticed a hint of Aiyana looking back at him through her brother's eyes.

"Get out of here," he hissed. "Go, before someone sees us."

Akano rose, confused, and began to slowly back away, maintaining eye contact. Then he turned his body, looking at Wakiza gratefully just one more time before sprinting away as fast as he could. Wakiza dropped the obsidian blade, and, upon feeling his knees buckle beneath him, gave in and fell to the ground. But before relief could overtake him, he heard a familiar voice from behind.

"I cannot believe you, Wakiza." Wakiza felt his blood run cold. He turned around, only to find Chief Taima approaching him. "I cannot believe you would let Akano live and just leave like that. Don't you know who he is?"

Wakiza thought carefully before answering. "No, who is he, Chief?"

"Don't play with me. We both know that's a load of bear crap. You know just as well as I do who that man was, who he was destined to become. You had him in your grasp, Wakiza, and you let him go. Why?"

"He said his wife had just had a baby, and I just couldn't…"

"You lie again. That's twice now you've lied to me, Wakiza. I saw the whole thing. Akano was one of the last men still fighting. The rest were either killed or driven away, back to the Sun tribe. All thanks to you and your commotion this morning. Awfully fishy, if you ask me. One might think you knew something was going to happen. And after witnessing this, well, I'm very inclined to think that."

"How much did you see?" Wakiza asked, a lump forming in the back of his throat.

"I saw your father running away, so I came to investigate what had happened. I'd seen him fighting with Akano, so I was surprised to see he survived that battle. I wondered how he could have defeated such a strong, viable warrior. Then I came over here and saw you, my prized Wakiza, one of the most honored warriors in the tribe become a traitor to our people. And to think I actually believed that one day you would take over as the leader of our tribe. You've made a fool out of me, Wakiza. You've made a fool out of all the Thunder people."

"Chief, I'm sorry."

"If you are a traitor, I should kill you right now. But first, Wakiza, I want you to answer me one question."

"What's that?"

"Why did you do it? Why did you let him live?"

Wakiza paused, and looked into Taima's eyes, but said

nothing.

"Very well. Wakiza, I cannot in good conscience kill a man who, in the past, has done so much for our people, who was once so revered as a warrior. But you are henceforth excommunicated from this tribe. You are no longer welcome in our village. May the Earth grant you more mercy than I have."

With that, Taima turned his back on Wakiza and walked away, back to the shambles that were once the Thunder tribe's encampment.

Wakiza sat numbly on the ground as the whole magnitude of his predicament settled upon him. He'd been banished from his family, the only home he'd ever known. He wondered if he would ever see his parents again in his lifetime.

He stayed there, motionless, for quite a while, listening to the distant sounds of his former tribe recoiling from the surprise attack. Tears welled in his eyes at the sobs of devastated wives and mothers, and the cries of grown men who had lost a brother, son, or friend. Many had died protecting their families, as Siwili surely would have had Wakiza not intervened. The destruction would have been far worse without his impromptu warning; but in the end, it didn't matter. He was alone now.

Finally realizing there was nothing he could do to remedy his current predicament, Wakiza picked up his blade, pulled his body up, and began to walk.

He walked away from the Thunder tribe, and ventured in a direction far even from the Sun tribe. If he had been excommunicated from his own people, he figured there wasn't much of a chance of him being accepted by Aiyana's tribe either. Sure, he had saved Akano, but he was still likely considered an ally of the Thunder tribe, given his status up until recently. If he chose to approach Aiyana's tribe, the best he could hope for would be that her father, Chief Etu, would kill him and spare him the shame and loneliness that he was now destined to face. But even that sounded undesirable to him, and he had a feeling that although he was shunned, there might still be hope to have a decent life on his own—if he created that existence for himself, that is.

So Wakiza walked, and walked, and walked, until eventually he came upon what appeared to be some kind of makeshift shelter deep in the woods.

Wakiza approached the tent, which was made up of tightly woven branches and leaves, with a drooping bear's hide for a door. He crept up to the entrance slowly, taking care not to crunch down on any sticks, but his attempts at remaining silent were futile as the hide swung open and Wakiza found himself face to face with a snarling wolf's head.

Wakiza started to back away, but as the wolf emerged from the doorway to the hut, he realized that it was not in fact an actual wolf, but rather a stocky old man wearing a wolf's hide. He froze, then decided it might be best to try to reason with this wolf-man and see if perhaps he could provide him with any kind of enlightenment on where he was, or where he could go from here. He did not want to impose on the man, but was simply curious as to why the wolf-man would go to all the trouble of building such an intricately designed house in such a remote location of the forest.

"What is it?" the man growled, much like a wolf might if Wakiza had in fact come upon an actual wolf.

"Hello… My name is Wakiza, of the Thunder tribe. Well, formerly of the Thunder tribe. I was hoping you might be able to help me."

The man pursed his lips, and stared at Wakiza inquisitively. "What do you want?"

"Um, well, I was sent away from my tribe, and am looking for a place to stay. Might you have any idea where a good location would be? You see, my tribe is at war with another tribe, and I don't want to live anywhere that might intersect with either one."

"So old Chief Taima cast you off, did he?" the man harrumphed. "Typical. No wonder the Earth never blessed him with a son. He doesn't know how to treat them well, now, does he?"

Wakiza said nothing. He had no desire to speak ill of his former chief, even despite his most recent interaction with him. Though he was deemed a traitor, Wakiza was far from one, even in his excommunication.

The man glared at Wakiza for a moment before sliding the wolf's hide off his body. "I, too, was once a member of the Thunder tribe. But unlike you, I chose to leave. I am not the kind desperate for glory born from violence." He cocked his head at Wakiza slightly and winked.

Wakiza squinted his eyes, and suddenly recognized the old man as the former shaman of the Thunder tribe. "Muraco?" He asked inquisitively.

"That's me," the man, whose name meant 'white moon', replied.

"What are you doing all the way out here? And by yourself?"

"Well, like I said, I chose to leave."

"Aren't you worried, being out here and all?"

"Worried about what? The Beast?"

"Aren't you afraid he'll try to eat you?"

"He's not interested in eating my old meat!" Muraco chuckled. "Now, enough questions about Kajika for now. You'll learn about him soon enough."

"What does that mean?"

"Now, have you managed to become the great warrior you

were foretold to be yet? Judging by your current predicament, I'm inclined to think otherwise."

"I guess I sort of was. Up until recently."

Muraco furrowed his brow. "I don't know, Wakiza. I have a sense you might still have a chance. But it won't be easy, of course."

Wakiza mustered a small grin and chuckled. "Nothing ever is, right?"

"Right. Now, come on in, would you? It's almost dark, and I'm sure you're hungry and thirsty by now, after all your travels."

"Thank you," Wakiza replied, following the shaman into his home.

The interior of the tent was dark except for a small fire burning in the very back, below a tiny hole in the roof that allowed the smoke to disperse from the inside. A bed composed of leaves and animal hides on the ground extended down the side of one of the walls, while on the other side stood several clay pots that likely contained food and water. Wakiza gazed from pot to pot, wondering what could possibly lie within their hollows.

"Now, have a seat," Muraco said, pointing to his bed. "I think I may be able to help you."

"How?" Wakiza inquired.

"Well, there's quite an easy way to find the answers you seek."

"And what way would that be?"

"A journey of course!"

"Journey to where?"

"Not an actual journey somewhere, although I can't guarantee that's not what you may discover along the way!"

"Please, Muraco," Wakiza nearly pleaded, rubbing his

temples in exasperation. "I'm not so keen on the folklore and riddles and such. Can you just tell me outright, please?"

Muraco laughed. "Typical moose-headed warrior. I'm speaking of a spiritual journey."

"A spiritual journey?" Wakiza said, though part of him wasn't surprised. "You mean, like taking mind-altering substances?"

"'Substances'? Boy, Taima sure has done one over on you. It's mushrooms, to be exact. A special kind of mushroom. One that can take your mind to places never thought possible." Muraco harrumphed again. "Mind-altering substances," he muttered mockingly.

"But I am not a shaman!" Wakiza protested.

"Of course you're not. But a lot of people in your very position do it, too. To find themselves, or their life's purpose, if you will. If you're unable to on your own, that is. Most people are, but you're one of the lucky ones that, so far, has not been able to. So here we are."

Wakiza sighed. "I guess what do I have to lose at this point, right?" he lamented.

"Exactly!" Muraco exclaimed, opening one of the clay pots and removing a few pieces of dried, brown lumps. "Chew and swallow, if you please."

Wakiza took the mushrooms from the shaman and sniffed them. They oddly enough did not smell as terrible as he expected. He took a quick lick of one, and found it didn't have much taste. Reluctantly, he plugged his nose, opened his mouth, and dropped one in. As he chewed, he found it wasn't horribly offensive to his taste buds, and when his saliva had broken down the mushrooms significantly, he swallowed.

"There you go," Muraco said. "Now we wait."

Wakiza lay down, and allowed his thoughts to gradually drift away. He pondered his predicament, explored possible outcomes, and—at last, when he couldn't bear to think of the real world any longer—allowed himself to daydream of Aiyana.

Just as he was finally feeling like he might fall deeply into sleep, he slowly became aware of slight color changes within Muraco's house that seemed to shift before his very eyes. Each color intensified, and began to trace across the room, trailing an aura of mist behind it. Sounds began to fluctuate within his mind, sounding very distant from him, then instantly loud, ringing and echoing in his ears. Then the colors cascaded down the walls, and patterns began to form that represented nothing to Wakiza's eyes but pure perfection.

"Wakiza. Wakiza, do you feel it? Just visualize." Muraco's voice trailed across his brain. Wakiza sat up, looked around with wide, dilated eyes, then fixated upon the shaman.

"I feel… strange," he whispered. Muraco laughed.

"Well, let's get up then, and walk around the forest," the shaman replied.

"No!" Wakiza protested instantly. "I… I can't."

"Nonsense. What kind of journey is spent just lying around? Get up, and let's go."

Wakiza reluctantly obliged, and followed Muraco out of his tent. The two men walked into a thick patch of trees, the songs of birds and the rustle of leaves surrounding them, and twigs cracking beneath their feet. The proximal noises violently assaulted Wakiza's ears, and he couldn't help but notice a faint chanting and pounding drums in the far distance.

"Here we are," Muraco announced when the two had reached a very large and ancient-looking oak tree. "Sit. And close your eyes."

Wakiza sat cross-legged on the ground, his eyes darting around and his torso whipping back and forth with every sound that came at him. He shut his eyes.

"Tell me, desperate warrior," the shaman said softly. "What do you see?"

Wakiza squinted, hoping for some apparition or visualization to just appear out of nowhere, but all he saw was the pure darkness of the insides of his eyelids. He began to grow impatient, but instead took a deep breath and sighed. He relaxed his body and waited.

Suddenly, Wakiza got the distinct feeling that he and Muraco were no longer alone. There was a new a presence, though not a human one. Wakiza tried his hardest to focus on the visitor as its energy swirled around him. Within his mind, he attempted to reach out to the being, hoping to discover its identity.

Who are you? he asked fervently within his thoughts.

A voice, deep and gnarled, growled in reply, echoing only in his mind. *I am the Spirit of the Mountain Lion. I've come at your request for guidance. What do you seek?*

I seek the knowledge and wisdom necessary for peace within myself. I do not know who I am anymore, Wakiza replied.

I do not agree, the Lion snarled. *You do know who you are, but your tribe chose not to accept you. I can help, if that is what you desire.*

Wakiza opened his eyes, half expecting to snap out of his daydream and find himself sitting alone with Muraco. But he found to his surprise that Muraco was nowhere to be seen. In his place was a faint vision of a mountain lion—though much larger than an actual lion. The apparition floated distinctively before him, glaring him straight in the eye, staring through his entire soul. The forest around him had also grown eerie, the air was still and stale without a hint of wind, and an overall mist enveloped through the canopy of the trees.

Wakiza felt uneasy about the sudden change, but knew this was likely his only chance to communicate with his spirit animal totem directly.

"Please. I desire your help, Mountain Lion," the warrior said aloud, to which the lion narrowed its eyes and nodded. Then the lion dissipated into thin air, and an image of a dark cave, rooted in the base of the northern mountain appeared, and an enormous, lizard-like monster emerged from the cave, its sharp, jagged teeth dripping with drool.

Here is where Kajika lies. Slay the Beast and reunite the inhabitants of this forest. Fail, and bear witness to the destruction of all the tribes within these trees.

So the Beast is real… Wakiza thought.

But remember, the lion added, *Kajika walks without sound, so use your other senses to guide you. And whatever you do, do not look into the Beast's eyes.*

The energy then shifted, and Wakiza felt his stomach turn. He blinked, then looked around and found that once again Muraco was sitting beside him, and the forest had returned to its former normalcy.

"Well? How was it?" Muraco asked, excitement apparent in his tone.

"Very insightful," Wakiza replied. "I think I know what I need to do now."

"And what is that?"

"Slay Kajika. I guess he does exist, after all."

"Then get on with it!" the shaman exclaimed, throwing his arms in the air. "I will leave you now. But you know where to find me if you need anything."

"Thank you Muraco. And if I succeed in my quest, I hope you will to return to the Thunder tribe."

"If the fighting has ceased, I just might. Goodbye." And with that, Muraco rose from his seat, turned from the warrior, and walked away.

Wakiza set off to the north. His mind was still unsure that this was the right path, yet something within his heart urged him to follow it. Though the vision of the spirit of the Mountain Lion had passed, Wakiza could still feel a hint of his almighty presence, looming over him and watching closely as he traveled. Every so often, Wakiza would stop, look around, and whisper some brief words of gratitude, expressing his appreciation for the lion's invisible appearance and silently pleading with the spirit not to leave his side. His rhetorical offerings seemed to be effective, for all the while that he traveled, he was accompanied by his animal totem.

As Wakiza walked, he found himself thinking of nothing but Aiyana, recalling the moment he had first met her over and over within his mind. It had been spring, and both tribes were eager to resume their hunting and gathering routines after the long winter. Wakiza had been hiding behind a blackberry bush, spying on a family of rabbits in the distant clearing, poised with his bow and arrow and ready for one to draw close enough to provide him a suitable shot.

One of the larger rabbits had moved away from the group, drawing closer to Wakiza's hiding place. He readied his arrow, tense with anticipation, ready to loosen the taut string at a second's notice. Then he felt a slight shove, and lost his crouched footing, falling to his rear with a loud thump. The family of rabbits perked up, eyes wide, then instantly scattered back to their burrows.

Wakiza stood up, angry and indignant, but his rage quickly dissipated as he found himself gazing directly into the shimmering eyes of Aiyana, who had been picking blackberries from the other side of the bush. Apparently he had been in her way, and was blocking a prime batch of berries, which prompted her to try to move him rather than request his relocation. Rather than protest, Wakiza had been so stunned by her beauty that he was at a loss for words.

"Very articulate, I see," Aiyana teased, flashing a quick wink in his direction.

"I, uh, um…"

"The hunter speaks!" Aiyana giggled. "Or, judging from your arm tattoo, I should call you the brave warrior, yes? From the Thunder tribe?"

"That's right. I'm Wakiza."

"Aiyana. Pleasure to meet you, great warrior."

"I… I'm sorry that, um, my body happened to be in your way," Wakiza stammered.

Aiyana smiled. "It's not a problem. Luckily for me, my meal isn't able to just up and hop away." She delicately plucked a few more berries from the bush and dropped them into her basket, then glanced at Wakiza once more, her eyes sparkling. "Sorry about your rabbit. I'm happy to share some of these ripe berries with you, if you'd like."

Wakiza felt his face flush, and took a deep breath. "Thank you," he nearly squeaked out. "That will be better than returning home empty handed."

"This batch over here looks the best. Why don't you grab some of them?"

Wakiza inched forward, and held out his hand to select one of the berries from the batch. To his surprise, Aiyana reached her soft hand toward his, guiding it to the ripest, juiciest berry of the bunch. The two locked eyes, and Wakiza felt a chill radiate through his entire body. He couldn't look away from Aiyana, and knew at that very moment that this was the woman he forever wished to look upon. Not just for the remainder of his life, but in his heart he knew it was for all of eternity.

"Aiyana! Aiyana, where are you?" An unfamiliar female voice rang out, and Aiyana quickly pulled her arm away from Wakiza, and quickly stood up.

"I have to go," she said. "My mother can't see me talking to you." She began to hurry away.

"AIYANA!? AIYANA, WHERE ARE YOU?!"

"Coming, Mother!"

"Aiyana, wait!" Wakiza called out, and Aiyana whirled around. "When can I see you again?"

"Meet me by the oldest oak that marks the line between our tribes. Tomorrow night just after the sun sets," Aiyana hollered back before darting off and finally disappearing within the trees.

After that, the two of them began to meet in secret, disappearing from their tribes for short periods of time to walk through the forest together, sharing stories and laughing. They would always meet at the same tree, and with each passing day they fell deeper and deeper in love.

Wakiza's eyes teared up as he walked. He swallowed, then within his mind begged the Mountain Lion to help provide him the strength to survive so that he could see Aiyana once more. Even if fate decreed that the two could never be together, if he could just see her one more time, he could die happy.

The Mountain Lion gave no reply, but Wakiza harbored a strange feeling of an entrance into his body, and assumed the Mountain Lion had imparted into him some of its energy.

By late afternoon, Wakiza had finally reached the foot of the northern mountain. It loomed over him, much like the Mountain Lion's spirit had during his spiritual journey. But there had been a innate sense of comfort from his animal totem, a security and eagerness to help, that the mountain certainly did not seem inclined to provide. Jagged rocks jammed out of the mountain's side, poised to slide down upon Wakiza's head at any moment, and there were no plants around its base, as if even the spirits of the plants found the blackened dirt not suitable enough for nourishment.

As Wakiza scanned the mountain, he could feel the presence of Kajika within it, though perhaps it was the spirit of the Mountain Lion that allowed him such sensitivity to the energies around him. But somehow, by some means—Wakiza inherently knew that he was in the exact place he needed to be.

Wakiza approached the mountain cautiously. He had no desire to give Kajika the advantage of sensing his presence before he was able to furnish an initial attack upon the Beast. But as he turned a blind corner around a particularly large boulder, he very quickly found himself looking into the infinite blackness of the mouth leading into a deep, dark cave.

"This must be it," he whispered softly to himself, but before the warrior could even ponder a possible advancement into the cave, he was startled by a very low, resonating growl from deep within the hole in the mountain.

"Who dares enter my lair?" the voice boomed.

Wakiza stood frozen in his tracks, unsure of what to do next. In his mind, he was kicking himself for not using all of his warrior training and experience he had accrued over his many years of life, but something about this Beast was paralyzing, and he found himself unable to exert any form of aggression upon the creature in his current state. His body was still, yet his mind and mouth were able to work properly. Wakiza realized he would need to snap out of his condition, and asked the Mountain Lion for assistance within his thoughts.

Call the Beast out, he heard within his mind.

Are you crazy? Wakiza thought.

Do as I say, O great warrior.

Wakiza hesitated for a moment, then called out, his voice

shaky, "Kajika?"

"Fool!" the Beast taunted, though still denying the warrior the chance to look upon him. "How desperate your pitiful intentions are. I know why you're here, young warrior. Killing me will not save your people. Why, you've merely saved me the trouble of traveling out of my humble home to hunt my dinner! Your tribe resides quite far from here, you know." Kajika laughed, a raspy hiss. "I must say, you are quite brave to sacrifice your own life to save just one of your... *tasty* people. Tomorrow I will hunt again, and all your efforts will have been in vain."

Wakiza quickly considered his options. He knew that if he could lure the Beast out of its cave and far enough into the sunlight, he would have a better chance at fighting him. If he succumbed to Kajika's attempts at mind-trickery and attacked him in the darkness of the cave, he would surely fail. But most importantly, he needed to avoid looking into the Beast's eyes!

Wakiza had always been a warrior acting out of desperation, but perhaps in this particular instance patience and ingenuity could lead to his success, much like the delicate ambush-hunting methods of the Mountain Lion. Wakiza fully embraced the spirit of his animal guide within him, took a step back, and ducked behind the large boulder. Suddenly he understood what he needed to do.

"Kajika!" he called out, his voice sly and mocking. "O great Beast, if fresh human meat is what you desire, I suggest you get off your lazy rear and come get it!"

Kajika roared angrily at the warrior's insolence, then silence followed. Wakiza turned his head slightly, peering just the corner of one eye around the boulder. He did not hear any footsteps approaching. In fact, there was no sound at all.

But as Wakiza continued to watch, a pointed snout emerged

from the darkness, silently sniffling hot breath as it swung around in all directions, trying to catch a whiff of where the warrior was. Then a set of jaws became visible, smacking thin lips around long, jaggedly sharp teeth that spanned the whole perimeter of the Beast's mouth. And finally, two eyes, yellow and slitted, surfaced from the cave, reflecting the sunlight, pupils retracting their dilation from the dark.

Remember, don't look directly into his eyes, Wakiza heard within his mind, though he didn't have time to consider whether the voice he heard was his own, or that of the Mountain Lion, whose spirit he felt within him. Kajika was becoming more and more visible.

The Beast was a lizard, though enormous, and he scuttled over the dirt and rocks in the exact manner of his smaller counterpart. Wakiza knew for sure, now, that this was the same creature he had seen in his vision. Muraco's spiritual guidance had led him true.

Kajika's tail was thick, and provided the majority of his balance as it dragged along the ground. Acuminous claws protruded from long, spindly fingers, but there was still no noise, no scratching to be heard as his feet moved across the rocky surface. The Beast indeed walked without sound as he slunk further and further out of his lair.

As Kajika approached, Wakiza knew that he would have just one perfect opportunity to make a first strike. There was no room for error. Failure was not an option. He clutched onto his obsidian blade tightly and desperately prayed to the Mountain Lion.

Just a few more steps this way…

Kajika had ventured out of the cave completely, and crept around the side of the boulder. Wakiza counted his heartbeats, timing the Beast's soundless approach. Then he leaped forth, his eyes squeezed tightly closed to avoid Kajika's glare. The blade connected, slashing Kajika across the face. The Beast wailed, and thrashed around, whipping his tail in all directions. The flailing limb slammed into Wakiza, tossing him a good distance backward.

Kajika, blood streaming down his reptilian features, watched the warrior fall. Then he stampeded over, mouth opened wide to reveal his razor-sharp teeth, jaw gnashing in anticipation of the impending ferocious bite.

Wakiza rolled back on his feet, snatching an arrow from its sheath and drawing back his bowstring. He sailed the arrow through the air, glancing only at the Beast's shoulder as he lunged forward. Kajika reared back, and Wakiza turned to retreat, but the Beast bit down hard onto Wakiza's ankle, latching onto the warrior's flesh. Wakiza howled in agony.

Wakiza slashed his blade at the Beast, cutting through the thick skin that hung from his throat, while buying himself a little extra time to avoid another chomp from the Beast's jaws. Though it was not a deep wound, it was enough to cause Kajika to recoil, allowing Wakiza the opportunity to right himself.

The warrior crouched low, much like he would if he were hunting, and prepared himself for the next impending strike. Kajika charged back at him, but this time Wakiza ducked and managed to stab his blade upward as the Beast passed over him, slicing a large, gaping hole down the ventral length of Kajika's body. The Beast looped around and, with a quick flip of his neck, smacked into Wakiza and sent him flying.

Wakiza landed heavily on his feet. His ankle screamed in pain from the wound, but Wakiza didn't have time to tend to it now. Kajika stormed back at him, opening his enormous jaws as he took a swipe at the warrior's head, attempting a clean bite to behead the warrior. Wakiza whirled around and leaped as high as he could, using his good ankle to brace himself. His blade slammed forcefully down through Kajika's head, stabbing straight into the Beast's brain through his thick skull. Kajika shrieked and moaned, body thrashing around violently. Then suddenly, the Beast halted, looked Wakiza dead in the eye, then rolled to his side before collapsing in a heap upon the ground.

Wakiza exhaled deeply. His arms hung at his sides, heavy with exhaustion, but he could move. He was surprised by the fact that he had not turned to stone, and wondered if the Beast was indeed able to paralyze one with simply a glare. Or perhaps at the exact moment that Wakiza looked into the Beast's eyes, it was possible Kajika was already dead, and therefore his glance would not have affected him. All that mattered now was that the Beast was dead. He shrugged, then chuckled wearily to himself. Maybe some folklore was worth paying attention to, after all.

Wakiza's attention then turned to his injured ankle, and he began holding pressure on the bite wound to stop the bleeding. He ripped some fabric from his loin cloth and wrapped the gash tightly before pulling himself up and surveying his victory. Kajika had fallen by his hands, and now he just needed to prove it. So the warrior took his obsidian blade and began slowly sawing off the Beast's head. When the gruesome task was completed, he tucked the head under his arm and began to limp in the direction of his former home as the sun began to set, far off in the distance behind the western mountain.

Wakiza walked through the night, but as he drew closer to his former home, he decided to take a slight detour. He couldn't stop thinking of Aiyana, and the longer he traveled, the more certain he was that there was something he must do before approaching Chief Taima. So Wakiza ventured in the direction of the Sun tribe, and upon arriving found to his utter surprise that there was already quite a commotion going on.

As he approached, Wakiza could hear sounds of a battle, the hoots and hollers of both his tribe and Aiyana's, as well as the sounds of blows being thrown, arrows whizzing through the air, and blades being wielded about. Wakiza halted in his tracks, and chose to creep very quietly toward the irreverent sound of war. Given the fact that he was heading toward the Sun tribe, Wakiza could only assume that it was his former tribe that had prompted the attack.

Wakiza peeked around a thick tree trunk, and witnessed his former chief, Taima, actively fighting against both Akano and his father, Chief Etu. Taima was doing a fairly decent job of holding his own against the two braves, but from the looks of it was beginning to weaken considerably. Wakiza took a deep breath and stepped around the side of the tree.

"Stop! There's no need for fighting anymore!" he cried, holding up the head of Kajika for all to see.

The two chiefs and Akano paused, staring as incredulously at Wakiza as if the warrior had, in the time of his absence, magically sprouted two more heads upon his shoulders. But Taima quickly snapped out of his stagnation, and aggressively pointed his blade directly at Wakiza.

"Traitor! I knew you would come here. To turn on your own people and join our most hated enemies!"

"I have done no such thing, my chief. Look before you! This is the head of Kajika, the Beast that caused all this fighting."

Wakiza held his breath, waiting for a reply. Finally, Etu took a step forward, gently placing his hand on Akano's shoulder

"Shunned warrior," Aiyana's father spoke softly, "this war was caused by your chief, Taima, blaming us for the disappearance of his people."

Taima looked at Etu, clearly appalled by his words. "Don't

listen to him!" he cried. "Etu and his people started this war by praying to the Beast Who Walks Without Sound! They caused Kajika to devour our people, and I'll be damned if my tribe has to share our land and resources with a bunch of murderers!"

"Taima, listen!" Etu, whose name meant 'sun', implored. "Our people have also gone missing! Kajika did not only attack and devour your tribe. Our people were victims of the Beast as well!"

Taima grew quiet—more quiet than Wakiza had ever seen in all his years living under the Thunder chief's rule. Taima's face looked pensive, pondering Chief Etu's words as his eyes moved back and forth from the Sun tribe's chief to the severed head of Kajika delicately dangling from Wakiza's fingers. He closed his eyes for a brief moment, then suddenly opened them and looked directly into Wakiza's eyes.

"Desperate warrior, you have slain the Beast who caused the trouble between the Thunder and Sun tribes. If this is indeed true, then there is no longer a reason for us to fight. You have unified our tribes." He smiled at Wakiza. "And for that, I accept and encourage your return to the Thunder tribe. You will be welcomed with open arms, and my offer for you to receive one of my daughters as a wife remains."

Wakiza gazed back at Taima, his mouth agape, unsure of how to reply. Out of the corner of his eye, he noticed a slight movement around one of the trees behind Akano and Etu. Then, a flash of shiny black hair, and a set of beautiful, sparkling eyes peering back at him.

"Aiyana," he whispered, his breath suddenly taken from him, his ankle no longer throbbing. Taima turned, noticed the woman, and his demeanor seemed to shift.

"I see," he said quietly. "Then none of my daughters can possibly be the wife you seek."

Etu turned and noticed his daughter standing behind him. He whirled back to glare at Wakiza, but instantly, he softened.

"So you're the reason my daughter refuses to take a husband from our tribe," he chuckled. "I've been trying to arrange a match with our best warriors for years. But she always found a reason to disapprove of them."

"Father, this is the warrior who spared my life," Akano spoke up, looking solemnly at Wakiza. "Now I know why."

From the ranks of the Thunder tribe's warriors, Siwili appeared and rushed to his son's side. He stood behind him and placed his hand on Wakiza's shoulder. "My son," Siwili said. "I am so relieved to see you. But what made you come here?"

Wakiza said nothing, but turned to smile at his father, then glanced over where he assumed Aiyana stood, watching them.

Aiyana stepped out from behind the tree, then approached her father and brother. "Please forgive me," she spoke tenderly, "for I cannot help whom it is I truly love." She embraced her family, then turned to Wakiza, gently taking Kajika's head from him, dropping it upon the ground, and slipping her soft, tiny hand into his.

Tears filled Etu's eyes, and he walked over to the two. "O desperate warrior," he said softly, "I cannot think of a better match for my precious Aiyana. Will you take her as a wife, and unite the Sun and Thunder tribe for all eternity?"

Wakiza beamed, his face flushing a bright red as he swung his arm around his bride and drew her in for a passionate kiss. "Nothing on this earth would make me happier," he declared, amid whoops and cheers from the members of both tribes who had gathered around them.

Taima and Etu embraced, and from that day forward, the Thunder and Sun tribe forever lived in peace, sharing the land and resources bestowed upon them from the earth, and each and every day expressing their gratitude to the brave man who unified their people.

And, with the everlasting love of Aiyana, the brave warrior Wakiza was no longer desperate.

Gale

LYSSA CHIAVARI

"This rough magic I here abjure.
. . . I'll break my staff,
Bury it certain fathoms in the earth,
And deeper than did ever plummet sound,
I'll drown my book."
- PROSPERO, *THE TEMPEST*

When I opened my eyes, I was outside in a storm. Rain pelted my face, huge droplets slapping my skin hard enough to sting. I rose shakily from my knees as the wind howled around me. It seemed to be shouting strange words in my ear, but I couldn't understand what it was trying to tell me.

I racked my mind, desperate to remember what I was doing out here. The sky above me was pitch black, far darker than it should have been from the storm alone. It must be after nightfall. That was more terrifying than the storm raging around me now, because going outside after sunset was forbidden. I dreaded to think what would happen if the Watch discovered me out here.

Even worse, though, was the thought of the other monsters that prowled the dark on Gale. We locked our doors after nightfall for a reason.

As my eyes adjusted to the darkness, I looked around and tried to get my bearings. I was standing in the middle of an unfamiliar street. The windows of all the buildings were blackened; I tried the door of one, and was unsurprised to find it bolted shut. I couldn't stay out here. I had to keep moving, try to find my way home before somebody saw me out here.

Heart pounding, I ran down the street, my wet hair plastered to my scalp and dripping down my neck. The powerful winds pressed against my back, spurring me on, at times nearly lifting me off my feet, but the strange street seemed to go on forever. It felt like every step I took sent me three steps backward. Where was I?

A bolt of lightning illuminated the sky over my head, followed almost immediately by the deafening crash of thunder. I screamed in pure fright, cowering and flinging my arm over my face. After a moment, I opened my eyes, and discovered I was no longer on the strange street. Now a flat, barren plateau stretched out before me. A short distance away, the ground dropped off steeply, disappearing into shadows.

I stepped forward, hesitantly. As I peered into the darkness, the sky lit up again, revealing the huddle of dark buildings nestled in the valley far below. I was in the bluffs outside town. But how?

My frustration reached its peak. "What's happening?" I shouted in exasperation. At this point, I didn't care if the Watch did find me. It would be better than dying alone out here. "Someone, please, help me!"

There was a rumbling sound, but it was different from the thunder. It seemed to emanate from the air around me. The ground beneath me vibrated, and I backed away from the edge of the bluff, struggling to maintain my footing. "Hello?" I cried. "Is anyone out there?"

"I'm here," a voice whispered gently in my ear, and I nearly screamed again.

I looked around, but there was nothing. "Who was that? Where are you?"

"I told you. I'm *here*."

The rumbling grew louder. I was certain it was going to rip the air around me into shreds. Then the clouds parted, revealing a creature the likes of which I had never seen before—a massive winged thing, like the dragons of legend. One of the monsters of Orbe. It had to be. I collapsed in terror as the creature descended before me.

The voice in my ear was back, a soft, reassuring sound. It was a girl's voice. "Don't be afraid," she said.

The beast opened its jaws, and I was blinded by radiant light.

"Miranda? Miranda, wake up!"

There was a hand on my shoulder, shaking me roughly. I could still hear the wind, but it was muffled now. I blinked a few times as the light faded back into darkness, and numbly realized that I was lying on my own pallet, across the room from my parents' in our small home. My father was saying my name over and over. I tried to answer him, but my jaw was clenched shut, and I couldn't make any noise other than an amorphous grunt. My body shuddered irregularly; they were just small twitches now, but my muscles ached with the memory of more violent spasming. Suddenly, I understood what was happening. I must have had another fit.

But that didn't explain that strange dream I'd just had. If it had been a dream.

"Hold on, Spero, I'm going to light a candle," my mother's voice interjected.

"But the Watch—"

"Just for a moment," she said firmly. "The windows are blackened. With all the lightning out there, they shouldn't notice anything as dim as a candle."

There was a scraping sound as she struck the match, then a small orange prick of light fizzled into life. My mother lit the wick of a small candle and came closer, peering at me in the dimness. She must have seen that my eyes were back in focus, because relief melted over her face. "Miranda, can you hear us?"

With effort, I managed to nod my head. My father exhaled. "Good, she's coming out of it."

The two of them ran their hands over my stiff arms, my mother murmuring, "Just focus on relaxing, Miranda. Relax…"

I closed my eyes, urging my fingers to stretch; then my hands, my arms, up through my shoulders. I repeated the process with my toes, and, at last, I felt the tightness in my body begin to loosen. There was a final shudder, and then I lay still.

I swallowed and said, "I think I'm all right now."

"What a relief," my mother sighed. "That was the worst one I've seen. You stopped responding to us. You were just lying there thrashing."

"I saw something," I replied, my voice cracking. My throat felt hoarse and dry, as though the screams from my dream had been real. I blanched as I realized I might have screamed in reality, and that would bring the Watch down on us for sure. "I didn't call out or anything, did I?"

"What? No, you didn't make a sound. You just thrashed around like your skin was on fire," said my mother. She seemed shaken, but I breathed out in relief.

My father broke in, "What were you saying about *seeing* something? Like a dream?" His voice had an edge to it, something I couldn't quite put my finger on.

"Yes, it was like a dream. It was after nightfall, and there was a storm. I was outside. And I saw… a dragon or something. I thought it might be one of the monsters of Orbe."

There was a long pause. My mother watched my father fretfully. My father stared down into nothingness, a frown drawing heavy lines around the sides of his mouth. At last he nodded and patted my hand. "It was just a nightmare."

"Spero, what should we do?" my mother asked at length.

"She's never lost consciousness during a fit before. Maybe we should bring her to the Healers…"

"No!" my father and I cried in unison. There was a moment's silence as we froze, glancing around as if for any tangible sign as to whether we were being too loud, whether the neighbors had heard and reported us. But of course there was nothing. If the Watch were to descend on us, we would have no warning.

"I'm fine, honestly," I said, struggling to keep my tone as level as possible. "I was half asleep when the fit came on as it was. I'm sure it was nothing."

My mother seemed unconvinced, but eventually she put the candle out and she and my father returned to their pallet.

I'm not sure how long we lay awake in the dark, surrounded by uncomfortable silence. I tried to push the dream out of my mind, ordering my body to relax. It seemed I would never fall back asleep, but the next thing I knew, I was waking from a doze to the sound of whispers from my parents' side of the room.

"Nai, you know we can't bring her to the Healers. These fits aren't on the approved list of treatable ailments. If we alert the Brotherhood to her condition, they'll just send the Watch for her."

"I know that. I wasn't thinking the Healers so much as… one of your former colleagues."

Silence followed, so abrupt that I almost rolled over to see what had happened, but I didn't want to draw attention to myself. With effort, I forced myself to remain absolutely still, my breathing as shallow and even as I could manage.

"No. That life is behind me now. I forswore the art and did my time. Twelve damned years of it. I can't go back now, the Watch—"

"Yes, but did you hear what she said? She 'saw' something."

"That doesn't mean anything. She probably just lost

consciousness and had some sort of lucid dream."

My mother was persistent. "But, Spero—"

"It isn't possible. She's been inoculated. Besides, these fits are like nothing I've seen before. None with my… talent"—his tone sounded weary and regretful—"ever experienced anything like this. It must be something else."

They were quiet for so long that I began to wonder if they'd fallen back asleep. Then, at last, my mother whispered, "I just don't want anything to happen to Miranda. If these fits keep getting worse—"

"We'll deal with that when the time comes." My mother made a sound of protest, but my father cut her off. "It's all we can do, Nai! I won't risk her life or yours by doing something rash. Our family is already at greater risk because of my past. It's simply too dangerous."

My mother didn't respond. I longed to see what her face was saying, but I still feared betraying that I'd overheard a conversation that didn't belong to me. Instead I stared at the featureless wall in front of me as worry turned my stomach sour. I hadn't understood anything they'd just said, but it had frightened me nonetheless. I'd thought that my fits were just some sort of freakish disorder, that they'd only come over me by a one-in-a-million chance, but now I was no longer so sure. My parents were keeping something enormous from me, and the thought made me both angry and terrified.

Trust was hard to come by on Gale, with the Watch looming over us at all times, demanding unwavering conformity. But I'd always believed I could trust my own family—it was just outsiders I needed to fear. I could see now that had been a childish mistake.

I felt as though I were back out in the storm from my vision: cold, afraid, and utterly, utterly alone.

The storm had subsided by the morning, but the wind was high as always as I walked to the education center. It whipped around my ankles and bit at my ears. Most of the dark clouds had blown away overnight, leaving behind an abnormally blue sky—and an unsettlingly clear view of Orbe. It hung suspended over the towering Citadel of the Brothers, larger and brighter than the sun. Inescapable.

On days like this, when Orbe was out, I usually felt on-edge and anxious being outside. The Admonitions of the Brotherhood, warning of the dangers of Orbe and its cunning monsters, would ring in my ears from the moment I left shelter to the moment I returned. Today, though, I felt like I was sleepwalking through a patch of dense fog. My mind kept wandering back to the whispered argument my parents had had the night before. My father—my ordinary, unobtrusive father—had done something long ago to cross the Watch. And now he was afraid.

That very imminent fear weighed on me more heavily than the distant threat of dragons ever had, regardless of my nightmare.

My one consolation was that my parents showed no sign of knowing I'd overheard them last night. They'd behaved completely normally this morning, though the tension between them was painfully obvious. Before they left for their daily labor, my father had reminded me, his voice forceful, that the vision had been nothing more than a nightmare. "Every child dreams of the monsters of Orbe," he'd said. "It's normal."

I didn't believe him.

My eyes flicked unconsciously upward, toward Orbe. It was so massive that it almost seemed poised to devour our tiny world. The milky colors of its atmosphere swirled together, pale yellows tinged with hues of pink and orange. Occasionally snatches of blue and green became visible through gaps in the clouds, providing a small glimpse of what lay beyond our view.

I'd never considered, really, what it was like on Orbe. The other world was a place of monsters, somewhere to be feared. It was Hell. Better to not think of it at all. But suddenly I found myself wondering what the view was like from the ground. Gale was so rocky and barren, with barely enough patches of greenery to sustain our small community. It occurred to me for the first time that Orbe might be different.

Unbidden, an image appeared in my mind, of a lush green landscape, covered with plants tall enough that they seemed to brush the colorful sky. I froze, transfixed by the unexpected vision.

What is this? My imagination? Or… something else?

Against the yellow-tinged clouds, a black beast soared, its wings leaving a vibrant trail of light. It was so distant that it seemed little more than a speck, but I gasped nonetheless at the sight of it.

"Miranda? Is something wrong?"

The sound of the voice made me jump. One of my peers, a boy named Ari, stood next to me. I blinked and my eyesight seemed to realign itself. I realized that I'd been standing stock-still, staring intently at Orbe. A fresh wave of disorientation washed over me as I wondered whether that black speck among the clouds had been my imagination, or if I'd actually seen something there in the planet's skies.

"I thought I saw—" The words came out involuntarily, and I broke off in horror. I supposed Ari considered me his friend—as much as one could have friends on Gale—since he always made a point of walking and talking with me on the way to education, an easygoing smile ever-present on his face. But it was dangerous to tell anyone too much, especially now.

I needn't have worried, though. Ari was gazing at the planet above our heads a bit nervously himself. "Don't look," he advised, turning back to me and placing a hand on my shoulder. "Let's just get to the education center as quickly as possible. We'll be safe there."

I nodded, hurrying along next to him. I didn't say another word. I felt strange; an odd, hollow sensation was building in my stomach. I'd never felt anything like it, and I hoped with all my might that I wouldn't have a fit during education.

It wasn't until much later that I had a name to place with the sensation I felt that day: *longing*.

The educator began the lesson with ten verses from the Litany of the Brotherhood, professing the defeat of the Pantheon and the expulsion of the monsters from Gale three hundred years ago. The first line read, "*The dark night sky grew blacker still, as the bodies of dragons filled the air.*" It seemed too much of a coincidence. Anxiety pricked viciously under my skin. I tried to focus on keeping my face an expressionless mask—something I'd spent a lifetime practicing.

Upon finishing the passage, the educator reverently closed the volume and looked out at my peers and me, grim-faced. "This chapter of the Litany deals with the two Brothers, Nio and Bastian, vanquishing the monsters of Orbe," he said, "but their defeat was only temporary. The threat is real, to this day. The monsters still live, and they are constantly seeking to reclaim Gale for themselves. The Watch has given me a warning to pass on to you today, my students: last night, a dragon was spotted in the skies over Gale."

I nearly choked, but somehow managed to restrain myself. My peers reacted with similar alarm, though, I was sure, for different reasons.

"Now, settle down," the educator said. "I understand that this is concerning, but it is the reality that we deal with every day. The old gods wish to reclaim what was once theirs. But we must put our faith in the Brotherhood, and their sentinels, the Watch. They will protect our people, as ever."

I tried to calm myself with the educator's words, but my heart was still beating out of control. My skin tingled, and drawing a deep breath seemed impossible. I was used to the constant companionship of anxiety, but this felt different. This felt like a fit was imminent.

Not here. Not now.

The educator was still speaking. In the back of my mind, I numbly heard him advising everyone to make sure their windows and doors were secure, reapply blacking to any opening in their house, and to contact the Watch if they heard or saw anything suspicious. Ordinarily I'd be paying him strict attention, taking down diligent notes, but right now I couldn't think of anything but getting away from the classroom.

Somehow, I managed to get to my feet without shaking too much, and incline my head deferentially.

"Forgive me, educator," I said, relieved that my voice was convincingly steady. "I'm afraid I need to use the lavatory."

He narrowed his eyes, but nodded curtly.

Stiff-limbed, I hobbled down the corridor to the lavatory. I kept my fists clenched, willing the tremors to hold off with all my might. I never thought I'd make it, but against all odds, I managed to get into the washroom and close the door behind me before collapsing to my knees in a fit of spasms.

Contractions rolled up and down my body. My muscles ached from exertion. My breath came in short bursts, hissing in through my nostrils and out through clenched teeth. A fresh wave of nausea erupted from my stomach, and my ears rang.

Each pulse along my body was like a bolt of electricity, of lightning.

And thunder.

And wind...

In a blink I was back out in the storm. Short brown hair whipped around my face as the wind howled mournfully in my ear, keening once more in that language I couldn't understand.

Not again, I thought, gazing across the rocky terrain. Last night, I might have been able to fool myself into thinking this was only a dream—even the landscape I saw this morning could have just been my mind wandering—but this left no room for doubt. My fits were causing this, whatever *this* was.

Are you there? It was the girl's voice from the night before, and I recoiled in shock.

Summoning all my courage, I called out, "Who's there? Show yourself!"

As if in reply, a bolt of lightning streaked down from the clouds, charring the rocks at my feet. I screamed and leapt backward, my eyes squeezing shut automatically.

When I dared to open them again, a girl stood on the blackened earth where the lightning had struck. My heart caught in my throat. She was unlike any girl I'd ever seen: tall and elegant; her fair hair long and streaming with colors, soft greens and dusky pinks. Her clothes were even more vibrant, a stark contrast to my dingy beige linens. Whoever she was, she was clearly not of this world.

She looked around herself, as if she were as confused by her sudden arrival in this place as I was.

"What are you?" I asked her, my voice trembling. "A... a goddess?" According to the Litany, the Brothers had banished the old deities to Orbe, so that all men would be equal. But if the monsters still existed, perhaps the Pantheon lived on as well. It was the only way my brain could reconcile this otherworldly creature before me.

The girl blinked at me in bewilderment, then scoffed. "What? No, of course not! I... my name is Ferda." She spoke with a strange accent, and pronounced her name like 'fair-deh.' I repeated it, my tongue tripping over the foreign syllables.

"Why are you appearing to me like this?" she asked. Her question caught me off guard, because I was going to ask her the same thing. "Who are you? Is this... is this Gale?"

I froze, suddenly wary of answering her. Perhaps she was not divine at all. The monsters of Orbe had strange tricks, the educator had warned. Could one of them be using me to try to get a foothold on Gale?

But she was in my mind, probing, seeking the answers out herself. Against my will, I heard myself replying, "This is Gale. And I... I am..."

"Miranda!"

The sound of my name shocked me out of the vision. I was lying on the cold stone floor of the lavatory, my limbs still jerking and writhing uncontrollably. A knock came from the door. "Miranda, are you all right?"

It was Ari's voice. I ran a stiff palm across my abdomen, softly urging the shuddering to slow. "I'm all right," I called back in as level a tone as I could. "I'm just feeling a bit sick to my stomach. It's, um, it's my menses." That ought to afford me a few more moments' privacy.

"All right," Ari replied uncertainly. "The educator sent me to check on you. I'll report back... unless you need anything?"

"I'm fine," I answered. My body had almost stilled. If I could just lie here for another minute or two, I'd be all right to return to the lesson. I hoped.

When at last the twitching tapered off, I struggled into a

sitting position and rested my head against the closed washroom door. My heart was still pounding, both from the vision and from my secret almost being revealed. This was the first time I had ever had a fit in public, but I knew it wouldn't be the last. It was only a matter of time before I got caught.

I couldn't keep on like this.

Shakily, I rose to my feet, brushed off my breeches and inhaled deeply. I was certain, now. I was going to have to talk to my father.

The educator stopped me after the lesson, as I attempted to retreat into the throng of my peers. "Miranda," he said, "if you're having trouble with your menses, you should see the Healers. It's a treatable ailment."

I thanked the educator, but inside I derisively wondered—not for the first time—how anyone could decide to treat one ailment but not another, and still call themselves "healers" without a trace of irony.

To my surprise, Ari was waiting for me outside the eduction center. "It's dangerous to walk alone," he explained, "after last night."

I froze momentarily before realizing Ari meant the supposedly real dragon that had been spotted, not the one from my vision. I gave him a tight smile and we set off. Ari didn't talk much, apart from asking if I felt better, to which I nodded noncommittally. My head buzzed with the questions I would have to ask my father when he got home from his labor.

I stopped short when I came through the front door of our home and realized I was not alone. My mother sat placidly at the table next to the cooking hearth.

Bewildered, I asked, "What are you doing here?"

She smiled, her mouth a tight line. "I was waiting for you.

I've found someone that I think can help with your fits."

My heart stopped. "What?"

"An acquaintance of your father. He… owes him a debt, of sorts. We can trust him."

"Does Father know?" I managed at last.

"No. And it's very important that he not find out. He wouldn't approve of this method of helping you, Miranda, but I feel we have no other choice."

I thought about what had happened during education today and couldn't help but agree. I couldn't afford to wait for another solution. I knew my father feared the Watch, but at this point the Watch was undoubtedly going to find out about me—probably sooner than later.

I felt uneasy as my mother led me through the streets to an unfamiliar part of town. I was certain someone would notice something amiss, realize that I was trying to keep something unauthorized a secret, but no one paid us any mind.

Finally, we arrived at a nondescript gray building, no different from the row of buildings on either side of it. My mother knocked, and a broad man, olive-skinned like me and with dark hair peppered gray, answered the door. He was taller and wider than any other person I'd seen, but seemed otherwise ordinary, with his close-shorn hair and plain linen clothing.

The man led us down a short hallway into a room with a private door. As he moved, a high-pitched noise seemed to echo his motions. Step, beep. Step, beep. I could feel the right side of my face twitching involuntarily at the repetitive sound. What was that?

A stone-topped counter ran along one wall of the enclosed room, its surface covered with glass bottles and implements that I could only guess the purpose of. I sat beside my mother on a rough wooden bench while the man shut and bolted the door behind us. In this small space, the beeping of his movements seemed to grow louder, reverberating around the room. I flinched, my right hand flying up to my ear.

My mother put a hand on my shoulder. "Is something wrong, Miranda?"

I started to open my mouth to ask if she heard the sounds as well, but froze. The man was watching me intently. My mother claimed this man would help me, but how was I supposed to believe he could be trusted? Something about the intensity of his gaze made me uncomfortable. He looked like he wanted to make a meal of me.

I said, "No, nothing."

She stared at me quizzically, but did not press the matter.

The man pulled up a stool and sat across from my mother and me. I braced myself for the mechanical shriek that seemed sure to accompany the scraping of the stool legs on the stone floor; but, just as suddenly as it had begun, the noise stopped. The ringing in my ears slowly faded.

The three of us sat in silence.

Awkwardly, I said at last, "Um, hello. My name is Miranda."

"Yes, Miranda," the strange man said. "I am called Ban. I am an assistant at one of the Brotherhood's healing centers." His voice was deep and rich. For some reason, it reminded me a bit of my father's. "I understand that you've been experiencing some... *unusual* symptoms recently. I'd like to help you."

"Is that all right?" I asked hesitantly. "There won't be a problem with the Watch, or anything?"

"Not so long as you do your part. There are secrets all over Gale, Miranda," Ban said, "you just have to know how to keep them."

His words sent a chill down my back, but I nodded. I'd become quite a master at secret-keeping, these past few weeks.

Ban asked me to describe my symptoms, which I did—omitting the part about the visions, as well as what had happened that day during education. I still did not entirely trust this strange man, despite his claims that he could help me.

Ban said nothing while I explained the fits, merely nodding and occasionally running a large brown thumb over his chin. Then, at last, he cleared his throat. "Yes, this would definitely not be considered a treatable ailment. It is too aberrant. However, I do have some ideas for things we could try, to see if we can alleviate some of the symptoms. I will have to retrieve the supplies from the healing center. And I will need time. If we are to keep this a secret, we will have to space our sessions carefully. People will notice if you come here every day."

My heart sank. Of course I understood, but every day that passed was another chance I might get caught having a fit in public.

As if he'd read my mind, Ban stood and began to rummage through the bottles on the countertop. "In the meantime, I've made this for you." He held out a small vial of amber liquid. "This is a muscle relaxant. Drink some if you feel a fit coming on. It will contain the spasms. It may make you sleepy, but you should be able to conceal that more easily than a fit. If anyone asks, tell them you have been prescribed that for menstrual pain."

I nodded, clutching the bottle tightly to my chest as Ban escorted us back down the hallway and out the door.

Later, my mother and I sat at the table in the kitchen, the vial between us.

"Maybe you should take some of that tonight before bed," she said. "To make sure it's safe. I don't want it to give you side effects if you have to take it in public."

I said, "Mother, these fits... do they have something to do

with Father?"

She wouldn't meet my eyes; she fixed her stare on the milky amber liquid in the glass vial instead. "I don't know."

I sighed and lifted the bottle, shaking it and watching the layers of yellow swirl together. Something about it reminded me of the pastel clouds in Orbe's sky. "I thought I knew everything there was to know about our family. I guess I was wrong. Father's past is his own, but if he did something that's causing these health problems for me, don't you think I deserve to know the truth?"

Mother stood up and moved to the cooking hearth. The conversation was over. She poked the embers from this morning's fire and tossed some fresh kindling on, and I sourly reached for my satchel, pulling out my book to start my reading for next day's lesson.

I almost didn't hear her whisper, "It's not my truth to tell, Miranda."

After dinner, I surreptitiously took a spoonful of the amber medicine. Then I hid the vial in my satchel.

I spent most of the evening waiting for something to feel different. I wasn't sure what to expect—would I start retching, or faint? Or would I start to miraculously feel better, healthier, *different* somehow? I wanted some sort of sign that would let me know for certain whether the medicine worked or failed.

But there was nothing.

I didn't have a fit, either, though. Truthfully, I just felt *normal.* This, I supposed, was novel in and of itself, considering how strange I'd felt for the past few days. I read my assigned segment of the Litany, and my father and mother played a game of draughts by the fire until nightfall. I knew I needed to talk to my father—there were so many questions I needed him to answer—

but when it came down to it, I lost my nerve. Perhaps I wouldn't need to, after all. If Ban could heal me, maybe I could forget about the whole thing.

By the time we went to bed and I'd felt no dizziness, no tingly skin or heart palpitations, I was beginning to wonder if Ban's medicine might be all I needed to make the fits disappear. I drifted off to these elated thoughts and woke in a strange, green place.

It was after nightfall, but I felt calm. This dream world was not Gale, and there'd be no Watch on my heels here. It was like the place I'd seen in my vision—or had it been just a daydream?—that morning on the way to the education center. Tall plants surrounded me, their leafy tops brushing the heavens. They were different than the dry, scrubby wood-plants that grew in the desert of Gale. Alien. I pressed my hand against the trunk of one. Its skin was coarse under my palm.

I made my way between the plants, looking up at the night sky. The clouds were thin and silky, not the roiling storm clouds I was accustomed to; and there was nothing more than the slightest hint of a breeze. I realized, gazing upward, that the immense yellow globe of Orbe was nowhere to be seen. I breathed a sigh of relief—no dragons here, either. In Orbe's place, a smaller sphere was just visible through a patch of misty clouds. It shone bluish-white, like a large star.

I walked only a short while before I came across a clear blue pond. A small creature sat on a giant leaf in the center of the water. It fixed its round eyes on me and croaked. I smiled in wonderment, moving closer to get a better look.

"What are you doing here?"

It took all my effort not to scream. The creature, on the other hand, leaped off its leafy perch in a panic and dove into the water.

The girl called Ferda was standing behind me, holding an odd lantern that glowed with no flame. How could she be?! I hadn't even had a fit tonight! Had the medicine suppressed my physical symptoms, but not taken away the visions? How was that possible?

"Hang on, there's no need for violence!" she squeaked as the light ran over my form. I'd picked up a heavy limb from one of the tall plants and was brandishing it at her.

"So you say," I growled. "But you're the one who keeps turning up in my mind, uninvited. What do you want from me, anyway? Why can't you just leave me in peace?"

"Wait, please, Miranda," Ferda protested. She set the lantern down and held up her hands in supplication. "You've got it all wrong. Please, let me explain. Can't we just talk? And I promise, I won't go in your head this time." I tentatively lowered the branch at that. She smiled, moving a few steps closer. "Honestly, I'm really sorry about that. It was an accident. *Meige* aren't supposed to enter without permission, but I'm still a novice, and, to tell the truth… you kind of scared me."

I dropped the branch onto the ground where I'd found it and said, "Same here."

Ferda grinned and moved over to the side of the pond, where one of the tall plants had toppled long ago. She sat, folding her flowing skirts around her, and kicked off her sandals, dipping her toes into the dark water. "I didn't realize there were any *meige* on Gale."

"What's '*meige*'? You said that word before."

"A '*meiga*' — singular — is what you are," Ferda said, as if that were any sort of satisfactory explanation. When I stared expectantly at her, she laughed and went on, "Sorry. Someone with the ability to enter others' minds, among other things. Travel the sixth plane. Project your form across long distances and such."

"I… *what*? You mean… magic?"

She smirked. "Roughly."

"But I haven't entered anyone's minds. It's been *you*. You keep appearing in my thoughts."

"That's because *you*"—she waggled a finger at me—"keep calling me. Even now, you just popped in while I was *trying* to do my nightly meditation." Her words seemed cross, but she was still smiling, and her voice was light. She patted the trunk next to her invitingly. I came and sat beside her.

"So," I said, "if you didn't bring me here, how did I get here? And what is this place, anyway?"

"This is the woods outside the palace of Nápule. On Orbe."

I gasped. "*Orbe*? This is Orbe? Oh, dear Brothers, I can't stay here!" I jumped to my feet, frantically looking around. "How do I get out of here? How do I get home?" I closed my eyes. "Wake up! Wake up, Miranda, come on—"

"Wait, Miranda, please!" Ferda hurried after me and caught my hands in hers. "Don't panic. You're not actually here, it's just your psyche. Honestly," she added with a laugh, "this would probably be hilarious to a non-*meiga* right now. I must look like I'm talking to myself."

Self-consciously, I looked down at my hands in hers. My olive skin stood in relief against pale fingers adorned with jewel-encrusted rings. Two different worlds.

I slipped my hand out of Ferda's, but didn't run this time.

"Just hear me out, Miranda," she said in a gentle voice. "I think you have the same abilities as me. Which is incredible, because everyone always says that no one on Gale has been able to project since the revolution. That's why we haven't been able to communicate with any of the people trapped there."

I rubbed my fingers against my temples. I wasn't sure what

was harder to comprehend about Ferda, her strange way of speaking or the even stranger things she said. "I only understood about half of that," I sighed.

"Okay. Sorry. Let me backtrack a little." Ferda clenched her fists in front of her face and pursed her lips in concentration. "So you know that Gale is Orbe's moon, right?"

"Yes."

"But do you know how your people came to be there?"

I quoted the Litany. "The people of Gale were created by the deities of Orbe thousands of years ago to be their servants. But three centuries ago, the Brotherhood rose up against the Pantheon and banished them from our world, so that all men could live as equals. Ever since then, the gods have sent their monsters out after nightfall to try to reclaim us, but so far..." I trailed off. Ferda's eyes had grown rounder the longer I'd spoken, and now she looked up at the shining light in the sky—obviously Gale, if this was Orbe.

"Stars and galaxies," she muttered. "Miranda, I have to tell you something. But you might need to sit down for it."

I remained standing. "What is it?"

She gnawed her lip so ferociously that a small droplet of blood appeared in the corner of her mouth. "Gale is... that's not..." She exhaled and looked down at her pastel skirts. "Miranda, I know that's what they told you, but it's not true. Until twenty-five years ago or so, Gale was a colony. Of explorers. From Orbe." I opened my mouth to protest, but she cut me off. "I know it's hard to believe, but I know it's true. Their governor, Prosper, was a *meiga*, and he was a friend of my father's. But there was a revolution—I'm not sure everything that happened, it was before I was born—and Prosper got overthrown. And after that, we completely lost contact with Gale. No communications, no projections from the *meige* that had lived there, nothing. We knew someone was still there, because whenever any of the kingdoms of Orbe send scout ships out, they get shot at. But we had no way of knowing who it was, or how many people were still alive, or what kinds of lives they were living, or *anything*."

Ferda trailed off as my knees started to give way. She caught my elbow, bracing my weight against herself. "See, I told you to sit down!" Gently, she helped me to sit on the fallen trunk again and crouched in front of me, looking up into my face.

"Why should I believe you?" I asked raggedly.

She shrugged. "No real reason to, I guess. But…" She looked down at our feet. "I'm not lying, Miranda. I promise."

I pulled my knees up into my chest and rested my cheek against them. My eyes burned, so I squeezed them shut. I had no reason to trust this strange girl, with her odd mannerisms and her multicolored hair. But by the same token… I knew my father was lying to me about something. And there had to be a cause for everything that had happened to me, both the fits and the visions.

What if Ferda was right? What if my father had once been a *meiga*, and he'd passed it on to me? But if that was the case, why hadn't he recognized the symptoms of my fits?

"This is too much," I said into my knees, my voice muffled. Hot tears seeped into the fabric of my breeches. "Why is this happening to me? What did I do to deserve it? All my life I lived by the edicts. I never wanted to be different."

"It's all right, Miranda," Ferda murmured. She still crouched in front of me, and I felt her hand brush my foot, an awkward gesture of reassurance. "I know this is probably really weird, but there's nothing wrong with you."

"That's not what they'd say on Gale. If the Watch finds out about me, they'll…" I couldn't finish that thought. I was too exhausted. The last few weeks had been too much for me. The fits on their own were bad, but trying to *hide* first them, and now these visions?

I just wanted to rest. When was I ever going to get any rest?

"Shh, Miranda, everything will be okay." I felt Ferda shift, slide onto the stump beside me. Her arm came around my shoulders, warm and comforting, familiar in a way I couldn't describe. "We can talk about this another time, if you want. Just call me, any time. If you can't figure out how to get back, call me and I'll come find you."

A humorless laugh shook my shoulders. "That simple?"

She poked me lightly in the ribs with her free hand. "It has been so far. Two for two, right? Here, close your eyes and relax. Think of home, and envision yourself waking up. That should be all you need to do to end the projection."

I stilled myself, breathing in Ferda's warmth for another moment, and blinked. When my eyes opened again, I was back in my parents' home. Starlight gone, only the smoldering embers of the cooking fire in the next room illuminated the house.

My muscles felt relaxed, and my parents were still sleeping, so I must not have thrashed. I'd had a vision without a fit, just as I'd first had fits without visions. Were the two unrelated, after all? My head ached too much to think about it tonight.

I tried not to think of Ferda as I lay in the quiet, willing myself to sleep. But one thing she'd said had stuck out in my mind: *two for two*. I'd seen her twice, but I know I had heard her a third time—in my first vision, the one with the dragon. Had she not had that vision as well?

And if not, then what did that mean?

Before I could consider it for too long, sleep claimed me.

"Hello, Miranda. How are you feeling today?" Ari asked me as we walked to education the next day. I gawked at him, and he clarified, "Your menses?"

Oh. Right. That.

When I told him I felt well, he smiled, but the movement of his lips did not seem to match his eyes. "I'm glad," he said. "I was a trifle worried. You know…" He hesitated, then added, in a much quieter voice, "There's a side of Gale that the Watch doesn't want you to see, but it is there. People care about others, for reasons besides the Brotherhood."

I stared at him in utter bewilderment. He colored. "I guess what I'm trying to say is, I've always thought of you as a friend, Miranda. So if there's something wrong, I hope you would trust me enough to tell me."

My pulse shuddered. What was he getting at? I thought back to him knocking on the lavatory door, how concerned he'd been after education yesterday. Had he seen my fit? Dear Brothers…

I smiled hollowly, attempting to mask my inner panic. "Of course, Ari. But truly, there's nothing wrong. I feel fine."

Ari nodded. He seemed disappointed, but did not press the matter. When we turned onto the education center's street, he broke away from me, calling cheerfully after a group of our peers.

I watched him as he went. Ari had always been so much more carefree than I ever dared to be. He flitted impetuously among our peers like a spirit on the wind. I always appreciated his open smile, but something about it had always made me a bit nervous. Between the Watch and the monsters of Orbe, it seemed like happiness was something that took more courage than I had. Ari's openness felt unnatural to me.

It had never occurred to me that maybe *my* reaction was the abnormal one. The fear that was ever-present in my home—was that something that was unique to my family? My parents' constant whispered warnings about the Watch suddenly seemed inextricable from the possibility that my father had once been a *meiga*. Maybe the oppressive anxiety I grew up under was not the norm, even here on Gale.

Maybe the only one that lived in constant fear—desperate to break no edicts, constantly looking for the Watch over her shoulder—was me.

A storm was forming over my head. The clouds were thick and dark, obscuring Orbe from view. The sky looked ominous, with nothing but the roiling steel-gray clouds to offset the black stone of the Citadel of the Brothers towering over the city. For the first time in my life, I wished that I could see the other world.

I wondered what Ferda was doing now.

A short distance away, Ari's laughter bubbled back toward me. And then, there it was again, the hollow sadness in the pit of my stomach, the longing for a life different than the one I had. Everything had been so much easier before these fits started, before I began to question my life. Before the visions. Before learning I was a *meiga*. I hadn't asked for this change.

But the changes weren't what bothered me the most. What I really resented were the people who had lied to me for so long, who had made my life into what it was. Who caused me this life of fear in the first place.

I resented my father.

The education center was still and quiet after the noisy chatter and whistling wind outside. The classroom looked foreign to me. I was seeing everything through new eyes. We all sat in our tidy rows, dutifully pulling our texts from our satchels, as the educator took his place at the pulpit in the front of the room, master of all we were to encounter that day. He would guide our minds to think only what we were instructed to, and none would question.

"Good morning," he said. "Let us begin today with a recitation of the Litany, book two, chapter seventeen."

My peers read the words aloud in a monotone drone. I moved my lips along with them, but my mind was preoccupied. Reciting the Litany made the questions of last night fresh and raw. If Ferda was right, the Brothers broke away from Orbe less than thirty years ago. Nio and Bastian must surely still be alive. The current Brotherhood weren't the descendants of the Brothers, they *were* the Brothers.

The only thing more incomprehensible to me than these two men fabricating a false history for the entire world was the fact that everyone went along with it. Most of the adults on Gale today would have to have been alive at the time of the revolution. Certainly the educator, with his graying temples, had been. So why did no one talk about it? Why did it seem like no one remembered?

The Watch.

The pieces fell into place with a sudden clarity. That was the true purpose of the Watch, then. Why everyone on Gale was surveyed so closely, why people's actions were so tightly controlled. Why differences could not be tolerated. The story the Brothers had formulated would be repeated, over and over, until everyone believed it was true. No questions asked.

"Educator, I have a question."

My stomach lurched at the voice. The heads of all my peers swiveled in unison over to Ari, who stood beside his desk. His head was bent deferentially, but his expression was firm.

The educator quirked an eyebrow, though he did not seem overly concerned. "Yes, Ari?"

"Sir, this passage of the Litany..." Ari ran a finger thoughtfully over the words on the page. "It talks about how all men are equal. That the deities were driven out so they could not control us any longer, so we could all be free. Is that not the case?"

"Indeed it is."

Ari swallowed. "But there are parts of our society that do not seem equal. Like the Healers, for example. Why do they treat some patients, and terminate others?"

This was about me. It had to be. He'd seen, damn it all, he'd seen. I should have known when he said those things on the way to education. But why, *why* was he asking the educator about it?

My muscles felt taut with panic, and I struggled to calm myself, to breathe evenly. I could feel my body wanting to move, to relieve the anxiety with a tic or a thrash, and I couldn't, especially not now.

Miranda? Are you okay?

I gripped the edge of my desk so hard my knuckles turned white. Ferda's voice. I was certain that I must be falling into a fit now, and my secret would be out; but Ferda must have sensed my panic, because I felt her retreat. She didn't disappear entirely, but stayed in a corner of my mind, listening, trying to sense what was the matter. I didn't mind her presence this time. It wasn't like the first time, when she probed my mind against my will. There was a hesitancy, waiting for my permission, and she did not pry. As before, in the woods, it felt like she was steadying me—an invisible hand to my elbow, or an arm about my shoulders.

Though I felt certain that my emotions must be written all over my face, a blaring klaxon to alert the Watch, the educator did not even glance in my direction. His gaze was riveted on Ari.

"Resources, my boy. This was discussed in an earlier lesson, but perhaps you misunderstood. All people on Gale are given the same amount of resources. Food, shelter, healing care. The

Healers have determined which ailments can be treated with any person's allocated amount. If someone takes more than their portion, it is a drain on the community. It would be taking from someone else. Would you want your resources drained?"

I squeezed my eyes shut, begging Ari to stop talking now, to agree with the educator and sit back down. But he just kept on.

"Sir, I wouldn't mind giving up some of my share to help someone who really needed it. If someone is ill, that's not their fault."

"That is noble of you, Ari, but you have to understand. The Brotherhood is wiser than all of us. Certainly wiser than a child like you, who has not experienced the hardships of life. This is why Brothers Nio and Bastian were granted the providence to rule. They could see what you don't. Their edicts have created the fairest system humanity has ever known. A system of equality."

Equality, my eye, Ferda snapped in my ear. *They just want to monitor everyone's medical conditions so they can make sure no* meige *slip through.*

My breath hitched in my throat. *Of course.*

"There's a difference between 'same' and 'equal,' Educator," Ari protested. "If we are to be truly free, the Brotherhood must take that into account!"

The room was absolutely still. Then the educator snapped his text shut.

"Everyone save Ari is dismissed. Ari, please stay behind. I would like to discuss this with you in further detail. I believe that, with further discussion, we can come to an understanding."

My peers rose without a word, although a few looked over their shoulders at Ari as they went out the door. My knees shook as I passed him, this boy I barely knew but who called me his friend. Who now was defying the Brotherhood and the Watch because of me. I wanted to say something to him, beg him to back down, but I couldn't find the words.

Ari's eyes caught mine as I passed. He didn't look sorry. He looked defiant.

I'd been right about Ari. He was far braver than I.

You're wrong about that, Ferda whispered. *Give yourself a chance.*

Then she was gone.

The house was empty when I got home. I wasn't sure what to do with myself. We'd never been sent home from education early before. I paced from one room of our small dwelling to the other, back and forth, the morning's events playing over and over in my mind.

I stopped only when the chill in my fingers and toes could be ignored no longer. The cooking fire from this morning had burned out, so I knelt in front of the hearth and began to mound fresh kindling inside the fireplace. I knew it was wasteful to start a fire when I was the only one home, considering how little kindling we were allotted each month. But I needed to do *something.*

You just "drain everyone's resources," don't you? Perhaps you should have just told the Watch to begin with. If you had, Ari would be safe right now.

But even as I thought the words, every fiber of my being violently rejected them. I didn't want anything to happen to Ari. But I didn't want to give myself up, either.

I wanted to live.

I sat on the hard floor in front of the slowly growing fire. I didn't know what to do anymore. I needed to talk to my parents. I'd planned to corner my father about the *meige,* but they'd already gone when I'd awakened that morning. The thought of the conversation filled me with dread, but I had to be brave this time. I needed answers.

I didn't want to be alone anymore.

My eyes stung. I squeezed them shut, blocking out the tears.

Then I thought of Ferda.

She'd said that was all I needed to do to call her again, and sure enough, as soon as I thought of her, I could see her in my mind's eye. But it wasn't the same as when I'd been asleep. My body did not come with me this time. Now it was as if I was seeing her world through her eyes. When I looked down, my fingers were pale and jewel-covered, and I could hear her voice echo in my own ears when she spoke, like I was the one doing the talking.

She stood in a large, bright room with golden walls and high ceilings. A man I didn't recognize, clad in vibrant robes like Ferda's and wearing a narrow silver circlet across his brow, paced a short distance away.

"Papá, you have to understand, I didn't do any of this on purpose." Ferda's voice reverberated in my skull, vibrating off my teeth. The sensation was no different than when I spoke myself, but it felt alien because the voice was not my own. "She's the one who reached me. She doesn't know how to control her abilities. She'd never even heard of *meige* before."

Ferda's father halted midstride and leaned against a table that appeared to be made out of glass. Colors winked across its surface, changing constantly. "If that's the case, then they truly must have purged the populace. Oh, Bastian, how could you do it?"

The name leaped out at me. Ferda must have caught it, too, because she stepped forward tentatively.

"Papá, that was one of the names I heard the Galecian man say. He called them the Brothers, Nio and Bastian. The rulers of

Gale."

Her father scoffed. "The Brothers. Yes, in more ways than one. Ferda, I'm afraid I'll have to tell you. I didn't want to get you involved with this—and certainly not so young—but I'm afraid there's no choice, now."

He turned to the glass table and ran his fingers across it. In an instant, an image appeared, suspended in midair over the surface. I gasped, but Ferda did not react.

The Brothers. Not in a drawing in a text, nor even in a statue outside the education center. As real as life itself.

"This man," her father said, gesturing to the figure on the right, "is Bastian. My brother."

Ferda's knees faltered, and I found myself reaching out with my mind, to steady her as she always did for me.

"You mean… the war with Gale was started by our own family?"

Her father nodded grimly. "I am afraid so, Ferda. My brother and the brother of my dearest friend Prosper, together. Prosper and I were both *meige*. Nio and Bastian were not. Growing up, I'd always suspected that Bastian resented me for it, but I had no idea of the extent until it was too late."

As he spoke, the images above the glass table shifted. Different angles of both Nio and Bastian, and then one of four men together: Ferda's father, the Brothers, and someone I knew all too well.

My father.

Ferda furrowed her brows, the muscle movement echoing strangely across my own forehead. "Who is this man?" she asked, pointing to my father's image.

"That is Prosper. The old governor of Gale."

I tumbled backward from Ferda's mind, my body pulling into itself in a violent fury of convulsions, my vision blurring black.

I don't know if Ferda's father's words caused the fit. Maybe it was just the built-up strain of the day. Maybe this was how my body was choosing to cope with stress. Maybe I'd used my *meiga* abilities too much today, and it was more than my body could handle.

Or maybe there was no reason. Maybe it was pointless to speculate, when this was just the way things *were*.

I lay there on the cold, hard floor, collapsed in front of the dying fire, feeling overwhelmed and unmovable long after my muscles finished spasming and my head stopped spinning.

I shouldn't have been surprised. After everything that had happened over the last week—everything I'd seen and learned—this really was the most sensible answer. It all came together, now: my parents' fear, the way they hid from the Watch, the desperation with which they guarded my ailments from discovery. And especially my father's reluctance to get in touch with any of his "former colleagues," as my mother had put it.

The Brothers weren't just mythical figures. They weren't the heroes of Gale. They were just two bitter men with a thirst for power and a hunger for revenge.

But one of them was my uncle. And the other was Ferda's.

If they knew about me, they would kill me. I knew that for certain. I couldn't fathom how my father had escaped death the first time, but I knew that if the Watch learned the truth about us, it would not happen again.

My muscles ached as I pushed myself up off the floor. I staggered across the room to the kitchen table, where I'd dumped my satchel. The vial of amber liquid was nestled safely at the bottom. I withdrew it and took a small sip. I still didn't trust Ban, but it seemed like the medicine had worked for a short time, at least. I wanted to be able to speak with my parents when they got home from labor without a fit interrupting us. I could only hope that the liquid's effects would last long enough to let me think of a solution.

After swallowing the medicine, I wandered into the bedroom and sat on my pallet, mentally rehearsing the evening's conversation. The thin light through the blackened window grew dimmer as midday shifted to late afternoon. My eyelids felt heavy, and I belatedly remembered Ban's warning that the medicine would make me drowsy. I hadn't noticed the night before, since I'd taken it right before bed.

Surely a short nap couldn't hurt. My parents will wake me when they come in.

I drifted off, my mind bobbing gently on waves of emptiness.

"Miranda?"

The ground was soft and damp beneath my body. Leaves rustled in the breeze, and unfamiliar animals whistled.

"Miranda, wake up."

My eyelids were so heavy that I didn't think I'd be able to lift them no matter how hard I tried. But someone was prodding me persistently, and her voice cut through the stupor of my sleepiness.

"Ferda?" I asked groggily.

She looked down at me in concern. "What are you doing here?"

I was collapsed on the ground in the same woods I had found her in the night before. The sky behind her head was tinged pink, with yellow-orange clouds. Nearly sunset? Or was Orbe's sky always this color?

With effort, I replied, "I was asleep."

"I can see that. But I've never seen anyone sleep on the sixth plane before. Are you all right?"

"I feel strange. Like I'm half-in and half-out of my body."

Even my voice felt heavy, and moving my lips was a struggle.

Ferda crouched beside me and rolled me into a sitting position, slinging my arm around her shoulders. "Are you ill?" she asked, hoisting me to my feet.

"I think it's the medicine."

Ferda frowned. "Medicine? Miranda, am I missing something here?"

"I took the amber liquid for my fits. It made me sleepy." Even as the words came out, my brain grew more alert, and I instantly regretted them. I tried to say something, to take it back, but my tongue tripped over itself.

"'Fits'?" Ferda repeated. "You mean, like *seizures*? Miranda, all that stuff your friend was saying this morning—was he talking about *you*?"

"No. I mean, he was, but it's nothing to concern yourself over, Ferda…"

She put her hands on my shoulders and looked me square in the eye. "Miranda, please. You are in a very dangerous situation. You have got to tell me everything that's going on."

I sighed and pinched the bridge of my nose between my fingers. Every part of me wanted to fight her on this. I'd never been able to tell the whole truth to anybody. I wasn't even sure I knew how.

But I was sick to death of being alone. I couldn't carry this by myself anymore. And if I had to have someone share the load with me, for some reason… I wanted it to be Ferda.

So I told her. Everything.

The truth was draining. It poured out of me like water from a sieve, exhausting me completely. When I got to the end, I felt even more tired than I had when she'd woken me, but my soul felt light in a way I'd never experienced before.

Ferda's arms were around me, holding me up and enveloping

me with warmth. "Damn it, Miranda, you can't stay there," she said softly in my ear. "This is too much for any person. We need to get you off Gale."

I smiled into her shoulder. "Wouldn't that be nice?"

She pulled back and looked down at me. "I mean it. You'd be safe here on Orbe. And we have actual doctors here who might be able to do something about your seizures. None of that 'treatable ailment' nonsense."

I blinked. "Truthfully?"

"Of course! Papá has starships at his disposal. We can bring you here tonight. But we can't get into your city, it's too well armed. Can you get out?"

The excitement I'd felt at the idea of leaving was dampened immediately by a fresh wave of anxiety. My stomach flip-flopped with nausea. I swallowed it down and said, "I'll have to speak with my parents first. If I leave, they'll have to come as well."

"Uh, no, no no," Ferda interrupted. "I needed to talk to you about that. I didn't want to say anything while you were feeling ill, but... I sensed you, earlier. I know you heard what we said. Prosper is your father?"

I looked down at my feet. "Evidently."

"Everyone on Orbe believes Prosper was killed by Nio and Bastian. If he's alive, then..." She hesitated, then blurted, "Then maybe we were wrong. Maybe his brother didn't betray him. Maybe he was working with them all along."

I gaped at her. "Of course not!"

"Can you be sure?"

I bristled. Yes, my father had lied to me, but he'd been trying to protect me. His fear of the Watch and the Brotherhood was real. I didn't know how he'd escaped them, but he must have, somehow. I couldn't believe he would have voluntarily forced not just our family, but the whole of Gale into the lives we led now. There was a reason for everything that had happened, and I needed to know the truth. I couldn't just abandon my parents to the Watch.

"We can't take any chances, Miranda. It's too dangerous. Maybe sometime in the future, we can go back for them, but—"

"No," I said firmly. "I'm not going to leave my family, and certainly not before I even get a chance to talk to them. Even if my father is guilty, what about my mother? And what about Ari? I can't go until I know he's safe, too."

"Miranda, every minute you stay on Gale, your life is at risk."

"You think I'm not aware of that?" I snapped. "That's been my entire existence from the moment I was born."

Ferda's eyes glistened, but she fought back resolutely. "I just want to protect you," she said.

The openness in her voice made my heartbeat stumble. I wanted to reach up and wipe the tears off her cheeks. I balled my hands into fists instead.

"But I have to protect my family," I said.

"Miranda," Ferda protested, but I shut my eyes and closed the connection.

My parents did not return home that night.

It was past midnight when I awakened after my argument with Ferda, but they were not in the bedroom beside me. It took some time for the effects of the amber liquid to wear off enough for me to rise from my pallet and investigate the kitchen, but they were not there, either.

I couldn't understand why my parents had not returned home. Or had they come home, found me unconscious, and left to get help? Travel was forbidden after nightfall; perhaps they got caught by sunset and would not be able to go out again until daybreak.

Or maybe Ferda was right, and they couldn't be trusted after all.

I sat awake for the rest of the night, worrying. My body felt sluggish and heavy, and it was difficult to think clearly. I didn't know why the medicine had had this effect on me, but I was certain that I would not be taking it again.

Throughout the night, I heard sounds I'd never heard before, like whispered voices. Snatches of conversation here and there, though when I strained to listen, the sounds would vanish. I couldn't be sure if it was the wind or my imagination, but I felt unsettled.

At last, the sun began to rise, but still my parents did not appear. I wasn't sure what I should do—stay and wait for them? Education was compulsory, so if I skipped I would be sure to receive a visit from the Watch. And I couldn't guarantee my father and mother would return, even if I stayed here.

I was beginning to regret not accepting Ferda's offer of escape.

Finally, I could wait no longer. I would just have to go to education and try to figure out what to do next afterward. At least this would give me the chance to check on Ari and make sure he was all right.

The throng of my peers seemed louder than usual as I walked to the education center, as if there were more voices speaking than there were people on the street. They echoed bizarrely, reverberating out of sync. The muscles on the right side of my face tightened again, the way they had that day at Ban's home. I needed to focus on something else.

Eventually I settled for counting my footsteps. One hundred twenty-seven down the street. Sixty-three through the square. Up the steps, thirteen. Down the hallway to my classroom, twenty-nine.

I passed through the doorway and froze, taken aback by the complete silence that I encountered inside the classroom.

The neat rows of desks had been rearranged. The day before, the room had held five rows of five. Now there were six rows of four. I realized, with a lurch of my stomach, that a desk was missing.

Ari.

My peers hesitated in the aisles, glancing at the educator for instructions. His smile was pleasant and unwavering. "Come, now," he said, "we haven't all morning. Take your seats. Alphabetical, as usual." He suddenly laughed, making my innards drop out from within me. "Now, now, Azer, have you forgotten yourself? You take the second seat, not the third. Behind Adriana, like always."

The color had drained from Azer's face, but he laughed hollowly along with the educator. "Like always," he repeated. "How silly of me."

Whispers echoed across the classroom. "He really did it." "Poor Ari." "I've got to be more careful."

I looked around in alarm. Were they really so reckless as to speak aloud? Then I realized, gooseflesh forming on my arm, that none of their mouths were moving.

I was hearing their thoughts. All of them.

"Excellent," the educator said from the pulpit. "Now, to begin. Before we turn to the Litany, I would like to ask the lot of you a question: what is disease?"

The sound of shuffling as my peers glanced at one another was muffled by an indecipherable mishmash of disembodied voices in my mind. Finally, a girl near the back of the room hesitantly stood and inclined her head. "A disease is a disorder of the body, sir. One that causes the body to no longer function properly."

"Would you say that a disease could be something that causes the body to no longer correctly respond to the proper impulses of the brain?"

"I suppose so, sir."

The educator smiled. "Very good. Have a seat, Uxia." He flipped open his text.

"The Litany of the Brothers, book one, chapter forty-three, line two hundred and eleven. *'And so the Brothers created the world anew, one living body. Each member a part, each part bound together.'* We are all one, my students. But we must remember that a body can only live with a head. The head rules the body; the brain controls every aspect of its being. Without the brain, the heart cannot beat. Blood will not flow. Life cannot continue."

He spoke evenly, his smile never fading, as blithely as if he were discussing the pleasant warmth of a summer day. "The Brotherhood is the Head of the Great Body of Gale. The Watch are their Eyes. We cannot live without their guidance. Remember, any part of the body that does not respond correctly to the proper impulses of the brain can be said to be diseased. And diseases can be infectious. For the health and wellbeing of the body as a whole, diseases must be cured… or eradicated."

I stared resolutely at my knuckles, the taut skin white against the dark wood of my desk. I couldn't bear to look at the educator, not when his thoughts were radiating such giddy delight at the grief of Ari's friends and the terror of those who feared making his same mistakes. If I looked on his face now, I was sure I would do something I might not live to regret.

There was a dry crackling as the educator began to turn the pages of the heavy tome on the podium before him. At last he spoke, his voice throaty and somber.

"Now, let us begin our studies. Book three, chapter nine, line ninety-two: The Lamentation of the Shunned One. *'What shall become of me, who opposed the Will of Destiny?' the usurper cried.*

"And the storm whispered to him, 'Alone, alone, ever alone. In misery 'til the fierce winds of the tempest blow the ashes of your bones to the sky.'"

My head was pounding as I left the education center. The disjointed thought-voices of my peers had assaulted me all morning, and between my own fears and the grief over Ari, I felt like my brain was going to explode.

I was so preoccupied, I didn't notice him until it was too late.

"Miranda," said Ban, falling into step beside me as casually and naturally as an old friend. "I'm so glad I caught you. If you don't mind, I need you to accompany me back to my domicile."

"I'm afraid I can't, Ban," I replied, hoping my voice did not betray my contempt—or worse, my fear. "My mother is expecting me."

"Indeed she is, but you will not find her at your home. She is at mine."

I stopped in my tracks. "*Your* home? But why?"

"I will explain when we get there. The streets are not safe."

I was reluctant to follow him, but my eagerness to see my mother—and find out why she and my father had not returned last night—outweighed any doubts. I allowed him to lead me through the streets to the same small, gray building as before.

But when I crossed the threshold into Ban's house, my mother, of course, was nowhere to be seen.

"Where is she?" I asked.

Ban merely chuckled in reply. And then the electronic noise from before was back, but a thousand times louder. It was in me, around me, crushing me with its intensity. I could not even hear the sound of my own scream as I fell to my knees and blacked out.

All my life, I'd thought I could recognize a monster. They were the otherworldly creatures from the legends and the Litany, dragons and evil gods. Something Other.

How foolish I'd been. If only I'd known, then, that the most deadly of monsters are the ones who can conceal themselves in plain sight. The ones who just look like ordinary people.

My body felt heavy as I awakened, the way it had after taking the amber medicine. I tried to raise my hands to rub my throbbing temples, but I found I could not move them. My arms were strapped down to the table I now lay on.

"I'm glad you're awake, dear Miranda," Ban said. I turned my head to look at him. He stood in front of the stone-topped counter, mixing some liquids in a glass cylinder. "I wished to speak to you before my brethren from the Watch arrive."

"Ban," I murmured. My voice was thick from saliva pooled at the back of my throat. I swallowed with difficulty. "Where is my mother?"

"Ah, not here, I'm afraid. You'll have to forgive the deception. I believe that she was apprehended by the Watch yesterday, along with your father. They should be in the Citadel of the Brothers awaiting judgment by now. The Watch likely is on their way for you, as well, but I had some unfinished business that I wanted to tend to first."

I attempted to focus my eyes on him, but just keeping my lids up took effort. "What do you want from me? I never did anything to you. You promised to help me…"

"Of course I did. After all, as your mother pointed out, I 'owe' your father."

"But why? How do you even know my father?"

Ban snickered. "You haven't noticed the family resemblance?"

My foggy mind snapped to attention. "What are you talking about?"

"Poor, sweet Miranda. Just a child, really. Too young to know the other side of Gale, the game all we grownups play." He came over and stroked my forehead with mock affection, but his ragged nails scraped and scratched my skin.

"I know it's all a lie," I spat. "I know about the revolution. And about the *meige.*"

"Oh, excellent. That will save me quite a bit of time. Do you know, then, that your father was once the most powerful man in the land?" He nodded when I said nothing. "But what you might not be aware, little one, is that there was more to Prosper's old life than just palatial finery and parlor tricks. The man called Spero has much hidden in his proverbial closet. For example, another family. One he abandoned."

The breath left me. "What?"

"It's true, little sister, it's true. Prosper may have been a great *meiga,* but he was surpassed in his power by another. A woman named Cora. My mother." Ban had still been stroking my forehead as he spoke, but now he grabbed a chunk of my short hair, yanking it so hard my scalp burned with pain. I yelped, but he did not relent. He leaned close, his breath hot and oppressive.

"They called her a witch, you know. They put her to death for it. But her power was the same as Prosper's. Why should one die while the other lived? Dear Uncle Nio believed he'd done his brother in, but I knew. I *knew* he had escaped. Zalo helped him."

"Zalo? My grandfather?"

"The very same. He used to be a member of our father's cabinet, in the olden days. He secreted Prosper away, helped him create a new life, a new identity. He even offered his own daughter as a bride. Such a generous soul." His voice dripped sarcasm. "Prosper thought he could hide, but it was only a matter of time until I found him. It's why I joined the Watch. I won't rest, not until all the *meige* are dead. Just like my mother."

"I don't understand," I stammered. Ban had drifted back toward the counter and resumed stirring his concoction. I didn't want a sample of whatever was in that cylinder. I had to keep him talking, try to preoccupy him until I could find a way to escape. "If both your parents were *meige*, shouldn't you be one, too?"

"I was inoculated. And unlike *you*, my inoculation took. It's very fortunate, you know, that you happened to be a cripple, Miranda. If it weren't for your fits, it might have been years before I finally found Prosper again." He turned to me. "Although it's too bad for you, really. If not for your affliction, I might never have known another *meiga* lived."

I started to protest, but he interrupted me. "There's no point in denying it, little sister. My"—he smirked—"'Watchman's Helper', if you will, has no effect on ordinary humans." He pulled a small device from the breast of his tunic. With the press of a button, the electronic noise blipped in my ear once more. I flinched.

"That sound operates on the sixth plane," said Ban, "which only people like *you* can sense. That's why I used this to test you. You twitch like a *corllo* every time it goes off. No doubt about it. So I'm afraid there's no other alternative for you, my dear. The *meige* must be purged."

I twisted my head left and right, trying to discern if there was anything in the room I could use to my advantage, but it was difficult to see anything, strapped down as I was. Frantic, I reached out with my mind in an attempt to probe Ban's, searching for some sort of crack in his psyche. But I hit a blank wall.

"That won't work, Miranda," he said, not even looking up. "I may not have the power, but that doesn't mean I don't know how to keep others out."

My blood ran cold as I belatedly realized that I hadn't heard anything since I'd entered Ban's house. It was the first respite I'd had all day. He was right; he could keep me out.

I was trapped.

He turned to me, a syringe in his hands. "Technically speaking, I'm supposed to turn violators of the edicts over to the Brothers for judgment. But in this case, I really think the honor should be mine." His lips turned up pleasantly. "I'm sure Uncle Nio will understand."

He stepped toward me, his thumb on the syringe's plunger.

No.

I screamed, and everything in me let loose.

The energy erupting from my body was more intense than anything I'd felt before—stronger than the fits or even the visions. It was like all my energy, my whole will to live, exploded from me in a burst of power. Ban staggered backward as if flung by a giant. His body slammed into the counter, the glass vials and bottles shattering with the force of his impact.

I looked down at my hands, free now from the leather straps that had been binding them. I didn't know how I'd done this, but there was no time to contemplate it. Ban was unconscious and bleeding from a wound on his forehead, but I could see from the rise and fall of his chest that he was not dead. I needed to get away, quickly.

I burst through the door, moving swiftly but calmly as I could manage down the street. As soon as I was free from Ban's house, the sounds of others' thoughts rushed back in, but they were more muted than before, and were quickly overridden by

Ferda's frantic, disembodied voice.

Miranda! Thank goodness. Where were you? I could sense you were in trouble, but I couldn't reach you. What happened?

I tried to keep my expression blank and my pace steady as I walked and thought-spoke at the same time.

The Watch found me. I need to get away. Is… is it too late to accept your offer from last night?

She laughed, sounding almost hysterical. *Of course not. We're already on our way.* Then she added, apologetically, *I… I wasn't trying to spy on you or anything, but I was worried, so I've been checking in throughout the day. When I couldn't find you, I panicked. I just didn't know what I would do if something happened to you, Miranda. I hope you're not angry.*

I fought to hide my smile, but inside, my heart was light. *Of course not, Ferda. Thank you.*

Though I couldn't see her, it felt, for a moment, like she wound her fingers between mine and squeezed my hand.

You'll need to get outside the city and hide somewhere. I'll contact you when we're close.

Getting outside the city—that would be the difficult part. The Watch had guards posted at all the exits. I'd never attempted to leave the city limits before. How would I manage now?

I'd walked blindly through streets I didn't recognize, and I was now in a part of town I'd never ventured to before. The road was lined with workshops and storehouses. I wondered if I could sneak out in one of the storage crates that I often saw stacked on wagons headed out of the city.

I'd just begun to move toward the storehouse when a new voice, distant but intense, caught at my mind. *Someone, help me, please!* it shrieked. *I can't breathe!*

I stopped in my tracks.

It was Ari.

I followed the disembodied voice into a seemingly abandoned workshop. Its one room was dark. Unrecognizable shapes filled the shadows of the small space.

"Ari?" I whispered, reaching out with my mind as I spoke. "Are you in here?"

Miranda? Yes, I'm here! Can you find me? It's so dark!

I crept forward, reaching out with my hands toward one of the dark masses in the room. My fingers brushed wood. As I ran my hands over the strange lump, I realized what I'd stumbled across. This was a woodcarver's shop. These masses were unfinished sculptures.

They sealed me inside one, Miranda. As punishment. The Brothers, they're not like the legends say. They don't care about Gale. All they care about is themselves.

"I know." I frowned, and closed my eyes. "Help me, Ari. I can't find you unless you show me where you are."

A large wood-plant trunk in the room's center stood out in my mind. It was still rough; the carver had not begun to shape it yet. I rushed over to it, grabbing one of the carver's tools off the workbench as I ran. Quickly, I began to hack at the wooden mass.

Hurry, please. I'm running out of air.

Each slam of the long metal implement echoed around the room. Finally, the solid wood began to splinter. With one last deafening crack, the trunk split apart and Ari tumbled out, gasping for breath.

I knelt beside him, bracing his shoulders as he frantically sucked in air.

"Thank you," he choked. His cheeks shone with dried tears. "I thought I was going to die. They meant for me to die."

I glanced around the room at the other half-finished

sculptures. How many of these, I wondered with a sick stomach, were other victims of the Brotherhood's wrath? I tentatively reached out with my mind, but sensed nothing. If any of these statues contained people, it was too late for me to do anything for them now.

"I heard you in my head," Ari said, his voice ragged. "I know that sounds crazy—"

"It's not crazy."

He stared at me a moment. "Is that why? Why you were... writhing like that in the lavatory?"

I sighed, remembering how Ban had called me a cripple. "No. Well, I don't think so. I'm not sure. I suppose it doesn't matter, in the end. All these things are a part of me, for better or worse."

Ari looked down at his feet, bare and filthy with dirt and wood shavings. Then he nodded. "All right. So what do we do now?"

"We need to find a way to get out of here. Quickly, before the Watch finds us. Help is waiting for us, if we can manage to get out of the city first."

"I might know a way," Ari said. I looked at him in surprise. He shrugged. "They brought me to the Citadel yesterday. I saw... things. I suppose they thought it wouldn't matter, since I was to die. But there is a way out of the city through there."

"In the Citadel?" I sat heavily next to him, resting my head against the shattered wood and looking up at the black ceiling. It was impossible. The Watch must be searching for us—Ban said they were coming for me, and even if he was lying then, I knew he had to have regained consciousness and alerted them by now. And as soon as they discovered Ari had broken free from his prison, they would be looking for him, too. To go to the Citadel would be walking straight into their hands.

As if on cue, my muscles tightened, and the familiar tingling nausea began to form in the pit of my stomach. Of course I would have a fit now. I shouldn't have expected anything less.

But the fit didn't come. Instead, I fell into a vision.

I was in a storm again, just as I was three nights ago.

And this time, when I awoke, I had the answer.

Is that possible? I whispered to Ferda in my mind.

I don't know. Nothing you've been able to do is like anything I've seen on Orbe. Maybe the meige *on Gale are stronger, for all the Brotherhood's attempts to destroy them. There's no way to know for sure, Miranda. You'll just have to try.*

Ari was kneeling over me, looking down in worry, when I opened my eyes. "Miranda? Are you okay?"

I nodded, sitting up and rubbing my stiff arms with my palms. "Yes," I said. "I have an idea. But I'll need your help. Will… will you help me, Ari?"

Ari grinned and clapped his hand on my shoulder. "Of course I will," he said. "That's all I've ever wanted to do, Miranda."

I smiled back. A part of me, deep down, still had trouble understanding Ari's easy offer of friendship, but I didn't want to push him—or Ferda, or anyone else—away anymore.

I would try. And if I succeeded, we all would be free.

Ari and I crept down the dark granite hallway as quietly as we could. I kept my internal ears attuned for the sounds of anyone approaching. This new ability to hear thoughts was proving quite useful for keeping us concealed—as long as I didn't come across anyone else like Ban, who could block my powers, we were safe.

We moved forward until I found the voices I was looking for. My parents'.

They were in a cell together, but they were not alone. Two

men were with them, arguing.

The Brothers. Bastian and Nio.

I held back for a moment, listening and fretting. I knew what I needed to do, but I was afraid. Greater than even my fear of facing the Brothers, I was scared to talk to my father again. I didn't know how he would react, but worse was not knowing how *I* would react. If I could keep my anger about his years of deception at bay long enough to do what needed to be done.

But I couldn't put it off any longer. So I closed my eyes and concentrated.

Father.

There was a slight hesitation. *Miranda? Is that you?*

Yes.

But how? You shouldn't be able—

There's no time for that now, Father, I interrupted him. *I'm here to help you and Mother escape. But I need to know something first. Are you still a* meiga?

His response was immediate and flustered. *No, I forswore the art. I did my time. I vowed I would never use my powers again.*

I didn't ask you that, Father. I asked you if you still have *the ability.*

Silence.

Then, *Yes.*

I nodded, the hint of a smile playing at my lips. With my father's help, we just might succeed. Silently, I told him my plan. Then I nodded to Ari. "It's time," I whispered.

The storm was building outside. Even through the thick stone walls, I could faintly hear the howl of powerful winds.

I crouched outside the cell door, listening with my mind for my father's cue. As I focused, the small room opened itself up to me: my mother, despondent on a rotting pile of straw, her knees pulled to her chest; my father, beside her, gazing calmly up at two men before him.

In person, the Brothers seemed smaller than they had in the legends. Less powerful. They were flesh and blood. I could see the resemblance to my father, now, in Nio's lined face. He looked more aged than my father, though his hair was not completely gray yet. Years of treachery had eroded him.

"I always knew Zalo was not to be trusted," growled Bastian, "but even I would not have thought him capable of such a deception."

My father replied archly, "He is just one of many, my friend. Your grip on Gale is tenuous. You'd be better served attending the ranks of the Watch than wasting your time on me. I posed no threat to you in my exile."

Nio scoffed. "So says the wizard. You'll have to forgive me for disagreeing."

"I have much more to forgive you for, Brother." It was barely more than a whisper. "And I do, as unnatural as you are."

"*I'm* unnatural? You dare to—"

"Don't let him goad you, Nio!" Bastian hooked his arms under Nio's shoulders, restraining him. "He can do nothing to us. He's lost his magic. He is defeated." He loosened his grip as Nio calmed, then turned to face my parents. "Now it is simply a matter of eliminating the two of them."

My father closed his eyes and hung his head. Just as defeated as they said.

And then he worked his art.

"Nio. Bastian."

It sounded like nothing more than the howling wind, but my uncle grew still and narrowed his eyes. "Did you hear that?"

"It's the wind. Don't worry about it, I need you to help me secure them."

"Nio. Bastian."

Bastian froze this time as well. Then he whirled on my father. "I thought you said you'd been inoculated."

My mother looked up with bloodshot eyes. "He has. We all have. We've done nothing but live by your edicts, for more than twenty years."

"Then who's doing that?"

My parents stared at each other in bewilderment. "Doing what?"

"Nio. Bastian."

Nio charged forward, grasping my father's tunic in his fist and dragging him to his feet. "Stop that, dammit!"

I pulled back and, with a quick glance at Ari to ensure he was ready, slammed my fist down on the door handle. The lock shattered under the concentrated force of my *meiga* energy.

Ari kicked the door open and raced in, but it was no longer Ari who crossed the threshold. In his place was a massive black creature, winged and fierce, too large for the room that now held him, as if his mere presence bent the space around him.

The Brothers cried out in fear, toppling backward together onto the pile of straw. "What the hell is that?"

My mother cowered, sobbing into her hands, "A dragon of Orbe!"

"Don't be ridiculous!" Nio shouted at her. "There's no such thing. That's just a tale we invented to keep the citizens away from Orbian starships."

"Are you sure?" Bastian asked, his voice quavering. "I'm having trouble remembering, now, what we made up and what we didn't."

"Of course I'm sure. This is just one of Prosper's tricks. It's not real." Nio staggered to his feet and rushed forward. Ari roared ferociously. Behind him, I thrust my hand forward, palm flat. A burst of energy, like the one I'd used on Ban, knocked Nio backward.

"Come on, Nai." My father quickly pulled my mother to her feet and they rushed past Ari into the hallway. Nio and Bastian lay dazed on the straw pile. Before they could recover, Ari had retreated and my father pulled the heavy door shut behind him.

"Here, Miranda. Help me." I placed my hand over the top of my father's, and together, we bent the broken metal of the lock to our will. It was badly damaged, but it would hold. Long enough for us to get out of the city, I hoped.

I turned, ready to run, but to my surprise, my father stopped me and pulled me into an embrace.

"Father?"

"Miranda, I never meant to put you through any of this," he murmured into my hair. "All I wanted was to protect you."

My mother came up behind me, wrapping her arms around the two of us. I was thoroughly cocooned between the two of them.

"We should have told you," she said. "We should have realized… you're not a child anymore. You're strong. And that strength saved us all."

My eyes burned. I closed them, resting my head on my father's shoulder and allowing myself this one moment without fear. Nothing within me but love.

Then, sniffling, I pulled away from them. "Hurry. We still have to find a way out of the city. Ferda and her father are waiting for us above the cliffs." Just like I'd seen in that first vision. That night hadn't been a warning—it had been a promise. Just as it had today, the sixth plane had given me an answer that night. A vision of the future.

And this time, when the "dragon" opened its jaws, I would run into the light with joy in my heart.

After.

I ran my hand along the sleek black body of the winged beast—the starship, rather; one of the many under the command of Ferda's father, King Lon of Nápule—and gazed up at the night sky. The stars were brilliant, tiny diamonds peeking out behind the gossamer threads of Orbe's effervescent clouds. I'd come here every night, to the airstrip. To admire the beautiful machines I'd once feared as dragons, and stare up at the sky.

"It's still so strange," I said, glancing over my shoulder at Ferda's approaching form, "being outside after dark. I never saw the night sky on Gale. Except in my dream, of course."

Ferda leaned against the starship beside me, fixing her eyes on the blue-white sphere glowing over our heads. "Thinking about going back?"

I laughed. "Definitely not."

"Your friend Ari plans to. He speaks of nothing else."

Friend. That was a new word for me. It was still hard to adjust to, having people I could trust.

"He's free, now," I said. "And now that he's had a taste of it, he wants to share it with everyone else. That's just how Ari is."

"He'll find a way. I'm sure of it. Your father believes that the Brothers' grip on Gale is slipping. There are sure to be other *meige*. We're as resilient as weeds. Having a parent with the talent helps, but others are just born with it. And it seems that the Brothers' precious inoculation doesn't always stop the power—it just changes it. Strengthens it." Ferda gazed at me steadily, unblinking. "Gale will be free soon. I'm sure of it."

I shrugged and turned away. It was hard for me to associate Gale with anything but the oppressive fear I'd been crushed under for fifteen years. But there were good people there, I knew. People like Ari, his friends and family. They didn't deserve what my uncle—and Ferda's—had done to them. I knew Ari would never be completely happy until his loved ones were safe as well.

"Maybe 'home' isn't just the place you live," I said softly. "Maybe it's more about the people you care about. That's why Ari misses Gale so much."

Ferda laced her fingers through mine, looking at me in concern. "Are *you* homesick?"

My skin tingled, but I knew it wasn't a fit this time. The palace doctor had given me medicine to control my seizures, one that didn't make me sick like the amber liquid had. Only time would tell whether I could ever be cured; but now, at least, I didn't have to live in fear just for being myself.

"Orbe is my home now," I said. "I think it always was meant to be." I remembered the first vision I'd had of Orbe, and the strong sensation of longing that had accompanied it. Maybe my heart—or the part of me that was *meiga,* anyway—had been trying to tell me.

I looked up at Ferda and smiled. "But I think anywhere would be home if you were there."

Ferda grinned back, her eyes crinkling at the corners. "Strange. I was just about to say the same thing."

She squeezed my hand, and I was sure.

I was free. And I was home.

About the Authors

LYSSA CHIAVARI can trace her interest in Shakespeare back to her *Gilligan's Island* obsession in elementary school. She could still sing all the songs from "Hamlet-a-Go-Go" if you asked her to. Lyssa is the author of The Iamos Trilogy, a young adult sci-fi series that has nothing to do with Shakespeare or *Gilligan's Island*, but she hopes you will like it anyway. When she's not writing, Lyssa enjoys exploring the woods of her home state of Oregon, designing book interiors and covers, and losing an unreasonable number of life balloons on *Donkey Kong*. You can visit her online at lyssachiavari.com.

T. DAMON has always harbored an immense passion for not only writing, but animals, nature, and the paranormal. Her added interest in all things magical and mythical inspired her to create The Forest Spirit series, which incorporates of a little bit of everything she loves. Her educational background is in the zoological field, but she maintained her love of writing throughout almost two decades of working with and among many different species of animals. When she's not befriending animals or creating mystical stories, she enjoys studying astrology, tarot, spirits, magic, and past life regression, things her mother refers to as her "hocus pocus". Her favorite activity, however, is spending time with her husband, daughter, and pets at her home in Northern California.

ALLAN DAVIS is a meek and mild-mannered computer geek by day, but... by night... he undergoes a bizarre metamorphosis, and, without warning, creates worlds so the other people who live in his mind have somewhere to play. Science fiction, fantasy, and horror all come creeping out of the dark and twisted corners of his brain, with the occasional political essay or offbeat humorous work thrown in just to keep people guessing at his true identity. His ramblings have appeared in Stupefying Stories, TheFridayChallenge, and LewRockwell.com. When he's not doing unspeakably horrible things to databases or sharing his fantasy worlds at allandavisjr.blogspot.com, Allan can be found hiding behind his camera, or chasing the kids around with fuzzy dice and air guitars. Never, under any circumstances, allow him to sing after midnight. Or before midnight, for that matter.

HEATHER DIXON works as an animation director, a story artist for Disney Interactive, and has written the books *Entwined* and *Illusionarium*. She is a huge *Mary Poppins* fan, is addicted to salt, and has the dream to establish a national Talk Like Lina Lamont Day. You can learn more and read her crazy comics at story-monster.com.

JON GARETT lives and writes in Minnesota with his inspirations: three cats, a parakeet, and his wife. RICHARD WALSH is a full-time husband, father, and accountant. He lives with his family and a pack of basset hounds in the suburbs of Minneapolis. Together, Jon and Richard are the creators of *The Adventures of Seamus Tripp*, an adventure-comedy series that combines monsters, treasure, magic, and mystery.

ALEX IRWIN is a twenty-something recent college graduate who enjoys writing despite what her procrastination habits might lead others to believe. She began writing while in school to weird out fellow students with strange science-fiction stories, a habit which has translated over to her adult life. She was born in Dublin, Ireland and now resides in Meath with her family, where, contrary to popular belief, the weather isn't all that bad.

However, this only makes it all the more difficult for her to avoid procrastinating. "Star Walker" is her first foray into publishing and hopefully will not be her last. You can follow her on Twitter at @irwinwriting.

ALICIA MICHAELS has been a lover of mind-bending fiction ever since she first read books like *Goosebumps* and *The Chronicles of Narnia*. Wherever imagination takes her, she is more than happy to call that place her home. The mother of three and wife to an Army soldier loves chocolate, coffee, and, of course, good books. When not writing, you can usually find her with her nose in a book, shopping for shoes and fabulous jewelry, or spending time with her loving family.

SELENIA PAZ spends a lot of her time working at a library surrounded by awesome books, and uses the rest of her time to read, write, and run with her dogs. She finds inspiration in everything from history to science and especially loves magical realism. Her manuscript "Broken English" was selected as a 2012 New Voices Honor winner by Lee and Low Books. She is also the author of *Life and Death*, the first book of the Leyendas series. You can find her online at seleniapaz.com.

PATRICIA SCOTT lives and does most of her writing in Nebraska. She is the author of "The Stars Were Stolen", which was turned into the short film "First Stars I See Tonight", which aired on the first season of *HitRecord on TV*. She also wrote the story "Saguaro" which is featured in the Campfire Stories Handbook published by HitRECord and the National Park Service. In between her day job and moped rides, she collects dragons and books.

JESS R. SUTTON is a queer nonbinary writer who is rooted in Northern California. They write short stories and poetry inspired by fairy tales and the everyday magic of the West Coast. They have an abiding love for menswear, Sameen Shaw, and other people's dogs. Their work has appeared in The Auburn Circle, The Fem, and Spectrum Lit. You can find them on Twitter @queeralto.

JANE WATSON has loved Shakespeare from a young age, *The Taming of the Shrew* being a particular favorite. She attended the University of Puget Sound, where she encountered many untamable dudebros. When she is not writing, Jane loves to sew, draw, read, and obsessively shop for purses. She lives in Oregon with her menagerie of pets. You can visit her online (and learn more about the continuing adventures of Kurt and the rest) at janewatsonauthor.com.